MUSIC
of the MILL

OTHER BOOKS BY LUIS J. RODRIGUEZ

Fiction

The Republic of East L.A.

Poetry

Poems Across the Pavement
The Concrete River
Trochemoche
My Nature Is Hunger: New and Selected Poems, 1989–2004

Nonfiction

Always Running: La Vida Loca, Gang Days in L.A.
Hearts and Hands: Creating Community in Violent Times

Children's Literature

América Is Her Name
It Doesn't Have to Be This Way: A Barrio Story

Anthology

Power Lines: A Decade of Poetry from Chicago's Guild Complex
(edited by Julia Parson-Nesbitt, Luis J. Rodriguez, and Michael Warr)

Luis J. Rodriguez

HARPER PERENNIAL

NEW YORK • LONDON • TORONTO • SYDNEY

MUSIC of the MILL

A Novel

HarperCollins books may be purchased for educational, business, or sales promotional use. For information, please e-mail the Special Markets Department at SPsales@harpercollins.com.

A hardcover edition of this book was published by Rayo, an imprint of HarperCollins Publishers, in 2005.

First paperback edition published 2006.

Designed by Daniel Lagin

The Library of Congress has cataloged the hardcover edition as follows:

Rodriguez, Luis J.
    Music of the mill : a novel / Luis J. Rodriguez.—1st ed.
       p.   cm.
    ISBN 0-06-056076-2 (acid-free paper)
    1. Mexican American families—Fiction.   2. Steel industry and trade—
Fiction.   3. Children of immigrants—Fiction.   4. Iron and steel
workers—Fiction.   5. California, Southern—Fiction.   6. Mexican
Americans—Fiction.   7. Yaqui Indians—Fiction.   8. Immigrants—
Fiction.   I. Title.

PS3568.O34879M87   2005
813'.54—dc22   2004056971

ISBN-10: 0-06-056077-0   ISBN-13: 978-0-06-056077-5 (pbk.)

HB 02.14.2020

But steel had to be made. No matter how many men were hurt, the furnaces must be kept going. A furnace that lost its fire was like a dead thing. It had to be torn down to the ground and built anew. . . . So the new men, like the new men before them, worked and some of them died. But the flow of steel did not stop. . . . The fire and flow of metal seemed an eternal act which had grown beyond men's control. . . . This hard metal held up the new world. . . . Steel is born in the flames and sent out to live and grow old. It comes back to the flames and has a new birth. But no one man could calculate its beginning or end. It was as old as the earth. It would end when the earth ended. It seemed deathless.

—William Attaway, *Blood on the Forge*

CONTENTS

Part I

PROCOPIO'S PRELUDE

ESTAMOS CHINGADOS

Procopio Salcido walks along a dirt path heated white by the sun. He's wearing dirt-encrusted trousers and a well-worn print shirt; he has a maguey fiber rope for a belt and a ragged straw hat over a red bandanna on his head. Procopio strides through the brusque Sonoran desert with sweat beaded on his forehead, the dust beneath his feet dry and ashy. Walking is what he always does—walking everywhere, all the time, although up until that singular moment, when he felt a pull from the North, his steps have never taken him very far.

The eighteen-year-old is surrounded by land that speaks in words older than sky. There, the blood of the earth rises to feed plants, trees, shrubs, animals, and the people he calls family. Nature, to his people, is their best teacher, companion, and challenge. Those who are closest to nature's rhythms, its crescendos and lows, its hollers and whispers, have no buffer between themselves and the patterns, laws, languages, and songs of the world. They live simply, but densely. When they think, they think in layers, every thought compacted, to where the soul is thinking.

A milpa—a small plot of corn—appears on Procopio's left, beyond a smattering of desert cactus and thornbushes. He strolls past it, past the withered stalks, brittle and unyielding since its blood has long since dried, and the earth and its creatures have become what thirst does to those not yet dead.

It's 1943 and Procopio lives in Yaqui country, in the northern Mexican state of Sonora. The Yoeme, or "the people," as the Yaqui Indians call themselves, are known as some of the fiercest warriors in all of Mexico. They were never conquered by the Spanish—and before that, they were a thorn in the side of the Aztecs. Later, Mexican and U.S. government efforts to tame them seemed fleeting.

The Yoeme are stoutly built, dark brown, with strong facial features and course black hair. They are extremely reserved and distrustful, having lived through years of abuse from strangers, especially strangers with light skin and those who cater to them.

One of many extermination campaigns occurred between 1905 and 1907, with the removal of thousands of Yaquis; they were forced to work as slaves in the Yucatán henequen plantations and sugarcane fields of Oaxaca. Yaquis—along with other tribes such as the Mayos, Opatas, and Akimel O'odham—were rounded up, jailed, and then shipped off to the nearby state of Nayarit. From there, the Indians were herded on foot across Mexico. Many died.

By 1910, Yaquis were driven from their ancient lands to Arizona and other locations in Mexico and the United States, a distance of some 3,500 miles. Still, even with their numbers decimated, the people survived.

Then in 1941 the Mexican government finished construction of the Angostura Dam, which diverted much of the water of the Río Yaqui. For generations, Yaquis had planted crops tied to the river's natural flooding cycle. Soon after the dam was completed, their way of life was gone. Thousands of Yaquis found themselves starving in their neglected and impoverished villages. Although the land was rich with flora, fauna, and alluvial soil, capable of supporting intensive cultivation, the Indians had no education, no tools, no political power.

Procopio walks and keeps on walking. Although he does not know where he's going, he leaves his small stone home where he lived with his elderly father, a younger but exhausted mother, and three small siblings. He does know this much—without water there's no corn. Without corn there's no life. For years there's been little of all three in the village where his family lives.

So he walks.

Hours become days. Days weeks, and Procopio enters villages and a vastness of land he's dreamed of but never knew existed. After wrangling a burro, he rides to a train, which then takes him to the border. He walks some more, this time across to Arizona. He has no intention of staying in Arizona. Procopio wants to work. To find life. A new life.

Procopio settles in southern Arizona. Other Indians, Mexicans, African-Americans, and Anglos are thrown into his life for the first time. At first he stays in Barrio Libre—the mostly Yaqui neighborhood in the Tucson area. Then he ends up in the copper mines of Bisbee, Morenci, and Douglas.

Frightened but unable to turn back, Procopio enters the dangerous shafts deep belowground where Indians and Mexicans labor to extract copper for the world—then a world at war. He is alone and without family.

At first Procopio is apprehensive about the copper mines. The mines have steel-mesh elevators that drop vertically into a deep abyss. Men enter the elevators, their every breath a prayer. He thinks how a copper mine seems to tear the heart out of the earth, leaving massive openings that are then abandoned. As he, too, descends into these giant wounds, he feels guilty—because of his need to work, the land, his earth, may never heal.

At least once a month, the copper miners and their families come together.

One day Procopio spots a young Mexican girl, Eladia, at a local gathering of Yaqui and Mayo Indians exchanging greetings and stories from home. He finds out she's fifteen. While Procopio was raised among Yaqui and mixed-Yaqui dwellers of scattered settlements in the Yaqui reserves of Sonora, Eladia's family consists of Mayo and mixed-Indian migrants from the same state. Her mother is Mayo and her father is a mestizo—mixed-Indian/Spanish/African—who worked the cows and horses for various ranchers in their village. Her whole family moved to Arizona during one particularly hard summer in the Sonoran outback.

Eladia works at home, taking care of her father and five brothers, her mother having recently died of tuberculosis. She's a second mother to the smaller ones and a maid to the rest. Eladia is bright despite her lack of schooling, and although not pretty, she has a strong face and, for her age, a mature body. Her hair is glossy black, streaming past her waist. She dresses plainly with little color. Yet there seems to be a vibrant spirit ready to live through her. Procopio senses this when they first meet.

Procopio also notices how much of a rein her father and older brothers seem to have on her. They don't allow her solitude for a single minute. They make menacing gestures to every young man that eyes her. Procopio senses that even though surrounded by family, Eladia has the kind of eyes he can relate to.

Her family must need her real bad, Procopio reasons. She's a girl in a household of machos—the kind of men who won't lift a finger to cook or clean while there's a woman around.

Procopio finds a way to introduce himself by chumming up to her brothers. He and Eladia talk briefly when they see each other. He hopes that over time they may get closer. Procopio waits patiently, time his endearing ally.

A year later, the copper miners begin to strike. A group of Yaquis, Mexicans, and other Indians decide to pressure the mine owners to improve wages—at the time they make only a few cents an hour. It's a bloody conflict. Many people are beaten; others are fired and replaced by scabs from nearby shantytowns.

Procopio, now nineteen, becomes active in the strike that pits Mexicans, Yaquis, Mayos, Apaches, and Navajos against the white mine owners and their goon squads. One late night, Procopio meets with other strike leaders in the dark outside one of the dilapidated workers'-housing units. In the middle of a heated discussion, and out of the shadows, a group of masked men rush in on them with rifles and handguns. The shooting begins. Procopio quickly drops to the ground. His leg is wounded, but he's alive. Others aren't as lucky. Three of the strike leaders are killed; the rest are wounded or disappear entirely.

In the commotion, Procopio is carried out and taken to a wood-plank hovel in a dusty mining community to be cared for by Yaqui *cu-*

randeros, or medicine men. After the ambush, Procopio learns he has a price on his head. Any vigilante white man can pull in a hundred bucks if they can capture, dead or alive, any of the strike leaders.

Procopio must leave. He becomes a fugitive. His new life in his new land is no more.

After hiding out for weeks while healing from his wound, one night Procopio knocks on the wall of Eladia's windowless adobe hut; her home has no electricity and an outhouse in the back. She gets up from bed, the cold desert temperatures forcing her to wrap herself in a blanket to find out who stands at the hole where a window should be. Although they have spoken only sporadically over the months, Procopio, appearing desperate and determined, asks Eladia to go with him to Los Angeles.

"I don't have much—as you can see. But I've got strong hands and a strong back," Procopio explains. "I can work hard. I know if I stay here, I'll be killed. But in Los Angeles, I can start over. Find decent work to provide for a wife and family. I know we don't know each other that well. But I'm leaving and I won't come back. Would you go with me, Eladia? That would make me proud—to be your companion."

"Estás loco!" Eladia quickly responds, almost shouting. She looks around then lowers her voice. "How can I leave? I have family here. They depend on me."

"Listen, I don't know much but I know one thing—you are not happy," Procopio continues. "I saw that the first day we met. You are beautiful, but you have such sad eyes. I'm not just saying this for me—I believe you need this as much as I do. But I would understand if you don't come with me. I'm leaving tomorrow morning. I'm on the first train. I have money enough for both of us, at least until the next train stop. But you have to be at the station with me."

"How am I going to get there?" Eladia says, exasperated. "My family would know I was missing and look for me . . . no, Procopio, this is too much. I can't possibly go with you. I wish you hadn't asked me. I hope this is just a dream. You know I like you. I'd rather you stayed here, but you are right—people will come after you. Don't ask me to turn my back on my family. It's true, I'm not happy. But that's my lot. My happiness is not important; I'm in this world to serve my loved ones. I'm sorry. I pray for you."

Procopio doesn't know what else to say. They stare at each other for a short spell; without words, their eyes speak volumes. Procopio leaves without saying good-bye.

The next morning, Procopio arrives at the train station while it's still dark. He buys his ticket and tries to bide his time until the train departs; he has on an old borrowed suit and hat, much different from the work gear he wears most of the time. He walks over to a bench, with a slight limp from his wounded left leg. Procopio looks around at the mostly empty waiting area and wonders if anyone will recognize him. The few people there seem preoccupied with their own problems. Procopio picks up a couple of newspaper pages left abandoned on the bench, sits down, and begins to read.

Someone gently pokes a finger from behind the newspaper. At first Procopio thinks it's a fly. But then the poking starts again and he slowly lowers the newspaper. To his surprise—and extreme delight—Eladia is standing there, her thick hair in braids. She wears a clean long patterned dress and carries a small hastily wrapped bundle. Procopio springs to his feet, disregarding the pain in his leg, and hugs her. Eladia doesn't know how to react, so she doesn't do anything. Procopio holds her desperately as if she were a large rag doll.

When Procopio lets go, Eladia says she hopes she's not making a grave mistake—to leave her house at sixteen—but she's been abused by her father and her two older brothers ever since her mother passed away. She cries and says she wants to be with Procopio. She feels if he leaves without her, she will ruin her first and only chance to get out of her misery.

"I couldn't sleep after you left last night," Eladia relates. "I was so angry you came, but then this powerful emotion overwhelmed me. I was afraid I would miss out on the most important decision of my life. I prayed and prayed, but the emotion stayed with me. It was a hunger. It was a deep pain in my soul. I figured that was God's answer—the feeling that I had to go with you. I couldn't get it out of my mind. So I got up, washed as quietly as I could, and put a few of my things in this bundle. Now here I am. I'm turning my life over to you . . . you damn Indian. I won't let you abuse me, but if you're good and decent, I'll be there for you."

Procopio can't ask for anything more. At that moment he feels alive with love as well as fear.

It takes trains, buses, and even some truckers to take them miles at a time until they finally arrive in Los Angeles a week and a half later. Before they finally get there, they stay in a small town in Nevada close to where California and Arizona meet, to get more money. There was always somebody in need of some cheap Mexican help. As they prepare to leave, Procopio decides to convince Eladia to get married in that town. This is the only way to legitimize their union, he argues. Eladia finally agrees—if she has to confront her family again sometime in the future, it's better if she does so as Procopio's wife.

They find a justice of the peace and marry. After several days of trains, buses, hitchhiked rides, and cheap motels, they arrive in Los Angeles, tired but still hopeful of a new life. They enter the City of Angels as Mr. and Mrs. Procopio Salcido.

Procopio and Eladia step out of the bus station in downtown Los Angeles and walk a few blocks to a restaurant on Broadway Street, smack in the middle of a colorful, theater-laden, high-rise section of the city. The place is called Rifton's, a cafeteria with a seemingly endless number of tables and a small waterfall and fantasy hut where children and their parents climb up to enjoy the diorama of forest and animals that graces its interior.

Earlier somebody at the bus station told the couple, who had no place to go, that indigent people could get bread, soup, and coffee for a nickel at Rifton's. Procopio, whose English is heavily accented but adequate from the short time he's spent in Arizona, communicates their dilemma to the cafeteria's host; they are then taken to a table and served.

"I've never been in a place like this, *mi amor,*" Eladia comments, whispering since she doesn't know whether it's okay for her to speak;

Rifton's has high ceilings and a dark decor with an almost churchlike quality.

"*Yo tampoco*—but it sure is nice, compared to those hot and dusty joints in Araisa," Procopio responds.

Many well-dressed people sit around long tables or are lined up at the start of the cafeteria line. The few blacks and Mexicans they see are at the indigent section, where Procopio and Eladia receive their portions.

After the brief meal, the couple walk out into the crisp air. Hundreds of people stroll about, most in nicely pressed suits or well-fitting dresses; there are sailors and servicemen among them. L.A. is a port town, known for entertaining the troops on leave.

It's been almost two years since Procopio first walked out of his village. The world war is still raging. What the two of them aren't aware of is the violent tensions between servicemen and sailors—and white people in general—and the Mexican barrio gang youth known as pachucos. These "baby" gangsters, as they are called, wear a stylized form of the "zoot suit." They also converse in their own street slang— *Caló*—a mixture of Spanish and English and newly invented words. They create a walk and a stance—an attitude with their dark skin, tattoos, pompadours, and ducktails; all of it quite a sight. They live in barrios with names like La Primera Flats, Tortilla Flats, Clanton, Happy Valley, La Diamond, Los Avenues, White Fence, La Maravilla, 38th Street, Watts, Macy Street, La Bishop, Palo Verde, and La Loma.

Procopio and Eladia knew about pachucos—there were a few of them in the copper-mine communities of southern Arizona. But they didn't know how bad it had gotten for these loud and rebellious youth in Los Angeles, one of the most race- and class-divided cities of the time. Or that pachucos would become precursors of what would later be called, from the 1950s to the present, *cholos*—a street-life culture that many sons of the present migrant generation would eventually absorb.

As the couple stand there taking in the sights, people walk around them, some with serious expressions, in a hurry, none acknowledging them or excusing themselves. A few shoot them looks of disdain. A young, dark, and wide-eyed Mexican couple is an anomaly standing there, even in Los Angeles.

The couple walk a few blocks, shyly absorbing the blinking lights, honking cars, streetcar whistles, neon signs, and shoppers with bags on one hand and the small hand of a child in the other. With elaborate facades, the multistoried water-stained Victorian buildings around them appear to puncture the clouds. Procopio looks up at one particular building that seems wrapped in a kind of turquoise skin with Gothic-like spires. He feels dizzy.

At dusk, the lights on the various theater marquees, the streetlamps and office windows, make the whole place open up like a city in a dream. Shady characters emerge from the darkened alleys and from newspaper-strewn building alcoves. War news and war posters are the primary business of corner news and magazine stands. A few tuxedoed and evening-gowned couples rush past them on their way to the theater.

This is a city—the biggest, most wonderful city Procopio and Eladia can imagine. They have grown up in simple ranchos in Sonora, Mexico: indigenous-rooted, land-worked, and mostly unyielding. Although they once lived close to each other in Mexico, they only realized it after they met in Douglas, Arizona. But that's all in the past—their future is now bound up in this massive web of glass, cement, brick, and cars.

Not long after they arrived in L.A., Procopio finds work in the warehouse district, loading trains and trucks for the growing industry south, east, and northeast of the city's center. Procopio and Eladia stay in a back room of a house where Eladia cleans; it's situated in a nice section of the city just west of downtown. Their pay is minimal—a quarter an hour, just enough for food, personal things, and a few articles of clothing. On some of the nicer evenings, the couple amble around Bunker Hill and downtown, always amazed at the buzz and activity there, considering how rural and backward areas like Watts and East L.A.—where most of the Mexicans live—are at the time.

One day, Procopio is loading vegetable crates onto delivery trucks when he notices three fellow Mexicans talking among themselves near a pile of wood pallets. Procopio, trying to keep an ear open for more work, dawdles over, pretending not to listen. But he picks up a few words including *acero*, the Spanish word for "steel."

"What are you talking about?" Procopio manages to ask, unable to contain himself, sensing they are on to something.

One man, slightly older than Procopio, pulls him in and says, "Look, there are jobs at a steel mill south of here. We'll include you since you bothered to find out what we're doing. But don't tell anyone else. This is for your own good. We've heard they're hiring lots of *paisanos*. The place is Nazareth. Nazareth Steel. It's dirty work, but the pay is the best anywhere. We're going over tomorrow to apply. You can come along if you want. But remember—don't tell anyone."

The next day a beat-up '32 Ford truck pulls up in front of the house in the back of which Eladia and Procopio live. Procopio stands on the driveway, having watched the dawn rise as he waits for the men, not knowing if they will actually show up. But here they are—his three new-found friends in work clothes, their skin all varying shades of Mexican.

They greet Procopio in a familiar, slow-drag Spanish, suggestive of the country folk many of these migrants actually are. The guy who had invited him to come along is a twenty-five-year-old named Eugenio Plutarco Perez de Garibay. Originally from Zacatecas, Eugenio happens to be the most skilled of the group, having worked as a mechanic in junkyards and repair shops in the silver-mine village where he was born.

When the truck pulls into Slauson Avenue, Procopio sees blocks and blocks of foundries, mills, and corrugated metal structures. Plumes of smoke from towers look like massive black birds on both sides of the street. He's unsure about this kind of work—it looks dangerous and intensely hot. But he understands it would mean better pay and a better life.

When the truck approaches Nazareth Steel, the place appears monstrous to Procopio. The site goes on for blocks, enormous compared to the smaller shops that surround it. The buildings are a hundred feet tall; they stretch for a quarter mile to a half mile long. The truck passes the row of red-hot ingots on the street side of the soaking pits, near the mouth of the 32-inch forge. The heat sweeps over the men in the truck and they groan in unison.

"*Estamos chingados*," Eugenio remarks. "Man, we're fucked."

The plant is located in one of many small enclaves that make up the industrial corridor of Southeast Los Angeles. Most of L.A.'s primary metals industry developed during and after World War II when the Port of Los Angeles became one of the largest shipbuilding facilities in the world, including Liberty and Victory ships, for the war's Pacific theater. Massive shipbuilding yards include one run by Nazareth Steel Corporation with steel pressed from its Maywood facility—their shipbuilding yard alone constructed and outfitted twenty-six destroyers during the war. After the war, Nazareth Steel moved from steel for ships and cannons to steel for skyscrapers, bridges, and piping.

After several more kilometers, the four *paisas* in the truck spot a line of men, all Mexican except for a few blacks and downtrodden whites, near the entrance of the main mill offices. They park the truck on the street near the building and walk up to the line. A handful of office workers, in white shirts and ties, move through the throng, handing them application forms. Procopio, Eugenio, and the others make it just in time to receive their paperwork. A large number of laborers is needed to sweep, shovel, and haul materials in and around the plant. For years, the mill has been largely worked by whites. But the war has pulled many of them away. Although the war is virtually at its end, the mill needs to fill the lowest-paid positions with those who will work like slaves and not complain. Newly arrived Mexicans fit this bill perfectly.

Although the jobs appear dangerous, physical examinations aren't given. The applications are simply used to obtain an address on file; most don't have phones. Hired hands don't have any special safety gear or work clothes to wear—they sometimes start work wearing the clothes they have on. The personnel staff picks out the sturdier-looking men and hires them. Procopio is one of them; Eugenio is another.

A cluster of new wooden structures near the plant sparks Procopio's interest. A personnel clerk tells him this is workers' housing. He's told his family can apply to live there; although there's a waiting list, the list is surprisingly short. The rent will come out of his check, and he'll be walking distance from the mill. It seems too good to be true.

By the time he gets home and tells Eladia, he's already having her pack their meager possessions. She's disappointed, having just begun to feel comfortable cleaning house for the white couple she works for—the man works in banking and his wife is a school administrator. Procopio won't entertain questions or hesitations. He has gotten a notion, and that's that. He's off in the mill's direction no matter what—a pull he's felt only once before, walking all over again.

Unfortunately, it takes a couple of weeks for the housing to clear—something Procopio didn't understand. Still Procopio and Eladia are one of the first families permitted to move in. Of course, this means they have to return to the house where Eladia cleans until then; they explain to the owners that their fast departure was due to Procopio's eagerness, that's all. The white couple shrug, relieved they don't have to sweep and mop for two more weeks.

The mill housing is cheaply made, with wood planks as walls. Each house has one bedroom, a bath, and a combined kitchen and living room. The cottage-type homes face one another. Some of the other tenants have children, but most are like Procopio and Eladia, young couples from the old country starting out in the new.

Roosters greet most early risers at the housing units. Procopio starts working rotating shifts—days one week, afternoons the following week, and nights the third week. There are at least two days in that schedule when Procopio barely has a shift off at home before he has to return to the mill.

Eladia stays at home, cleaning and getting to know the other women who live in the housing units. They put wash up on long clotheslines after scrubbing by hand the filthy work clothes of their mill-employed husbands. The mill goes strong day and night. In the afternoon, Eladia will go outside and bring in the wash; she and the other women have to battle the small metal flakes clinging tightly to the sweaters, towels, blankets, and clothing. Everywhere there is steel. On the ground are pieces of a brown material that she later learns is coke, which is derived from coal and used to raise the heat in the mill's furnaces. In those days, there was no way to keep the fumes and flakes from raining down on their small community.

The mill has equipment brought over from older steel facilities in Pennsylvania—most of the forges, dies, hearths, and furnaces in L.A.'s Nazareth plant are from the turn of the century. Procopio does some of the dirtiest work in the mill, his leg long improved. He and his fellow laborers are sent to clean out toxic boiler tanks, rusted water piping, and the accumulation of grease-slag chips and who-knows-what-else beneath the large shears, hotbeds, and rollers—junk to make hardy men retch. They shovel, sweep, haul, and sweat—backbreaking labor at a backbreaking pace.

His friend Eugenio, however, figured a way to get out of this kind of work. Once when he was near a repair job next to fairly young and impressionable white mechanics, he pointed out a way to fix a broken motor part. A foreman later walked up to Eugenio and asked him how he knew what to do with the motor. He told him he had worked with machines in Mexico. In a week, the same foreman offered Eugenio a position in the millwright craft units—the guys who repair and maintain the mill's equipment.

Eugenio jumped at the opportunity; the craft guys got paid more than what both he and Procopio made together. It was also something rare—at the time, Eugenio was the only Mexican working a skilled job. There were a couple of blacks, but all the rest were whites.

As a laborer, Procopio works with mostly Mexicans and blacks. Ever alert to new English phrases, he picks up one from a group of black laborers: *No money, no honey.*

He likes the sound of that. Pretty soon, Procopio is saying this everywhere he goes. When someone asks him a question, he'll answer with an accented "No money, no honey." If a non–English-speaking *paisa* wants some new words, he'll tell him, "No money, no honey." He begins to drive Eladia mad, using that phrase to punctuate most of his arguments. It's his way of saying "you know what I mean?"

"*Mira, mujer,* if you get more eggs and bread at one time," he tells Eladia one day in their tiny kitchen/living room, "we won't need to keep going to the store every other day—no money, no honey."

After months of this, Eladia and his friends try to stop him from repeating the phrase. They figure if they make some strange noise every time he quotes it—a yell, a moan, or a catcall—he'll stop. After a while, it begins to work, until, that is, he picks up another phrase in the mill: *You snooze, you lose.*

For many months, Eladia forbids Procopio to speak any English when he's anywhere within earshot.

On weekends, when most mill employees are not working—many of the major repairs are done on Saturdays or Sundays—the housing units come alive with circles of family and friends who sit on home-made chairs in the space between the cottages. They drink beer, enjoy a goat roasted in an earthen pit or grilled chicken from their own coops, all the while strumming guitars and singing romantic boleros or those minstrel-type *corridos* that often tell of their plight as migrant workers caught in the shadowed places between two worlds.

Laughter, Spanish curses, and children's yells emanate from the cottages, often heard by the craft workers on the catwalks or towers overlooking the soot-stained streets, brick hotels, small shops, and mill housing. In the mill, the Mexicans do their work and don't say much when others are around. But when they gather together, there are songs, *zapateados,* poetry, jokes, beer-induced tears, and one hell of a fiesta.

Procopio sits next to Eladia, a guitar on his lap, his round fingers playing Mexican chords and a few bars of tunes that speak of the Mexican revolution and other sorrows he learned about when he was a child. At one point, the men and women begin to share popular sayings they remember from back home.

"How about this one: *No hay mal que dure cien años, ni tarugo que lo aguante* (There is no wrong that will last a hundred years, nor an idiot who will bear it)," recites one of the seated men.

"I got a better one," remarks a woman from an open kitchen window. "*Si tu mal tiene remedio, no te apures; y si no tiene remedio, para qué te apuras?* (If your troubles have a solution, don't worry about them; if they have no solution, why worry about them?)."

Others contribute more *dichos*. Soon off-color jokes and memorized poems follow, bringing the neighbors to guffaws and *ahhs*.

Procopio snickers at someone's glib remark while glancing at a guitar he picks at; then he looks up toward the mill to see several men standing around on the walk-around that grips the side of each of the cooling towers. The men just stare at the gathering across the street, not saying or doing anything. He can't make out who they are, but he can see they wear blue hard hats. Millwrights. What must they be thinking? he wonders. Some may have never seen Mexicans before. Many of the craft workers had been brought in from East Texas, Arkansas, Louisiana, and California farmlands. They are young, blond or red-haired mostly, arrogant at times, and some are even downright mean.

Procopio recalls once scraping the hardened slag off the rails of the slag cars where the furnace heats had been poured. Eugenio was nearby, monkeying around with broken-down equipment, when two smug millwrights showed up.

"Yeah, that Rex—he knows enough to be dangerous," said one millwright. The other laughed. The millwright crews began to call Eugenio that name when they couldn't pronounce his real name. "Rex the Mex" is what they actually called him. Despite the attention, Rex didn't say anything as he continued wrenching apart the machine.

It was well known that Rex knew what he was doing, although it would take him years before he became a full-fledged millwright, longer than any other millwright in the mill's history. But he never made an issue of it. He kept carrying out his work assignments, finding easier ways to do things than the other—supposedly more experienced—millwrights had been doing.

"Yeah, Rex ain't afraid of no work," the other millwright added. "He'll lay right down next it anytime."

Rex looked up, smiled, then continued his job; his command of English wasn't solid. So much of this banter he didn't understand.

"Ah, Rex is all right; the rest of the world is fucked up, that's all," the first millwright retorted as he motioned to his friend for them to leave.

Procopio later learned that one of those young whippersnappers was Earl Denton. He's a boisterous and obnoxious millwright who seems to be the ringleader of an anti-Mexican group among the craft workers. When the Mexicans first came into the mill in large numbers, these millwrights glared at them, made comments about "*panchos*" and "burros," and generally gave them a hard time.

Procopio decided to stay out of their way until one day he came across one Mexican laborer, a much older man, who happened to be by himself shoveling grease, oil, and slag chips from beneath the 22-inch hotbed. Denton and four other millwrights were there pushing him around, overturning the container of junk he had already filled up, and making fun of his Spanish when the Mexican tried to protest. Procopio didn't know what to do at that moment, although he raged inside. He had seen too much of this in Arizona. Denton looked over and spotted Procopio. The two were nearly the same age.

"What you looking at, greaser?" Denton snarled.

Procopio knew he didn't have a chance at doing anything just then. So his rage festered for a long time, even now as he continues to witness Denton's crew inflict more humiliations on the darker-skinned folks, and worse on Mexicans.

Procopio thinks of this as he slides his fingers across the guitar frets, fooling around mostly, as the others sit around, talking or eating grilled meat with mashed beans and freshly cooked tortillas.

He thinks of how his compatriots have a deeply rooted culture: ways of seeing and being, of thinking and acting, some of which link back tens of thousands of years before the Spanish conquered. They embody elaborate traditions and customs; the children, for example, are having fun, playing games, yelling, but still behaving. A mother's look or a father's stern warning will be enough to pull a child back into line if he or she happens to cross over it. For the most part, Mexicans still retain their respect of elders, giving just due to the older sages among them. They hold dearly to extended family, seeing aunts and uncles almost as parents, cousins as siblings, godparents as blood relations. Respect is everything. They keep their songs, their idioms, their social habits. They maintain aspects of their Mexican-style Catholicism, full of indigenous symbols and patterns of worship that annoy the mostly Irish priest and Irish-American nuns who run the small Catholic church nearby. The Mexicans rarely show up there—all the services and catechism classes are in English or Latin. Useless to Mexicans.

The previous Sunday, Procopio and Eladia decided to attend mass to consider worshiping there. As soon as they walked into the sanctuary, the white congregation turned around and stared. The couple stood in the back, looking around, seeing that none of their people were there. Nobody walked up to them and offered them a seat. Nobody asked what their names were. The room was as silent as the moment after Procopio had asked Eladia to leave her family for him had been.

"God doesn't live in this church," Procopio said before they turned and quietly walked out.

At the end of the row of cottages, the families have built an altar with the Virgin of Guadalupe's likeness, candles, branches, bowls of water and dirt, and photos and letters from loved ones in the old country. On Sunday, the women gather there to pray while the men stay in front of their homes, drinking beer, playing dominoes, or keeping time on an old guitar.

Procopio feels at home among his neighbors. But in the mill he feels he has entered another universe. At home, he's man and provider, keeper of house and family. But in the mill, he's a thing, a mule, somebody to be humiliated when Denton and his buddies feel like it, to be yelled at whenever his bosses want to yell. His sense of manhood, of being Mexican—of being human—is always on the line when he enters the mill.

In time, the mill and its bosses clash with many of the ideas and ways brought over from the old country. Industry destroys the tribal and village elder system and replaces it with the boss–worker system that eventually dictates one's life, one's relationships and aspirations, including how one deals with family, one's wife, and even with one's own worth.

Whatever the workers may think, the mill becomes primary; family, children, music, and community become secondary. To maintain the pecking order, some men come home demanding that wives do what they say, that children keep quiet and out of their face, that all will have to tolerate their late nights drinking, hanging out, and maybe even having another woman on the side. Their excuse—"I work in the mill. I bring the money. I take shit at work; I'm not going to take any shit at home."

Procopio is one of those who avoids these scenarios—he remembers his promise to Eladia to be good and to love her all the days of his life. But over time he sees the effects: There are days or nights when men in the cottages yell at the top of their lungs, often drunk, frightening children, beating walls, sometimes having to be restrained from knocking their wife's teeth out. The mill gets under their skin: The monotony, the long hours, the changing shifts, and the treatment they receive, as if they are less than others. Most handle it as best they can; far too many let it eat them alive.

After a couple of years, Procopio saves enough money to move his family out of the mill's housing units and rents a small home in the South Los Angeles community of Florence, named for the main thoroughfare in the community: Florence Avenue. This area is opening up to Mexicans and blacks as large numbers of whites move out of the older-stock housing to nicer, newly constructed homes in places like the San Fernando Valley, which was then developed from mostly farmland.

Procopio and Eladia begin to have children. Boy after boy, one a year, from 1945 to 1950. In fact, Eladia was pregnant, although she didn't know it, before they moved into the mill's cottages. The first child is named Severo, born with the aid of a *curandera*/midwife. Then Procopio Jr. comes. By the time the family makes it to Florence, Rafael is ready for the world. Then Bune and later Juan arrive in succession.

The couple stop having children in 1952: This is the year their only daughter is born. They name the baby Azucena. She is a beautiful brown child with a head full of curly dark hair. Since he has had nothing but boys before, she shines special to Procopio. But two years later she's gone, having drowned in a bucket of dirty mop water when Eladia was hanging the wash and the boys were playing in the front yard with neighborhood children.

It wasn't but fifteen minutes after Eladia thought she left Azucena safely in her high chair. But the girl somehow climbed out and made it to the floor before ending up headfirst in the water.

Procopio was working at the time. He didn't get the news until he arrived home at midnight; in those days it was hard to communicate with workers during the day, especially since most didn't have phones. When Eladia came in from the backyard, the girl had already stopped breathing. Eladia snatched her up in her arms and then ran into the street screaming. People rushed out of their homes to find out what the screams were about. A neighbor agreed to drive mother and daughter to East L.A.'s General Hospital, some ten miles north of their barrio. Other neighbors said they'd watch the boys.

When they arrived at the hospital, Eladia tried frantically to get emergency assistance—the steelworkers hadn't yet acquired medical benefits. In any event, a doctor and a couple of nurses hurriedly took the girl from her mother and tried to revive her, but it was too late.

Azucena was buried in a newly opened Catholic cemetery in Montebello, where Mexicans from all over buried many of their dead; a number of Procopio's neighbors from the mill housing units and his fellow laborers in the mill attended the wake and funeral.

Procopio shut down emotionally after Azucena's death. Where once he was playful, funny even, now he is silent. He often wrestled with the oldest boys and swept the younger ones up in his strong arms. But after the funeral, he seldom reaches out anymore. He also stops being intimate with Eladia as well, something she endures for years in silence. It's a painful rejection. On that same fateful day, she lost both a daughter and a husband.

Over the years, Procopio gets to know and rely on Nazareth Steel as one would rely on an old friend. Many laborers move up into other positions in the plant—mill hands, furnace operators, and overhead-crane operators. But not Procopio. He likes the hard work, the laborer's lot, the constancy of sweat and muscle. Nazareth becomes his one comfort. Not home, not wife, not even memories of Mexico.

The few photos of Azucena are put away, deep in a carton below stacks of other boxes in the garage. Eladia wants her daughter's picture in a frame, in the middle of the room, over a makeshift altar. Procopio will have none of this. But what does it matter—he spends hours upon hours, double shifts, as much time as he can, in the plant.

The boys grow up without a father. For the older boys it's devastating—they recall a caring and nurturing dad. Neither their father's body, nor his spirit, is around anymore.

The youngest boy, Juan—or Johnny, as he's later called—is too young to remember such a father. He was four years old when Azucena died. He remembers having a baby sister, but beyond that not much.

One day, when Johnny's about six years old, Eladia finds a reel of eight-millimeter film and she decides to put it on an old projector. Procopio's at work at the time. All the boys gather to watch the film with their mother. As the film flickers on a cracked blank wall, Johnny's surprised to see his dad holding him, at age two, smiling and bouncing him in his arms. There are also shots of Azucena, tiny in a crib. Eladia cries and Junior moves to turn off the projector, but Eladia stops him and insists that he keep the film rolling.

There are scenes of the family on the beach, their dad, dark and large, running back and forth into the frothy edge of ocean, the boys following behind in fits of laughter. Eladia is so young looking, slouched back on the sand, unwilling to stand up and display her old-fashioned bathing suit, which Procopio is playfully prompting her to do. There are scenes of their first apartment in Florence, before the family finally bought a larger house where they now live. Again, Procopio smiles, dances, and teases. He seems happy and alive. All this before that day, the day his daughter passed away.

It was the last eight-millimeter film the boys ever saw in the house.

The United Steelworkers of America, Local 1750, is located across the east parking lot of Nazareth Steel. It's August of 1959, and the normally quiet union hall is abuzz with activity. Hundreds of mill workers pack into the place, although the majority have rarely ever shown up to union meetings. But this is different. The international union has embarked on the largest strike in its history—more than a half-million union members have walked out on their jobs across the country.

Procopio is crowded in with the others—all races and languages—listening to loud and harried conversations. Like him, most of the men are worried yet excited. While Procopio has been in strike battles before, this one, he knows, is going to be huge. Up until then, labor crews made slightly more than a dollar an hour—the union feels it's time that Big Steel, whose members have become profitable conglomerates, provide decent standard pay and benefits to the men of steel. The large number of workers out at one time will probably have the effect of crippling the steel industry, as well as related industries such as auto and construction. It can also destroy the union—it's a world-class gamble. As Procopio stands there, he spots an old friend—Eugenio.

"*Oyé, paisano—que piensas de este lio?*" Procopio says to get Eugenio's attention.

"We're in for a battle, *compa*," Eugenio responds. "This isn't going to be easy."

In minutes, international union representatives pull the men together to address them. The local union leadership is also there—made up of conservative white racists who use the local hall to get out of work, have parties, and hold perfunctory and ineffectual meetings. They aren't happy about the strike, but they can't say or do anything against it as long as the international reps are present.

Strategies are worked out and men are allocated to different strike positions. Procopio becomes one of the picket captains—his first major participation in the local union since he was hired into the mill fourteen years earlier. He is slated to work with mostly laborers in early-morning strike detail, armed with picket signs and standing next to fiery metal trash cans in front of the plant's main entrance. There are no strike funds for those who man the pickets; at the most, they may get canned goods or other food items.

That night Procopio relates the news about the strike to Eladia.

"Qué chingao vamos a ser con este pinche estrike?" Eladia responds. *"No podemos hacer nada con la sopa que la unión da."*

"Ya se, I know, but this is what we have to do," Procopio answers.

The boys, varying in age from nine to fourteen, don't understand what this is about, except that their father will not be working for a while.

But having Procopio present doesn't mean he's "present." Sure, he dictates the rules in the house. He reprimands the boys so they'll obey their mother. When the boys get in trouble, he disciplines them with a belt. Eladia hardly does that. She yells, threatens, but mostly she tells Procopio and then all hell breaks loose. The boys learn to behave—or at least to do their best to get away with whatever it is they're doing.

But beyond that, he doesn't relate much to the boys.

Except with Severo.

Procopio dotes on his oldest son. Ever since he was a child, Severo has always been close to his father. When Procopio comes home in the late mornings from the picket line, Severo is the only one who runs up and hugs him. A stocky, chubby-faced athlete and fast learner, he stays out of trouble in school and routinely does what he's told—the good son among his brothers.

The other boys continue their play while Severo sits close to Procopio in the living room as he relates mill stories, strike stories, and jokes (the funny parts are mostly due to Procopio's heavily accented corruption of the English language—like calling the Supreme Being a "string bean").

Johnny, the youngest, is the most distant from his father. On top of that, his older brothers—Junior, Rafas, and Bune—often beat up on Johnny when Procopio or Eladia aren't looking. Johnny doesn't have a problem with Severo—he's too old for the much younger Johnny to hang with. Besides, Johnny looks up to Severo. The age difference allows Johnny to elevate Severo to the position of "good" brother.

The next three boys, however, take their wrath out on little Johnny. Johnny's scared to tell his parents—warned that he'd get it worse if he did. They throw balls aimed at his head and push him off rooftops. One day Junior invites Johnny to hang out with Junior's friends. Johnny thinks it's nice for Junior to suggest—maybe he's not so mean after all. But as soon as he hooks up with the older boys behind a small plastics factory, Junior encourages his friends to beat up on Johnny, all the while laughing as they punch him black and blue.

Instead of the strike bringing father and sons closer together, Procopio's rage fills the small house. He seems more irritated than usual during the strike—not working, but walking picket lines, freezing in the early mornings.

Meanwhile, the bills pile up. Gas, and therefore heat, is sacrificed. And extra car parts and other junk in the driveway and backyard are sold.

After a little more than four months, the strike ends. And, to the surprise of most observers, the steel corporations give in to the union's demands—a landmark event that lays the groundwork for major changes in steel and other industries for years to come. The boys, on the other hand, have had their fill of their father at home during the strike. All except Severo.

Things for Johnny only get worse. He steals, he talks back, he runs away. In a few years, Johnny ends up in the streets, driving his mother mad with worry and forcing Procopio to place ultimatums on Johnny's behavior. Eventually, he's kicked out of school at age thirteen, joins a *cholo* gang, the Florencia Trece Locos, and is arrested for stealing cars. In a few years, Procopio turns his back on him completely.

Most of Johnny's troubles start around 1963. That year, after Procopio had become active in the union during the '59 strike, he runs for union office and briefly participates as part of a slate of Mexicans and blacks for local union offices—the first time the local has ever run a nonwhite slate. It's a hell of a struggle—one that keeps Procopio away from home even more than before.

Johnny's life, on the other hand, spirals downward. At age sixteen, he spends months in juvenile hall awaiting hearings on a robbery charge. Eladia is the only one to visit him regularly; his brothers come from time to time. As she and her son sit in a room with other boys and their parents and siblings, Eladia feels inadequate, only able to communicate with small talk. Johnny doesn't know what to say either. But finally he asks how his father's doing.

"*Tu padre? Muy bien, m'ijo. Trabajando como siempre, ya sabes,*" Eladia says.

"Why doesn't he visit me?"

"Oh, *m'ijo*, he too busy. Too much work. He miss you. Too much work," Eladia tries to say in her best English. "*No es que no quiere.* It's not that he doesn't want to."

"I'm not sure he wants to," Johnny says, a tinge of bitterness in his voice. "Honestly, *amá*, I hate that steel mill."

"Why you say that, Juanito? Steel mill good. Good for family. Need money."

"I know, I know, but Dad's never got time for me, or for my brothers. He's working there all the time. Then with the union elections . . . forget it."

"Don't hate mill. You work in mill someday—*sabes?* When you get out of this thing. You work like your brothers work."

"I don't want to be like my brothers," Johnny almost yells. "I'd rather be locked up. Dad don't deal with me anyway. Might as well be put away and forgotten."

Eladia's eyes tear up. She wants to say so much to him, but can't seem to find the words, even in Spanish.

"*Estás equivocado.* You wrong. We need the mill. *Tu papá ha sacrificado tanto para ti y tus hermanos. Mira cómo estás. Tienes mejor idea? Tienes otro remedio?*"

"You're right, Ma. I don't have a better way."

While the rest of his brothers eventually fall into line, entering the steel mill one after the other, Johnny only sees what the mill has done to his family: pull Procopio away, closing him off, driving a wedge between his mother and father, between father and sons, between the danger and excitement of street life and the sure-thing nature of steel work, with its relentless schedules, long days, and body-damaging workloads.

The day Johnny is sentenced to the California Youth Authority, Eladia and his brothers are there, but not his father. Procopio never shows up, despite Eladia's declarations to Johnny that he is on his way. This puts a greater distance between them, a distance not easily bridged, a distance that can cause a lifetime gulf between father and son.

Johnny spends the next few years, until he's twenty, at a Youth Authority prison. On her visits, Eladia tries to convince her son to forgive his father and consider working in the steel mill when he gets out.

"You have to stop this trouble you get into," Eladia pleads on one such visit. "Think about the mill when you get out. It's your only chance."

"We'll see about that—I got lots of time to think about it," Johnny responds, not wanting to commit to work in the same place as his father.

Eladia, in turn, pressures Procopio to see that Johnny's going to be all right—that he shouldn't be written off.

"*Es tu hijo—procúrale,*" Eladia tells her husband one day at dinner.

"*Y por qué?* He'll never amount to anything. Forget about Johnny—*ya no es hijo para mi,*" Procopio replies coldly. "He's no longer a son of mine."

But Eladia can't turn her back on Johnny. She knows there's one thing that can possibly bring father and son together again, one thing that when Johnny gets out, he can try for, one thing that has given their family, their community, their world the worst and best of everything, that feeds and takes away, but also forgives. She's seen this over and over again—that one thing is the steel mill.

Part II

THE NAZARETH SUITE

CLOCKWORK

An overhead crane with massive iron jaws lifts several tons of red-orange forged-steel ingots from their soaking pits. The crane moves across its tracks and lowers the ingots onto stainless-steel rollers that push them into the pounding forge of the 32-inch mill. With enormous force, the forge rams down on the ingots, shaping them into long beams to be transported to other mills for more precise shaping—into I beams, H beams, plates or rods of various diameters. Nearby, a gondola car on a narrow-gauge track brings in more newly formed ingots for the soaking pits inside Nazareth Steel Corporation's two-man-high chain-link and corrugated steel fence that faces Slauson Avenue.

Johnny Salcido looks on from across the street, although he doesn't stay long; the heat from the ingots—known as "hot tamales" because of the high temperatures and their shape—penetrates the clothing and skin of anyone standing there, even at that distance.

But for as long as he can, Johnny eyes the steel mill. He watches as waves of heat rise into the air from each virgin ingot. This is where he's going to work. Work he desperately needs. It's May 1970. He's been married for a month and unemployed for a lot longer. Lanky but muscular, Johnny has sharp dark features, a thick head of hair that he wears combed back, and a whisper of goatee under his bottom lip. But he also has a streetwise stare at age twenty. After surviving drugs, stealing, violence, and jail, his ready-for-anything demeanor is sensed by all who know him. Now Johnny's ready for a new wife, a new job, perhaps even a family.

Although he doesn't have a clue as to how to start this new life, Johnny is prepared to do whatever he has to. Working at Nazareth Steel is his one chance to straighten up and to prevail—not just survive. This is what his mother, Eladia, has told him repeatedly while he was behind the razor wire and barred doors of the California Youth Authority prison. He had argued with her—he didn't want to cave in to the mill, where his father, Procopio, had spent a quarter of a century. This is the same father who kicked Johnny out of the house when he was fifteen, forcing Johnny to fend for himself in the trash-lined streets, crash in friends' pads, and sleep in the drug dens of his neighborhood. Procopio expected his sons to be working men, not bums or petty crooks, like Johnny seemed to be.

Yet, after his release, Johnny figures that if he doesn't find work in the mill he may have to return to stealing, the drugs, and, most likely, a jail cell . . . what a plan to fall back on, he thinks.

As it is, Johnny's four older brothers also toiled in the mill—three of them are still there: Junior, Rafas, and Bune; the other, his oldest brother, Severo, died within months of being hired at Nazareth.

Ever since Johnny has been exiled from the family, they all only came together for him once—at his wedding. But the estrangement lessened when word got around that Johnny had been hired at Nazareth—without a recommendation from his father, which would have been a surefire way to get hired. A fact Johnny's particularly proud of, and something his father didn't like hearing at first. Deep down, though, Johnny knew that Procopio felt relieved his youngest son was following in his steel-toed footsteps.

The mill is a hard nut to crack; thousands line up weekly to apply for whatever shoveling or hauling jobs are available. Johnny, however, is assigned to the maintenance crew, a prestigious prospect in the poor South Los Angeles barrio where he grew up. Not everyone is allowed to work on these crews, and he knows it.

By the time Johnny's hired, Nazareth Steel has been continuously running its powerful electric furnaces, rolling mills, wire mill, warehouses, and scrap-metal yard on several acres of prime land for thirty years. Generations of fathers and sons and grandsons have already toiled in the mill by then. Nazareth feeds off the large number of Mexicans in surrounding communities, including East L.A.; blacks and Mexicans from South Central L.A.; and blue-collar whites and Mexicans from communities like Bell, South Gate, and Lynwood. The workers come from far-flung Southern states like Texas, Arkansas, and Louisiana; from Indian lands in Oklahoma and Arizona; and distant Mexican states like Durango, Sinaloa, Sonora, Chihuahua, Jalisco, and especially from Zacatecas, where silver has been mined for centuries.

Mexicans and blacks work in the low-paying, backbreaking labor crews on all three shifts—the plant never sleeps—while the higher-paid construction, maintenance, and electrical crews consist mostly of Southern whites, brought in specifically for the skilled jobs. Most of the foremen and all of the management are also white.

By 1970, after a decade of bitter civil rights battles, including the 1965 Watts riots and disturbances in East L.A., Nazareth begins to break down its own racial barriers. A consent decree has been signed with the United Steelworkers of America that demands blacks, Mexicans, and Indians enter the once-restricted repair crews; a similar decree will later allow women to work in all areas of the plant (besides clerical positions, that is).

That's why Johnny Salcido—badass ex-*cholo*, ex-*pinto*, and onetime druggie—manages to get a position in the "oiler-greaser" gang, the first level of the millwright craft crews at Nazareth. Although the term *oiler-greaser* sounds derogatory to Johnny, he knows this is good news. After his release from the CYA facility in Chino, his parole officer said factory and foundry jobs awaited wards of the state—prior to his release, he was trained in basic mechanics. His bride is a beautiful eighteen-year-old South Central L.A. girl, formerly named Aracely Velasco. Everything seems to be looking up for Johnny. Everything.

It's hard for Johnny to believe he's got the job. The day before, he'd taken his referral papers from the parole office and walked into Nazareth Steel's personnel offices in a soot-covered brick building next to the plant. It still had that old early-1940s look and smell; nothing appeared to have changed in thirty years. His interview went well—the man behind the counter barely questioned Johnny about his interests or his skills. It didn't matter. He was to be trained as per Nazareth's program. Johnny knew he was simply a quota number for the consent decree. Johnny also got the impression the plant administrators didn't care about this decree. Everyone at the personnel office seemed to comply because it was their job. Get the bodies—who cares how—and meet your quotas, Johnny figured. This way they can stop hiring any more blacks and browns than they had to for the skilled jobs. Luckily, Johnny got accepted into the craft units before the Mexican quotas were filled.

That same day, Johnny filled out tons of paperwork, got photographed and fingerprinted—a flashback to his mug-shot days in prison—then he was off for a quick physical; his one embarrassment was handing the secretary a plastic bottle of his own urine.

"No, don't give it to me," she shrieked as she pulled her hands back. "Leave it at the lab window."

The only words missing were, *you stupid.*

After passing the initial examinations, Johnny drove a few blocks from the plant to pick up his uniform. The company referred him to a shop that catered to the many foundries, forges, packing plants, and assembly lines in the area by leasing out and cleaning uniforms. With the tremendous amount of grime his uniforms could accumulate in a day, Johnny soon learned how often he would need to have them cleaned.

He received a set of dark green shirts, and pants to match, with his first name embroidered on the left side of the shirt. He also got steel-toed shoes and a green hard hat. The green signified apprentices—different-colored hats mean different crews and levels of employment in the plant. As a member of the maintenance crew, he also had to buy a leather tool belt that he took to Sears so he could pick up a basic set of wrenches, channel locks, ball-peen hammers, locks, and pliers.

Johnny soon learned that Sears is the place for tools; their Craftsman line has a lifetime guarantee. If any of them break you simply bring them in to be replaced. That's why the craft workers are fond of declaring, "You can't beat that with a stick."

The safety gear is the other must-have: safety glasses, earplugs, and gloves along with hard hat and shoes. Johnny recalled seeing a cartoon at the personnel office that had a squashed figure of a mill hand with a felled I beam over his body. The hard hat, gloves, shoes, and protective eyewear, however, were still intact.

I'm glad I wore my safety gear, read the caption.

Later, Johnny came home before Aracely had returned from the assembly plant where she worked. He put on his uniform, hat, shoes, and belt with tools. He stared into the mirror at himself, his body weighted with equipment. He stood there for the longest time. He looked like a soldier, Johnny thought, only his battlefield was the steel mill, his weapons were tools, his victory consisted of well-oiled, well-greased equipment.

Johnny didn't notice Aracely entering the house. But soon he heard her moving about the living room in the small apartment they rented in the Florence neighborhood of South L.A. He walked in on her in his new getup and practically gave his wife a heart attack.

"Shit, Johnny, I thought you were a burglar or something," Aracely said, half surprised she'd be so startled.

"Nope, *mujer,* I am your local steelworker guy—that's right, I'm now in the 'oiler-greaser' gang at Nazareth Steel," Johnny responded with a wide smile, revealing a missing left tooth among a clutter of teeth. His thoughts suddenly turned to his father, Procopio, who had put in those many years in the mill.

"*No me digas*—you got the job!" Aracely exclaimed. "Right on, *mi amor.*"

The following Monday, Johnny feels oddly nervous. He's so jumpy he can't even eat breakfast. It's his first day on the job. He once briefly worked in a meatpacking plant, hosing down the innards from butchered animals. But, as Johnny knows, Nazareth is considered bigtime in the barrio. There are several big plants like this around—producing autos, tires, bridges, airplanes, or bombs. To keep the facilities at peak levels, half a dozen federally subsidized housing projects were built in South Central L.A. after World War II to house the mostly Southern black workers for many of these plants; another half a dozen housing projects in East L.A. house mostly Mexicans.

But Nazareth is the granddaddy of all the big plants, the largest steel mill west of the Mississippi. And Johnny's now part of it.

Aracely checks him out before she dashes off to her monotonous day-shift job assembling washing-machine parts.

"You look sharp, *ese*," she declares, eyeing him in a way that makes him more self-conscious. Aracely has short curly hair, a honey-brown complexion, and a sweet face; her body is small, with disproportionate hip size in comparison to her chest. But she's good-looking, not over-weight, with a strong personality and an intelligence Johnny has al-ways respected—Johnny's as much attracted to her mind as to her humor and natural beauty. And he thinks: If he had known a uniform, hard hat, and tools could turn women on, he would have worn them a long time ago.

Johnny and Aracely rent a back apartment on Maie Avenue near Florence Street behind an old wood-shingled house. The Florencia barrio is one of the oldest and poorest Mexican neighborhoods on the Southside—a former pachuco 'hood of the 1940s and 1950s, it's now home to one of the most active barrio gangs in Los Angeles: Florencia Trece. Their elaborate and cryptic graffiti, mostly the tag *F13*, can be seen on every wall, trash can, and telephone pole in the area.

Several families live in the front house—there are old charcoal-filled barbecue pits in the yard, dirt-laden plastic children's toys, and frayed fold-up chairs. Their landlord, who doesn't live anywhere near here, comes by once a month to get his rent from several homes and apartments he owns up and down the street.

Johnny walks out of his apartment like a leather-and-rhinestone vaquero, only he's decked out in steel-mill regalia. He soon realizes he's showing off, so he hurries to his car and backs out of the driveway.

He drives a short distance to Maywood. He turns into a street in the middle of the mill, flanked by two large parking lots for Nazareth employees; with all shifts going strong, the lots are never empty. Johnny parks his ratty two-tone '58 Impala in a space and steps out. He can see smoke curling away from various towers. Air whistles blast loudly at varying intervals. A resounding roar from the electric furnaces and the boom of scrap metal being dropped into the back of railcars rounds out the amazing cacophony of mechanical sounds. From the parking lot, Johnny sniffs the sulfur and limestone smells, the iron and coal dust, and he realizes what a powerfully sensual world the mill is. It has its own music, seemingly senseless but over time coming together in harmonies all its own. It's an otherworldly place, far removed from his Florencia neighborhood with its small ma-and-pa stores, liquor stops, and taco stands.

Johnny enters a corrugated tin-covered shanty before walking through the main gates of the plant, guarded by uniformed security officers. Inside the shanty is a time card with his name and plant number—a number he'd come to remember like his Youth Authority prison number. He pushes the card into a time clock in a row of similar clocks. It stamps a date and the hour on the card, marking the beginning of his shift. Johnny then places the card next to several others that have also recently been punched in. A few workers leaving the night shift trudge into the shack to remove their cards and place them close to where he placed his; they punch their cards into one of the clocks and then stack them on another section marked for employees whose shift has ended. Everything is routine—schedules, operating procedures. Everything like clockwork.

Directed by the guard, Johnny walks into what appears to be a small city. Workers are leaving the plant; others, like him, are coming in. Forklifts drive past. He walks over numerous rail tracks embedded in the ground. Dirt and scrap crumple beneath his feet. Huge cranes with magnets at the end of their lines fill the awaiting train beds with tons of scrap metal. He can see the molten liquid steel being poured from a massive ladle onto empty ingot molds on top of other railcars. This sight almost takes his breath away. He has seen images like this before, maybe in magazines, in a movie—who knows where—but to actually witness this is really something. Maybe, he begins to realize, this is why his father has spent so much of his life here.

Johnny heads toward another large corrugated steel building, the millwright shanty situated next to the four gigantic electric furnaces and the 22-inch rolling mill. Inside, he sees half a dozen new maintenance crew members. They wear uniforms similar to his, only they are different colors and sizes. The men sit around a heavily carved, grease-stained wooden table, awaiting the day foreman to arrive and conduct orientation.

Johnny walks up to each man and shakes his hand.

"Hey, I'm Johnny Salcido," he greets.

One guy is a Seminole from the Oklahoma Indian country. The other men are two Chicanos, a black, a Colombian, and a young white guy. Except for the Colombian, Seminole, and one of the Mexican guys, they seem to be just out of high school. The white guy stands up and walks off to one side to smoke a cigarette. Johnny thinks they all look cool in their clean, pressed uniforms, although the black and one of the Chicanos have on flannel shirts and jeans. Various kinds of tool belts are wrapped around their waists or flung on the table.

"Grab an empty locker," one of the Chicanos, named Ray Garcia, instructs Johnny. A few locker doors are open and Johnny spots one in the middle of the others. He peers inside; there's graffiti and bumper stickers on the metal. A partial magazine photo of a naked girl is taped to one side. Johnny throws his tools inside and closes the locker door, snapping on the lock he bought the day before.

Just then a red-faced older man wearing a blue-striped white hard hat enters the shanty. Next to him stands a full-fledged millwright wearing a blue hard hat—you can tell he's a veteran in the mill, his tool belt worn and his tools long tarnished, his hard hat scuffed raw.

"Welcome, men," the red-faced man begins. His name is Emmett Taylor; he runs the oiler-greaser crew. Johnny later learns he's a West Virginia coal-mine recruit from twenty years ago. The mustached millwright next to him spits tobacco crud into a trash bucket in a corner near the lockers.

"My name's Taylor," the foreman explains. "I don't have much to say except that you do what I tell you to do, you don't come late, you don't leave early, and you don't give nobody any lip. You got grievances, take them to the union. This here is Bob Michaels, your union rep. You can get more details from Bob about the union, benefits, and pay increases. From me you'll get clear instructions and work schedules. You'll get daily repair sheets and also the daily rounds you have to check on. There will be two men on every job, unless I say different. We have twenty-five men on this crew. You'll get to see every nook and cranny of this mill. After a while you'll get to meet the other oiler-greasers—right now they're getting their work assignments. This shanty is where you'll change your clothes, put your tools away at the end of the day, grab other tools you may need, and get your assignments. There are showers and restrooms down on the left. This is also where you eat. Keep it clean. If you run out of work and there are no more assignments for you, you mop these floors and clean the tables and lockers. Mops and buckets are over there in one of the toolsheds. Each tool you borrow will be marked, and it'll have to be returned as soon as you've finished with it. All tools must be returned cleaned of grease. There are turpentine vats just outside the shanty for you to wash your tools. You'll also be assigned a grease gun and copper-pipe cutters. For the next few weeks you'll work the day shift. After you've gotten the routine down and have proven yourselves on the oilin' and greasin', we'll put you on repair crews for different shifts and different parts of the mill. That's for later. Right now you'll concentrate on being the best damn oiler-greasers this plant has ever known. Questions?"

A few *nos* and *we're okay* arise from the men.

In Johnny's mind, Taylor's a good ol' boy, no doubt about it. Johnny can practically hear country music and stock cars racing as Taylor speaks. But he is also a straightforward, take-care-of-business kind of guy. Strongly built for an older man—his eyes asquint like Clint Eastwood—Taylor looks like he can handle his own.

That night, Johnny lies in bed staring at the ceiling. Aracely snuggles up close to him, her right leg draped over his body. Earlier, Aracely had put on a sexy nightie and robe and did a slow strip tease for Johnny. He laughed and laughed—Aracely was actually quite funny. She would drop pieces of her clothing and say, "Oops, how did that happen?" or "My, these clothes are slippery," as she bent over to pick up her underwear. By the time she stood naked at the end of the bed, her brown skin glistened with sweat, strands of hair across her face, the moonlight through the window silhouetting her body against the far wall. Johnny could hardly contain himself.

The steel-mill uniform, tools, shoes, and hat he wore when he came home really did help.

Johnny had met Aracely when he hung around Fremont High School with his homeboys, even though he had already dropped out. He stayed in touch with her over the years; even after his incarceration, they kept writing to each other. Aracely found something in Johnny she didn't find in other guys—a depth of feeling, loyalty, and a kind of nobility she couldn't even name. When Johnny got arrested, she let go of him for a while; later she decided she really wanted to stay in touch with him. She became Johnny's girl—Eladia sometimes took her to see him at the California Youth Authority. As soon as he was released, they got married.

As Johnny begins to doze off, he thinks about the money the mill will bring in. The pay in the unskilled labor crews is relatively good; better, if you are a mill hand or operator. But to be in the craft division, this is unheard of. In the barrio, this is the pinnacle of success, the I-made-it-now kind of work that is supposed to last a lifetime . . . no, several lifetimes. Generations dependent on the mill are legion in Florencia. As it was, steelworkers were some of the best paid in basic industry—following a tremendous strike in 1959 that over the years would lead to lucrative contract agreements in exchange for relative peace in the mills.

But the money from being in the craft units—including the best health benefits and retirement—are what Mexicans had been denied for so long. The consent decree changed that for a chosen few. And Johnny is one of them. One of the prime candidates, the lucky ones, the few who can walk proud down the well-worn Florencia streets and actually command a measure of respect.

Unemployment in the neighborhoods is rampant, despite the factories and forges that surround these streets. There are far too many winos and junkies in the alleys next to liquor stores, and *cholos* with nothing to do as they hang out on the street corners.

Johnny understands he's making a place for several more generations of Salcidos. You never give up a Nazareth Steel job. It seems unbelievable, but at such a young age, Johnny's going to be set for life. How many people in his barrio can say that? He and Aracely, Johnny thinks, are going to have it made. They can buy a new car. Maybe even save up for a new home. Or have a baby. He figures they can afford a baby with his new benefits and pay. No more newlywed poor for them. No more small dingy apartments with landlords who won't fix leaky roofs or backed-up toilets. No more feeling like he isn't worth anything, only good for trouble and stealing. Johnny doesn't have to steal anymore. He's a steelworker. *A steelworker*. Imagine that.

Johnny smiles as he glances over at Aracely, so peaceful and beautiful in his arms. Eventually, he falls asleep. A most wonderful, well-earned sleep. The sleep of his life.

"Hey you, Fire Hazard!" yells out one of the older millwrights from the top of an overhead crane on the 10-inch mill.

Johnny has just emerged from below the mill bed, where electrical motors, crankshafts, bearings, and couplings are caked with grease, wet with oil, and speckled with flakes of steel slag. He looks down on himself and realizes he's soaked with oil and grease from his hard hat to his steel-toed shoes.

"Don't have a smoke or you'll blast off, Fire Hazard," mocks another millwright.

Fire Hazard becomes Johnny's new mill name—everyone in the craft crews has to have one. In a short time, Johnny gets to know many of these characters.

There's Dirty Harry, an old Appalachian-bred millwright who never seems to be free of dirt and grime. Another is One-Wrench

Mike, who's the direct opposite: He always leaves work with the same spotless pressed clothes and dirt-free hard hat that he comes in with. Instead of a well-worn tool belt, he has one shiny stainless-steel wrench sticking out of his back pocket, thus his moniker. He somehow manages to stay clean regardless of how dirty his assigned jobs may be.

There is Rex the Mex—the one Mexican millwright who already has twenty-five years' time in the plant. Rex is an old-timer who calls everything he sees a *chingadera*.

"Give me that *chingadera*," he tells his apprentice while pointing to some tool. Or, "Get those *chingaderas* over here," he says as he signals the overhead-crane driver to transport some equipment. Or, "If I see another one of these *chingaderas* on the floor, I'm going to punch somebody," he declares when he steps on a piece of aluminum foil in the millwright shanty. The foil has pieces of a burrito from the "garbage" truck—or lunch wagon—that parks inside the mill during lunch breaks (the one cafeteria in the plant serves only office employees).

Then there's Heavy, a 350-pound millwright working days on the electric furnaces; he is known to have the best stories in the mill, sitting for hours on the graveyard shift or during the daytime repair days, telling stories to anyone who'll listen.

Johnny realizes that Fire Hazard is not a cool name. But until he grasps how to work without being a magnet for every kind of flammable liquid and glob of grease he comes across, he's stuck with this name.

Pretty soon everyone calls him Fire Hazard, even the new oiler-greasers who are only slightly better in keeping the grease off themselves.

Johnny's first days on the job are marred by his clumsiness. He learns the hard way that he has to pay strict attention in the mill. A wrong move, a forgotten instruction, a lapsed moment can prove deadly. One alleged incident involved a drunken overhead-crane operator. Everyone knows that many of the crane operators are drunk half the time while they maneuver their equipment. This one particular time, the crane operator was too drunk to notice that bricklayers were repairing the damaged firebricks inside one of the furnaces. The operator moved a load of scrap metal over the opened furnace roof and then let it go, burying three bricklayers beneath tons of crumpled cars and metal junk.

From then on, cranes moving over the furnaces automatically send out flashing lights and sirens as a warning to anyone below.

Johnny's mishaps are far less serious. He once drove a forklift over to pick up equipment, but he kept the lifting section high, tearing up water pipes, which caused streams of water to spray everywhere. At the following month's safety meetings, the mill instructor drew a forklift and stick figure to show others what "not to do" while driving a forklift, making Johnny the butt of that month's joke.

Another time, Johnny stood on the floor of a warehouse area where an overhead crane was hauling tons of metal piping across the bay, held by a worn-out wire rope strap that Johnny, in his inexperience, used to hold everything. Suddenly Johnny got the urge to piss and he ducked into the men's bathroom just before the wire rope gave way, dropping the massive pipes onto the very spot Johnny had been standing just seconds earlier.

Once he was supposed to move the overhead crane that strips the ingots of the slag shells they're in before being placed into the soaking pits. Johnny and his partner for that week, Ray, were to set up an air-powered grease gun on a platform and grease all the bearings on the stripper crane's "jaws." But as Ray began to unravel the grease gun's hose, Johnny moved the crane toward the platform, in his haste forgetting to lift up the iron jaws. The jaws struck an ingot on the railcar, which keeled over onto the one next to it. That ingot hit the next one, and on and on—a domino effect—toppling several ingots onto the ground.

Johnny swiftly climbed down the crane while Ray mumbled, "*Puta madre*," over and over again. They rewound the hose onto the grease gun and quietly walked away as several workers gathered to see what had happened. Taylor almost fired Johnny for the incident.

The closest call was when Johnny almost lost an arm in the 22-inch mill's overhead crane. The heavy metal door leading to the operator's cabin closed quickly as soon as someone opened it to enter. All operators, oiler-greasers, and millwrights were supposed to be warned about it. One day, Johnny opened the door and walked through, thinking nothing of it. The next instant the door came crashing shut. He barely pulled his arm out of the way when the frightening bang behind him made him jump. Instantly, Johnny realized how close he had come to losing a limb. He was angry for days because nobody had told him about the door before he climbed up there.

In time, Johnny will get the hang of working with the equipment and watching what he's doing. But he almost destroys whole sections of the mill before he learns the right and wrong ways of getting the job done.

Heavy pushes back against a creaky, grease-stained metal chair inside the millwright shanty beneath the floor of the electric furnaces. He talks slowly, revving up for a story, as a couple of millwrights and two oiler-greasers, Johnny and Ray, stand around him amid the muffled roar of the machines. Heavy adjusts his mountainous weight and looks up at the wobbling ceiling fan and the fluorescent lights hanging by wires; his fingers lace like so many sausages across the canvas of blue work shirt on his chest.

"One thing you got to keep in mind," Heavy states in his deep Southern accent, "is watch what you do around the 'lady.' Everything gets paid back."

"What's the lady?" Ray asks.

"It's the mill, son," Heavy instructs. "This mill becomes your main squeeze. You spend more time here than at home or the bar. You treat her right, and you'll be fine. But play any tricks, mess around, don't do what you're supposed to do, and she'll come get ya."

The other men just listen.

"Got a story for you, gents," Heavy continues. "A lesson in *re-lay-sion-ships*. There was a melter, Mexican dude, who had an affair with the pit boss's wife. That happens. No big deal around this place. But the problem was this melter lived directly across the street from the pit boss. He decided to see the dude's wife anyway, with not a care in the world. One night, just before the graveyard shift began, the melter kissed his own wife's round face and left his home, headed toward the bus stop. As he walked down his driveway, a loud hollow sound split the air and a bullet pierced the melter's hard hat. The dude fell onto the pavement like a sack of potatoes. The moral of this story: Never have an affair with someone whose old man lives within shooting distance."

Slight smiles and knowing winks greet the end of that story.

Heavy waits to let the story's impact seep in before he embarks on another.

"Some of you weren't around when the next incident happened, maybe five years ago," Heavy continues, between strained breaths. "I was there. What I'm about to tell you is the damn truth, swear to sweet Jesus if He don't strike me for swearing. There was a foreman on the labor crew who the other guys didn't like. His name was Sanford Duncan. Yes, sir, that Sanford was an old cuss, pain in the ass, who thought he knew everything. Don't even tell him he's wrong. If he said the moon was green, doggone it, the moon was green. He had a mean word for everyone. For one thing, he called everyone a Polack. Don't matter if you weren't a Polack. You were Polacks to him. And he would yell. Man, he could yell. You could hear Sanford clear to Cucamonga. He'd yell at the laborers for not cleaning up all the slag chips from the mill floors, or at the slag men for not moving fast enough when a heat was tapped after hours of the furnaces cooking iron."

Heavy moves again slightly to the side to relieve pressure on his diaphragm so he can breathe more easily and continue his tale. A couple more men have poked their heads through the shanty opening where a window should be, but isn't, to hear what Heavy has to say.

"One day, old Sanford had a crew of young bucks, barely off the farm, go with him up to the roof of the furnace building where the bag house is. He was yelling at them about this and that. The youngsters weren't totally out of it. One of them insisted to Sanford it was dangerous to walk on the tin-roofed panels; any one of their weights could cause them to fall about a hundred feet into the gaping mouth of a furnace below. You think Sanford would give him credit for this? No, he got upset and told the crew, 'Nonsense, you're all a bunch of lazy Polacks.' Sanford then proceeded to walk across the roof as the men stood nearby with their jaws hanging, next to the safety of side beams. 'See,' Sanford admonished as the hydraulics moved shutters up and down to capture the sulfur dust and other crap in the bag house. 'There's nothing to this.' Then Sanford stepped forward again, and before anyone could shout his name, the fool crashed through the roof, screaming like a stuck pig, right into a reddened pot of molten metal. The oxygen in his body made popping noises as it entered the vat of liquid steel. The furnace operators couldn't do a thing but keep dropping buckets of scrap iron to melt. They skimmed the slag off the top, and when the heat was ready, they poured the molten mass into ingot molds. There was nothing they could do for old Sanford. Things had to keep moving."

Heavy stares at the men listening to him, now including a group of hard hats standing at the shanty entrance. Even one of the foremen stops and gives a listen.

"Somewhere," Heavy says, leaning forward and scanning the room with eyes pushed deep back into his fleshy face, "there's a building in downtown L.A. with steel beams made from ingots with Sanford's body inside. Somewhere there's a bridge or underground pipe bound up forever with his sorry remains. The moral of this story: Don't ever think you know more than what the mill knows. The lady always knows."

"Okay, 'nough lounging 'round," the foreman says after a particularly long pause. "Get back to work, all of youse."

Johnny picks up his tool belt and his grease gun and clambers up a ladder to the furnace roof; he can't shake the story of old Sanford, whose presence—perhaps ghost—seems to brush past him as he moves toward the next piece of machinery that needs greasing, one of many on his work-assignment list.

"Come on, man, you slowin' everythin' in here," Robert yells up at Johnny, who's eighty feet in the air and holding on for dear life in between the huge electrical arms on top of one of the electric furnace roofs.

The temperature is around 250 degrees, even though the furnace has been cooling for hours; Johnny can see smoke rising from underneath his steel-toed boots. He reaches up to a "button" on a bearing so he can fit the end of his grease gun onto it. With a few pumps of the gun, the bearing is greased, and he can move on to another button. But a lot of the fittings are smashed or broken off. Using his channel locks, Johnny removes old buttons and replaces them with new ones. Sometimes he has to hammer in a "tap" to remove a worn button that is stuck inside the threaded hole.

But the heat is unbearable. And Robert's shouts from the furnace floor don't help matters.

Robert Thigpen started work as an oiler-greaser six months prior to Johnny; he is another beneficiary of the consent decree. Foreman Taylor tries to have new men on the crew work alongside more experienced men for the more complicated computer-generated assignments. The men will learn to rely on one another, to learn from one another, and at times to put their lives in one another's hands.

Johnny accepts this as truth. On several jobs, his oil-gang partners literally hold the power of life and death over him. Once when they were greasing the wheels of the soaking-pit cranes, Johnny had to hang over the railing to get to the bearings. While they often use safety belts for the jobs that are high up, these are cumbersome and can be a hindrance. They find ways not to use them but then have to rely on one another for safety. This time, Johnny's partner had to brace himself while holding on to Johnny's legs so he didn't fall over. Whether they want to or not, they have to trust their partners, even if they don't know them. Feeling vulnerable is an understatement.

Robert is Johnny's "mentor." He's a sixty-year-old black man who yells out instructions and humiliates his coworkers. Robert is tall, with a distinguished-looking thin mustache on his upper lip and long fingers. Johnny has worked with him for a couple of weeks and he's already tired of him—he can't imagine having Robert hold on to his legs while working in jobs on the soaking-pit cranes.

For one thing, Robert rarely lifts a finger to help in normal working conditions. Robert barks out orders and then jumps up and down when Johnny doesn't get it quite right. Standing there without a safety belt, on top of the hydraulically opened furnace roof, revealing the red glow of the firebricks inside, Johnny has just about had it.

"You do this, then," he yells down at Robert.

Robert looks up at Johnny with scorn.

"You silly bitch," he says. "I knew you didn't have what it takes for this job. A girl could do better than you. Whatever happened to the real men—all I get is these chickens that can't get their feathers ruffled."

"Fuck you," Johnny responds. "I'll get these last fittings. Then I'm coming down to kick your ass."

At this, Robert smiles.

"About time you wised up," he says. "So hurry up so we can see whose ass is goin' to get kicked 'round here."

"Fuck!" Johnny yells out as he tries to grease another bearing and comes across another smashed-in button.

After he finishes greasing the roller masts on the furnace roof, Johnny painstakingly climbs down from the roof, onto steel ladders and catwalks surrounding each furnace. His asbestos-lined gloves hold off some of the heat as he grabs on to the handrails, but he can still feel the warmth penetrating his hands. On his way down, he's picturing smashing Robert's face with a well-placed punch.

But as soon as Johnny hits the furnace floor, a major commotion breaks out over at the next building; an air whistle blasts several times, signaling danger. Robert stops pulling in the grease pump's hoses and looks over to where he hears yelling. He sees people scrambling.

"Shit, somethin's happened over at the 10-inch mill," Robert exclaims. "Come on, let's see what's goin' on."

Robert and Johnny tear off toward the rolling mill that makes steel bars and rebar for construction. Tools clanging at their sides, the men race down metal stairs and across a roadway that runs between the furnaces and the mill.

Men in yellow hats crowd around someone on the floor while redhot coils of steel rod sizzle in the air around them. Normally, the coils run in and out of a die system that shapes the bars into their proper size and strength. But as Johnny has learned during his first days working there, the rods will often run off their tracks. Labor crews will use long poles to push them back in or—if the steel begins to bunch up—shut down the mill and use acetylene torches to cut up the coils into small pieces, which will later be placed into scrap heaps and reused for the furnaces.

But this time one of the fiery red rods has run off its track, piercing the stomach of a yellow-hatted crewmember who had been unable to get out of the way. The rod runs out several feet on the other side of him before the mill can be shut down. A couple of men hurriedly use their gas torches to remove the pieces of steel from in front and behind the man; they lay him down as gently as they can until Nazareth's emergency medical team can arrive.

Johnny looks over the huddle of men surrounding the Mexican, a man in his midthirties, who's grimacing in pain and gasping for breath. He can't believe what he sees—the rod has gone through his body and out the back. No blood flows as the rod practically cauterizes the wound's opening, although burned intestines and other tissue have come out from behind him. The man shivers and mumbles a few words as fellow hard hats hold his head and hand. One man tells him in Spanish that it's going to be okay—that it isn't so bad. The injured man seems to calm down a little; his mouth agape, like that of a hooked fish, his eyes opened wide, yet not really appearing to see anything. Time stops. The roar from other parts of the plant can be heard, but Johnny feels as if a bubble has enveloped the injured man and everything around him. He hears someone praying.

Johnny has seen a lot of things in his life—friends shot, drug overdoses, shankings in prison. But something about this is more frightening, perhaps because it feels so random. Accidents like these are quite common, it turns out. But the mill keeps churning out steel, keeps blasting and pounding, to meet its production goals. The one issue for everyone is not to let any section of the plant be shut down for any significant amount of time. Profit, and therefore payday, means the mill has to keep going, day and night, no matter what.

White-and-yellow-stripe-hatted foremen from the 10-inch mill arrive and pull everyone away from the dying man. A medical wagon pulls up next to the area and parks; two uniformed paramedics rush in and make their way through the widening arc of men. Nobody says anything as the paramedics study the situation; there's a certainty in their gaze that this man isn't going to make it. Still they bend down to the ground, trying to make things as comfortable as possible for him.

Just before the man goes into convulsions, he yells out a name, his wife, his girlfriend, somebody: "Elena." The paramedics squat next to him, holding his head and hands as the others had done before, while the man expels his last breath and then eases onto the ground. "Elena" is the last thing he says.

Elena must be a remarkable woman for her name to be the last to escape his lips before he dies, Johnny thinks. If Johnny were to die, he'd think of one name, too. Aracely. To die in the mill, surrounded by friends, with a woman's name on his lips—that's a decent way to go, Johnny figures. For Johnny, thinking these things is a way to escape getting sucked into the emotional vortex that seems to exist around them as the man's body lies motionless on the ground. For what seems like an eternity, workers stand around without saying a word. Robert has a look on his face as if he himself has been speared by the rod.

Johnny feels sick to his stomach and turns away.

2

PAYDAY

Every two weeks on a Friday, the millwrights and other craft workers line up at the pay shanty to pick up their checks; the other workers obtain theirs on alternating Fridays. The structure is an unpainted wooden shed. Nazareth clerks open up the locks and go inside, setting up their boxes and paperwork on splintered, partly rotted shelves, laden with spiderwebs.

Workers show up in their dirty work gear and hard hats. In their hands are metal key-chain tags with their employee numbers stamped on them, proof of who they are before they can receive their checks.

The clerks hand out some rather juicy checks—a result of the tons of overtime and double shifts that most of the employees have accumulated. There was so much work then that steel beams and rods practically flew out of the rolling mills and forges while machines had to be repaired and sometimes taken apart and replaced, keeping repair crews on hand twenty-four hours a day.

Of course, on payday, without fail, the racing forms pile up near the feet of the waiting men. It's the early 1970s and Hollywood Park and Santa Anita racetracks are big draws for the construction, assembly, and mill workers throughout the Southland. In addition to the racing forms, there are flyers from nearby bars and card clubs offering "mill" specials on drinks and card games. And the redbrick fleabag hotels on Slauson Avenue open up for hourly rates while prostitutes stand on the sidewalk or in doorways soliciting the men on their way home.

Some wives wait in cars while their husbands collect their

checks—women with crossed arms, unkempt hair, and piercing stares making sure their men don't make any detours. But for the rest, there's nothing to stop them from enjoying the fruits of their labor; more than likely this means spending most of their checks before they even get near a bank or check-cashing outlet.

Collaborating in this are the bars and hotels willing to cash the mill's checks. Who can resist having their checks cashed and a tab started? Few do, except perhaps the superfanatic Holy Rollers—many a man ends up at church on Sunday after two days of carousing and carrying on.

Steel mills pay well—this is common knowledge. But many of the men don't know what to do with their wages, having that kind of money for the first time in their lives. So they end up throwing much of their hard-earned cash at the horses, booze, and prostitutes.

Johnny catches on quickly about payday expectations. At first he brings his checks straight home to Aracely, proud to show off the numbers, the most money he's ever made legitimately. But this doesn't last long. He, too, gets snagged, the bars being his particular lure.

"Johnny boy, how 'bout we get a few brews after," Clyde Four-killer suggests as the men move up the line in front of the pay shanty. Clyde is a tall, long-haired Cherokee Indian from Oklahoma, a mill-wright apprentice, a notch up from oiler-greaser. (Soon after the consent decree was enacted, Nazareth hired a crew of Oklahoma Indians for the craft trades, some of whom had cut their teeth on oil rigs and Texas shipyards.)

"Not sure, Clyde, I think I should get this check home before I lose some of these zeros," Johnny replies.

"We won't spend much—we can hustle our drinks with pool games."

"To be honest, I'm not much of a pool player."

"Hey, neither am I," Clyde responds. "That's never stopped me."

Johnny has no arguments left. He nods at Clyde just as his paycheck slides across the small opening at the pay shanty, along with a pen so he can sign a receipt.

Wild Woolly's is one of the local dives; nothing but country and western on the jukebox. Redneck territory. The blacks have their rowdy joints farther down Slauson toward South L.A. Mexicans have theirs closer to East L.A. and some South and Southeast L.A. main streets. Clyde likes country music. Although as a Cherokee he has his issues with whites, he's lived in their culture on the outback farmlands of Indian Territory in Oklahoma. He talks Okie and walks Okie, but is painfully aware of being a "Skin."

Johnny and Clyde met when they got to talking in the millwright shanty where the oiler-greasers, apprentices, and classified millwrights come together to hang, eat, or get ready for assigned jobs. They became fast friends and Clyde often seeks out the brown-skinned Mexican "relative," as he calls Johnny, even though Clyde has strong Indian features on lighter skin.

"We'll play eight ball," Clyde says. "We'll play lousy. That'll corral some studs so we can take 'em for beers. Don't worry about us losing; you'll see what I mean."

Johnny pulls up behind Clyde as they spot an empty pool table. Johnny can play pool, just not as good as some of the others. He doesn't have to pretend to play badly. But Clyde has more up his sleeve than he lets on. As soon as two bar patrons challenge them, things begin to change. Johnny continues to make his mediocre if somewhat lucky shots. But Clyde becomes a pool shark. He makes shot after shot. Beers come their way a few times. Before too long, a group of hustlers gather around the two darker men, and Johnny knows trouble's not far behind.

"Don't you just hate them beaners coming into this place as if they had an invitation," one of the white men says to another, not addressing Clyde or Johnny. They figure Clyde's Mexican. He glares at them for a few seconds, then remarks, "I ain't no beaner. I'm Cherokee. And as far as I'm concerned, I don't need no fuckin' invitation."

"Mexicans or Cherokees, you're beaners to us, asshole," another man, wearing a flannel shirt, chimes in.

Johnny feels the adrenaline rush through his body. He's a fighter. He likes the feeling, the way the blood dances beneath the skin and a kind of red fog gathers in his head. He looks up and sees the battle will be uneven, but he's game. Why not? Few things excite him in this world as much as a good scrap. Johnny stands by Clyde and dead-stares the five dudes surrounding them.

"I'm Mexican," Johnny announces. "Which one of you is going to try and throw us out?"

"Hey, this punk speaks English," the first white dude says to his friends. "But he don't understand shit."

Normally Johnny would've thrown the first punch—and kept punching until the man was on the ground and mostly out. But with whites, he has to be seen as not having started anything. The white men keep talking and harassing, but he notices they aren't moving on them. Their aim, he figures, is to get Clyde or Johnny to throw the first blow, a signal for the rest to get in on this.

"Well, I'm tired of the stink in this place," Clyde chimes in. "Let's mosey on over to the bar across the street."

One of the men looks behind him. There at the bar counter is an older, red-haired mustachioed man whom Johnny recognizes as a veteran millwright—an old-timer. He's known as Dent. His real name is Earl Denton. He's the one person his father, Procopio, warned him about when Johnny first signed on the mill. Dent doesn't say much, but seems to draw a measure of respect from the younger men in the bar. Dent looks up, gives a half smile, and nods.

Just then all hell breaks loose. Johnny feels a fist strike his chin and blood trickle from his lip. Clyde gets hit from both sides. Johnny picks up a cue stick and starts swinging it around, hitting the knuckles of one guy whose hand is on a pool table and poking the large end of the stick into another man's face. But he's also pummeled with fists coming at him from all angles. Clyde manages to regain his balance and starts throwing blows of his own. He can fight. Johnny picks up a chair, but someone snatches it from him, and another fist hits the side of Johnny's face. He begins to throw blows wherever he can, knocking the teeth out of who knows who. More dudes jump in, pulling him to the ground and raining blows on his face, neck, chest, and back. He loses track of Clyde as he tries to crawl toward the door. He's kicked, mostly his ribs and stomach. Steel-toed shoes are making their impact as he feels his ribs sting with pain; at one point, he hears one snap. A couple of blows from cue sticks also land. It seems like the whole bar is getting into it. Johnny tries to get up, but is knocked down again. He grabs one man's shirt to take him down with him, but the shirt rips in his hand.

Johnny's hurting; he has some broken bones, he can feel it. He can't see Clyde. All he can think about is getting out, crawling his way to the door. He touches the cement sidewalk just outside the bar and then feels several hands push him farther out, with kicks to send him off. Clyde soon follows, thrown out on his ass, blood all over his face.

Someone slams the doors shut behind them. Johnny and Clyde gaze at each other, looking like shit after a tornado. Nobody else is on that sidewalk. Johnny starts to laugh, but his side burns as though hot irons are being pressed against it. It isn't long before an ambulance arrives, before people gather and gawk and both men are transported to the nearest hospital. Being steelworkers, they have good insurance. The mill pays for everything.

Aracely arrives at the hospital, mad as hell.

"Where's Johnny Salcido's room?" she demands from the first attending nurse she can find.

Johnny has been placed in a room at the Kaiser Hospital in Bellflower after triage and emergency treatment.

Aracely jumps into an elevator and anxiously presses the button to the floor the nurse says Johnny's on. When she finds his room and sees Johnny, tears form in her eyes. Yet they trickle down her cheek more with rage than relief.

"Who the fuck did this?" she inquires as if she herself were going to locate the culprits and beat them to a pulp, an act Johnny believes she's capable of, despite her small stature.

"Don't worry about it," Johnny tries to say from behind the bandages and tape around his chest; his face is red and swollen. "Some *gabas*—a few I remember from the mill. They'll get theirs. Hey, baby, meet Clyde."

Clyde is in a bed next to Johnny, straps of tape around his head and a sling around a broken arm. Aracely just looks at him, thinking he looks white but then realizing he isn't.

"You can't keep getting into these brawls, Johnny," Aracely says. "I know you like to fight; I know you're good for it. But I get tired of hearing that you've been stomped on all the time."

"I know, *muñeca*, I know," Johnny says in between clenched teeth. "Just trying to have a good time. Somebody's always got to come along and mess it up."

"I'm also tired of you spending your weekends away from home," Aracely then adds, with more anger in her voice. "You ain't going to be a *pendejo* wino like my dad, you understand. You come home and you won't be sitting in any hospital room or jail cell on weekends."

Johnny looks at Clyde, who has a Mexican girlfriend at home. Clyde knows the wrath of a Chicana and they glance at each other knowingly.

"You listen to me or I'm going to beat you worse than those *pinche puto gabachos*," Aracely assures.

Johnny and Clyde don't say anything. They aren't in any position to argue. And they know she means it.

Johnny finishes recuperating at home, losing precious days of work. His brothers Junior, Rafas, and Bune come by to see how he's doing. He receives phone calls from his oiler-greaser friends, including Robert Thigpen. He doesn't like Robert, but after working so long with him, arguing and almost coming to blows at times, Johnny's begun to warm up to the man.

"You've got to be the dumbest Mexican I ever met," Robert kids on the phone one day. "You go into Wild Woolly's without some brothers? What you thinkin', fool? Them honkies gonna give you a reception?"

Johnny laughs. "Hey, we did all right. I broke a nose or two. Besides, payback is a motherfucker."

"Don't look at me for any of that," Robert says. "I'd never have sat my ass down in that joint in the first place. Nah, you on your own for this one, cuz."

Weeks pass and Johnny's itching to get back to work. Finally, the doctor gives him the okay and Johnny gets up extra early that day, puts on his freshly cleaned uniform, picks up some coffee and *pan dulce*, sweet bread, on Florence Avenue, and pulls into the parking lot.

Soon after, he walks into the millwright shanty. The foreman, Mr. Taylor, is there with a scowl on his face. He seems to know what happened to Johnny but doesn't say a word.

Robert approaches Johnny as Johnny begins to put things into his locker. Despite his kidding on the phone, he shows Johnny respect.

"Don't look too much worse for wear," Robert says. "Next time, bring an army."

Ray and the other Chicanos on the oil gang come by as well. Ray leans over and whispers to Johnny, "We're going to raid Wild Woolly's Friday night. You don't need to come, Johnny. You've had enough. We'll finish it for you."

"If you go," Johnny tells him, unconcerned for the moment about Aracely's warnings, "I'm going with you."

"All right, you men, get your assignments and get to work," Taylor commands over the din of voices and the roar and rumble of the mill.

Robert is Johnny's work partner again. They both look at the assignment sheet. They are supposed to grease and oil all the massive rocker arms, couplings, motors, bearings, and bushings beneath the hotbed of the 22-inch mill. It's a lot of work, but relatively cozy. They labor below the surface and are able to take long breaks if they want to. Johnny thinks this assignment is a good way to return to work.

They sign out for a power grease gun and various crescent wrenches, large channel locks, and pipe wrenches. They move themselves and the equipment a few yards to the 22-inch mill, which is shut down for repairs. They both climb into the hotbed pit, caked with grease, oil, and the metal flakes that often fall from the red-hot steel being shaped into rods. After the electrical boxes are locked off (to make sure nobody starts up any motors or gears while they're working on them), Johnny and Robert start at one end of the hotbed pit and move toward the other end, greasing buttons and oiling gearboxes along the way. They also take apart ripped piping and copper fittings, replacing them with new ones.

Before too long, the two men finish the job with a couple of hours to spare. Instead of going to the millwright shanty to pick up another job assignment or clean up the shanty, like they are supposed to, they decide to find a couple of relatively clean spots and take a nap. It's a perfect place for this unless somebody goes down into the pit to check on them, something a foreman would rarely do.

As Johnny climbs out to gather the air hose for the power grease gun, he notices someone on the catwalk above the hotbed. He has on a scuffed blue hat and a heavily tooled belt around his waist. A cigarette dangles from his mouth and he looks down sternly at Johnny. It's Dent.

Johnny knows that Dent heads the Ku Klux Klan group in the mill. The Klan has been in the mill since the early 1950s. They keep an eye on all the "troublemakers," particularly the few Communist organizers and the staunch union men. The Klan is an extralegal terror group—they threaten, they set people up to get fired or hurt. They make sure the workers aren't united and strong enough to exact any positive changes from the Nazareth Steel Company. They are the company's unofficial eyes, ears, and even arms. They are particularly hated by the Mexican and black labor crews, especially since Black Panthers and Brown Berets have begun educating and organizing in some of L.A.'s neighborhoods.

Johnny looks away blankly. He doesn't want to let on that he gives a crap whether Denton's there or not. It's at that moment, though, when he realizes Denton's keeping an eye on him, which is never good.

After he climbs back down into the pit, Johnny tells Robert about Denton.

"That's not cool, man," Robert says. "That dude is a stone-cold peckerwood."

"I know," Johnny responds. "He was there the night I got jumped at Wild Woolly's. I saw him give those guys the signal to beat on Clyde and me."

"You saw Dent at the bar?" Robert asks. "Shit, man, why didn't you say something. He's going to target your ass—to make sure you don't get any revenge. He's going to be watching your every step. One false move and you're a goner."

"What do you mean?"

"He's known to set people up. To lie to the foreman about guys they consider trouble in the mill," Robert explains. "I don't just mean to get them fired. He's done plenty of that. I've also heard he's had people lose limbs and get killed around here. He carries a lot of weight, man."

"You think he's watching to see if we sleep so he can get a foreman down here and bust our ass?" Johnny asks.

"I wouldn't put it past him. He's bad news. He ain't got a mercy bone in him."

Johnny and Robert decide not to take a break this time. What a waste, Johnny thinks, to have such a gravy job and not take advantage of a good long snooze. But with Denton standing overhead, they know he'd find a way to mess with them. If he had it in for the Mexican and black labor and mill crews, he's even more likely to be incensed that a few Mexicans and blacks have made it into his precious skilled trades.

Ever since the consent decree had been agreed to by union and company, a war had been waged—in the mill, in the bars, and in the union hall. The way some of the white guys dealt with the decree was to make it so no black or brown person ever wanted to work in the well-paid craft positions. Violence was their form of persuasion.

One day Johnny saunters into the millwright shanty as a discussion with a half-dozen men flourishes at one of the wood bench tables near the lockers. Johnny wanders over to his locker. While opening it and reaching for his tool belt, he catches snippets of the conversation.

The loudest voice is that of Harley Cantrell, a tall, well-built warehouse maintenance worker in his late twenties with long, dirty blond hair. Harley's one of the radicals in the plant, a member of a Communist group. At first Johnny sees him as one of the many colorful characters the mill produces—all kinds of religious, political, and social types work here, a concentrated microcosm of the rest of the world.

Harley's group has members in the warehouse, masonry crew, the electrical crews, and a few in the labor crews, mostly young Anglos. Harley's actually a college graduate who quit postgraduate study to get hired in the mill and, in Johnny's estimation, to stir up trouble for the "revolution."

"Racism is a tool to keep us divided," Harley declares, his hands in front of him emphasizing key points, his eyes sweeping across his listeners' questioning gazes. "The men enter the mill with black skins, brown skins, or white skins. They come out coated with oil, slag chips, and dirt, and most can't be told apart. They are the same—'brothers in grime.' But when they leave for home, they sleep in different racial neighborhoods, drink at segregated bars, and hang out with mostly their own people. Society has us believe that we have more in common as 'race' than we do as workers. In the mill, these divisions are reinforced by the job allocation system—which is slowly being broken down by the consent decree, but not much. Not enough."

"Yeah, but we do have problems with race," Ray, the Chicano oiler-greaser, chimes in. "You know whites have most of the skilled jobs and union positions—look at who runs the plant! It's *gabachos*. Don't tell me race doesn't matter."

"Of course it does; I'm not saying it doesn't," Harley responds. "Race is important. Racism is something we should oppose everywhere. In fact, white workers need to be in the forefront of this—white privilege holds us all down, whites included. The fact is white people are also exploited for their labor—maybe not to the extent that blacks and browns are, but this is mostly to keep us at each other's throats."

"Does that work here at Nazareth?" Johnny, never one to stay quiet for long, interjects, now turned toward the seated men. "I mean this exploitation you're talking about. I'm getting some great pay in this place! I've never had it so good. Look at the funky jobs that most of my *gente* elsewhere have to do—it's clear they're getting shafted. Or even that lots of blacks and Mexicans have a hard time finding any kind of job at all. There are problems in the mill, sure, but I don't see how we can complain about being exploited."

"It's complicated, man, but let me try and break it down." Harley brightens, eager to take on the challenge. "There are only two ways to make a living in this world—you either work for it or you steal for it. Us steelworkers know how we got our money; tell me how the owners of the factories and mills get theirs. Of course, corporations and banks and all don't steal by putting a gun to your head. They do it through laws—through the legal license of the so-called free-market system.

"Here's what I've learned," Harley continues, taking in a deep breath. "Steel mills don't make steel; they make profits. They don't just do this by adding price to the costs of production. They can only truly make profits if they improve their technology and cut costs, which many steel corporations are doing, laying off workers everywhere. They also cheapen the manufacturing process—in other words, paying workers far less than what their labor produces. They do this by breaking union contracts or by moving their plants to cheap labor areas in the South, Mexico, or Asia."

"I don't know about all that," Johnny interrupts. "I thought profits are how we get paid."

"Well, it's actually your labor that produces profits," Harley explains. "For example, a steelworker's labor can bring, say, around a thousand dollars in profits in an hour. Those profits in turn pay for machinery, maintenance, debt, buildings, operations, and salaries. Paying for machines and debt don't bring any returns. But salaries do because you never pay a worker what they're really worth. Now it's true that steelworkers are some of the better paid of all industrial workers. But even if they get around twenty-five dollars an hour with pay and benefits, this is only a fraction of the thousand dollars his work may bring in that same hour. Again, a good portion of this goes to pay for capital expenditures, loans, dividends, and such. But there's still a lot left over. The owners—set up in corporations with stockholders, law firms, and fancy offices—pocket the rest. That's how the owners steal without working. That's why they can play golf all day, fly to Europe, build mansions in different parts of the world, work on other mega-business deals, and create associations that lobby for their interests in government and society. That's why they're considered the ruling class. They run the show and reap most of the benefits."

Johnny decides to listen for a while as others shower Harley with more questions. Harley is in his element. Johnny concedes the guy makes sense. But his theories also seem too neatly tied up—Harley seems to have an answer for everything.

Life can't be that easy to figure out, Johnny thinks, and walks away, the din of Harley's voice behind him.

Procopio works on one of the labor crews in the electric furnaces. He has already put in more than two decades in the mill; dark, squat, and wary-eyed, he's considered an "old soldier" and is highly respected among the labor crews.

One Saturday, he walks up to Johnny as his son greases some bearings and oils a few gears and pistons.

"*Cómo estás, m'ijo?*" Procopio asks. Normally when the mill is in full swing, one isn't able to converse. It's just too loud. The mill hands use hand gestures and nods to communicate. For example, two fingers across the arm from a foreman mean he's inquiring if the worker wants to work a double. The worker has only to nod and the deal's done. Pointing to the eye and then upward indicates a "crane overhead"— the noise will even drown out the sirens that blare as a load of steel is being passed.

But things are down for repairs and the mill is unusually quiet this day.

"Hey, *apá*," Johnny says after looking up to see who's addressing him. "Not much—just a few copper fittings and couplings to change so I can finish oiling and greasing. *Y usted—cómo está todo?*"

"*Aquí nomás,*" Procopio responds. He hesitates, watching Johnny work as if he's interested in what he is doing, but his eyes indicate he has other things on his mind.

"*Mira,* I got word that Dent and his boys have their eyes on you," he finally blurts out. "I know they were behind your beating. I told you before: Be careful with that guy, *m'ijo*."

"I'm not scared of those *pinche gabas*," Johnny says, standing up. "I'm playing it cool, but when I get my chance, I'm putting a drop on them."

"I'm just telling you, Juanito," Procopio says with more concern in his voice. "You can get them, but you have to be smart, not just tough. I know you're tough. I've known a lot of tough guys in this place. But they aren't around anymore. The smart ones are still working here, though."

"What are you saying, Pops?"

"I'm saying . . . listen, I never told you how your brother Severo died. Not the whole story."

"Dad, I know he got killed in the 32-inch mill—he lost his footing and fell in between the rollers. What else don't I know?"

"I can't tell you too much, but I will tell you this," Procopio says, with an intensity Johnny has not seen in his dad's eyes before. "I got active in the mill. You know, in the union. The *paisanos* got organized after being treated like dogs for years. We threatened a strike by the labor crews. By then Severo had started to work here. I've done battle with Dent and those guys since I began working at Nazareth. We got the upper hand sometimes; sometimes they did. But in the early sixties, we started to take over the union jobs. We had a lot of grievances settled and made some changes. We took part in national steelworkers' conventions that eventually led to the consent decree. That was partly our doing, *m'ijo*. Around the country, the Mexicans who had been working in steel mills in Chicago, Pennsylvania, Indiana, and here in California, we flexed our muscles. But at Nazareth we had to deal with those KKKers. They really couldn't get to me, you know. We stuck together real good. But Dent and them knew that Severo had started working here. He was a *mocosillo*, barely getting his feet wet. He was so young, eager, and hardworking. I don't know everything that happened, but I'm convinced Dent and the Klan had something to do with Severo's death."

"*Chingao*—you never told me this before, Dad!" Johnny exclaims, shocked at what his father is telling him—and in the middle of a shift, as though there really were no time like the present.

"How could I? I don't have any real proof. But now that you work here, you may as well know. Dent threatened me and the other *paisanos*. We weren't scared of him. We challenged him and his thugs to try and stop us. Then later in the week, I'm on the furnace floor cleaning around the furnaces when I get word that Severo has been killed in the 32-inch mill. It's a 'freak accident,' they say. Some freak accident! He supposedly slipped, but I know there are guardrails all around there. Somebody had to push him over. The only other way is to jump. And he wouldn't have jumped. I know in my heart it was Dent."

"What did you do, Dad?"

"Oh, I did plenty. Don't forget, I've been here a long time. But I never could prove anything. Mostly I've been waiting. That's why it made me angry that you were hired without going through me. I needed you to be prepared, but you're *terco* like your mother. Stubborn. But since the beating, I knew I had to tell you. You've gotta be careful. They may be messing with you to get to me. I don't want to lose another son."

Tears begin to well in Procopio's eyes, but he wipes them away quickly before they spill over. "We'll talk about this some more later, *m'ijo*," he says as he walks away. "For now, don't do anything. Let's figure things out first."

Johnny watches as his father retreats. Procopio's not much for words. They've hardly spoken since he moved out of the house with Aracely and, especially, after the wedding. But now he's in his father's domain. He'd better know more about his dad and what he knows and doesn't know. In the mill, the old-timers know pretty much everything. They are the wise elders, although they mostly keep to themselves. But if they offer knowledge, you have to listen. Like Heavy always reveals in his stories—the mill has seen a lot. The old-timers know what the mill has seen and what it all means. If a green hat is interested in knowing about these things, fine. If not, he'll have to find out the hard way.

After Johnny listened to Procopio talk about how Severo died, his thoughts turned to his oldest brother. When Severo started working in the mill, he was eighteen and Johnny was thirteen. He recalls his mother's screams when his dad told her the news of Severo's death. His brother had been working there only a few months. But that was what Severo had been groomed for—to become the second generation of steelworkers in the family. Johnny's other brothers followed within a few short years of Severo's death.

Severo's death impacted Johnny in ways he couldn't express. Soon after the incident and funeral, he started getting into trouble at school and in the neighborhood. He hung around the older Florencia Trece gang leaders. He saw something heroic in them; a vacuum had been created by Severo's passing, which he wanted to fill. And perhaps he felt the great injustice—why a good person like Severo had to be taken away from this world, already too full of hurtful and untrustworthy people.

Several busts, drug addictions, and broken hearts later, Johnny is now in the very mill his brother died in, completing a circle he had never anticipated being part of. Finding out more about his brother's death is now a priority, as is having a hand in some long-due retribution.

Aracely and Johnny sit rather uneasily in Robert Thigpen's living room as Robert attempts to cook some collard greens and ham hocks, old Southern recipes he brought to L.A. when he moved from Alabama some ten years before. In the kitchen is Robert's irate girlfriend, Wanda, who's yelling at him while Johnny and Aracely exchange awkward glances.

Robert had downed close to two six-packs before they arrived; the lifeless beer cans lay all over his coffee table and floor. When Robert answered the door to let Aracely and Johnny in, he was already soused. His girlfriend arrived later, fuming while ignoring the young couple in Robert's home.

Robert tries to appease the woman, but she pushes his arms back and then throws him against the refrigerator.

"I don't know what I'm going to do with you," Wanda yells. "You're just a no-good drunken fool. I should walk out on you right now."

"No, baby, you don't wanna do that," Robert counters. "I looves you, man. You're all I have, baby. Don't talk that way. Come on in and meet my friends. We'll have a nice dinner together, just you, me, and my—"

"In your condition!" Wanda yells back. "No, thank you. I could care less about your steelworker friends. What bothers me is your drinking. You're always out of it. I'm tired of picking up after you. Of wondering whether you're going to run off to the bar, or go lounging with some skank, bringing in all kinds of nasty shit to my bedroom."

"Wanda, baby, please . . . we got company." Robert tries to talk low, but it's still loud enough to hear in the living room. "These are nice people. Come on, stay awhile and have something to eat."

"I'm taking my things," Wanda says, eyeing Robert with an evil glare. "This time you ain't gonna stop me. I've had it with you. Understand? I'm done! You can get your pussy somewhere else."

Aracely almost laughs just then but holds back; she looks at Johnny to see his expression. He's speechless, not knowing whether he should intervene or just let it all take its course.

Johnny knows about Robert's troubles with Wanda. For some time that's all his oiler-greaser partner would talk about. Wanda's been driving Robert crazy, but he won't do anything about it. He loves that woman. The way he handles the situation is to keep on drinking, which makes Wanda even madder. It's a match made in steelworker hell.

Robert's had a drinking problem for some time. Often he shows up to work with his eyelids practically closed and his coordination off-kilter. Johnny's had to leave him in some dark hole or behind a pile of beams to sleep it off while he finished the assigned work for both of them. It's a pain in the ass, Johnny thinks, but then he also feels bad for Robert. He knows how the work they do can tear a man down to nothing.

Robert is aware that Johnny's covered for him. He has become more open to his work partner and tells him his troubles with Wanda. As a gesture of gratitude, one day Robert invited Johnny and his wife for dinner.

"I make the best Southern soul food anywhere," Robert bragged.

"Okay, I'd like to try it," Johnny accepted. "I'll let Aracely know. Let's do it soon."

When the evening for the dinner arrived, Johnny and Aracely got nicely dressed and drove several blocks to 107th and Avalon, in the Watts section of South Central L.A. where Robert lived. It's a mostly black community, but Johnny and Aracely have no problem with this, having been in South L.A. all of their lives.

But as soon as Robert opened the door, the couple could smell his intense beer breath. They walked inside and Robert was talking a mile a minute—offering them beer, which Johnny accepts but Aracely passes on.

With Robert talking away and pots boiling on the stove, Wanda made an unexpected visit—and the drama unfolded.

After a long while, it becomes evident that Johnny and Aracely aren't going to have any collard greens and ham hocks that night. By the time Robert begins to beg and cry, and Wanda softens up, cuddling Robert in her arms, Johnny and Aracely get up from the sofa and quietly walk out the door.

Earl Denton gazes at the faraway sparks of welding torches and of men hammering away at rail tracks for the slag cars. His blue eyes mirror the electric blasts of an arc weld from a distance. Deep in his bones, however, he feels like he's slipping off a steep mountain. That world he has staked so much on appears to be coming to an inglorious end.

Back in the 1940s and 1950s, members of the Communist Party had been hired at the plant. Dent became part of a pro-American group that made sure the Communists were identified and weeded out. There were threats, fights, and the handing over of names to government officials. Denton did this because he loves his country. Because he sees how great it can be—but he's also aware of the myriad enemy forces that exist in the world, determined to destroy these United States. He's been told they often start in places like a steel mill. In Denton's mind, anyone who tries to tear Nazareth Steel down is tearing down America as well. He has never married. He doesn't want to be tied down. Nazareth Steel is his life. It is his wife. He doesn't need anything else.

In the early 1950s, a group of Kentucky and West Virginia ex–coal miners had been brought in to work in the millwright positions. They were a loud, funny, and hardworking bunch; among them were Emmett Taylor, Bob Michaels, Hank Cheatham, and Heavy. A few of them also brought the tenets of the Ku Klux Klan, a secret society dedicated to white supremacy, God, and country. Denton soon joined them and in time proved to be their greatest asset.

The small group terrorized mostly blacks and Mexicans who got out of line. A few beatings, nothing more. Dent recalls one particularly violent kidnapping of a black union organizer. They took him from his home in the dead of night. They put a gunnysack over his head, drove him to an empty garage, and then beat on him until he couldn't stand up anymore. Then they dropped him, bloody and unconscious, onto the railroad tracks that divided the all-white South Gate from the mostly black and Mexican Watts community.

Los Angeles in those days resembled a Jim Crow town in the South. Restrictive covenants kept blacks, Mexicans, and Filipinos in the worst housing, segregated and neglected. The police force was filled with many Southern white migrants and California farm boys looking for work and positions of power and respect. They had a green light to do whatever they wanted in the poor black and brown communities. Sometimes they clashed with fellow whites in the scattered "Okie" and "Arkie" impoverished camps in and around the farm fields that surrounded the city. But they also recruited from among these "po' folk" to help keep the "coloreds" in line.

Denton sees Nazareth as part of the great American ideal that he feels should rule the world. Over the years, he became the company's eyes. When increasingly more blacks and Mexicans joined the workforce, he put in extra time to make sure they wouldn't undermine the big mill's production plans.

For his part, Denton hates blacks, their easy manner, their loud voices, how their skin glistens in the heat of the communal battle with steel. He hates the dusk-faced, mostly Indian Mexicans, their shifty dispositions and strange language that grates against his sensitive "white-bred" ears. The "minorities" sing too much, laugh too much, they are always too quick with a word. Denton is the guardian of American might. He protects the great American way of life, which in his view is the "Great White Way."

The company loves Denton. The union will never be a challenge to the company as long as men like Denton dominate it. There's a link between the steel mill's corporate heads and Denton. The same blood seems to flow between them. Only one owns the mill; the other acts as its guardian.

Yet Denton's relations are no different from those foreign-tongued migrants, Cherokees, and Mississippi men he scorns. Texas born and raised, he made his way to the West from a difficult environment to make something of himself. It was the same reason most every other man had come. But Denton didn't see it that way.

Denton is a millwright. He knows his craft. He uses his brains. He's no lowly laborer. He's a knight of the forge. He stands above them all, often from a view on high. He slings his tools over his shoulders and walks the mill like he owns it, as if it doesn't own him. The mill is his goddess. Denton is its protector, brother, friend, and loyal lover.

For years Denton has mended its machinery. What would it be without him? And then these blacks, Mexicans, and pinko whites come along who don't know the meaning of work, but are the first to make trouble.

"They're all leeches," he bellows more than once to anyone who will hear him. "They only take; they won't give any more than they have to."

From his metal perch, Denton eyes their work, their audacity, making damn sure they pay for their "crimes."

Wives, kids, houses, boats, cars, and some good drugs now and then—all of them make for an upper-working-class life. But when it comes to the mill's own needs, the workers become expendable. The mill has its own demands, its own addictions. Sure, the mill makes all these things possible; some of the steelworkers own two or three homes (a good many of them have as many wives). But when the "lady" calls, you come arunning.

The mill keeps eternal hours. On top of that are the shift changes—the mill managers place most of the workforce on a rotating shift schedule. This alone means most steelworkers can't sustain a healthy family life.

In one week, a mill hand or craft employee is assigned the day shift; the following week, he'll work the afternoon turn. Then the week after that he's on graveyard. He barely gets used to the change in sleep patterns and he has to do it all over again—week after week, month after month, year after year.

This makes the men tired, cranky, and downright mean at times. Domestic trouble is the number one problem in the mill, linked to high levels of alcoholism and drug use—again, the mill has its own counselors and recovery programs, mainly to ensure the men are not given sick leaves for such problems by independent professionals.

Drug dealers, including some from Florencia Trece, make a nice business selling amphetamine pills—"whites"—to the men in the parking lot just before they enter their shift turns. The pills are used to keep the men up as long as possible. Sometimes this distorts their logic and how they make decisions. They often get drunk when they aren't in the plant, then drop whites like they were gumballs at work to stay awake. *Unpredictable* isn't close to the right word for their constantly shifting behavior.

In the beginning, Johnny avoids most of this as an oiler-greaser since this is one unit of employees that works during the day. But he begins to see other problems his lot faces. For one thing, after a few months of oiling and greasing, the majority of oiler-greasers are assigned millwright apprentice positions. This means higher pay and benefits (along with rotating shifts). Johnny notices that while others are moving up, most of the Chicanos, blacks, or Indians in the oil gang are not.

One day the company hires a group of young Anglos. Johnny's assigned to train them to perform various grease and oil jobs. A few weeks after the training is over, these neophytes are moved into apprenticeship positions. Johnny isn't.

The mill finds complex ways to discriminate and keep the workers of color from breaking too many barriers. Johnny gets really angry. He decides to submit a discrimination grievance to the union.

This act gets the attention of the plant's director, Lane Peterson, a balding, white-shirt-and-tie-type administrator in his midforties, originally from Erie, Pennsylvania, who controls the mill as if he were an old Western sheriff. He runs it the way he wants to, with little interference from the main offices except when production isn't going as smoothly as it's supposed to. Peterson rarely gets involved in management issues; but when he perceives there's organized trouble, particularly discrimination grievances, which he feels have to come from outsiders, he gets personally interested.

Unfortunately, the plant's bosses are not the only problem for Johnny.

The union is in the hands of the most conservative old geezers the mill has produced. Even Dirty Harry has a position as sergeant at arms. The millwright's union steward, Bob Michaels, is from the same clique. They don't do anything but hold bingo games and conduct boring meetings where nothing seems to get accomplished.

When his grievance gets turned down—and the union refuses to do anything about it—Johnny tries to muster up support at the union meetings to demand some changes. He starts with the labor crews on the jobs he works on.

"Aren't you tired of all the bullshit around here?" he asks a group of brown hard hats in the wire mill during lunch when he gets assigned there for a few weeks. The wire mill is like the Siberia of the plant— Johnny begins to feel this assignment is meant to keep him from talking to the more volatile furnace and mill workers who work in the main plant.

"Yeah, but what we do don't make no difference," one vocal black man named Al Simmons remarks. "I've been here fifteen years—don't you think we've tried our damnedest, son?"

"But I just can't see you giving up. They keep us down, pretending to have a consent decree, then finding all kinds of ways to undermine it."

"You're not telling us nothing new," Al continues. "But as long as the union is in the hands of those old peckerwoods, we're not going to get anywhere."

"Well, let's change that," Johnny argues. "Let's get our own people in there."

Al looks at Johnny as if he's out of his mind.

"And what about Denton and the KKK? They make sure anyone who tries to change anything gets set up and thrown out—or worse."

"I'm not scared," Johnny asserts. "I'm willing to take them on."

"You may have balls of steel, son, but unless you get more people behind you, you're not going anywhere."

"Well, help me out, then. I know I can get people interested. We'll run a slate at the next union election. A slate of blacks and Mexicans—what do you say?"

"Blacks and Mexicans? Man, you haven't been here too long, have you? Don't you know we're always at each other's throats? When are you going to bring together blacks and Mexicans in this mill? In this city? You're dreaming, man."

"We have to start somewhere," Johnny insists. "I can probably get my dad to help. He was around in the early sixties when the blacks and Mexicans ran the union. He remembers how it was back then and all the changes that they made. Sure, that's no longer the case. But we can do it again. We have to. If not, we're always going to be screwed."

"Okay, okay, tell you what," Al challenges. "You come to me with representatives from the labor, mill, and craft units in all the rolling mills, forges, the wire mill, the warehouse, and furnaces—show me you got the numbers and I'll back you up. Call a meeting somewhere—

I don't care where, at the local church if you want. But if enough people don't show up—and believe me, I'll know what's enough—I'm walking out."

"Fine, good, that's a start." Johnny brightens up. He looks at the other men, all black, who listen to but don't participate in the conversation. He knows Al wields leadership and respect among these guys. "I'll get the word out. We'll call a meeting and then we'll see who shows up. If I don't get enough support, you can walk away. No hard feelings. Deal?"

"Deal," Al says. "Now let me finish my grub before the whistle blows, will ya?"

Later that night, Johnny walks over to his parents' house on Nadeau Street, a few blocks from his apartment. Procopio and Eladia live in one of a row of six cottages that face one another; it's a one-bedroom place that is perfect for his mom and dad. The house they had lived in, and the one where Johnny grew up, is long gone and rented out to strangers.

Procopio's in the living room watching TV with the door open. Johnny walks up and knocks on the doorjamb.

"*Qué hubo, apá?*" Johnny greets.

"*M'ijo*, what brings you out here? You don't hardly come by anymore," Procopio says, rising up from the plastic-covered couch he's sitting on.

"Don't get up, Dad, let's talk," Johnny says. Just then his mother walks into the living room wearing a food-spotted apron. She wipes her hands and kisses Johnny on his cheek.

"*Y tú—sin vergüenza*—where you been lately?" she asks.

"Working, just working, like Pop and everybody else in the mill."

"Do your ribs feel better? You know—the ones that were broken."

"They're fine, mamá. I've been back to work for a while now. I'm doing fine."

Johnny moves to the sofa next to Procopio, who has since sat back down. Johnny watches TV for a few minutes just as a courtesy—he isn't interested in the stupid Mexican variety shows that have the dumbest clowns and silliest jokes he's ever seen.

"Listen, *apá*, I'm going to put up a slate of some active Chicanos and blacks for the next union election," Johnny finally blurts out.

Procopio moves in his seat to face Johnny.

"*N'ombre*. You think you can do that? I mean with Dent and them keeping an eye on you?"

"Exactly, that's why I'm doing it. I'm tired of watching my p's and q's around those guys. It was bad enough I had to tell my friends not to raid Wild Woolly's when I returned to work. I think it's better this way. We need to take over the union and make it work for us again. Make it meet our needs, not just the racist *perros* who've made a mockery of what it means to be a union man."

"It's going to take a fight—people will get hurt," Procopio cautions.

"I know. But we have to do this. Just look at my case: I can't move up into the millwright units. The company just comes up with excuses. They say I know the oil and grease jobs better than anyone else—so they keep me there with no extra pay. If I'm going to make it in the mill, I have to become a millwright. That's just one of many issues. You know what I'm saying, right, *apá*?"

"I understand, *m'ijo*. I just want to make sure you know what you're doing."

"Listen, I'll get the support. I'll talk to my friends in the craft units. I can also get to the melters on the furnaces and labor crews on all the mills. But I'm going to need your help. Everybody knows you. With you there, I can call a meeting and talk about all these concerns. I even got Al Simmons willing to join in."

"Al Simmons?" Procopio scrunches his nose. "You can't trust that guy. He's only in it for the blacks."

"That's right—the problem is Mexicans and blacks don't see eye to eye. That's how the company has us coming and going. We end up fighting each other for the crumbs while Dent and the Klan take up the best positions, and the company gets away with murder."

"You mean like Severo?"

"Yeah, *apá*. I haven't forgotten what you told me about Severo. I've heard there are others. Dudes who were left alone in jobs that somehow became 'accidents.' I also found out how Dent and his goons forced the last Chicano president of the union out—by stealing funds and putting the blame on him. I know what they're capable of doing. But I'm willing to fight fire with fire. We don't have a choice. Even if I get kicked out, it'll be worth it."

"I'm not worried about you getting fired. I just don't want something to happen to you. Losing Severo was hard enough."

"I know, Dad. But we can avoid that. We can keep an eye on each other. Watch each other's back. Like in the barrio—I learned a few things being in Florencia. Those dudes still keep an eye on me. They know I'm not involved in the 'life' anymore, but they still watch out for our house and Aracely. Remember when that guy broke in while Aracely was asleep. She woke up and called Popeye and Chivo from the barrio, not the cops. They came right away and took care of that *pinche* thief. Those guys still treat me like one of their own. They're even proud that I'm working at Nazareth. Not many of them can find work, so I'm like a hero to them."

"*Órale, m'ijo*, I guess I'm just tired and old," Procopio says. "But I used to be like you. I'm really glad you're in the mill. You got that old spirit. I think it's worth a try. To be honest, I'm tired of those *hueros* controlling everything. They're a small minority, but they think they can run the union and whatever happens in the plant. Just remember—you have to be smart. You got *huevos*, but you need some brains, too."

The next few weeks, Johnny talks to as many laborers, mill hands, millwrights, and other Nazareth employees as he can trust. Since he's all over the mill, he can convey messages to the various sections that normally don't communicate. He gets Ray and the oiler-greaser Chicanos behind him. Clyde Fourkiller and the Indians in the oil gang and repair crews agree to work with him. He talks to Tigre Montez, a leader among the 10-inch-mill workers, and Pepe "Mosca" Herrera, one of the key melters on the furnace floor. His brothers are more hesitant, but after Procopio clues them in, they say they'll help.

He even gets the old millwright Rex to pay attention to him. Only Johnny can tell that Rex is giving lip service to whatever they are going to do. Rex has already seen it all. He isn't going to invest any energy in any upstart union struggle. But he believes in it, having been the only Mexican in the craft units for several decades. He understands the need.

All of this, of course, gets back to Lane Peterson. He has heard from his spies in the mill that Johnny's going around talking to key people. Peterson sits at his desk and pulls an empty file folder from his supply closet. He writes *Johnny Salcido* on the top of the folder and puts it in a locked file drawer that only he has keys to. It's his way of keeping tabs on potential problems among the millworkers.

One day, Johnny's in line for the the Mexican-food truck that parks at the millwright shanty during lunch break. Harley Cantrell walks up to Johnny as he orders a *carne asada* burrito.

"How's it going, Johnny?" Harley greets.

Johnny glances over to see who it is. He doesn't know entirely what to make of Harley and his group. They are nice enough fellows. He likes that Harley sits down with the oil gang—something few other workers would do—and has political discussions with them. Johnny's fascinated by these talks, even in agreement most of the time, but he also notices how the millwrights avoid Harley like the plague.

"What's up, Harley? What's the latest?" Johnny asks, not really interested, but recognizing why Harley would have anything to do with anybody—to feed them Communist propaganda.

"I understand you're gathering support for a union takeover," Harley says.

"Oh, you do?" Johnny responds, wondering how Harley got word of this. "Yeah, well, I'm talking about a takeover involving only the Chicanos and brothers in the plant—I'm sure you get it."

Harley is used to being put off. It doesn't deter him a bit. Every worker is important, every worker a challenge. He knows being a Communist in an American steel mill is like jumping into a pit of rattlesnakes. But he has a vision, he has a source of knowledge—and he has a plan.

"That's fine, but you're still going to need help," Harley explains. "We don't want to do anything you don't want to do. But I can get a lot of support from workers who may not have supported you in the first place. We all have a stake in this. We're in this mill together. We know the injustices that exist—and if one worker's under attack, all of us are. Besides, we hate that right-wing clique that's running the union. It'll be best for all of us to get rid of those clowns."

"Well, I'm not against anyone's support. We're going to need as much as we can get," Johnny says. "But I hope you understand we don't want to turn over any control to you or your Communist friends. You're welcome. But we're calling the shots."

"Hey, Johnny, we don't want to run anything," Harley says with a laugh. "We hate the capitalist system and we're for a workers' society. Beyond that, we're willing to support anyone that's bettering the lot of the millworkers. There are a lot of things we can do to help. Ronnie— you know the Japanese electrician on the furnaces—he's with our group. He knows all about where the mill gets its money, the stock- holders, their pension plans, and their relationship with the local union. We'll get you as much information as you need. We'll also get the word out all over the plant. The fact is, change is something many of the white workers want as well—not just Chicanos and blacks. As Benjamin Franklin once said, 'Let's stick together or we'll hang sepa- rately.' "

"Okay, Harley," Johnny says, just to make their relationship as clear as possible, something Procopio told him to do in dealing with people like Harley. "I just don't want this to be some kind of Commu- nist takeover. The company will cut our throats if we do that. We need to make this bigger than that. There are Catholics, Evangelicals, and anti-Communists among these mill hands. They're brown, they're black, and, I'm willing to admit, they're also white—we're going to need all these groups if we want to get rid of those fuckers. So you can help, but don't make this into a Communist thing. If you screw this up, we'll never want to hear about your commie talk again, no matter how right you might be at times."

"You got some misguided ideas about Communists," Harley says. "But what the hell—I agree, this is not about us. It's about justice and equity in the workplace. We're with you if you want what we have to offer."

Johnny knows the Communists can be of great help. They are learned men of the working class, while the vast majority of the mill hands have barely finished high school, if that. Smart guys are always good to have on your side, he reasons, taking what his father tells him to heart.

"All right, you're on," Johnny says. "I'll let you know when we're going to meet. I want this invitation to go only to people we can trust. On the down low, you know. If our plans fall into the wrong hands, we'll lose before we get started."

"We know who's who," Harley says. "I'll get back to you."

As Harley leaves, Johnny thinks this is becoming more important than he had originally thought. He wonders if he can really handle the ramifications of what he's attempting to do. But he can't back down now. His credibility's on the line. He has to come through. Anybody can talk tough. Now he has to make something happen.

3

NIGHTS, WALLS, AND A BABY

racely sweeps the dust balls from under the box spring and mattress, held up by cinder blocks, in the one-room apartment she shares with Johnny; she can hardly bend down, gasping for air—she's eight months pregnant—as she uses the broom to pull out a dirty sock, cigarette butts, and a squashed beer can.

"Smoking in bed," Aracely says to herself. For some time now, she worries about Johnny's smoking and drinking. He won't do anything to harm her or the baby, that isn't it. It's that whenever he is home—most nights he's not—he needs at least a six-pack to fall asleep.

Aracely stands up and places her hand on her hip, her back and legs aching; premature varicose veins ink up the back of her knees. Johnny and Aracely decided it was time to have children, something they've always wanted. And with the extra hours Johnny's working, Aracely has left her monotonous assembly-line job so she can be home full-time.

Johnny's also finally made millwright's apprentice. This means higher pay but also those dreaded rotating shifts. The windows in the small bedroom are covered with aluminum foil to keep out the sunlight while he sleeps during those weeks he works nights.

The one saving grace in all this is the incredible health plan that Nazareth provides for its employees. The plan covers the prenatal and maternity care. Aracely and Johnny are even taking free Lamaze classes at a health center in Huntington Park, on the other side of L.A.'s Alameda tracks, a slight step up from barrio Florencia.

Although surprised, Aracely is glad that Johnny is really getting into the Lamaze classes; he carefully goes over all the breathing methods and reads the various pamphlets on baby care. The union workers have fought for these kinds of benefits on the national level; but the struggles in the local union are far from over.

Johnny's been working for months to organize a group of black and Chicano candidates for union-officer positions. Aracely shows up at the first meeting of his fledgling movement, held at a church front in South Central L.A. Mostly blacks attend. The Chicanos and Mexicans don't come in the numbers Johnny knows he needs. The word he gets is that most of the Mexicans don't trust working with blacks. Johnny argues that they can't win without one another's participation and backing; but at the first meeting only a few *Raza* go along with him.

Al Simmons steps through the church doors, glances around the room, taking in the mostly black group, and almost walks out. But Johnny convinces him to stay.

"You telling me you're going to lead a revolt in the union and you can't even get your own people out here?" Al inquires soon after Johnny begins the formal part of the gathering. Other blacks nod.

"Well, you said it yourself, Al, blacks and Mexicans don't get along around here," Johnny explains. "It's not going to be easy. But I'm willing to get some things going. This is only the beginning."

"Hey, don't forget there are *some* Mexicans here," Junior shouts from his seat in the back of the room.

"The Salcido family is here," Al adds, provoking snickers from others in the audience. "Okay, I know it ain't easy getting people together. But I did my end of the bargain; I want to see what you got to offer. If we take these honkies on, we're going to need some forces. I got mine; where are yours?"

"I understand, but I think people are waiting to see how things work out at this meeting," Johnny says. "If we can come up with some overall plans and action steps, and perhaps some ways to draw in more workers, I'm convinced we can get them here."

"You're trying my patience, young man," Al interjects. "I don't want to be left holding the bag. We'll take those fools on, but we'll make it a black thang. That's who's here anyway. We ready to roll, so let's roll."

Johnny knows this is what Al's position has been all along. Al has little need for Mexicans. He's been organizing the black labor crews and feels they don't need anyone else involved.

At that point Robert Thigpen stands up. He hasn't said anything so far during the meeting—and prior to this had indicated to Johnny he wasn't interested in any union takeover. But he shows up for the meeting anyway. Slightly drunk and red-eyed, but he shows up.

"Yeah, brother, we can do that," Robert manages to say, bringing out the words slowly and thoughtfully. "But we're still a minority in this place. The Mexicans—they the majority. We need them; they need us. I've worked with Johnny for a long time. His word is good. He's our best link to get a strong showing from the mill against those lame union hacks. You want it to be a 'black thang,' bro'; you'll lose. I say we send out more flyers—in Spanish and English—and bring our brown brothers into this. We can start the ball rollin'; that's fine. But let's make sure it rolls in more people from the mill. Our power is in our numbers. We better do all it takes to bring those numbers in, brother."

Johnny's impressed by Robert's reasoning; usually he is too juiced to say anything serious. Somehow, though, Robert gets it right. This quiets down the others in the room. But not Al.

"Look around you, *brother*," Al responds, emphasizing the last word with a sarcastic tone. "You can see the bloods is the only strong group here. We don't need Mexicans; they can't get they own selves together. And we definitely don't need any whites."

Al turns around and points his head toward Harley Cantrell and four other radical white workers from the mill who had just begun to sit down in the back of the room.

"We sure as *hell* don't need white people," Al repeats. "We can do this our damn self. In my book, there ain't no good whites; there ain't no bad whites. They just white people—peckerwoods and racists. We can't trust them as far as we can throw them."

Johnny can see the splits among the mill workers, wide as several Grand Canyons. The Chicanos, the "bloods," the "Skins," the "Woods"—everybody in their own worlds, although they face the same seemingly monolithic power of the corporate mill and the union hacks who work for them. Johnny's dad had warned him about this—how the conservative whites used these divisions to take over the union in the late 1960s.

Johnny feels his heart drop. Perhaps this is all a mistake. How can he go against years of bitterness, rivalries, hatred? That's how the powers that be win all the time—they count on the distrust. How dare he think he could repair the damage racism, fear, and the unrelenting competition for survival has done over the generations? The Mexicans who don't want to show up; Al, who depends on this to do what he wants—Johnny must have been crazy to think he could rise above such deep divisions.

Johnny's about to sit down and give up when his dad, Procopio, slowly rises from his seat; he's in battered overalls, a large gray work shirt, his dark skin accented by mostly gray hair, cropped short, on his head. In strongly accented English, he addresses Al and everyone sitting around him.

"You say you hate white people?" Procopio challenges, his voice resonant and loud. "You have no idea what hate is. I saw what racist *perros* and their corrupt flunkies have done in Mexico and later when I worked in Arizona. I've seen my own son Severo killed because of Dent and those KKKers. I tell you—you have no idea about hate. I may not know much—I'm just a labor guy on the furnaces. But I know one thing—hating people kills you, not them. My father saw thousands of people shot, hung, and tortured during the Mexican revolution. He saw the Yaquis, our people, enslaved and pushed out of their land like fleas. He hated so much that the alcohol that eventually killed him could not break through his stone heart. He hated his wife—my mother, a beautiful and wonderful Indian woman—and he hated us, his own children. He couldn't stop hating once he started . . . that was his problem. And that's your problem, too, Al. I agree with my son Johnny. I agree with his friend Robert. We have to do what they don't expect we'll do—we have to unite. Can you imagine, *hermanos*? If we ever united—*válgame Dios!* And as far as not working with whites—*fíjense*, if we have people like Harley and other whites willing to go against the ones in the union offices, isn't that to our advantage? Why do we want to keep splitting up the poorest people by color and language, yet we treat whites like they are as solid as a block of granite? They're not. They don't all agree. They aren't all racist. Some of them, as you know, are as poor as we are. If we unite— all the poor, regardless of color—and we split our enemies up, that's the winning combination. Like playing the ponies, amigos. You bet on the long shots—you don't win most of the time, but when you do, you win big. We have to start winning big. This is one election. But what about after that? *Necesitamos estrategias.* We need strategies. We need tic tacs . . . I mean tactics. We can win these things, but we have to think big, not small."

Procopio pauses for a couple of beats, then adds: "That's all I have to say."

At that a number of the men, including some blacks, begin to clap; Harley and his friends in the back clap the loudest. Johnny gets up and joins in, slowly, in unison, clapping like he recalls seeing the United Farm Workers union strikers do after his hero Cesar Chavez finished speaking. Didn't Chavez have whites, blacks, Filipinos, all kinds, in the 1965 grape strike that helped bring union recognition in the fields? he asks himself.

Al sits back and listens as others speak, articulate men who mostly agree with Procopio and who lay out ideas to wrest control of the union for the benefit of the majority. Al doesn't seem as perturbed as before; perhaps this unity dream is possible after all?

Johnny begins to smile. So this is what the beginning of victory looks like. This is what he's wanted to set in motion. The pieces of the puzzle are starting to fit, to make sense. He calls on others who offer more advice. There is some hard-won wisdom in that room, including from those who participated in strikes in other industries or had similar battles in other big plants. The fact is, this kind of struggle is going on all over, not just at Nazareth.

Eventually Johnny moves on to propose a slate and a platform highlighting the changes they want to see take place for the campaign, to make this meeting productive so that most of them in the room will come back to the next meeting . . . and the next and the next.

That day Aracely witnesses a certain strength and patience in Johnny she did not know he had before. And she sees strength and experience in her father-in-law, Procopio, a mostly silent man who now appears to her like a steaming volcano. She feels proud of her husband and the family she married into, but also sad. Johnny's a good man. Maybe too good. He's going to get hurt. He's going to get disappointed. And she wonders about how she gets the notion to even think this—has she been disappointed, hurt, by Johnny's attention to the mill instead of to her and their budding family? She tries not to consider this much as she sits and watches the meeting.

"Thanks, Robert, I appreciate the support," Johnny remarks to his work partner, who's approaching him as everyone else moves chairs around to leave.

"Listen, man, I ain't as fucked up as you all may think," Robert says. "You got something here. I think it's worth a try."

Johnny then turns around and embraces his father, something he has not done since he was a little boy. Procopio feels awkward, out of place. But he manages to hug Johnny briefly, a contented gleam in his eye. The other sons stand around, smiling. Aracely learns something about men—how they can love but don't always express it the way women do.

Other meetings follow. With flyers to get the word out—and the influence of the Salcido brothers and their father—more of the Mexican labor crews become interested; by the fifth meeting about half the group is Mexican, most of the other half black. Al appears willing to hang in there. Even more white workers show up. It looks like most of the mill is going to be represented after all.

Eventually, after several meetings, arguments, missteps, and misunderstandings, the group comes up with a slate of officers to run against the old guard at the local union. The slate consists of Al Simmons for president; Johnny for vice president; Tigre Montez, from the

10-inch mill, for treasurer; Jacob Wellborne, another black labor-crew leader, for treasurer; and, since some people feel they need a progressive white guy among the nominated group, Harley Cantrell as sergeant at arms.

This means they can't keep calling people honkies and *gabachos*. This is fine with Johnny. If they are going to win against the small, entrenched, right-wing union members of whatever color, they will need a significant number of whites on their side.

Union steward nominations go to various blacks, Mexicans, and—taking into account their freshly acquired insight on the matter—a few whites who support their platform of equality and fairness for all workers, regardless of color.

Of course, the old guard's not just sitting around watching this happen. As their cushy union jobs are on the line, they move more quickly than they have ever moved on any legitimate grievance. They place their stickers and flyers in all the work shanties. One of their slogans, with an image of the American flag underneath it, is, "Trust the Tried and True."

On another level, written threats are being stuffed into various people's lockers and on their car windshields—Dent's gang is also organizing. Johnny receives a piece of paper with the figure of a hanged man pushed into his locker. And false word gets around that the Communists are trying to take over the union, exactly what Johnny feared when he invited Harley to participate.

One setback involves Mosca, a leader among the furnace floor operators; he does a complete 180-degree turnaround. He goes from supporting the movement to being totally against it, telling people the whole thing is a dangerous waste of time. Procopio, who's helping his son get the word out about the campaign to the labor crews, says Mosca was put up against the wall by Denton and the KKK. This is unfortunate since Mosca wields a considerable amount of influence. But he isn't much for principles, a parasitic fly, as his nickname implies. He's the main one calling the new slate a "bunch of Communists and pinkos."

Another key activist, Gerardo Reyes, from the 32-inch-mill labor crew, is found badly hurt when he supposedly slips and falls to the floor, about a twenty-foot drop. Again, it doesn't appear to be an accident; somebody had poured a fresh, unused can of oil on the metal walkway. Gerardo breaks both legs, but he vows to remain active in the struggle for the union takeover after he recovers.

"Fuck 'em," Gerardo says from his hospital bed the day Johnny goes to visit him. "They should have killed me. But they didn't, so fuck 'em."

Johnny isn't immune to the attacks. His first day as a millwright apprentice, he is assigned to work with a journeyman millwright named Steve Rodham. He's one of the biggest racists in the plant, and Johnny feels something's up.

On Johnny's first morning as an apprentice, Steve doesn't say anything to him as he gets up and walks to the repair job site where they're stationed. Johnny stands up and follows. For most of that day, Steve has Johnny go back and forth between the tool and supply sheds, picking things up. Johnny feels like a mule.

At one point, while Steve is arc welding two pieces of metal, he has Johnny hold the pieces together with channel locks. But he neglects to tell Johnny not to look at the arc-welding light—which has about the same energy as a lightning bolt—as it melds the metal pieces and a welding rod together. While Johnny watches intently Steve is stone silent.

Johnny stares at the "little sun" at the point of fusion between the rod and metal; he has only his safety goggles on to protect his eyes. Steve makes a perfect bead along the seams; he's been doing this for two decades. It's a hell of thing, Johnny thinks, the artistry involved in making a simple weld.

What Johnny doesn't know is that he needs an arc-welding helmet, which fully covers his face and has a special window area for his eyes—like the one Steve is wearing. The safety goggles are no protection from an arc weld. In fact, Steve has a leather cover over his torso and arms; without them, he can get the equivalent of a sunburn. Johnny is without the added skin protection.

Later that evening, as Johnny drives home, he has trouble keeping his eyes open. He somehow makes it home, but his condition worsens. His eyes sting as if tiny needles are being pushed into them. He can feel every bit of lint, dust, and particle scraping against his eyeballs. Aracely is alarmed, but Johnny pretend it's no big thing. Then the pain becomes unbearable. Finally, pushing his pride aside, he asks to be taken to the emergency room. Aracely drives him to the Kaiser Hospital, where the doctors, after examining his eyes and getting an account of what happened, report that Johnny has burned off the lubrication in his eyes. If he had stared at the arc weld any longer, he could have permanently damaged his eyesight.

That night in bed, he's held gently in Aracely's arms, gauze and tape over both eyes, until he falls asleep. It takes several days until the lubrication comes back and his eyes are properly moist and protected.

As before, Johnny loses several days of work. And again some racist dog's the culprit behind his injuries. Johnny wants to take a gun and hurt somebody, but he knows he needs to bide his time. Steve Rodham isn't going to take responsibility for what he's done; he has already told everyone that Johnny should have known better—insisting it isn't up to him to give him basic safety lessons.

Johnny will need to be two steps ahead of Steve and his friends if he wants to carry through with the local union elections fight. He needs to be ready for anything.

And, of course, Aracely's pregnant. This puts a damper on Johnny's plans, but he decides to continue with the takeover campaign. Aracely, on the other hand, worries about how Johnny's being targeted.

As Aracely moves to the kitchen to put the broom away, her worries and chores make her tired. The L.A. sun is beating down on the apartment. She puts a small fan next to a rocking chair and then places a milk crate by her feet. She sits on the chair, her belly extending out so far that she can't see her toes.

The battle is on. Aracely's part of it, whether she likes it or not. If something bad happens to Johnny, she'll be alone in raising her soon-to-be-born baby. But she also believes in him; she believes in the struggle he's taken on. What she has learned most from life is that you have to fight for whatever dignity and respect you get in this world. Staying out of trouble because it's "trouble" isn't an option. It will never be an option for Aracely and Johnny. Not when it comes to winning what others take for granted, to getting your just due as an American worker. As a human being.

She puts her feet on top of the wooden crate and, minutes later, falls asleep, her worries a dark tint to her dreams.

There's something about the graveyard shift. Johnny can handle days and afternoon turns—in fact, the afternoon shift works best since he can sleep late and take care of things during the day that he can't do any other time.

But the nights—strange things happen at night.

As a child, like many children, Johnny had learned to fear the darkness of night, the unseen dangers, the creatures that stirred, the eerie silence, punctuated by crickets and owls and bats. It's also dream time, magical time, the realm of spirits where one can't control anything. He fears the night. He recalls several times as a child knocking on his parents' bedroom to ask to sleep with them. Eladia would get up and walk him back to his bed, suggesting in soft tones that guardian angels and Jesus Himself were standing over him, ensuring his safety. This scared him even more.

He remembers one particular dream when he was around four or five years old. He had fallen off the bed. Through the doorway, which opened into the dining room and kitchen of the small house they lived in by the railroad tracks near Florence Avenue, he saw a large, dark figure—an ominous ghost or monster, something too terrible to describe. It moved slowly toward him. But Johnny couldn't get up. He tried and tried, but he was stuck, as if by glue, to the bedroom floor. The creature neared and Johnny screamed, but the sound of his screams wouldn't come out. He was alone, helpless. He felt he was going to die. He never forgot that dream—it still haunts him.

So the night shifts are special for Johnny. Special in an unsettling way.

The first time Johnny walks into the plant at night, everything feels different; the cool air and dark sky fall across a brightly lit and noisy plant. He ambles over to the central millwright shanty to his locker. Nobody else is there. The place feels abandoned, not like the daytime, when oiler-greasers and millwright apprentices congregate, share stories and cigarettes, and prepare for their job assignments. Johnny feels wrong standing there, like he isn't supposed to be there.

Johnny takes out his tools, hard hat, and goggles and strolls over to the millwrights' shanty below the furnace floor. He's been assigned the electric furnaces for the week. As he nears the furnaces, he hears them bellowing their monstrous roar—all four furnaces going strong at once. He can see workers on the furnace floor shoveling coke and lime into the open mouth of one of the furnaces; eyeing the color and consistency of the molten steel inside the furnaces, a melter plunges a large rod into the same opening to blast oxygen into the concoction before he pulls it out and has the furnace doors closed. The bright yellow-red glow of melted steel shines on the furnace men's faces, the floor shadowed by their figures and of equipment lying about nearby.

Johnny walks into the shanty as Rex, Bob Michaels, another millwright named Frank Horner, and the night foreman for the furnace operators sit around drinking coffee, talking, and laughing at Rex's goofy jokes.

Rex is his work partner; Bob and Frank have dropped in from other parts of the plant to chat. Johnny hangs his tools up on a hook by the grease-stained, banged-up tool lockers in the shed. There are pipe-cutting machines, table clamps, stacks of different-size piping, turpentine vats, and a large metal desk that Rex sits next to in a worn office chair. Magazine pictures of naked women are tacked up on one side of a wall.

"Sit down, relax . . . we'll get started soon," Rex says without looking at Johnny.

Johnny sits on a painted wooden bench, carved throughout with years of names and love interests. "You got coffee?" he asks.

Rex gives him a hard look. "I'll get you some coffee this time, but next time, bring your own," he responds. "And bring your own sugar. Sugar is hard to come by in this place. People around here will kill for sugar. So keep it hid away in your locker. Remember, if you don't bring your own, you're out of luck."

Johnny makes a mental note: First rule of the night-shift crew on the furnaces—bring your own coffee and sugar.

It takes a while, but the men finally stand up and disperse. Johnny's almost falling asleep just sitting there, not used to staying up that late. Also, he couldn't get much sleep during the day in nervous anticipation of his graveyard-shift duties.

Rex stares down at some paperwork on the desk. He has a strong Indian face and nose, with short gray hair and a beer paunch below a muscled chest. Born in the old country, Rex had learned English and Anglo ways in the mill quickly. He rarely speaks Spanish to anyone, but when he feels like it, he'll rattle off complex curses.

Johnny's always thought Rex was a weird name for a Mexican, but then he's surprised to learn from reading the time cards that Rex's real name is Eugenio Plutarco Perez de Garibay.

Rex turns to Johnny briefly, opens a drawer, and throws a rectangular booklet filled with job assignment sheets on the desk. "You're to fill out these *chingaderas* at the end of every shift, detailing the work you've done here," Rex explains. "I'll tell you the names of the various jobs and equipment we'll be working on. Make sure you sign and put your employee number on each page."

Second rule.

"You just listen to what I tell you; right now you don't have to think about things too much," Rex continues. "But there are a few things you need to know. Don't go off to sleep anywhere without telling me. I need to know where you are at all times. If you go to the shitter or to visit anyone else in the plant, let me know. Pay attention to the air whistles. Different numbers of whistles mean different things. The signal you have to remember is five whistles—count them, make sure it's five. That's the millwrights' signal; it means there's some repair emergency. We get our tools and rush to the furnace foreman to find out what's wrong. Wherever you're at, drop what you're doing and go to the furnace floor. Repairs have to be done as fast as possible. These guys all have production quotas. Any downtime for repairs hurts their production. If we have to shut down a furnace, we make that call with the foreman. That's a major decision, so the foreman has to make sure it can happen. You follow my lead, you should be okay. *Entiendes, Mendes?*"

"*Simón*, that's clear," Johnny responds. Rules three to six, he notes in his head.

Rex is no-nonsense and to the point. Johnny likes that. Rex also likes to talk, unlike most of the hardened millwrights, whose motto seems to be "Don't explain; don't complain." He'll learn a lot from Rex.

There are routine checks to make on and around the furnaces when there are no repairs demanding their attention. They have to check all the gauges on the hydraulic machinery, which pulls the massive doors and roofs off the furnaces. They have to check the cooling towers that are situated alongside the furnace building—this is where the water that runs through various pipes to cool the furnaces returns (in a highly heated state) and gets cooled so it can go back and cool the furnaces once more. The most frequent repairs include the busting of water pipes around the furnace structures. They have to check oil and water pressures, the various electrical motors and gearboxes, and make sure the railcars and overhead cranes are in proper working order. At times, again when repairs aren't necessary, they change the wire rope on the outside cranes as well as the overhead cranes inside the furnace building. There is a lot to do at night.

And sometimes there's nothing to do.

When the furnaces are "purring," as Rex says, and all the routine checks have been made—"the rounds"—then Rex turns off the mill-wright shanty light, closes the door, and offers a bench for Johnny to take a snooze. Rex sleeps just fine in his old creaky chair. Johnny will be so tired he'll knock out in a matter of seconds. A couple of hours before dawn, Rex wakes Johnny up; he then orders him to do an errand so that he's pretty much awake by the time the day crew and foremen show up.

Most times when the sun rises, Johnny likes being on the water towers, or on the furnace-building's roof checking out the bag house and its multiple hydraulic arms. The sun sets the sky ablaze with an orange-red haze, similar to the color inside the furnaces. From where he stands on the highest points on the towers or roof, Johnny looks out at the horizon where palm trees, industrial buildings, stunted apartment complexes, and single-family homes stretch along for miles.

The world seems to open up like a cracked egg. Morning spells the end of the night madness. With the dawn, everything seems balanced, in place. Johnny feels renewed, alive again, blood flowing freely in his veins. As tired as his body is, his mind is sharp, charged, capable of anything. Perhaps because he was born at dawn, as his mother once told him, Johnny feels in tune with the birth of morning. Before first light, the birdsongs come. They call one another and then more birds, different bird voices, appear to bring up the sun from the blanket of earth that covers it. Although fatigue sweeps through him like a rising fever, dawn means a couple more hours at the plant, a short drive home, and the loving arms of his very pregnant wife. Every night is a battle; every morning the triumph of home over the job.

Before dawn, the shifts appear to last forever, unless he manages to get in a good snooze or is busy doing long repair jobs. All night long, but particularly after the foreboding midnight hour, he'll spot a clock and watch as it slowly marks the time over the course of the shift, torturing him. Time seems to stand still at crucial moments.

During a repair, however, it feels like being in a gun battle. People yelling. Hearts pumping. Pipes bursting. One night a door gets stuck on one of the furnaces. The furnace operators can't get the concrete-and-steel door to open so they can throw in the required coke and lime and oxygen blasts. The foreman screams at Rex and Johnny to get the repair done so they can continue cooking the molten scrap. Despite his speech to Johnny, Rex mostly ignores such admonishment. He actually doesn't care about their production quotas. Rex studies the situation, diagnoses the needed remedy, and then proceeds to direct Johnny to get the proper piping, tool, equipment, or other *chingadera* to get things working again. Rex knows his stuff. Most of what he does is called "Mickey Mousing." This means doing the most minimal repair job possible to keep the furnaces going until the day crew comes in to do a full and proper maintenance.

"We're like doctors," Rex offers. "We do routine checkups, perform emergency operations, and provide long-term care. Most of the emergencies here are stop-the-bleeding kind. If we do that, others can come in and finish up. Remember—the guys on the furnaces expect miracles. The same thing people expect of doctors. But we don't do miracles. If it can't be fixed, believe me, it can't be fixed. But I'll tell you from experience—don't say this out loud—almost anything in this place can be fixed. Almost anything."

Yes, Johnny learns a lot working the night shift with Rex. The daytime is more work intensive; the day crews work on the major repairs that can't get done at night. The afternoons also don't provide much room for Mickey Mousing. Despite the dread he feels staying up at night—fighting to keep his eyes open most of the time—he begins to appreciate working with Rex.

Rex works hard, but he also rests hard. Again, when things are going smoothly, the lights go off and they both end up cutting some major logs, snoring together in rhythm beneath the furnaces' incessant roar.

Johnny sits with his father and three brothers in the small living room of his apartment, planning out the final days before the union elections. Although the nominated slate members are having their own meetings, the family holds separate discussions to deal with the dynamics and details of the union takeover drive.

Regardless of what anyone else thinks, the Salcidos are the engine pulling the train.

There are already rumors that the old guard will stuff the ballot boxes. Johnny insists that members of the slate take turns at the ballot-box table in the local union hall to oversee the process. But they have other things to consider as well.

"Some major intimidation is going on in the mill," Rafas reports.

Rafas looks a lot like the rest of Procopio's sons—dark-skinned with a handsome face and a stocky body. Rafas, nickname for Rafael, was the tallest, although third from Severo in the birth line. Junior follows Severo; Bune, after Rafas. Junior is the stoutest—drinking beer like water most days. Johnny is in the best shape, being also the youngest and most streetwise. But he's also tall, and with years of hard labor and drinking—as well as Aracely's great cooking—he will eventually become hefty like his brothers.

"Dent and those fools are putting on the pressure," Rafas relates. "A lot of the guys aren't buying. Still, I'm afraid the majority of the plant won't even vote."

"I can't believe this," Johnny says. "They'd let a handful of fucking racists push them around! Don't they know those *perros* put on their pants the same way everyone else does, one leg at a time? They ain't shit. You have to stand up to these assholes."

"Well, *m'ijos*, you have to understand, the mill guys ain't scared of getting hurt," Procopio interjects. "They just want to work and keep their families fed. They don't want to lose their jobs. Why fight the union guys—as long as their jobs aren't on the line? They want stability, not change. We have to convince them that their jobs *are* on the line. They have to understand that with a weak union, the company will do what it wants to do. The bosses have already fired whole crews. They've denied people pensions and benefits. They've even hired some guys from Michoacán—*sin papeles*—to do some of the repairs on the new wire mill machines for real low pay."

"I'm going to talk to those Michoacán guys," Johnny says. "The millwrights want to fuck them up, but for the wrong reasons. I'm going to get them on our side—and we'll defend them as well."

"Dent and the Klan are watching everybody," Junior adds. "They stand on the catwalks, making sure nobody is talking too much, for too long. People have to keep shoveling or they let the company know who's not and write-ups start coming at people right and left. If you have enough write-ups, you can get canned. I wish we could do something about Dent and those fucking KKKers."

"Not now," Johnny says. "People would know it was the union takeover guys and they'd come after us. Someday, I don't know when, Dent will get his. For now, the only way we can deal with those guys is by focusing on the elections."

"It doesn't look good, 'manito," Bune offers. "Unless something drastic happens, the millworkers think it's just a beef between two rival union groups—and they could give a shit which of them wins."

"Then we'll have to make them give a shit," Johnny argues. "Harley is good at putting words together—that's one smart mother-fucker. He can come up with strong slogans and flyers. We'll keep getting flyers out, and spread the word. We'll keep talking to people every day until election day. And Tigre is pulling in more guys every day 'cause he's well known in the mill. Al and the bros will get what they can, although many blacks don't even like Al. I'm wondering if putting Al on the slate was a good idea."

"What could we do?" Procopio explains. "Al brought in his guys. He's out there every day with the blacks. We had to have him on the slate. I know most people think he's too much like a black version of a KKK guy. But he's tough and he's got pull. The same thing with Harley. Sure he's a Communist—something I don't care about myself—but he works hard, and he's bringing in a good number of the whites that don't want anything to do with Dent or the union hacks. We need them both."

"You're right, apá," Johnny agrees, wondering if his father's opinion of Harley has really changed. "Al and Harley bring in the groups we need—but the majority in the mill think those guys are too extreme to get behind. We need to make sure we present the issues in a way that convinces them to vote."

The pains come in waves—strong, deep, distressing. Aracely has been napping when she feels the first contractions. She isn't sure what to do; she knows about false labor. She doesn't want to call the mill to get Johnny to come home until she is certain the baby's ready to come out.

She stands up, puts on some clean clothes she has ready to wear to the hospital, pulls her overnight bag from the closet that she has carefully packed with everything she needs, and waddles into the kitchen.

She makes herself tea and then sits down, glancing over to the clock above the sink. It's 4 A.M.

Johnny is on the furnace floor, talking to the melters and furnace operators about the upcoming elections. He hasn't felt like sleeping the past few nights. When things are going smoothly on the graveyard shift, he walks around to talk to the mill workers wherever he can find them. Rex doesn't stop him; he stays back in the shanty, resting or talking to anyone who comes by, until the five whistles blare or morning breaks through.

A phone call wakes Rex from a short snooze, which is odd since the phone rarely rings on the graveyard shift.

"And what may I do you for?" Rex answers in a phony English accent. He listens attentively then hangs up. Rex picks up his tools and walks through a corridor with rows of pipes on either side to metal-and-cement steps that lead up to the furnace floor. He climbs the steps and asks the first man he sees if Johnny is around.

"Yeah, he's on the other end talking that elections stuff," the mill hand says.

When Rex reaches Johnny it looks more like he is joking than talking serious. Johnny notices Rex, stops smiling, and gives a nod of "what's up?" The sight of his work partner makes Johnny's heart skip— his thoughts immediately turn to Aracely and the baby.

"There's a hell of an emergency on the hearth in the 10-inch mill," Rex says. "They need our help. Dirty Harry and Frank Horner are already over there. The foremen here will keep us posted in case anything happens on the furnaces."

Rex and Johnny climb onto a battered forklift and get going. When they arrive at the hearth area of the plant, everybody seems in battle mode. A section of brick wall has fallen down from the hearth to the mill floor. Red-hot bars of steel are sitting in the massive oven, exposed to the air through the opening and cooling off to unworkable levels. Harry and Frank are up on top of the structure, with safety belts around their waists and an overhead crane holding a massive plate of thick steel to be fastened onto the opening until the hearth can be shut down and the masonry crew brought in to rebuild the walls.

Both millwrights are sweaty, dirty, and slightly burned on their faces and arms. They have been trying to put the plate on the opening for almost an hour; exhausted and hurt, they need Rex and Johnny to take over.

The overhead crane holds the plate in place so that Harry and Frank can pull away from where they have been standing, climb down a ladder, and let Rex and Johnny climb up and take their positions above the flaming-hot opening. Nobody says a word; Harry and Frank are too weak to do anything but get out. Rex and Johnny then clamp their safety belts to brackets near the ladder and try to determine the extent of the damage so they can finish the job.

Just then Johnny receives a blast of heat that makes him feel as if the flesh on his face will melt right off. He doesn't say anything, although he wants to yell as he looks over at his partner. Rex clenches his jaw, squints his eyes, and tries to determine what the problem is. Harry and Frank had been trying to fasten the plate with huge clamps to the remaining brick section of wall. But Rex can see they were only making the wall more likely to fall apart completely from the weight of the plate clamped to it.

Rex shouts for Johnny to walk across some piping to the other side of the plate so he can steady it. As Johnny slowly walks over, his pants feel as if somebody is ironing them with him inside. He grabs piping and brackets near his head and almost falls back when the heat goes through his gloves. For a moment, he feels he's going to die, but then pushes the thought from his head and continues along the pipe to the other side.

Rex spots the huge clamps and picks one up with his gloved hands, yet almost drops it because of the heat. He sees a section of beam from inside the hearth that he feels is strong enough to hold the clamps and the plate. He gives the overhead-crane operator signals to move the plate up and over. He gives Johnny a signal to hold the plate steady while he tries to clamp one corner to the beam.

As the crane operator slowly moves the plate into place, a corner of the plate above Johnny's head accidentally smashes against a galvanized pipe and hot steaming water pours out. This pipe is connected to the hearth's water-cooling system.

When the pipe bursts Johnny takes big drops of the boiling liquid on parts of his face and arm. He loses his footing and falls back—this time he yells—only to be held up from falling by the safety belt. He hangs there, some thirty feet above the mill floor, his skin stinging from the burns. Johnny realizes he's dangling toward his death. In his mind, he can only think of one thing—Aracely and the baby.

Aracely calls the mill soon after her water breaks. But she can't get anyone at the millwright shanty, the only number she has for the night crew. She phones her sister-in-law's house down the street. Patricia is married to Bune, who's out in an after-hours club with Junior that early morning. She's also Aracely's closest friend among the Salcidos.

"Pati, I need you to take me to the hospital," Aracely says. "My water broke and I can't reach Johnny. I've been having some strong contractions. Johnny's supposed to be in the electric furnaces, but I call the number and nobody answers. I called the plant number and nobody answers there either. I need your help, *mujer*."

"Sure, Ari, I'll be right over," Patricia assures her. "Let me get a few things. It'll only be a minute."

"Okay, but don't take long—I may not have more than a minute."

By the time Patricia makes it to Aracely's house, the woman is lying back on the couch, her legs wide apart, and her arms around her swollen womb.

"You're having the baby now?" Pati asks, alarmed as she sees Aracely on the couch.

"No, no, I don't want to have it here . . . take me to Kaiser Hospital in Bellflower, *de volada*!"

The drive to the hospital seems to take forever. It's only a few miles from Aracely's apartment, but the early dawn traffic is already picking up.

The labor pains become more violent. Aracely thinks something's wrong, but she doesn't want to worry. She prays to the Virgen de Guadalupe to protect her and the baby. She also wonders about Johnny—where is he? And she wonders whether he will be there for the baby's birth.

"Pati, please do me a favor and call the mill as often as you can until you get Johnny," Aracely says. "I want him to be with me when the baby comes. He worked so hard to be my birthing coach—it would be really, really bad if he missed this."

"*No te preocupes*, don't worry—I'll be calling until I reach somebody," Pati responds.

The hospital staff seats Aracely in a wheelchair. Her medical card through the benefits program is all she needs to get in, get comfortable, and have a baby. As a nurse's aide wheels her down the hall to her room, she hears one woman in labor in another room screaming for painkillers.

Pati goes to make a phone call. As soon as Aracely is on the bed and the nurse's aides are gone, tears begin to well up in the mother-to-be's eyes. Johnny, oh Johnny . . . where are you, *querido*? she wonders.

Johnny tries to reach a pipe or bracket with one of his tools and pull himself back to the hearth wall. Rex walks across the same pipes that Johnny did to get to the dangling figure. The overhead-crane operator has moved the plate away to give the men room. Several mill hands below are yelling. Johnny can't hear what they're saying. He feels weak, skin tight with heat, and there are patches of burns on his face and arm. Rex—although he's past fifty—is nimble and strong. He reaches out to Johnny's legs and pulls the young man in. Johnny can see the heat streaming from Rex's clothes and hard hat, his face bathed in perspiration.

Once they are on the wall, barely hanging on, Rex moves back to his position on the other side. Johnny thinks perhaps they might come down, but he sees that Rex means for them to finish the job. At that moment, Johnny thinks the hearth system should be closed and allowed to cool down completely so a repair crew can come in later and do the job right. But he knows Rex is pressured by production deadlines. Again and again, this is the overriding concern, even when someone is in danger of getting killed. The plant has a terrible safety record. The company has monthly safety meetings for the craft crews and some of the mill hands. They put up posters and billboards around the plant addressing safety. They have everyone convinced that injuries and deaths are the fault of the workers—someone didn't pay attention to this, or was not prepared for that. But Johnny knows better—the demand to keep the mill running and profits pumping is hurting and sometimes killing plant employees.

Rex and Johnny work faster, with the heat almost suffocating them. They don't give up. In a half hour, the plate is clamped onto beams on the other side of the hearth, helping to hold some of the heat inside. Then they work on the broken water pipe; putting temporary rubber clamps over the punctured section of pipe. The repairs—even if "Mickey Mouse"—allow the overhead cranes to pull out enough malleable bars for the 10-inch mill. Production is stalled, but not stopped.

The two men are dead tired. Nobody claps or acknowledges their efforts, or the efforts of Harry and Frank. They slowly climb onto the forklift and ride back to the millwright shanty; the sun now past the horizon is silhouetted by mill towers and corrugated tin buildings. Rex and Johnny wash up and put ointment on their arms and faces, tending to their burns. As the shift starts to wind down, Johnny thinks about his first thought when Rex said there was an emergency—about Aracely. He calls the house right away.

Pati is the only witness to tiny Joaquin Salcido's birth into the world; she can't contain her joy, despite being exhausted. Aracely is different though. The new mother comes through with flying colors, sticking to her Lamaze techniques despite not having Johnny there as her birthing coach. The baby seems extremely sleepy, causing Pati some concern. But he's fine. The nurse wraps up the purplish-skinned boy and hands him over to Aracely. The baby's eyes are closed and his mouth moves slightly; he is wrapped in a cocoon of warm blankets, with a baby cap on his head. Aracely looks down on her son and tears stream down her face; although they are tears of happiness, they are laced with a deep regret that Johnny was not present.

4

ELECTIONS

Joaquin's cries push through the hollow wood door from the living room to the bedroom where Johnny is trying to sleep in the middle of the day. A hole in the aluminum foil that had been spread across a window allows a stream of sunlight into the mostly darkened room, illuminating the dust and a section of pillow near Johnny's head. He slowly opens his eyes and watches the way the light appears to singe the delicate design on the pillowcase.

Trying to sleep during the day is difficult enough, but with the baby, it's near impossible. Joaquin is a colicky child—crying most of the time he's awake as if something is burning his insides; something, of course, he can't name. Aracely rushes to the baby and picks him up; she walks around with Joaquin on her shoulder, humming and rocking him at the same time.

Johnny's fully awake. He lies there for a while, wrongly thinking he'll get tired and fall asleep again. It never happens. Johnny sits up in bed looking around the room, finally focusing on the source of the light.

In a few hours, he'll be back at work.

Resentment had set in with Johnny ever since he was unable to attend to his wife during the baby's birth. On the morning Joaquin entered the world, Johnny showered, changed his clothes, and rushed to the hospital. By the time he arrived, Aracely and baby were resting comfortably with Pati nearby, waiting to be relieved.

Johnny strolls into the living room in his boxer shorts, adjusting his vision to the daylight that engulfs everything. Aracely glances over at him and sighs.

"Sorry, Johnny," Aracely says. "I tried to get the baby before he got too loud."

"That's okay," replies Johnny, half awake. "Let's just hope tonight's a smooth night."

He goes to the kitchen and pours himself a glass of water. A mirror above the drying dishes shows a dark mark over his cheek from one of the burns he got during the hearth-repair effort. He again thinks about missing his son's birth and anger knots in his gut.

The union elections are just around the corner. That evening before he starts his shift, he's going to Harley's house in Bell to meet with the Communists. Although he didn't trust them in the beginning, they are consistent and thorough during the campaign. They write strongly worded leaflets with facts about how the steel mill and leading members of the union are in cahoots. They describe the system of "race splitting" and how the workers with common interests and aims can be distracted into believing they have more in common with the company than with their fellow workers.

Johnny gets closer to Harley during those weeks before the election. Harley is intensely smart and articulate, and he never has a bad word to say about anybody, except the mill owners and their union puppets. Johnny is amazed by how Harley and the others carefully study the "big picture," then methodically share their understanding with their coworkers.

"Everything is a process. You have to go through all the necessary stages—there are no shortcuts," Harley constantly reminds Johnny.

Johnny observes that prior to making a move, these revolutionaries try to think everything through. And their efforts are bearing fruit: Harley and his friends have convinced a large number of whites among the mill hands and warehouse workers to join their struggle for new union leadership. This is crucial to defeating the racist whites, mostly from the craft units, who run the union.

When Johnny arrives at Harley's small square-shaped home, cars are parked in the driveway and along the curb in front of the house. Johnny has to park several houses down. He walks in the breezy summer evening—the kind of evenings Johnny likes the most. Even though he isn't a Communist, he's intrigued with their intellectual banter and sharp humor. Johnny has no idea what communism is, but he's finding out there is more to it than most people think.

His one previous experience with "Communists" involved a crazy sect in a meatpacking plant he briefly worked in. The group was called the United Communist Front (Revolutionary). They were college-educated whites working among mostly Mexicans, who were barely educated. But unlike Harley and his friends, Johnny felt these dudes were completely nuts. They brought red flags to the workplace and left Mao's *Red Book* on lunch benches. They would argue with everyone—mostly their fellow workers—deriding them for being exploited and manipulated by the "bourgeoisie." They had a knack for using words that other people never heard of, and ranting on and on regardless of whether anybody understood what they said.

On one occasion, during a campaign for union recognition—the plant was nonunion—they burst through the company gates in a truck with red flags and their members holding megaphones and screaming at the "stupid" workers for not "getting it" about Communist revolution. The end result was a sabotage of the union-organizing drive. Needless to say, they alienated more people than they ever recruited, remaining an insignificant yet highly annoying group.

Johnny is convinced they were police agents—they tended to undermine or destroy whatever they got ahold of. Besides, for being so bent on "communism," they sure turned everybody off to it, which made their actions all the more suspect.

At first, Johnny had judged Harley and his friends by this first encounter with the UCF(R). The Communists in the steel mill belong to different organizations, including, he finds out, the UCF(R). Harley belongs to a group called the Communist Labor Organizing Committee (CLOC) that stays away from the UCF(R) and other groups. Johnny now understands there are as many differences among Communists as there are among Protestants. Fortunately, in Harley, Johnny finds someone with immense patience, respect, and character.

At the meeting, Johnny recognizes a number of people from the mill, mostly white. One exception is Ronnie Nakamura, a Japanese-American mill electrician who is well known for his grasp of facts and figures. Harley spots Johnny and offers him a seat next to Ronnie.

"We'll start now that Johnny's here," Harley announces. "In the first hour, we'll go over the current world and national situation. This will help orient the practical things we have to address later this evening. I've asked Ronnie to begin this part of the meeting."

Ronnie looks up, clears his throat, and opens up a folder filled with newspaper clippings and lined paper laden with penciled notes.

"The most salient aspect in our world today is the growing rise of destitution and hunger among most people, while a decreasingly small class of people holds most of the world's wealth and power," Ronnie begins. "The United States, particularly after World War Two, emerged as the most powerful capitalist nation in the world. Since then it has embarked on controlling the world's financial markets and most of its resource industries. Today, however, with the impending defeat of the greatest military power in the world by the Vietnamese Communists, the ruling class in this country has resorted to greater repression and terror against the powerless and most exploited—particularly blacks and Mexicans, but including a growing number of whites. We're seeing class politics move to the forefront after decades of race politics dominating the social scene. This is a crucial development—the working class becoming aware of itself as a class as the necessary ingredient to advance the ripening revolutionary political situation."

Ronnie then brings in examples and statistics from news items he has been collecting and studying over the past few weeks.

Johnny listens. Much of what is stated he doesn't understand, but he catches the gist of it—this is a group willing to "break things down." Still, these guys speak a different language. To them, words are important—"the right word to describe the right thing," as Harley says. They are scientists of society and its motive forces. However, they aren't removed from the rest of the world like other scientists; they are a beacon of intellectual activity, integrated in the major plants, mills, and refineries, among the people communism is supposed to reach.

Johnny also isn't sure he can entirely agree with them, but he's interested. He likes the feel, the texture of these meetings, where words, passion, ideas, and visions burst out of normally stoic men and women. Yet years of living in the streets has also taught Johnny to be *trucha*, as they say in the barrio. This means "alert," "wary," "wise." You have to be trucha to survive *la vida loca*.

Johnny's aware that communism is considered the scourge of the world, the most un-American concept anyone can possibly believe. Certainly that's what he's learned in school and in the media.

At some level, Johnny feels strange coming to Harley's meeting— as if as soon as he steps outside, he'll catch a bullet. People around the world die for delving into such concepts, for simply breaking from the status quo. This is common in Mexico, Central America, Southeast Asia, and Africa. He feels he's entering a dark, forbidden place, a place that is labeled evil yet is strangely liberating. He knows government agents target such people. He also knows the KKK and the union stooges are determined to make sure no Communist ever gets a foothold in the mill.

What keeps Johnny interested is the inescapable truth of what everyone is saying, the intensely powerful logic of their analysis. They talk funny. They sometimes look funny. But damn, they illuminate reality in a way he's never experienced before.

At a certain point in the meeting, after a particularly heated discussion—nobody really disagrees with one another, but their intensity helps solidify everyone else's clarity and commitment—Harley moves the agenda to the local union elections.

"We are in the middle of a key battle," Harley begins, "the battle for true equity and justice at Nazareth Steel. Winning local union positions is a first step. But this won't be easy. The old guard is entrenched and desperate. The Nazareth management has joined in the fray by scaring most workers into not participating in the elections— saying they'll lose hours or even their jobs if they vote. Or they're coercing certain workers to support the present local leadership. The company has a stake in this, too. I'm afraid this battle won't easily be won, if we win at all. We *should* win the election, but the main thing we need to achieve is the unity to keep organizing and fighting regardless of the election's outcome."

At that moment, Johnny realizes the Communists have their own agenda. This is what he came to see. For Johnny, the election is a thing in itself. But for the Communists, it is a springboard to something else: power in the mill, perhaps. Johnny keeps his mouth shut, but this realization colors how he wants to relate to Harley and his friends. The rest of the lively discussion blurs in front of him. The Communists are using the elections for their own aims, he figures. Procopio has told him about this—keep the Communists close; they are basically well-intentioned people, but don't turn anything over to them.

Al Simmons has plans of his own.

He gathers a group of militant blacks from among the labor crews. They have their own study circles and community ties. They are meeting with Black Panthers and later with United Slaves organization members in South Central L.A.—although the Black Panthers and United Slaves had their own beefs with each other, manipulated by government agents that led to the killing of two Panthers on the UCLA campus a few years earlier.

Al preaches a firebrand version of black power. He tells his followers never to trust whites, even the liberals or Communists. To Al they are the worst. They make you drop your guard, but in the end they want to control things. He also claims blacks shouldn't trust Mexicans, who are mostly illegal and not adept in English, who only watch out for their own when it comes to work and, when push comes to shove, will join with the whites against the blacks.

Al wants to win the top union spot so that blacks can run the union the way the whites have done before them. Unlike Johnny and some of the others, including Harley, Al doesn't want to "change" the system. He wants blacks to be the top dogs. He doesn't advocate doing anything different from what the racist whites have done, except to make sure blacks get the best jobs and union positions.

But Al also realizes he needs Johnny, his family, and most of the Mexicans—and even the supportive whites—if he's to win the election. There was strong disagreement during the process that ended by nominating Al for local president. But at the time, he had the majority of people who came to the meetings. By the time this changed, Al had become the best of all possible nominees for president.

Al grew up on the streets of Watts in the Nickerson Gardens Housing Projects. He battled his way through South Central's mean streets against gangs like the Gladiators, the Slausons, and the Bounty Hunters. Al built up his rep as a man to be reckoned with. After a short stint at Chino Prison for burglary, Al worked in the massive Goodyear Tire Company plant on Central Avenue until he got fired for riling up the mostly black workers. As soon as he was hired on at Nazareth, he began pulling in the black laborers, getting them to black-power meetings in the community and connecting them with various militants in other factories and plants. For years prior to this, he was a leader of the Black Workers Alliance, with representatives from various large plants in L.A., until they became too "communistic" for him to continue.

Part of Al's agenda is to reconstitute a black workers' group at Nazareth that can spread across industrial L.A. and begin the process of taking over the political and social reins for their neglected and maligned communities.

One day just before the elections, Al meets with a cadre of black militants on top of the wire-mill cooling tower, where they can see for miles, but nobody can see them. Nobody knows they are there—his pull with the labor-crew foreman allows them to meet without being bothered.

"The election's almost here," Al proclaims. "We need to mobilize as many brothers as we can to vote. I know some don't want to be bothered, but we can show that our unity and beliefs will make a difference. I don't mind working with the Mexicans and liberal whites while we do this. But our goal is for us to be in control and begin to bring our people into all the major union positions."

"How we going to get rid of them *eses* and peckerwoods once the elections are over?" one of the men asks.

"They don't know what they're doing," Al responds. "We're the best organized and the most determined. We'll ramrod them. They won't even know what hit them. The Salcido family? They too nice to deal with what we have in mind."

As the men talk, one worker sits in the back, not saying a word. His name is Tony Adams. He's a recent hire, in his early twenties, and he quickly maneuvers himself into Al's closest ranks. He also happens to be Robert Thigpen's cousin, a fact the others aren't aware of. Robert suggested that Tony get close to the black militants and report to him. Robert doesn't care for Al and his black-power politics. He has begun to see Johnny as a true leader for everyone at the mill—black, white, and brown—and wants to make sure his efforts aren't undermined.

Tony nods his head in agreement as others, like in church, loudly proclaim their support of Al's militant stance. Tony partly agrees with what is being said—racism against blacks in America is deep, ugly, and pervasive. He understands why Al and the others can't work with anyone else, why they take such extreme positions against the world. But he also agrees with his cousin: If change is really to happen—real change, real justice—most everyone will have to be involved.

"We get into office then we move on all the honkies and any Mexican who stands in the way," Al says. "If a Mexican wants to join with us, fine, but they're under our leadership. We'll make the local union an outpost of true black power. We'll have classes on black history and organize rallies for housing, education, and political issues. Everybody with me?"

"Yays," "heys," and "black power" are shouted out. Tony joins in the chorus. He looks down from the water tower to see if anyone can hear them. The mill is so noisy and the traffic on Slauson Avenue so incessant, they are safe from being heard.

Even if the slate wins, they've already lost, Tony reasons. The various groups trying to get representation through that slate are united only on paper; they are as divided as they ever have been.

The Steelworkers Hall—Local 1750—is a one-story gray-and-brown building across the street from the east end of the plant. It has a large meeting room, a kitchen, and several offices. A parking lot in the back hits up against poor to moderate single-family homes in the working-class town of Maywood.

Frank Horner, Bob Michaels, Hank "Dirty Harry" Cheatham, and Earl Denton sit around a table in the empty meeting hall. Frank, a huge veteran millwright with a 1950s-style haircut, smokes filterless cigarettes one right after the other. Bob Michaels is smaller than Frank but carries himself like a tough hombre with a smart mouth and an edgy disposition. Hank is more restrained, an older, balding man; he doesn't say much but keeps order when things get heated. Earl Denton, of average weight and height, is clearly the leader among these men.

As they talk, Steve Rodham and Ace Mulligan push in the double doors to the hall and look at the table where their buddies sit. Steve is thin, although he eats like a horse, and Ace is stout and hairy.

"No wonder them niggers and spics want to get rid of you fuckers," Mulligan blurts out. "You are some sorry-ass old men—somebody should fucking kick you out of here."

Nobody laughs. Everyone just takes his words in stride. Mulligan is the local president. He's an overhead-crane operator on the scrap yard. He holds sway largely because of his ability to make light of any situation. Nobody takes Mulligan seriously, except when he drinks. When he drinks, that Irish blood surfaces to his face and hands and all he wants to do is fight. Most of his friends try to make sure he doesn't drink too much, but Mulligan always finds a way, often in bars far distant from the ones that have longed barred his presence.

Steve and Ace pull up two chairs and sit next to the men.

"We got some trouble brewing in the warehouse," Steve reports in his familiar raspy voice. "Now the fucking Reds have a study circle over at Harley's house. Most of the guys that go to it come from the warehouse. They've got a list of demands. They're getting others from the rolling mills and wire rope mill to sign on. It's just a way to get more people to vote this coming Tuesday."

"Don't worry about those fuckhead commies," Denton says. "We can take care of them. It's Johnny and those Mexicans. It's Al and his black militants. That's who I'm worried about."

Mulligan looks over at Dent and appears surprised. "First time I ever heard you fret about anything," he says. "I thought we had all this in the bag."

"We got most people not bothering to vote, that'll help," Frank responds. "But the ones who do vote, they can still pull it off. We'll need to get all our votes plus some. Otherwise, we ain't going to make it."

"We need a way to get more votes in the ballot boxes than actually vote," Bob asserts. "But Johnny and them plan to get their people in here when the balloting is going on. They're going to inspect the ballot boxes and then make sure only one vote is coming in per person. They also got the international to send a representative here to oversee the elections."

"Do we know who this fucker is?" Mulligan asks.

"I've got that covered," Denton insists. "We've got one of our guys coming in—Johnny and his compadres don't have the pull we have with the main international staff. But Johnny's still going to be one hell of an ass-fuck."

"What happened to all the threats and shit," Mulligan continues. "You losing your bite after all these years, Dent?"

"I ain't your fucking dog!" Denton retorts.

"Whoa there, pardner," Mulligan says, backing off, his face red. "I ain't questioning your abilities, Dent. But you were going to scare them Salcidos and Mexicans—use one of them as an example. I know it didn't work with the dude from the 32-inch mill. He's fully recovered and active again. What do you have in mind, is all I'm asking."

Dent ignores the question. He does what he does; he doesn't feel he has to answer to anyone, particularly that loose-cannon loudmouth Mulligan. But his tone is more uncertain than it has ever been in years.

"We got another problem," Dent says. "The consent decree has been challenged on the issue of bringing women to the mill floor and into the craft units. I just got word that the international union and the company have agreed to hire women into those jobs. You know what this means? Not only do we have to contend with these mud people, now we'll have fucking pussies working right next to us. This is fucked up. This is goddamn communism. Worse than hell."

"Shit, the days of whites, Christians, and men are numbered," Ace says under his breath.

The men stare at one another. This is their biggest fear. They have to hang on, they can't give an inch. In the South, where many of these men originally came from, they fought tooth and nail for their privileges, opposing civil rights organizers against desegregation and the black codes. What they didn't always understand was that they, too, were poor—sometimes poorer than some blacks. By putting their boots on the necks of blacks and others to keep them down, whites ended up in the same ditch.

But Dent and his cronies don't acknowledge this. To them, white is right and it doesn't matter how contrary to reality this belief may be. If they believe they're right, they're right.

"We got to scare the hell out of them ass-wipes before the election. You know, raid their meeting places or something like that," Bob Michaels proposes, spitting a wad of chewing tobacco into a trash can at the end of the table.

"Can't you guys think of something a little more creative?" Hank finally contributes.

"Creative, hell," Steve says, leaning back against his chair. "I'd like to get my hands around them pencil-necks and squeeze. Is that creative enough for you?"

"Listen, you guys keep working on getting the votes we need in here," Denton interjects. "I'll take care of those we don't want to vote."

"Sounds like a plan to me," Mulligan says, slightly bored.

Johnny hears the sizzle of the meat as several packages wrapped in aluminum foil are pulled up by wire from the side of the soaking pits.

Tigre Montez and his friends are cooking a couple of steaks inside the massive oven. Men in the furnaces and the hearth do the same thing. Sometimes, they'll drop a juicy steak in foil right on top of an ingot. You have to know when to pull it off or it will burn to a crisp. After years of practice, the men have perfected the right cooking time.

"*Qué hubo*, Johnny," Tigre acknowledges. "Care for some *carne asada?*"

"No, I'm fine," Johnny says. "But we should talk."

It's day shift. After the men gather around the floor of the 32-inch mill to have their lunch, Johnny sits next to Tigre to find out how the voting will go—the elections are the next day.

"We're down to the wire, Tigre," Johnny says. "How does it look with the crews and mill hands on the 32- and 10-inch mills?"

"It looks good, *ese*," Tigre says while biting into a steak sandwich filled with jalapeño peppers. "I got my troops ready. They'll vote. They ain't scared. Them fucking KKKers tried to pull some moves on a couple of dudes who were alone in the scrap yard. That's how they operate—they try to come at you when you can't fight back. But most of my guys have stayed together. They don't mess with us anymore. They know better."

"Sounds good. I got fairly good reports from the 22-inch, the warehouse, and the wire mill," Johnny says. "But I'm not sure about the furnaces or the craft units. It seems to me they've managed to intimidate the largest group of mill hands there. We'll need the labor crews to pull it off."

"Well, as you know, *carnal*, a few people are still wondering about the *pinche* Communists," Tigre declares. "I know they've been helpful, but you know these labor guys don't care for either the right-wingers or the left-wingers. They want to work; they work hard and they'll come through, but they also don't want to be in anyone's pocket. So as long as the issues stay in the forefront, I'll think we'll get most of the crews behind us."

"I know they won't vote for the old union guys; the problem is whether they'll vote at all," Johnny explains. "Management keeps a tight rein on the labor crews. They're the least paid and more likely to get kicked out of here. There are hundreds of guys in the street willing to come in and shovel junk all day long. They'll take their jobs in a hot second. So the crews know management has them by the balls."

"You're right, *ese*, they won't vote if they think management is keeping an eye on them."

"We have to courage them up," Johnny says. "So they can stand up to management for their jobs. Whether we win or lose, what could be done to protect their jobs once management starts making their move against them?"

"If we win, we can mount a fight at least," Tigre suggests. "But if we lose, nothing. These guys know that. They want a guaranteed win before they'll step up. But we can't give them that—can we?"

"*They're* our guarantee!" Johnny declares.

"Not really," Tigre adds. "Even if we win, those *putos* in the old union group will contest the results. They'll keep us in meetings and hearings. They'll make it so we can't lift a finger to help anybody. In the meantime, these guys get fired, harassed, pushed to the limits with work assignments. You see my point? So they're asking what guarantees do we have that they'll have their jobs once the election is over."

"I don't know . . . I guess we don't have any guarantees," Johnny concedes.

"That's right, *carnal*. So that's what's going to hurt us. Winning the election may be worse than if we lose. Either way, we're fucked." Tigre sighs.

"*Órale*, I understand," Johnny says. "But can we keep this to ourselves?"

Tigre looks up from his sandwich.

"These aren't trade secrets, my friend," Tigre comments. "People know what's up. They already know what it will mean whether we lose or not."

"I know, but we have to give them the other side of the story," Johnny continues. "The side where we have the union hall for our needs. Where we get union reps that walk these floors and file hundreds of grievances to defend our rights. Where we force management to stop and pay attention—and do something about the fucked-up situation here. The side that puts power in our hands and allows us to get more jobs and better pay for all the workers. We have to emphasize that no matter what, it's better to fight than to sit around and do nothing. Without us, this company wouldn't be crap, wouldn't make any profits. We, the workers, make this place go 'round."

"You're sounding like that Harley *vato*," Tigre quips.

"Well, he's got his problems, but essentially the dude's right. Anyway, do whatever you can to get your guys to the union hall tomorrow. *De acuerdo?*"

"*Simón*, agreed—just remember, win or lose, we better do something for these guys."

Roosevelt Park is crammed full of people on a warm Sunday afternoon. Vendors in carts selling *paletas*—Mexican-style frozen fruit bars—stand around as kids and their parents decide which ones to buy. The place is filled with Mexicans on blankets, next to beer coolers, setting up barbecue grills; a few black families can be spotted among the crowd doing the same. This is Florencia's main community hangout. Brown and black children scamper by; a few tattooed *cholos* stand beneath shady trees. Winos and junkies sit on weather-worn benches to *averiguar*—or "shoot the shit," as they say.

Aracely and Johnny lie on a blanket with tiny Joaquin next to them in a baby car seat. In the sun Joaquin calms down and falls asleep. This is rare and Johnny enjoys the relative quiet for a few minutes. Coming toward them, Junior, Rafas, and Bune haul coolers full of beer and lunch meat. Three women follow right behind them lugging paper bags with food and other items; they are Pati, Bune's wife; Sarita, Rafas's partner, with their three children behind her; and Junior's girlfriend, MerriLee, an African-American he recently met at a nightclub.

"*Qué hubo*, bros," Johnny greets as he opens his eyes slightly to take in his brothers and the women.

Aracely stands up and starts placing the food onto another blanket; she opens a bag with napkins and plastic utensils and puts them near bowls of homemade potato salad and rice. Next to the family is a small grill with hot dogs and chicken pieces over a fire that Johnny lit earlier.

Entering the park from another direction, Procopio and Eladia walk over with their two other school-age grandchildren—Pati and Bune's children. Procopio carries folded-up lounge chairs under his arms.

Everyone greets one another with smiles and small talk. It looks like a celebration, a gathering of family to signal some great occasion or purpose. But it's just a time to get out for a while.

The union elections had been held the Tuesday before. Johnny and the other candidates spent all day at the union hall, watching the voters and the ballot boxes. The international union representative didn't do anything but stay in one of the union offices jaw-jacking with Ace Mulligan or one of the other union hacks. Sporadic numbers of labor-crew guys and mill hands showed up. But almost all the craft units, crane operators, and furnace operators participated—all of them part of the mill strongholds of the old union leadership.

Johnny, Al, Tigre, and the others received indifference or hateful stares from many of the pro–old-guard voters. No real incidents occurred at the union hall, except when Johnny went to locate the international union rep to help with the count and he was nowhere to be found. Somebody later tracked him to a local pub and brought him back.

But things were quite different in the mill.

A couple of Harley's Communist friends were attacked and beaten in the warehouse area, forcing them to miss voting; the assailants turned out to be members of the rival United Communist Front. Johnny was further convinced they were paid agents who somehow knew when to do things to disrupt any possible change in the mill. Worse still, a couple of Harley's other friends fended off another attack in the parking lot and were promptly arrested—again, before they were able to deposit their ballots.

A group of Al's militants gathered in the parking lot and pushed aside a few whites who were on their way home. The militants came to the union hall as a group, forcing others to make room for them as they signed off to vote and placed their ballots in one of the boxes. But this only turned away whites who would have been supportive of the new slate.

What bothered Johnny the most was the large number of Mexicans who didn't bother going to the union hall at all. Sure, his friends and some of the people who told him they would back him showed up to vote. Tigre's supporters also took part in fairly large groups. But far too many of the other mill hands and crew members just punched out, went to their cars, and hurried home.

It took a day and a half of counting, arguing, recounting, and both sides threatening to storm out of the main union hall before the final tally was declared official by the international union representative. The vote was close—but not close enough for Johnny and his local union rebels. The slate of old union leaders won by a slight majority.

The following days had been discouraging. Johnny saw it in the faces of the men who went all out, hopeful for change, but were forced to return to the drudgery of business as usual. He also saw the faces of the men who didn't vote, some of whom refused to look him in the eye. The way Johnny figures it, most of the Mexicans at Nazareth weren't going to rock any boats. They had jobs—great jobs compared to their compatriots. And as bad as conditions were in the mill, these guys were determined not to let anything keep them from hanging on to these jobs. On the surface, having a new local union leadership didn't appear to have anything to do with this fact—so they didn't bother to vote.

And they were probably right, Johnny reasons. Union officers tend to form cliques among themselves. They rarely engage other workers except at election time. Why would anyone risk their jobs for a group of guys who rarely cared about them?

Johnny's father, Procopio, is also deeply disappointed in the election results; this particular election came close to those that took place in the heyday of struggles he had led in the early 1960s. Procopio, however, sees the writing on the wall—the divisions between the mill workers are too deep to overcome in one election. In an important way he agrees with Harley—you have to educate people on their class interests. Otherwise people vote—or don't vote—based solely on their immediate concerns.

Johnny thinks about this as he lies on the blanket at Roosevelt Park. He sure needs a break, there with his family. He knows that Dent and his thugs are going to make life difficult for the rebel leadership in the coming weeks. They are going to have their payback—firings, so-called accidents, beatings. First off, half a dozen Communists have been fired after the flare-ups in the warehouse and parking lot. Harley and Ronnie barely hang on to their jobs.

After the elections, Al pretty much attacks the whole effort, claiming he didn't want to do this in the first place. Tigre and his group go back to work as usual, playing the ponies or visiting the card casinos in Gardena and other nearby towns on paydays. And Lane Peterson, the plant director, puts out memos to key department heads praising them for keeping the "crazies" out of the union offices.

The only solid group, near as Johnny can tell, are the right-wing whites, who also happen to be the worst of the lot—the most destructive, narrow-minded, and mean-spirited force within the mill.

"People deserve what they get," Johnny remembers a Youth Authority teacher once telling him. He wasn't sure what this meant until now: If the mill is fucked up, and if only a few are willing to let go of their selfish interests to do something about it, then who are the rest going to blame? "Whatever you permit, you promote," Johnny recalls his teacher also saying.

"You care for *pollo* and potato salad, hon?" Aracely says to Johnny.

He stops his train of thought and opens his eyes. Aracely's pretty face is smack in front of him. Just then, love overcomes him. Enough for tears even. But he won't let it go that far. The mill is war; here is love and home and child. Here is family—at least they are willing to come together to make their lives richer. Johnny isn't sure he can muster up the strength to continue organizing his fellow workers. But, for now, the mill is the farthest thing from his mind. He has Aracely; he has his parents and brothers; he has his son. He has his barrio. He has this life.

For now, this will have to be enough.

For now.

5

NEW BIRTH

Years down the road, the Nazareth Steel Mill continues its song, the pulse of steel, cement, and stone, fusing lives from so many worlds into one, feeding new generations of families while tying them to *los hechos y deshechos* of the vast Southeast Los Angeles communities, far removed from Hollywood, from the shoreline, from marquee lights, holding everything up, skyscrapers and bridges, as part of a region's economic base, the lifeblood, easily written off, invisible to most eyes, yet melting and pounding and forging steel like there was no tomorrow.

In reality, the weight of many tomorrows has been closing in on the plant and its workforce. Johnny doesn't worry about such things. He plugs away for years, day in and day out, hoping to put in as much time as his father did at the plant, hoping for a large family, a large house, hoping to retire and do nothing until his last sacred breath, surrounded by children and grandchildren, rocking on a patriarch's honored chair on a wooden South L.A. porch.

The tumultuous union elections and its aftermath during Johnny's first three years at the plant are long gone. Those times blur into a dismal distant memory. Little has changed. The local union continues in its irrelevancy. But as Johnny sees it, it was a hell of a fight. Johnny and his team lost, but he has emerged as someone to be reckoned with. His skills as a millwright have also grown, envied by a few of the older millwrights and looked up to by many of the younger ones.

Johnny learns quickly and works hard. His prowess as a quiet but strong leader is also a topic of more than a few conversations. You may not like Johnny, but you have to respect him.

Two years after Joaquin's birth, Azucena is born. This time, Johnny's there as participant and witness. He stays with Aracely the whole day and throughout the evening while she goes through labor. A drenching rain buffets the windows and roof. The rain doesn't let up the entire time she's in labor, evoking damp emotions in the hospital room as Johnny does magic tricks and brings out a joke book to keep Aracely's mind on anything but the pain.

In the short lulls, Johnny manages to catch a few winks. At one point, Aracely asks him to massage the small of her back to alleviate some discomfort. But he doesn't answer. She looks over and watches her husband snore on the couch next to the bed.

Aracely, of course, has already mastered much of this—she gave birth to Joaquin nearly alone, without drugs to ease her pain. Natural childbirth is a sacred act. Even during the difficult "transition" stage, the stage when most women begin cursing the father of the child, Aracely goes through it solidly, bravely, without complaint.

She feigns interest in Johnny's simple magic tricks and tries to laugh at a few of his awful jokes—she sees how hard he's trying, *pobrecito*. This keeps Aracely somewhat amused until a particularly strong contraction hits her.

Finally, the time comes. A nurse stands next to a young doctor in a wrinkled white coat, huddled on the other side of Aracely's legs as Johnny nervously pushes his wife's head forward while she's sweating, red-faced and breathing between moans, until the infant girl's head emerges from her womb.

Then it's Johnny who almost doesn't make it. He's caught between the greatest joy he has ever felt and disgust. In a mirror facing Aracely's opened legs, Johnny can watch the whole birth. He hangs on as long as he can. He sees how strong Aracely is, working hard, pushing and gasping. He can't let on that a part of him wants to sit down and vomit. He's one tough guy, capable of standing on thin steel beams a few dozen feet in the air without a safety belt, but as soon as the baby's bloody and milky body emerges, it's enough to knock him to his knees.

At one point, Johnny's asked by the nurse if he wants to cut the umbilical cord, but he turns away. He has seen dead bodies and torn limbs at Nazareth—but something about doubting his own child will be normal, that she may be nothing but guts and blood vessels, makes him woozy.

Azucena enters the world with rainwater streaking down the outside window and a full head of straight dark Indian hair. Her eyes are elongated; her nose and mouth tiny and sweet. Staring at her, Johnny gathers himself enough to briefly hold Azucena before she's taken away by the nurses.

When Azucena's returned to father and mother, she is wrapped cocoonlike in a soft cotton blanket with a small beanie cap on her head— Aracely comments on how she looks exactly like Joaquin did when he was born. The baby's asleep. Red-faced but freshly cleaned, she smells like new life. Johnny forgets the nausea from moments before. Here's his daughter. A whole being. What a blessing. What a dream.

What will his role be with a daughter? he wonders, attempting to guess at the answer. Johnny stares at her and thinks he's never seen anything so beautiful.

In addition to Azucena's birth, other changes have occurred in Johnny and Aracely's lives since the union elections. For one thing, doctors believe Joaquin's initial inconsolable crying stems from Johnny's drinking—and consequent neglect. After his colicky first months of life, the boy becomes quiet and withdrawn. He's slower than he should be at that age. The doctors try to help. The situation with his son bothers Johnny to the point that he enters the alcoholics' recovery group at the mill.

His friend Robert Thigpen has already suffered a great deal because of his drinking. He also enters the recovery program, but, oddly, continues to drink. He comes in to work drunk once too often—after days of not showing up at all—and is finally fired. Johnny tries to stay in touch with Robert, but soon he stops hearing from him. Robert has moved out of his house and, according to Robert's cousin Tony, ends up homeless on L.A.'s massive downtown skid row.

Robert's story is so common it elicits more yawns than yelps in the plant. But it still bothers Johnny that Robert has nowhere to go, that a steelworker can end up as anonymous and forgotten as a wino on skid row.

Johnny's decision to stop drinking is thorny at first; the few active nondrinkers are inactive in other things, too busy attending sobriety meetings and things. To Johnny, this feels like another kind of death. The men are scared not to be in meetings, too scared to hang around old haunts and old buddies, convinced their removal from such temptations is vital to their health and sanity. But they stop having any impact on anyone else. Johnny understands these programs are necessary for one's own healing. "Take care of yourself before you can take care of anyone else," they say. But Johnny feels he needs to be among his friends, family, and work. He doesn't want to hide to get better, but learn not to drink and still stay important in the lives of those around him. Johnny soon leaves the plant's recovery program and embarks on a personal program dedicated to sobriety.

It's hard, but Johnny's determined to do this. Maybe it's his ego talking, but he has to try.

Within a year after the elections, Nazareth Steel has allowed a few women into the labor, mill, and furnace crews for the first time. Some women even make it into the masonry, electrical, and millwright craft units. None of them are managers yet or crane operators or furnace melters, but they do almost everything else.

Their presence is gradually but acutely felt. Johnny will be working on a machine and turn around and see a woman in hard hat with a shovel and gloves. He sees a couple of women training to lay firebricks or pulling wire with the electrical repair crews. It's disconcerting at first. They are women but dressed as men—flannel shirts, denim jeans, and steel-tipped shoes. But when they walk he can tell they aren't men. When they talk or smile, all of a sudden their feminine qualities shine through. Most aren't, as one might say, "model good-looking." The majority are big women—mostly black, some white, a few Mexicans. Physically strong, too. Many of them are former welfare mothers or waitresses.

The labor crews are the first to bring the women in; later some of the other departments. In a couple of years, they make their way to the repair crews.

Johnny's helping do repairs on the 32-inch mill one day when he spots two new oiler-greasers with grease guns and flashlights looking for "buttons" on the gigantic rollers. He looks at them for a spell and finally realizes they are women—a Mexican and a white woman.

The white woman is young, tall and thin, with loose work clothes and a half-falling tool belt. The Mexican is older, shorter, thicker, with long hair piled into her hard hat. Her tool belt sits easy on top of her relatively wide hips. Johnny cannot make out any terribly attractive features on these women. But he's fascinated to see females doing what he used to do when he first got hired at the mill, back when it was, like, the most fantastic thing he could have imagined doing.

Most of the men seem to handle the women's presence quite well. No real complaints as far as he can tell among the majority of mill hands and labor-crew members. But Johnny still feels tension and resentment from a few of the other men, particularly among the millwrights.

"I thought I'd never see the day," old Rex remarks one day when Johnny works with him on the furnaces. "We're going to see loose parts fly out of these machines and gears. Mark my word, son, this is a sad day for millwrighting."

Johnny doesn't see it that way. He's glad the women are coming in. With proper training they will do fine, he reasons. But that will be the kicker—can they be trained well by men who don't even want them there? The men won't share the blame; they will make it so the company will have to keep the women out of certain job assignments. Perhaps the safety issue will be raised—the millwrights work in some of the most dangerous places and jobs in the mill.

Rex notwithstanding, Johnny hears the loudest complaints from the old redneck millwrights, guys like Frank Horner, Bob Michaels, Steve Rodham, Dirty Harry, and Earl Denton. They are outright hostile to the new oiler-greaser women. They won't offer a hand to any of the women who have a hard time pushing their wheelbarrows full of muck.

"They want to work here, fine," Frank exclaims once in the mill-wright shanty. "They're going to have to pull their own weight, that's for damn sure."

Pretty much that's what the men say: The women aren't going to be treated any different. But that's a lie, Johnny figures. They are going to be given a *harder* time. As hard as it was for him when he first started, there was still some effort to assist, to teach, to make a way. Now, though, the men in the craft units close off, refuse to provide any support, act as if the women don't exist, as if they don't matter.

One day Johnny sees the new white oiler-greaser woman ask one of the millwright apprentices about how to use the air-powered grease gun. The dude looks at her, spits into a corner, and walks way.

Johnny stands up from his seat, where he has been enjoying a well-packed *carnitas* burrito. He walks toward the machine and proceeds to show the woman how it works.

"Thanks, I really appreciate this," she says. "By the way, what's your name? Nobody here wants to tell me theirs."

"It's Johnny. If you need anything, let me know. Don't let these assholes get under your skin. They treat everyone like shit. I think they're mostly scared. I mean, not having had women working with them before."

"My name's Darlene, and again, thanks. I just hope these guys un-derstand I need work just like them. I got a girl to feed. I got bills. I don't have no 'man' to take care of me. It's just me and my girl."

"Sure, you don't have to convince me about why you're here," Johnny says, "As far as I'm concerned, you belong here as much as anyone."

Darlene smiles. The rest of the day, this conversation carries her through some hairy situations. To Darlene, Johnny's kindness is like water to a thirsty woman in a parched desert.

Carla Perez takes three long bus rides to get to Nazareth Steel's massive gates on Slauson Avenue. She has just been hired at the mill. She's to be trained as an oiler-greaser, something she has no idea about. She shows some mechanical aptitude, so she's told this is where she will be placed.

Carla has worked in petty jobs, cleaning, wiping, mopping. Most of her mechanical abilities come from fixing things around the house. When her live-in boyfriend, Mateo, sees the ad in the newspaper about women being hired at the plant, he pushes the newspaper toward her at breakfast one morning. Carla knows why—he doesn't want to work himself, the asshole.

But the ad seems to offer another option for her: She won't have to be around this *vato* so much. And the money, the money's good. For the first time, the mill is offering women jobs in all the major plant divisions, not just in the offices. Carla looks at the ad for a long time. She isn't entirely sure about applying. Part of her is scared—she realizes this is rough work. She's seen the plant from afar—noisy, dark, hot, huge. It doesn't look like a place for women. It looks like a place for war, the kind men seem to like to create and get off on.

Mateo rises from the kitchen table in their one-room apartment in the Pico-Union district of Los Angeles and tells her, "*Vaya, pinche.* What's it going to hurt? If you get the job, we'll be set. Believe me, these jobs pay better than Vegas. You know we could use the money right now. We got bills up the ying-yang. *Hazlo por el amor de Dios*, do it for the love of God."

Carla hates his nagging, his put-downs, his demands. He's Chicano—he grew up around Burlington Street. He has dealings with the 18th Street gang, a large and dangerous gang that seems to penetrate every nook and cranny of the neighborhood.

Carla is from El Salvador, the department of Sonsonate, to be exact. Her mother brought her to Los Angeles when she was a little girl. While the Pico-Union and Westlake areas, just west of downtown, were home to many Central Americans, it was still mostly Mexican in the 1970s.

Carla's choices of where to go, how to live, and where to work seem limited. She took up with Mateo, her first and only lover, because her mother wouldn't have her in the house anymore. They had been fighting since she was small, mostly over her mother's many and strange boyfriends. Luckily none of them abused her, although a few eyed her with lascivious intent; as soon as she could, she found a way to get the hell out of there.

Carla told her mother she was in love with Mateo and wouldn't stop seeing him. Nineteen years old and mostly a homebody, she was pushed out into the street as if she were an unwanted animal.

Mateo invited Carla into his small apartment, a small world for a small mind. He only saw Carla as someone to fuck, to fix his meals, to go out and make money at any slop-and-mop joint so he could stay home and watch TV. Mateo is good-looking but arrogant. He is also selfish and uninspired. Carla hit the big time with this one.

In the beginning, Carla feels Mateo gives her the attention she craves. She never had a real father. The men around her mother could give a hoot about her. Mateo comes along, this *prieto bonito*, and she wants him, what he represents: freedom, a new life, possibilities beyond her mother's narrow goals.

Boy, is she disappointed, and fast.

Carla now longs for something bigger, better—something with wheels, a life that has its own steam, its own speed, its own direction. She's tired of going along with other people's programs, her mother's or Mateo's. In the first place, she never wanted to leave El Salvador, which she remembers fondly as a quiet place filled with family, chickens, dogs, and goats—only to have her stability disrupted when her mother is accused of some crime she has no comprehension of (an aunt later insinuates the incident may have involved an important older man in the *colonia*). So they run away. Fugitives from who knows what.

The want ad from Nazareth proves to be enticing in more ways than one.

Carla has a rather plain face, framed with short black hair. Brown-skinned, her body's not bad. She has everything smaller than it should be, but she is strong from having worked hard most of her life. When she bothers to make herself up, she can be strikingly beautiful. But she doesn't give much importance to this. Her plainness keeps her in the background, unnoticed, untouched. She likes that—she doesn't want any attention from most people even as she yearns for it from those she cares about. She is shy on the one hand, but not so shy when she wants something real badly.

The first week on the job becomes a test for Carla. She can't get things right. She moves her wrench the wrong way, tightening instead of loosening. The dude she's working with doesn't tell her anything. But when she steps on things she shouldn't, when she brings the wrong tool for the job, when she can't cut copper piping correctly with her handheld pipe cutter, he's all over her like a dog on bone.

The plant doesn't even have proper restroom facilities for the women. There are no women's showers. The company sets up a few temporary potties for the women to use, but Carla feels uneasy going into them. What if a deranged mill worker forces himself in and assaults her? she thinks. She only uses them when she can't hold it anymore. A few times, when no one is looking, she'll squat in the oil-and-grease pits below the rolling mills to relieve herself.

One day Mateo walks into the apartment after hanging out on the corner with the "boys" and sees Carla crying at the kitchen table.

"*Y esto*—what happened, Carlita?" he inquires. "Did something happen at the steel mill . . . or did your mother call again?"

"I just don't know if I can take this job, Mateo," Carla finally answers after wiping her eyes with a dirty napkin. "The money may be good, but I'm afraid I'm going to make a mistake and get myself killed or something. That place is complicated. There's so much to do, to learn, to pay attention to. I'm not cut out for it."

"Okay, but do me a favor," Mateo responds, smarter than he lets on at times. "Wait until you get your first paycheck. If you still feel the same way after that, go ahead and quit."

He has her there.

Two weeks later, when Carla lines up at the pay shanty to receive her check, she feels angry and confused about being shunned amid the loud talk around her, as if she's a lamppost. But when she signs for the check and holds it in her hand—a full two weeks' worth of taking everyone's bull—the numbers, the feeling of having that much money, the kind of money she never dreamed she'd have, change everything.

It's real. Her status as a steelworker is fucking real. Fuck these guys. She *is* a steelworker. Here in the palm of her hand is proof. She'll put in the time and sweat. The blood and tears. She will be as good as any of them *puto* bastards.

She hates to admit that Mateo—God bless his money-grubbing soul—was right.

Another adjustment for Johnny after the failed union battle is his relationship with Harley Cantrell. After the elections, Johnny doesn't want to think about struggle, justice, change. He doesn't hear any more from the guys who ran with him on the proposed slate, except Harley. Al doesn't want anything to do with Johnny; he has his own thing going. Same with Jacob Wellborne. Tigre and his homies pretty much just work, party, and work some more.

One day, Harley walks up to Johnny, who is busy repairing the overhead crane in the warehouse. Johnny has just climbed down when Harley walks up to him and shakes his hand.

"Long time no see," Harley says, smiling. "Been trying to call you, but you don't answer your phone, dude. Everything all right?"

"Yeah, I was getting threats from the KKKers," Johnny says. "It was better not to answer the phone after a while. If my family needs to reach me, they know where to find me. I guess I also haven't wanted to talk to anyone since we lost. How 'bout you? You doing good?"

"Oh, I'm okay," Harley explains. "We had our setbacks. And you know, some of our guys got canned. We filed to get their jobs back, but with those union fucks wanting us out, we didn't have a chance in hell. We still have our meetings, though. We've even recruited some new folks. This time it ain't so 'white,' if you know what I mean."

"That's good, Harley, great," Johnny says. "Listen, I got to get going. Say hello to the wife for me."

"Hey Johnny, don't leave so fast," Harley presses. "I'm going to be honest here. We need you. You have spirit, leadership, and heart. We can help. What we provide is knowledge: science, consciousness. With us, you don't do anything you don't want to do. Of course, what you agree to do you should do. But you understand this. You're disciplined—one of the most disciplined people I know. But you also need a collective—fellow activists and leaders meeting, studying, and strategizing together. You need a political touchstone to come back to from time to time, to get clarity and renew your fighting spirit. I'd like for you to come back to the meetings. Don't worry about taking on any assignments. Just come and study with us for a while. We meet every week. What do you say?"

"Harley, I appreciate the invite," Johnny responds. "I'll think about it. Right now I need to focus on work and family for a while. You understand. But when I feel up to it, I'll let you know."

"That's fine. I can't ask for any more than that. Let me know when you're ready. Remember, our doors are open to you anytime."

With that, Harley ambles off, his trademark long blond hair peeking out from beneath his hard hat. Johnny *will* think about it. The Communist meetings were one of the best things that happened to him during the union-takeover campaign—despite missing a few points, he learned a lot from their weighty discussions. But for now, he isn't going to hurry to think about this. He needs a break—a lengthy and stress-free one—for as long as possible.

A few weeks later, Johnny calls Harley.

"What do you say?" Harley says on the other end, glad to hear from Johnny. "You ready to study with us, dude?"

"Yeah, I've been hanging out, taking it easy, but—you know—I'm kinda bored," Johnny explains. "I'd like to get into something. I don't mean another campaign. But at least to talk with you guys again, to look at the world, to rack our brains. I'm not sure I can come all the time—my kids are quite a handful. But maybe every other week, depending, of course, on the shift changes. How's that sound?"

"Johnny, we'd be glad to have you join us whenever you can," Harley responds. "Every other week is fine. At least try to stay consistent as much as possible. Maybe you'd like to come by this coming Wednesday. Are you through with the afternoon turn?"

"This Wednesday works for me. I'll try to come as often as I can. I'll let you know my work schedule and we'll go from there."

"We'll keep this to ourselves. Don't go around telling people where we're at. We change the meetings around so that those fucking KKKers don't mess with us. We'll talk later about how to bring around anyone else you think should come. See ya around."

This relationship lasts several years; steel mills rack up years like prisons. Before Johnny knows it, another year has crumbled to the floor in the form of a naked women's calendar page the workers favor keeping track of the days with. He realizes how he has stayed out of the line of fire for a long time following the elections struggle. At least he keeps meeting with the "comrades"—as Johnny and Aracely call the CLOC members.

Johnny misses a few meetings here and there, but he tries to make most of them. The group in the mill grows over the years. More Mexicans and blacks get involved. People come and go. Regardless, it remains a relatively small organization. At one point, Johnny tries to get his dad and brothers to attend, but they don't want anything to do with the Communists. That's okay with Johnny. He loves his family anyway. This is more "his thing." Something *he* is interested in. Aracely doesn't mind. In fact, the one person he does manage to recruit to attend the study circle is her. She arrives at the first meeting with Joaquin in diapers and Azucena in a baby carrier.

For Aracely, those days consisted of home, babies, and meetings. She gets close to Nilda, Harley's Puerto Rican wife, whom he met when he was organizing in East Harlem in his earlier activist days. Nilda runs a whole district of Communists that pretty much covers most of Los Angeles—from the harbor to the Valley, from the shoreline to the desert. Nilda is totally into this, setting up other study circles, meetings, and distribution teams (the group has a nationally published newspaper—*The People's Beacon*) for various factories, sweatshops, poor neighborhoods, and political demonstrations.

"Aracely, I want to ask you something. You got a minute?" Nilda inquires one day when Aracely shows up to Harley's house for a meeting with the babies in tow.

"Sure—what's up?" Aracely says while putting down Azucena's carrier from one arm and the toddler Joaquin from another.

"We're creating a council of revolutionaries to help run CLOC. Do you think you can help us with this?" Nilda asks.

"What would I have to do?"

"We'll have some orientation meetings, then some advanced study sessions with various Marxist texts. We'll also have strategy meetings and make decisions for overall activity in the L.A. area."

"I'm definitely interested. I just have to talk to Johnny."

"Aracely, you should talk to Johnny," Nilda says. "But we're asking you as an individual, someone who has something to offer and can make up her own mind. I'm sure you need to work things out with your partner. But don't let anyone else make this decision. This is yours to make."

Aracely is pleased that Nilda puts things this way. It *is* her decision. Johnny will have to deal with it if he doesn't agree. But she also wants to make sure Johnny understands and is behind her decision. That's important to Aracely.

"I'm with you," Aracely responds. "I'll make my own decision, but Johnny and I share our politics. Let me talk to him so that we're together on this."

"That's perfectly fine," Nilda says, an air of authority in her voice, something she seems to have when she talks and moves. Aracely likes Nilda's confidence, her inner strength—the feeling she gives off, like she determines her own destiny.

Later that evening, Johnny and Aracely talk about Nilda's offer.

"Baby, I suppose that's up to you," Johnny says after he hears the proposal. "Right now you take care of the kids and the house—you need to get out and do something else, too. This is about as good as anything you can do. It will help you learn more about the 'comrades.' What they do. How they organize. I don't really have any idea about a lot of that."

"I think Nilda wants to teach me, to train me. She's such a good organizer. I'd like to learn how she does such things."

"Sure, go for it. As for me, I'll just continue with the study circle for a while before I get pulled into organizing things."

Aracely stares at Johnny for an instant as he shuffles around the bedroom looking for clean pajamas to wear on that cold winter evening. He looks tired. Not drinking keeps him up nights. He becomes more irritable at times. The babies bother him, for one. He will play with them but for only so long. Johnny often doesn't know what to do with himself in between work shifts. He watches TV. He reads the racing forms. At least the study circle keeps him busy for part of his down time. Yet at that moment, while Aracely tries to take in his presence, his smell, his body, his caring personality, she feels secure, wanted, alive with love.

She also feels good about Nilda's offer to help with CLOC's organizing efforts. It's a way to be part of something she believes in, something with purpose. For once in her life, she has somebody she can learn from and emulate. And she appreciates Johnny's support. She wants to rush over and hug him, but Azucena begins to stir and whimper from her crib. Johnny continues his search for pajamas. Aracely hurries into the next room to get a bottle for the baby.

When Carla first begins working at Nazareth, Darlene has already put in a few weeks in the oil gang. There are three women there now, including Angie, a heavyset Chicana from the Estrada Courts Housing Projects in East L.A. With the way the guys and their foreman, Mr. Taylor, are treating them, they begin to hang together. Taylor is often the subject of discussion.

"That fucking jack-off," Darlene relates one day to the other two women in the tool-and-locker area. "He gave me an assignment sheet yesterday, right? Then before the middle of the shift, he finds me and sends me on another job. I barely get that going when he has somebody come by with another assignment sheet. I had three job assignments and couldn't get any one of them done. Then—if you can believe this—he has the gall to talk to me this morning about not completing my assignment sheets. Fuck him and the horse he rode in on."

"You know what I don't like," Angie interjects, "is when they send us on these jobs by ourselves. How're we going to know which end is up? I thought there was supposed to be a trained oiler-greaser with us at all times."

"I smell something cooking and it ain't beef stew," Darlene adds.

"I just wish I didn't have to leave this place feeling like shit all the time," Carla adds.

"You got that right, *carnala*," Angie agrees. "It's bad enough I got dirt and grease in places there shouldn't even be sunshine. But the worst part is the humiliation."

Just then Milton, one of the veteran oiler-greasers, walks in. "Mr. Taylor says you guys have to get going. You're taking too long getting ready. I'm waiting for you over by the soaking pits. Come on now."

Darlene gives Milton a dirty look and answers back. "What does it look like we're doing—putting on makeup? We'll be there as soon as we get our gear on."

Darlene's getting a reputation in the mill as a "sassy bitch," what several guys in the oil gang and millwrights' crew call her. The other women complain but mostly to themselves. Darlene doesn't care who hears her. She talks loudly and directly, without any pretty ribbons attached to her words.

She is a working-class girl whose family once labored in the coal mines of Colorado. When she was a child, they migrated to Lynwood, at the time a poor white family in a mixed Mexican and white neighborhood. She gave birth to a child at sixteen and worked many low-paying and often demeaning jobs—including a stint as a nude dancer at Little Bo Peep's in Compton—before going on welfare. It was in the welfare office that one of the social workers pointed out the new hiring policy at Nazareth. Darlene was definitely interested. The mill sounded like a great place to work. Having had experience helping her brothers work on beat-up cars, she was offered one of a few oiler-greaser jobs available.

She doesn't mind the work. She has a tough exterior, although she is thin and doesn't look like she can carry her own weight. She is also politically inclined. The old-guard millwrights take a particular dislike to Darlene when they find out that Harley has recruited her for his meetings—the only woman among the new hires that shows an interest so far.

But that isn't all they're perturbed about. One time, Darlene noticed Lane Peterson drive into the plant in a sleek Lincoln sedan. She was sitting near piles of steel beams in the warehouse, waiting for some tools that her grease partner went to get. She eyed the sparkling-clean vehicle as it pulled up into the messy dirt-and-track area near the warehouse, and instinctively thought this was odd.

Peterson got out, opened up his trunk, and walked into the main warehouse offices. She didn't think much of it until two men pulled up in a forklift with two small electric motors on a pallet. They climbed down the forklift and placed the motors into the trunk, closed it, jumped back onto the forklift, and left.

A little while later, Peterson walked back up the tracks to the car. He began to open the front door when he turned around and spotted Darlene. Without thinking, Darlene gestured to him with a thumbs-up, as if she knew what he was doing and "hey, ain't you cool." But Peterson was far from delighted. He scowled, stared dead-on at Darlene as if he would like to pull her head off, and then entered his car and sped off, dust trailing the back of the wheels. Darlene shrugged it off.

After Milton's admonishment to hurry things up, Darlene, Carla, and Angie walk out to help an extra-manned crew on the soaking pits—to oil and grease the railcars and other machinery. Frank Horner looks down on them from the 10-inch-mill catwalk. Next to him is Earl Denton.

"That fucking lesbo Communist bitch is getting on my last nerve," Frank says. "I think we got to teach Darlene a lesson."

"Yeah, I'm working on that," Dent replies. "In fact, I got something I'd like to try. If we don't make an example of her, more of these women will start talking back like she does. We'll have more and more of them pushing their weight around and taking over these jobs."

"It just bothers the crap out of me to see them moving into the repair crews," Frank continues. "Who the fuck do they think they are? They held a wrench for some crab-assed boyfriend, and now they think they're mechanics! Fuck that!"

"Well, with what I got in store for that bitch, she'll wish she never got near a fuckin' wrench," Dent assures. "Taylor is going to help me on this one. He owes us big-time for getting him that foreman position a few years back. I just need to find the right time to make that call."

"Do it," Frank says. "If we don't move now, we'll be hard-pressed to push back on those broads later."

Just then Dent gets quiet while looking down from his perch. He motions his head to the ground for Frank to see. Below them Johnny is walking toward the soaking pits, where major repairs are being made on the crane and rollers. He carries a massive pipe wrench over his shoulder.

Frank looks over at Johnny and frowns. "I want to make sure he's around when we make our move," Dent says, walking away.

One day, Darlene and Carla enter the millwright shanty beneath the furnaces as Johnny grabs a metal coffee cup, coffee, and sugar from his locker. He's working days that week, helping with various repair jobs around the mill.

"Hey, Johnny, I want you to meet a friend of mine," Darlene says.

Johnny looks over and sees the brown-faced, nondescript, but fairly small—she must be five feet, he figures—Carla standing next to Darlene. She doesn't look too glamorous in hard hat and goggles.

"Hey, what's up?" Johnny answers. "You got yourself another partner in crime on the oil gang?"

"Yeah, there's three of us girls now," Darlene says, looking around at the shanty filled with tools and mechanical implements; the naked-women magazine pictures that once graced a wall have long been removed. "Before you know it, we'll be all over these repair crews. You ain't worried about your job, are you?"

"You can have my job . . . care for any coffee?"

The women sit down on one of the heavily marked benches. Johnny finds two other coffee mugs and pours water over them from a dirty sink by the lockers. He places the mugs on the bench and hands the women a bottle of instant coffee and a bowl of sugar while he boils water on a hot plate.

"What are you all doing over here in the furnaces?" Johnny asks.

"We're greasing the stripper crane on the ingot line," Darlene says. "Don't worry—we got the spiel about some oiler-greaser who toppled ingot after ingot because he forgot to pull up the crane's jaws."

Johnny turns around and winces when he hears this. He decides not to say anything about his role in that long-ago incident.

"Looks like a good job—if they leave us alone," Carla says.

"What do you mean?" Johnny inquires.

"They don't let us finish any jobs—as soon as we get good and going on something, Taylor comes along and gives us other work," Darlene explains.

"He's fucking with you, that's what he's doing," Johnny says. "He's trying to set you up to be fired. Be careful. He's a real snake."

"We know—that's why we're telling you," Darlene continues. "If we do get fired, we're going to need some backup to get our jobs back."

"I see, well, keep me posted. If there's anything I can do, you know I'll do it," Johnny responds.

Carla looks again at the handsome young millwright. He seems like something out of a dream. Johnny's nice, amiable, hardworking, and smart. Are there still guys like this in the world? she asks herself. She has heard that he's one of the best millwrights in the plant. Yet he doesn't throw his weight around. Of all the men on the repair crews, he's the only one who actually pays some respectful attention to the women workers.

The weeks pile up for the women. They are already all over the mill, greasing and oiling and cutting copper piping. They're getting good at what they're doing. Taylor even lightens up on them for a while.

"It feels like the calm before a storm," Angie says at the lunch truck one day.

"You think something's up?" Carla asks.

"I'm not sure. These guys haven't talked as much shit as usual," Angie explains. "Taylor gives us our assignments and disappears.

When did that ever happen? And we've been finishing our work. Don't you think this is strange?"

"Yeah, but maybe they're just realizing we can hold our own," Darlene interjects. "We've come through on everything. The more jobs they throw at us, the more we've proven we can handle them. I think they're finally seeing us for what we are—we're good."

Just then, Milton and Roland, another oiler-greaser, walk up to Darlene.

"Taylor wants you to work on the 22-inch overhead crane with us," Milton declares.

"We're in the middle of the shift," Darlene protests. "You think we'll finish before the shift ends?"

"Yeah, this is basic maintenance," Roland says. "We'll change the brake pads while you get the gears and couplings oiled and greased. With the three of us, we'll be done in no time."

"Okay, I'm ready," Darlene says.

She has never worked on the 22-inch mill crane before; neither have the other women. Darlene grabs her tool belt and stands by Milton and Roland.

The men look at each other for a moment then start walking, Darlene in step behind them. She turns around and waves at Carla and Angie, who are leaning against the corrugated steel wall of the main millwright shanty, drinking soda and smoking hand-rolled cigarettes.

The overhead crane is parked on the north end of the building where the mill is housed. It's several feet in the air, on rails that spread across the west and east ends of the building. Darlene, Milton, and Roland climb the metal wall ladder to the first cab door. Darlene waits for Milton and Roland to enter first, but they both make way to let Darlene through. She looks at them and raises an eyebrow, as if to say, *Woow—what gentlemen! I've never had this kind of treatment in the mill before*.

Darlene pulls on the cabin door, which is difficult to open. There is a kind of pressure that keeps the door almost stuck closed—she can't figure out what it is. She pulls it partly open, allowing enough room for her to walk through. She then moves into the space before the actual operator's cab, which has yet another door before you can enter.

As Darlene walks in she places her left hand on the edge of the doorway to balance herself, letting go of the heavy door in the process. In a fraction of an instant it happens—the door slams shut so fast that at first Darlene doesn't understand what she's done. The blood spraying onto the walls is the first thing she sees. Then the shots of pain.

Milton and Roland are on the other side of the door, standing several feet away. They see four slender fingers fall to the ground by their feet. They hear Darlene's screams. Roland tries to get to the door, but Milton grabs his arm for several seconds before he lets go and they both pull the door open. They pick Darlene up from the floor of the cab, where she holds her left hand in her right, pressing hard on her wrist to contain the blood from her severed fingers. She feels like she's going into shock as Roland helps her climb down the ladder and Milton holds the door open, yelling for one of the mill workers to get the company's emergency response unit there "pronto."

As soon as Roland and Darlene are on the mill floor, several mill hands surround the woman while one of them puts a temporary tourniquet on her arm. Milton is about to climb down from the cab when he stops, turns around, takes out a dirty rag that has been hanging from his tool belt, and picks up the fingers from the metal flooring. He covers the fingers up in the rag and puts them into his front pocket before descending to the furnace floor, already teeming with people, voices, and chaos.

6

EXILED

The wire mill is situated in a separate building west of the main plant facility; it houses several machines that weave wire rope and other wire-based materials. It used to be an independent company until Nazareth bought it and incorporated it into its vast system of forges, furnaces, and mills. The building has numerous conveyor systems, pumps, motors, and tanks.

Johnny is assigned to the wire mill as the sole millwright on the day shift during a reorganization of the mill's repair crews. He actually wants to be the night-shift millwright on the furnaces to replace his friend and mentor, Rex the Mex. He has learned everything about the furnaces from Rex and is quite capable of running the operation at night. Rex finally retired after more than thirty years. On his last night of working, Rex told Johnny he wanted him for the job.

But the powers that be decide otherwise.

The wire mill is like millwright purgatory. It has a separate tool shanty, separate time-clock area, and separate parking lot. Johnny can no longer interact with the millwrights and mill workers in other sections of the plant. He has to maintain and repair all the machines. He doesn't have any helpers, unlike the other plant divisions. Johnny knows why he was sent here—although he's becoming one of the most competent mechanics in the whole plant, the company and their union stooges want to keep him from organizing the other employees. This reassignment would have happened sooner, but an old millwright named Pete Rozansky wouldn't let the millwright job at the wire mill go—it was gravy compared to the other millwright positions (and if one was a hermit at heart). But then he also retired.

For Johnny, the assignment is slow death.

It's also punishment. After Darlene lost her fingers, Johnny figured she was set up by Dent, using Taylor to send her on the job with Milton and Roland as accomplices. Nobody told her about that 22-inch mill overhead-crane door, something most oiler-greasers are warned about early on. Although Johnny had also not been warned about the door when he first started, he managed not to lose any body parts. He sees how this is a way for the KKKers to set up the new hires when they need to.

After the incident, Johnny begins to speak out. Of course, without proof he can't do anything beyond talk. In the short and quick investigation into Darlene's injuries, Milton and Roland swear they alerted Darlene; they claim she carelessly went through the door without considering their cautions. She denies this, of course, but her end of the story is unimportant. Taylor leads the investigation and declares the incident "an accident."

Johnny won't let it go, but few millwrights back him up. He knows there is no legal recourse. As the KKKers have been doing for years, other means will have to be used to exact justice in the mill.

Johnny organizes a defense squad with people like Clyde Fourkiller, Ray Garcia, Tony Adams, and his own brother Bune. He doesn't involve the Communists—even if they're game—since he knows they will bring more heat than he's already going to get.

The group's first action happens while Darlene is recuperating from her injuries. None of her fingers were saved; they were in gross shape by the time Milton turned them over to the plant's managers. Johnny feels he has to start there—with Milton and Roland.

Milton and Roland are young white guys in their mid-twenties recruited from the family members of veteran KKK members in the plant. Milton is Bob Michaels's nephew; Roland is best friend to Hank Cheatham's grandson. Dent and the others try to get more bigoted white guys into the oil gang to offset the set-aside jobs for "minorities and women"—and to stop any commie whites from obtaining those positions as well.

In the oil gang, Taylor uses Milton and Roland to help keep the three oiler-greaser women in line and to check up on any "trouble-makers" among the men. This is well known among the millwrights. So Johnny feels confident that's where he has to start.

The alley behind Wild Woolly's at 2 A.M. is as good a place as any to begin. Johnny has noticed for some time that Milton and Roland like to drink there most nights, since they work days as oiler-greasers.

One early Thursday, when the bar is practically empty, four ski-masked men hide behind a roll of Dumpsters next to the joint. Before too long, Milton slams open the back door of Wild Woolly's, un-steadily eyeing the two cars to his side. Roland bursts through the door soon after, fumbling in his pocket for keys.

In a matter of seconds, the masked men appear armed with bats, chains, and belts. Milton looks up and freezes. Roland has enough presence of mind to start a run, but this doesn't help. The masked men pounce on the two men, striking them on their legs, backs, arms, and head. Roland cries and screams. Milton tries to throw a few blows, even picking up a broken milk crate and crashing it over the head of one of the masked assailants. But that's all he can do, suffering extra punishment because of it. When the attack is over, Milton and Roland lie moaning in the oil-stained alley. One of the masked men looks down on the two and says, "This is for Darlene, motherfuckers."

That's all that Roland remembers. Milton has lost all memory of the attack after spending several weeks in the intensive care unit. They both survive, but they aren't the same after that.

Dent has his suspicions: He figures Johnny's behind the beatings. So when Rozansky finally nears his long-awaited retirement from the wire mill, Dent uses his clout with the plant managers to get Johnny assigned there—exiled.

When Darlene's fingerless hand heals, she wants to return to the mill—she's not going to quit. Johnny admires her moxie; most any-body, he thinks, including most guys, wouldn't go back for all the money in the world. However, the company refuses to allow her her old job back because of her disability. Fingers are crucial in millwright work. With only a few months in, she's already out of the steel-mill business.

After the attack at Wild Woolly's, Johnny gets a shotgun for himself in case the KKK tries to come after him at home; Aracely isn't happy about this, but he hides the shells so that the kids won't accidentally find an armed weapon. Now Johnny has to think about what else he needs to do. Where his next steps will take him.

Aracely and Nilda get together about twice a week to follow up on meeting decisions and plans. CLOC is undergoing an aggressive campaign to build their organization among workers throughout the Los Angeles basin. Distribution teams and speakers are dispatched: to the large Cannery Row in the San Pedro Harbor area, to the many sweatshop sewing plants in and around L.A.'s downtown garment district, and to the large mills, factories, and production lines throughout the central industrial corridor of the city and its waterfront.

It's 1980. For some ten years, many changes have occurred in industry, including the loss of thousands of jobs to overseas competitors or to companies moving their operations to cheaper labor markets in the Southern United States, Mexico, Central America, or Southeast Asia. Other industries are automating, again throwing vast numbers of workers into the ranks of the unemployed and destitute. By the mid-1980s, such industry-laden cities as L.A., New York, and Chicago will become centers of homelessness.

The Communists, small in number as they are, stay busy during these transitions. Everything they have been saying about capitalism is coming to pass: The economic downturns and crises during this period are of a different quality.

"Advanced technology is changing the very nature of production," Nilda says during one of her talks with Aracely. "In the process, a new class of people is being created: permanently unemployed, permanently thrown out of the capitalist production process itself. They aren't just 'a reserve army of the unemployed'—that can be used against the employed at various times in the class struggle. This new class is a growing group of former workers who are unable to return to production even during the economic upturns and recoveries."

"But it seems that things are getting better in the U.S.," Aracely states.

"No, no, *mujer*—Ronald Reagan's election as president has opened up a new phase of political crisis that's not going to disappear," Nilda chimes in. "Reagan's efforts to undercut the safety net and to place more tax dollars and benefits in the hands of the rich and powerful has made matters worse. Major industries are leaving or being streamlined, more workers are entering the labor force from across the country but also from Mexico and other parts of Latin America and Asia. Yet power and wealth are being concentrated in fewer and fewer hands."

Aracely comes alive during these intense discussions with the comrades. She looks forward to hearing people like Nilda, Harley, Ronnie, and others lay out the bare bones of what makes the country and the world run. She has never been taught this way of thinking—never.

Although Aracely graduated from high school—unlike Johnny, who got his diploma and credentials in youth prison—she's always felt behind the eight ball in the real world. Aracely received good grades, and even joined an honors group at Fremont High School. But when she took the college entrance exams, she found out she needed to take extra classes just to pass them.

Aracely had grown up in a large Mexican household—she was a middle child of twelve siblings. Only five of them are her real brothers and sisters. The others are half siblings from her mother and stepfather, a hardworking, hard-drinking control freak. Aracely did well in school and obeyed her parents, but beneath this, she always longed for something more. An education. But in her family, an education is considered a luxury. She wanted to go to college but was discouraged by her stepfather. The children were all supposed to work to supplement the family's income—much of what her stepfather made as a low-level machinist went to the Caliente betting lounges or jai alai games in Tijuana, where he spent an inordinate amount of time.

When she realized she needed remedial classes even to apply, she lost interest in college altogether.

Aracely's one joy was meeting Johnny when he used to come to her South Los Angeles high school with his Florencia Trece homies. Although he had a gangster's scowl, he was polite and considerate. Aracely saw right away what he was truly made of, regardless of the image he wanted to convey. Once the connection was made, she stayed hooked—even during his incarceration.

Aracely ended up in assembly lines and domestic work before and after the marriage because she didn't qualify for anything else. Her frustrations were evident in the quiet downtimes when she could reflect for a few moments. It was then that tears fell from her eyes and she wondered what she was meant to do in this world, what great destiny evaded her, and why she always seemed to miss life's few precious opportunities.

Now, in CLOC, reading books—which used to be hard for her—has become one of Aracely's favorite activities. Johnny finds it odd when he comes home and there's Aracely reading a book on the couch while the little ones sleep or play nearby. Johnny likes the talks, but he isn't into reading much. He mostly learns from the words that come out of people's mouths, not from text on a page.

Nilda and Aracely have become friends. Nilda's skin is dark, her hair wavy and parted in the middle; she's strong and muscular. She's also well educated, having gone to college as part of the first generation of Puerto Ricans in New York City to do so in the late 1960s and early 1970s. Aracely notices a photo of Nilda from her high school graduation—she has an Afro hairdo and an intense look on her face—similar to the one she gets when she makes her points in meetings. Later she becomes part of the Young Lords Party in New York City; in another black-and-white photo with some of her fellow Lords she wears a dark beret with insignias. Now Nilda doesn't look as cool or as crazy as she did then, but she's never lost the intensity in her eyes.

"I think we have a pretty good idea about this week's activities," Nilda declares after a long session with Aracely. In the other room, Joaquin has climbed on a sofa to watch TV. Little Azucena pushes herself around in a walker, drooling because of new teeth breaking through her gums.

"*Simón*—I mean, yeah, I agree," Aracely says.

"Okay, we can stop for now. Care for some pie? I made it yesterday."

"Nilda, you made your own pie! I wish I could do that."

"It's simple—and cheaper. I'll show you how to do it. I even make my own bread."

"Right on—that would be great: to make my own bread. I mean, I don't know when I'll have the time with these babies. But I'd like to learn."

"Like I said, it's simple and doesn't take a lot of time."

Nilda shows Aracely some recipes and a book on making bread. Aracely rarely sees this side of her. She is all politics and business most of the time. Nilda is not just a freethinking person; she also has many interests and hobbies outside of her work with CLOC.

For many years, Aracely has taken buses and walked from her apartment in Florencia to Nilda's Bell home and back again. On the bus, as the kids fooled around or dozed off, she thought about being a woman like Nilda: knowledgeable, tough, active, aware—and still beautiful. That is so important, she thinks. Women should be beautiful. But she realizes it's more about feeling and thinking beautiful, not just looking beautiful. She always feels inadequate, although she's game to try different things. To take risks. She just can't entirely shake off the notion that she's less than others.

With Nilda around, however, she feels like she can do anything.

Rex dies within six months of leaving the plant. The news of his death hits Johnny hard. Rex had been enjoying his retirement at home, doing nothing, watching TV, alone with a few cats and birds, when, without warning, he suffered a massive heart attack.

"He died quickly," one of the paramedics says after Johnny rushes to the hospital after hearing about Rex's collapse.

Still, Johnny sees the unfairness of it all. How someone like Rex can put in more than three decades at a job and finally, when he's allowed to leave, can't even enjoy his free time. It's a common story among steelworkers; most steelworkers who retire are dead in less than two years.

Procopio is also nearing his retirement. Although Procopio and Rex came into the plant at the same time, Rex was six years older. Procopio plans to retire in 1980, after thirty-five years at the plant. Johnny knows his father is susceptible to the same fate as the others.

"You ever think about what you're going to do after you leave Nazareth?" Johnny asks his father one day when he's visiting with his parents.

"What do you mean, *m'ijo*?" Procopio says.

"I mean, do you have something you want to do? Some work or hobby. You're not just going to sit around all day, are you?"

"Listen, *m'ijo*, first of all, when I retire and all I do is sit around and do nothing, so what? As far as I'm concerned, I deserve it. I've worked hard for it. That's something I should be able to do if I want."

"Sure, *apá*, but to be honest," Johnny continues, "I'm worried that you'll end up like the other oldsters out of the plant. Rex just had a heart attack. Over the years, how many times have we heard of newly retired guys keeling over at the dinner table, in their gardens, or while they're taking a walk? Rex was sitting in front of his TV, for chrissakes."

"I know what you're getting at, but I don't have any intention of 'keeling over,' " Procopio explains. "I will stay busy. Work around the house. Maybe take up other work somewhere; who knows? Me and your mom, maybe we'll take some trips. I've never seen most of this country. Only Arizona and California. Las Vegas once in a while. I'd like to get around, you know."

"I understand, but I just feel bad about Rex. He was a good dude, despite his ways and backward thinking. He always treated me right. I feel bad he ended up with little to show for all his years of work. What does it matter to have a great retirement plan when you can't even live long enough to enjoy it?"

"I'm telling you, Juanito, those Communists are putting stupid ideas in your head," Procopio says, shaking his head. "Rex worked hard because that's what we all should do. He made his choices. He knew what he was getting into. I'm sure he wanted to live a long time, but that just wasn't in the cards for him. But I wouldn't say he didn't have anything to show for it. I don't like what happens in the mill, those KKKers and the union bosses, but I'm proud of being a steelworker. I wouldn't want it any other way."

"That's fine, Dad, I feel the same way. I've been in the mill eight years now. But still, we don't get any help staying healthy while we're working. I'm sure Rex had heart trouble for a long time. But everything is work and more work. Who tried to give him the preventative care he needed? That heart attack was a long time coming. And having to go from hard work all the time to doing nothing didn't help."

"Don't feel sorry for these guys, is what I'm saying," Procopio continues in an agitated voice. "We do what we're supposed to do. We do our jobs. We never give up. We don't have any reason to feel bad. If we don't make it—hey, that's life. But none of us would trade our jobs for anything else. Yes, things should be better. We need a better union. But our dignity, our self-respect, nobody can take that away from us unless we let them."

Procopio's like many of the older steel men with this logic; Johnny understands that. Despite losing Severo, Procopio never grieves or talks much about what happened, except for his few comments during the election campaign. He's also like so many Mexicans he knows—*se agüantan*, they take a lot of abuse and don't complain. To complain is a sign of weakness.

"The future's not here, so why think about it so much?" Procopio adds, in an effort to cut short the discussion. "Just work hard. Keep your end of the bargain. You come through no matter what. Don't forget, nobody respects a lazy worker. You work hard, do your share, and then I'll listen to what you have to say. Otherwise, you can't show me nothing."

"I don't disagree with you, Pops. . . ."

"You better not," Procopio says, laughing.

"But we have some hard cases here. We have these KKKers, and they don't play around. I know about working hard. I'm one of the hardest-working guys in the plant. I respect everyone and treat everybody the way I want to be treated. But tell me, what good does it do? What good did it do for Rex, for Robert—remember him? Or Darlene? To the bosses and people like Dent, no matter what we do, it's never good enough."

"*Sí, es cierto*, yes, it's true—but you're not doing things for them. You're doing what you have to do to be a decent person in this world. It's not about them. They'll never get it. Like I said when we were first organizing that union drive—hate only eats you alive. I'm not saying we shouldn't defend ourselves, that we shouldn't take those bastards on when they try to screw us over. But remember: Where's your dignity, your inner strength, your way of walking in this world? How do you carry yourself? Who cares what they think! You have to sleep well at night. To get up the next day and know you've done a good job and that you're healthy and mindful to do it again."

"Okay, you win, *apá*, like always," Johnny concedes, thankful that he and his father can finally talk with each other so openly. "At least you're consistent."

After Darlene's accident, no more women are hired into the oil gang. Women's safety becomes the issue, not women's equality. Most people know that's the company's excuse to undermine their agreements. Of course, every man risks life and limb working at Nazareth. Yet nobody stops men from coming in. But women are women—they aren't supposed to be in the line of fire. Instead of working on ways to make the jobs safer, the company blocks women from entering the more well-paid and skilled positions.

Carla and Angie stay on. Like Johnny before them, they get good at maintaining the machines, gears, pulleys, and motors. But they aren't moving up the ladder. Most of the men are becoming millwright apprentices. Like Johnny, Carla and Angie stay on to train others who then move up before they do.

At the same time, Carla and Angie find themselves working together more often than not. As if the men are avoiding having to partner with them.

One day, Carla's greasing the skids on the 22-inch mill. The mill is shut down and nobody else is around. Carla has a streak of grease across her cheek.

"Wipe your face—you got grease," Angie says while handing Carla a rag.

"What for, it's going to get dirtier later on. I'll just do it when we finish."

"Yeah, but it covers up your pretty face," Angie says while spitting on the end of the rag and carefully wiping Carla's face. Carla looks at Angie, aware of her tenderness, really needing it just then. Angie seems to be the only friend she has in the world. Mateo's no friend. No other person in the mill will talk to them but Johnny, and he's in no-man's-land. It's just Carla and Angie.

When Angie finishes, Carla keeps looking at her.

"Okay, I'm done . . . you can keep working," Angie says, appearing uncharacteristically shy.

"I want you to keep doing that," Carla responds, not sure why, not sure if she understands the words.

"Doing what?"

"Rubbing my face."

Angie looks up at Carla. Her shyness is now lifted. She takes her gloves off and puts her hand on Carla's face, gently caressing it. Carla feels something move inside her, something strange but necessary. A bright warm spot in the center of her being. At that moment she wants Angie to kiss her. But she doesn't know what to say, how to tell her. Angie seems to grasp this. She moves her face closer to Carla's. Carla doesn't move away. Then Angie opens her mouth and begins to kiss Carla's mouth, around the edges, in the middle, slowly, lovingly, gently placing her tongue into her mouth.

Something wants to burst inside Carla. Something that's sweet, powerful, sticky. Like honey from a glass jar that's about to break. Angie stops for a moment, but Carla says, "Don't stop." They kiss some more, moving closer to a dark section of the skids, moving to the cement steps that lead below the skids themselves. The grease, the oil, the dirt doesn't matter. They kiss, caress, move their hands to their breasts, unbutton their shirts and pants. From below the skids come moans and sounds of kissing. Words of "don't stop" over and over. They make love the way women make love: mouth to mouth, water to water; slowly, meticulously, planting kisses like seeds of flowers all over their bodies. The world closes off. No mill. No noise. No dirt. Just Angie and Carla, skins united, daring to risk their jobs, their reputations, everything. None of this matters. What matters is not stopping.

Dent stands on the overhead crane above the furnace floor. He's part of a repair team servicing the furnace machinery. He feels old that day. Almost sixty, he's been in the plant since 1942, not long after it began operations soon after America's official entry into World War II. In those days, the plant produced steel for ships, bombs, bridges, and planes. It was a powerhouse. Denton remembers those exhilarating times. Many in his family entered the war as soldiers. He came to Los Angeles and worked in the skilled trades—the pride of the industrial might that helped win a war and, subsequently, dominated a world.

From his roosts overlooking the mill, Denton says little but watches everything. He's been doing this for so long he can't remember when he first looked down from forty feet high or more to make sure nothing wrong happened to his precious mill.

That particular day Denton contemplates doing something dramatic, something that will shake the very core of the mill's foundation. He only has a couple more years before he retires. Besides, he's getting tired. For all their gruffness and bluster—and the myth that has been created around them—the KKKers at Nazareth Steel managed to kill only a couple of people. It was in the 1960s when the first real challenge to their power took place. One of those who got it was Procopio's son Severo. Yeah, they moved in on him when he was green and wouldn't know what hit him. Never in Denton's wildest dreams did he imagine, though, that Severo would reemerge in the spirit of Johnny, presently the biggest thorn in his side.

Denton wants revenge for the attack that took Milton and Roland out of his commanding ranks. He wants to get Johnny. But something else is on his mind as well. Perhaps the beating at Wild Woolly's—which Dent sees as a sign of desperation on Johnny's part—can open the door to finally discredit and remove the Communists. They had to be working with Johnny, he surmises. They had to be among those cowardly masked men who beat those two youngsters while they were drunk and defenseless. He will get Johnny soon enough, but for now he has his sights on those commie bastards. It's all-out war as far as Denton is concerned. They fired the first shot; he'll have the last.

Johnny keeps everything in the wire mill humming. Properly taken care of, the machines will produce without much time off. Johnny makes his rounds checking pumps, gauges, tracks, oil and water levels. He gets reports from the foreman as to how things are sounding, how the gears are meshing, what the conveyors are doing. The other employees in the wire mill like Johnny. He greets everyone, gets to know most of the workers by name. He keeps the wire-mill foreman off balance by taking into account his authority and suggestions, although most of them don't have a clue as to what's going on. When everything seems to be working well, he climbs the water tower with a book—he's trying to get some reading in, seeing as Aracely is so into it—or just to rest.

Once in a great while he'll spot Al Simmons. Al has moved up from the labor crew. He now runs one of the galvanizing tanks for piping and fencing next to the wire mill. It's a hot and heavy job. Through sulfuric acid fumes, the men in gas masks and heavy coats handle large tongs to push steel sheets or rods into rectangular molten zinc vats, or skim the slag off the liquid zinc's surface with close to hundred-pound iron spoons.

But it pays almost as good as a melter's job on the furnaces. Big bucks.

"What's up, Al? How's the family?" Johnny says when he walks into the tank area to visit.

Al looks over, a little surprised to see Johnny. After a couple of seconds, he smiles and says, "What'd you say, Johnny? We're all fine. Your dad and the rest of your family's cool?"

It's small talk. Johnny doesn't feel he can broach a more serious topic just now. Al isn't closed off to him entirely, but Johnny knows he doesn't want to revisit the union election fiasco. So Johnny just gives him the minimum of greetings.

He walks over to the wire rope-making section, where several machines are weaving the metal wires into the heavy-duty wire rope as if it were silk on a loom, only these machines are noisy, hot, and metallic.

As he walks by to check gauges and levels, he notices a long-haired woman being trained on one of the machines. She has an attractive face and shapely figure, highly visible even beneath a hard hat and overalls. Johnny tries not to look interested, but he feels her eyes behind his back.

Her name is Velia. She has just started, part of Nazareth's plan to bring more women into the wire mill. She stops listening to the journeyman machinist, who's telling her something about the machine, enough to notice Johnny as he checks out the hydraulic tanks.

"You paying attention? I don't like flapping my gums over here for nothing," the machinist booms after he has turned around to notice that Velia has her mind elsewhere.

"Sure . . . sure, I'm listening. Go ahead . . . I'm getting it," Velia stammers.

After that day, Johnny tries to check the machines and gauges more often than usual. Velia has creamy light skin with a street kind of look. She looks fine—a classical Mexican face. Her one drawback is a missing front tooth. Johnny can match this with his own missing canine. After a few days of just passing each other, Velia decides to strike up a conversation.

"Hey you, I think the spinner over here needs grease or something," she tells Johnny as he kneels to tap on a gauge window. "You're the maintenance guy, right?"

Johnny stands up, looks over at the machine and then at Velia. "I'm the millwright. And thanks for telling me. I'll check it out right away. By the way, I'm Johnny."

"My name's Velia. I just started here."

"I know. I just started at the wire mill. But I've worked in the main plant for years."

"No kidding—you've been here a few years already?"

"Yeah, almost ten years now. What'd you do before you came here?"

"I did odd jobs. Worked in assembly lines. I was mostly on welfare, though. I'm a single mom with two kids. Their father split on us. So it's just me and the kids. How 'bout you?"

For an instant, Johnny hesitates. He doesn't want to mention his wife and two children. But what can he be thinking? Of course he'll mention them. They are his family. Velia should know about his family. It isn't like she's trying to pick him up or something. They work together. She's friendly. He's friendly. That's all it is.

"I got two kids—a boy and a girl."

"You're married?" Velia asks, not seeing a ring on his finger and hoping he isn't.

"Ah, yeah, I'm married. I've been married as long as I've worked here. Aracely is her name. We live in Florencia."

Velia tries to hide her disappointment. She smiles and puts her hands in her back pockets. "Well, I'm glad to meet you, Johnny. So when you get a chance, check out that spinner, okay?"

"Sure, as soon as I can."

Despite this awkward first meeting, Johnny finds himself at the wire-rope building more often than not. Instead of kicking back on top of the water tower, he'll hang around the spinner machines, making small talk with the forklift drivers and machinists. He spots Velia and makes sure she notices his presence.

During lunch, he stops by the lunch area, where Velia is alone eating some slop from the lunch truck.

"How goes it?" he asks.

Velia looks up and is delighted to see Johnny, even though she knows their relationship can't be what she might like it to be. So she keeps her responses short and snappy.

"Fine. Just eating."

Johnny sits down next to her, tool belt clanging at his side.

"So, how do you like working here so far?" Johnny asks.

"Not sure. I'm still trying to figure things out. I just feel like I'm getting things all wrong. Hardly anyone to talk to here," she says.

"Yeah, I know—some of these guys act like they have the keys to the world's great mysteries. It's their way of having power over you. The more they know and the less you know, the more they think they're God or something. But believe me, whatever they know, you can figure out. There's no magic to running those machines. When these guys started, believe me, they probably knew less than you do now about how to handle them."

"You're kidding me. It doesn't seem like it the way they talk to me."

"They're not used to having women around. But they'll get over it. Once you do well, they'll bring in more females. You never know—this place may end up having nothing but women."

"Well, compared to other places, the pay is good," Velia says. "That's why I even bother to show up. There's been a few days this week when I wanted to grab my hard hat and toss it to the ground. But I guess you're right. I'll get it. I should just hang in there."

"Sure, that's the way to go," Johnny says, standing up to leave. "Remember, you can do anything these guys can do, and probably better than they can."

Velia watches as Johnny wanders over to the machine section. Nice guy, nice looking, too, she thinks. Maybe there could be a chance for them after all, she muses, a mischievous gleam in her eye.

7

DESPERATE

The bag house on top of the furnace building gathers the sulfur gases and debris from the furnaces, containing them in an elaborate system of bags instead of releasing them into the air. The structure was built after environmental regulations were imposed on industry to cut the smoke, dust, and contaminants that helped make Los Angeles one of the cities with the worst air quality in the world.

Harley, however, hears from a few mill hands about a practice the company institutes from time to time to circumvent the regulations. Late at night, on certain nights, when the smoke can't be seen, the gases and dirt are let loose. This saves the company thousands of dollars in monthly cleanup costs. It's also illegal.

On a few nights, Harley, Ronnie, and a couple of their fellow revolutionaries keep tabs on when the smoke and debris are let go. They arrange to have one of the Communists on the furnace floor climb up to the roof to see if the pollution is actually being released. At first, nights pass without anything out of the ordinary being spotted. But one night—and then for several nights after that—their suspicions are confirmed. Toxic gases and smoke are being released without the use of safety bags. Not all the time, but enough to cut back on having to keep the waste properly held and disposed of, according to regulation.

Harley and the others feel this is the way to force Nazareth's hand. They will go to the local press and media. They will pressure the company to clean up its act as well as provide safe and decent working conditions for all employees. It's their ace in the hole. But they need to have incontestable proof. They need to have a smoking gun—like the written orders from the company to a subordinate authorizing the violation.

They know getting their hands on that information is going to be tough.

One day, outside of work, several Communists at the mill meet to discuss what can be done. Harley and Ronnie are there. So is Johnny. Although Johnny never calls himself a Communist, he has been meeting with them so long that he is really one of them. His credibility in the mill forces him not to make a public issue of this. But to most anyone who knows him, he's a consistent CLOC participant.

"Maybe we can break into the main office and rifle through the files—we're liable to find something," one member of the group suggests.

"No, that wouldn't work," Harley counters. "If we found something, we wouldn't be able to use it—the evidence would be illegally obtained. Besides, if we get caught, everything we've been working for would go down the tubes."

"How about if we convince the mill hands who know about the practice to speak up?" Johnny says. "You said someone actually saw the bags open up on several nights. How about that guy? Maybe it's a simple matter of finding out who's allowing this to happen. We have to pinpoint the actual culprits."

"We know the culprit—it's Lane Peterson, the plant director," Ronnie Nakamura explains. "He's making sure this happens and trusts maybe one or two people to see to it. They're not going to talk. The mill hands, even if they stepped up, can only testify to what they saw. They can't testify about who made the decision and when. We need that."

"Peterson will make out like he's dumb," Harley adds. "He'll say he knew nothing about this and have somebody else take the blame. The company will sacrifice a lowly managerial staff person to save their butts."

"I propose we go ahead and leak this to the press—let them do their jobs for once," Ronnie says. "If they have an ounce of spit, they'll find the evidence we need. They have better investigative tools and paid employees to do this. Once it's in the papers, we can put the squeeze on the company. They won't know the leaks came from us—they'll think it was the work of some overzealous reporter. But we'll make the company pay from our end. They're breaking more laws than just this one."

Everyone agrees this is the best way to proceed. But they need to make sure the information they have—meager as it is—gets into the right hands. The *Los Angeles Times* is the newspaper to go to. But everyone feels the editors there won't initiate such an effort. It will have to come from an area newspaper and get followed up by the *Times*.

The *Huntington Park Advocate* is just such a newspaper, they surmise. And one reporter, who writes about local industry for the newspaper, is the man to call on: Charlie Cohn. The newspaper covers national news through its wire services and local news through a handful of reporters. Charlie has done pieces on Nazareth before, mostly based on their press releases and promotional materials. But everyone remembers that he did manage a fairly evenhanded reporting on the last contested union elections.

"Fine, we'll gather whatever information we have on the bag house," Harley summarizes. "Ronnie and I will communicate this to Cohn. Once we see articles in the newspaper, we can raise more issues with the company. Everyone with this so far?"

There isn't a dissenting voice.

The next few weeks, Johnny waits to see what will happen. He starts to pick up the *Huntington Park Advocate*. In the millwright shanty on the wire mill, after all the major rounds and maintenance checks are done, he'll read as much as he can, mostly spending time on the comics section.

One day, out of the blue, Velia strolls into the shanty, something a nonmillwright person will rarely do. Johnny is pleasantly surprised.

"Like them funny pages, huh?" Velia asks.

Johnny looks away from a *Peanuts* strip and can't believe his eyes.

Velia is still in her hard hat and work boots, but she now wears clean jeans and flannel shirt tied around her waist. She looks beautiful. He almost wants to tell her it isn't such a good idea to dress so temptingly in the mill. But he doesn't.

"Well, I'm really reading the news here, but I end up at the comics," Johnny explains, caught a little off guard. "What brings you here? Got a break?"

"I'm actually on my day off," Velia says. "I thought I'd come by and say hello. So . . . hello."

"You're kidding me? You'd come here on your day off," Johnny responds incredulously. "I'm flattered, but I'm not worth the effort. I wouldn't get near this place on my day off."

"Well, I got up this morning with absolutely nothing to do. I just felt like making the ride and visiting. When I'm working there's really no time to come by and talk with you."

"Okay, I'm in pretty good shape today as far as repairs go—sit down awhile," Johnny offers.

For the next hour or so, Johnny and Velia talk. He even invites her to the study circle, although she makes a face like *say what*! But he figures he may as well let her know what he's about. If she doesn't want anything to do with him after that, cool. But Velia listens. She isn't sure if she's interested or not, but if Johnny's into it, the group may be worth exploring.

"Well, gotta go—I have to get back to my kids as soon as they get out of school," Velia finally states as she stands up. "I appreciate you taking the time. Maybe we can do this again on another day."

"Sure, if I'm not busy with a job assignment," Johnny says, knowing that the way he has the wire mill running, he's more likely than not to be free.

After Velia exits the shanty, she leaves behind the scent of her perfume, which Johnny doesn't want to let go of. He sits there for the longest time just taking it all in.

Several more weeks pass, but the articles on Nazareth Steel's illicit release of mill contaminants don't appear in the *Advocate*. Charlie Cohn, although competent, is still beholden to his editors, who, because of advertising, are disinclined to publish damaging articles on local industry. But Harley and Ronnie's persistence is starting to wear him down.

One slow news day, Charlie picks up the phone to schedule an interview with Lane Peterson. Charlie has just finished looking at the file of information and letters that Harley and Ronnie have given to him on the sly during the previous weeks. He figures talking directly to Peterson is the best way to find out if the allegations are true.

Mr. Peterson is not usually in his office—nobody knows what he does, but he mostly lets others do the actual managing of the mill. Mr. Peterson does the presswork, the interviews, the regular "company letter" to the employees, and more visible promotional junkets. He travels to Japan and other Asian countries to study their steel-production facilities, which are much more modern and technologically advanced compared to Nazareth Steel's ancient enterprise.

He also travels frequently to Nazareth's national headquarters in Pennsylvania.

By sheer luck, Charlie is able to find Mr. Peterson in his office and schedules an appointment to speak with him that day. Charlie arrives at the company's main offices, around the corner from the mill, down several blocks and away from most of the plant's hustle and bustle.

The interview is short, although far from sweet. Charlie pointedly asks Mr. Peterson whether he's allowing the bag-house process to be sidestepped so the dirty fumes escape directly into the night air. Of course Mr. Peterson denies this and cites Nazareth's long record of keeping pollutants from the skies. But in the back of his mind, Peterson's thinking of ways he can find out who has given Charlie the bone. The way he does this is to trick Charlie into showing him the anonymous letters.

Mr. Peterson promises to give Charlie exclusive inside information about the steel business. Charlie in turn agrees to let him see the information he has, and Peterson tells him if he can find answers to some of the concerns, he will let Charlie know.

What Charlie doesn't grasp is how he is giving Lane Peterson the clues he needs to figure out the source of the leak. Peterson can immediately tell it has the stamp of Ronnie Nakamura and Harley Cantrell. Peterson consults his secret files of flyers, posters, and other communications on the CLOC members at the plant. He has been moving on CLOC from time to time, firing as many participants as he can. In addition, he keeps tabs on their comings and goings. Ronnie's file, for example, has lots of materials from his many years of producing propaganda pieces. The letters Charlie receives have Ronnie's distinct matter-of-fact yet engaging style.

Charlie won't do an article on the allegations unless he has solid confirmation or proof, Mr. Peterson reasons. In the meantime, he'll work on ways to stop CLOC. One way to handle this, Peterson figures, is to bring in Dent, Ace Mulligan, and Bob Michaels to discuss the options.

The meeting is held in Mr. Peterson's office. The union officers are known to go there every once in a while to discuss business with management. But this is no ordinary union–management matter.

"I have here information that was leaked to the *Huntington Park Advocate* by CLOC," Mr. Peterson begins. "They're trying to get an investigation into environmental violations involving the bag house. They don't know what the hell they're talking about. But I'm getting mighty upset at this level of intrigue and sabotage in the plant. I think it's time to get rid of the troublemakers once and for all."

"Sure, we're all for it," Mulligan says. "We can't stomach them either. But remember, Lane, we have union rules as well. We can't just work in cahoots with you to get rid of people you don't like. You have to have sound and solid reasons. You need to have something that can stand up in arbitration hearings. You know they're going to fight every firing like they have the last ones."

"We'll handle our end of this," Peterson persists. "I want you to handle yours. We'll find the reasons. We'll move on the main troublemakers—Harley Cantrell, Ronnie Nakamura, Johnny Salcido, and some others. I'm not telling you what to do, but you should know we're hitting them hard and fast this time. Do what you have to do—I don't even want to know what it is. But we're going to tear out this cancer once and for all."

The meeting doesn't last long. It's clear the men in that room have the same goal. Peterson is giving the union guys—and by extension, the KKK group—a free hand to deal with the latest problem posed by the Communists and their friends.

For Dent, this is all he needs. He has been thinking of ways to get to Harley and the others for some time. Now the company is going to look the other way. He aims to leave Nazareth in a couple of years with the relief of having removed the last vestiges of the 1960s from the plant.

Desperation, anger, fear—there are countless reasons why someone would kill. There's also money, revenge, power, status; some even do it for kicks. Murder is such a rampant occurrence in L.A.'s poorest communities, particularly during the strangling days of major industry in the mid-1970s to the mid-1980s. Domestic battles, gang wars, personal beefs, female problems, male problems, infidelity . . . the list is as long as there are people's names in a phone book. It's no different for Dent.

Dent has always had it in him. To murder, that is. He orchestrated the couple of so-called accidents that led to deaths when the right-wingers lost control of the union for a short time during Procopio's revolt. Police were powerless to do anything when the company declared these attacks to be "accidents"—even when Procopio tried to get detectives to investigate Severo's death. Dent and his cronies got away with it and celebrated for several nights at Wild Woolly's.

He even managed to escape a murder rap in Texas before moving to California. Dent and a friend committed the armed robbery of a small gas station near the East Texas town he grew up in. Before killing him, they managed to rob the proprietor of twenty-two dollars, big bucks for two poor white boys with the country in the middle of a war. That was one of the reasons he hightailed it to L.A. That case never caught up with him. Although he has threatened violence more than he has actually carried it out, Dent definitely has some experience under his skin. If he needs to hurt anyone, he will. If he needs to kill, he will. He also musters a small army in the mill that will do his bidding.

But something about this particular murder doesn't seem to come from Dent's less-than-subtle hands. His manner is crude, reckless. This killing is particularly cold, well planned, and ruthless.

The body is found behind several empty warehouses in the Union Pacific track yards of East Los Angeles. It lies motionless in the front seat of a Ford truck, five bullet wounds to the head. The police believe the victim was killed much earlier and somewhere else, then driven to the spot and left there. There are no fingerprints, no gun, no bullet casings. The body also has no identification. The body is that of a tall white male with long blond hair, somewhere in his thirties.

It doesn't take long, however, for friends and family to call the police and declare the victim to be Harley Cantrell.

Nilda tells police that Harley left the house late one evening to meet with Ronnie Nakamura at Ronnie's place in Gardena. But Ronnie said Harley never showed up. Both Ronnie and Nilda called around, but nobody saw him. Two nights later, the truck was found.

CLOC is devastated. After Harley's body is positively identified by Nilda, several CLOC members stop coming to meetings. Politics is fine, but death-squad stuff is another matter. Suspicions grow—most everyone feels that Dent and the KKK group are behind the murder. But others aren't sure; this has a professional killer's touch. Yet no other possible suspects are identified—it has to be Dent.

Johnny and Aracely are beside themselves after the killing. They have grown close to Harley and Nilda—their beautiful brown-skinned daughter, Matilda, with long curly blond locks, is close friends to Joaquin and Azucena.

For days, Johnny can't sleep. He wanders the wire mill in a daze, unable to focus on his duties, his rounds and assignments. Revenge fills Johnny's heart; day after day, he thinks of ways he's going to get to Dent. The urgency he feels comes from believing that Harley will not be the last of their victims; Johnny is probably high up on their hit list. He has to get Dent before Dent gets him.

One day, Velia walks in on Johnny as he changes a burned-out electric motor on one of the spinner machines. "I'm sorry to hear about your friend Harley," she says, genuinely affected. "How are you doing?"

"I'm fine," Johnny remarks quickly. He doesn't feel like saying more for fear his rage will turn to unquenchable grief. "You're not here on your day off, are you?"

"No, I'm working today," Velia says, wearing dirty overalls along with her hard hat, safety glasses, and steel-toed shoes. "I'll check with you in a couple of days when I'm off, okay?"

Velia walks away. Johnny doesn't say anything, but he really wants to see Velia again. She has come to the work shanty a few times on her days off since that first time. They communicate well, talking politics and even laughing at a few things. But as he sees Velia return to her workstation, Johnny tries to think of something else and keeps working.

Aracely finally gets the nerve to drop off the babies at Eladia's, the kids' *abuelita*, and visit Nilda. Azucena is now talking and running. Eladia can handle her and Joaquin better than when the girl was still baby-strolled around and carried in her arms.

Aracely doesn't know how to approach Nilda, but she knows she has to.

After transferring buses and walking, she ends up in front of Nilda's home. It's quiet, barren, void of any life. Nilda sits alone at the kitchen table. Aracely rings the doorbell and waits for Nilda to answer. It takes a while, but she can hear Nilda pushing back a chair, standing up, and walking slowly to the door. When Nilda opens it, Aracely sees her friend's face, and as if a button has been pressed, tears fall down Aracely's face. Nilda looks tired and beaten. She moves to embrace Aracely and at the moment of contact Nilda also breaks down, heaving so hard it frightens Aracely; she has never seen her strong and willful comrade become so compliant and tattered.

The women stand there in the doorway for the longest time, sharing with each other a world of tears—for Harley and all such losses suffered by women everywhere.

Things change after Harley's death. CLOC is pretty much in disarray, a shadow of its former self. Nilda eventually takes an indeterminate leave of absence; she returns to New York City with Matilda to stay with her family. No one knows if she'll come back. Johnny and Aracely keep going to meetings with CLOC members in the mill; but at one point only three people show up, and two of them are Salcidos. Eventually the other guy stops coming.

Ronnie, too, manages to sort of disappear.

One night, Johnny receives a call from Ronnie's wife, Ruth.

"You have to help me, Johnny," she says, her voice cracking in desperation. "Ronnie's been at the poker club for several nights now. He just won't come home. We're losing everything, probably our house. He's got the gambling jones bad. I tried to pull him away, but he tells me to fuck off. I don't know what to do anymore."

"I'll come by and see if I can talk to him—give me a minute," Johnny assures.

Johnny drives to a card club in Gardena and walks through the glass doors. After a short search, he spots Ronnie, his brow knitted, sweat falling down his face, with a hand of poker down on the table in front of him. This happens a few times. Late in the night, they'll talk. Ronnie implies he knows he needs help and that he doesn't want to lose his family. But regardless, soon after such talks he'll end up back at the card tables, again and again.

Eventually, Johnny hears the family has lost their home and Ruth has filed for divorce, taking their half-Japanese, half-Anglo son with her to another community far from the Southeast L.A. gambling joints.

Now it's up to Johnny and Aracely to keep the CLOC work alive in the steel mill and in their neighborhood. They aren't sure if they are up to doing so, but they decide not to give up. They communicate directly with CLOC's central offices in Chicago. They receive the *People's Beacon*, which Aracely distributes at a few shopping centers, parks, factories, and community events. Johnny keeps trying to get people at the plant to attend meetings; he's gotten a few labor-crew members to attend from time to time, but not many.

The one person who never shows up to a meeting or study session is Velia. Several months after Harley's death, she doesn't want anything to do with Johnny.

It might have started innocently enough. As friends. As coworkers. As two people with kids and other lives finding common ground in the wire-mill section of Nazareth Steel. At first it was probably just foolish attraction. But somehow they knew—Johnny and Velia were going to be with each other. It wasn't something they were both aware of as far as timing went. But they knew in their hearts it was bound to happen.

The temptation built up in Johnny for some time. Aracely became preoccupied with Nilda's emotional state as well as their growing kids' needs. Johnny had this raging ball inside his gut that needed to go somewhere, but he didn't know where or how. Velia was just lonely. She hadn't had a decent boyfriend since the father of her kids left her. She'd had one-night stands and unstable relationships for far too long. She longed for someone she could just hang on to for a while—for a long, long while.

One day on one of Velia's days off, Johnny had been in the pipe shop shed in the back of wire mill, where a pipe-cutting machine, piping, and other tools were located. Velia ended up there after one of the wire-mill workers pointed out where it was. Johnny was cutting several feet of two-inch black iron pipe. She looked sharp again, even with her hard hat on. She wore a tan blouse with tight tan jeans. And the fragrance—he looked forward to being enveloped in it whenever she visited.

Who knows why, perhaps because it was a different venue from where they usually talked or maybe it was its isolation, but Johnny simply walked up to Velia and kissed her. An array of burning emotions pushed him to explore Velia's lips, tongue, cheeks, and neck. Velia was surprised at first, but it didn't take long for her to respond in kind. She had secretly waited for this day for so long, not knowing when or even if it would come. Now they were in each other's arms and the passion between them pushed them beyond the limits where their own hearts weren't sure they should go.

Johnny moved toward Velia's breasts and she pushed them farther into his face like instinct, without thought, letting her body speak, think, move. Her hips began to pump, again as reflex. Her hips longed for this, longed to be held and pushed back with every one of their thrusts. Johnny managed to unbutton her blouse, where a large white bra held a pair of heavy cream-colored breasts. As he pushed the bra away with his hands, Velia's swollen and bumpy nipples showed through. He hungered for them, sucking and licking. Velia moaned heavily as his tongue encircled the engorged nipple of her left breast; the down of hair all over her body tingled with each watery mouthful. She could feel herself coming with his mouth on her breast and his hand between her legs. She pumped her pelvis harder and harder into his hand until she couldn't stand it anymore; suddenly she exploded with a powerful thrust of her body, a muffled scream emanating from her throat for what seemed like several long ecstatic seconds. Velia then squatted down in front of Johnny, her breasts still exposed, and pulled at his belt and top button in front of his pants.

Moments after they had brought each other to pleasure, the realization hit them: They had done wrong. They knew they could get caught. They knew so much could be destroyed. But they also knew they had to continue, despite the real reservations they both shared.

It felt like it just had to be.

Their lovemaking moved through the myriad dark tunnels beneath the wire mill. Lengths and lengths of them, these tunnels were hardly visited by anybody except Johnny when he checked on hydraulic equipment. Sometimes he went down there to take a nap. In time, it became Johnny and Velia's most frequent place to share intimacies, with a large flashlight illuminating the spot where they'd lie down, a broken-down cardboard box their only mattress. They couldn't do this anywhere outside the plant—the chances of being seen were far too great. But here in the entrails of the wire mill, without the knowledge of fellow worker or boss, they found their refuge on oil-stained ground, along the dark and mysterious concrete corridors, in another world away from the world.

A lanky, metabolically thin son of Slavic immigrants, Turk Corovic joins the oil gang at Nazareth Steel after leaving Chicago, where his father and uncles are union leaders at another steel plant. At nineteen years old, he needs to break away from his tight-knit family. His plan, in fact, is to get a college degree or an acting job in the L.A. area, a place he always wanted to visit, having seen Disneyland and Hollywood as the prize for any child's dream of potential greatness.

But all that disappears when Turk comes across an ad for oiler-greasers in the repair crews of the plant and he applies. Much to his surprise, he's called in for an interview.

After being offered the job, Turk walks for a long time around the modest streets of modest homes that surround Nazareth's personnel offices. His future is on the line—should he forget this job and continue his studies so he can return to Chi-town with a degree and perhaps his parents' approval on their lips? Should he just drop all this nonsense and get into a Hollywood acting workshop and consider a life on the big screen? (Yeah, right! he thinks.) Or should he take the job, following in his dad's footsteps, and then later return home to labor in the vast steel-production complexes that Chicago is known for?

At nineteen, such decisions can have devastating results. And, of course, he will probably make the wrong choice. But then again, isn't that what nineteen-year-olds are supposed to do?

The most immediate impulses determine which way he'll go. The money at Nazareth is good; he'll have to do this just to meet his rent and mounting bills.

Without telling his parents, Turk accepts the job at Nazareth and he soon enters the plant as its newest recruit in the oil gang.

By then much has happened at the mill: Harley Cantrell is gone;

CLOC has disbanded; Johnny is weeks into his affair with Velia; Dent and his cronies feel they are now in control even as many of them are preparing to retire. Turk knows none of this, of course. But he's going to play an integral part in the continuing drama that is then unfolding on more intense levels. This time, it has to do with the very life or death of the Nazareth Steel Mill in Los Angeles.

As it turns out, Turk is hired—as if by rote—at a time when corporate heads are planning to close the Los Angeles plant. Much has changed in American industry by the late 1970s. The microchip has introduced a kind of technology that threatens the way business, products, and social relations have been established up to that point.

For the steel industry, imports from the more technically advanced and financially secure plants in Japan and Germany—as well as the ones in Mexico and Taiwan that brought labor costs down—are undermining the domestic steel-production market. In effect, the U.S. steel industry, once the backbone of the most aggressive industrial power in the world, is being outbid in the global marketplace.

Nazareth decides to consolidate its various mills, forges, foundries, shipyards, and other production facilities that it maintains scattered around the country. In Los Angeles, the corporate offices first close the shipyards. Soon after, rumors abound in the Maywood mill about its impending demise.

Fear and insecurity spread among the mill hands, laborers, and craft workers. Those who can retire do so to get their pensions and other benefits. Some of the more skilled workers quit altogether to get work in other industries such as aerospace and auto, although in time these jobs are also cut. Production quotas begin to fall as many workers stop caring about killing themselves for jobs that may not even exist in a year or two.

For a time, Johnny doesn't worry about shutdowns in his isolated wire-mill shanty; everything seems to go well. That is until a notice appears one day without warning in the wire mill's time-clock shanty.

Dear Nazareth Wire Mill and Warehouse Employees:

Due to increased imports from Japan and other countries, and the prohibitive costs of revitalizing the whole plant with modern steel-production equipment, the Nazareth Steel Corporation has decided to close the wire-mill and warehouse operations in Maywood, California. We understand the nature of such a difficult decision and we regret any inconvenience this may cause any of our wire-mill and warehouse employees. Employees with seniority in their production units will be allowed to integrate to similar jobs in other parts of the facility. Those who are eligible for retirement will be asked to do so. More recent hires will be laid off and be eligible for unemployment insurance from the State of California. We are prepared to help all wire-mill and warehouse employees with other jobs that may be available outside of your present job description if you so desire. Again, we apologize for this decision. But we believe this will help Nazareth Steel become stronger in regaining our once-prominent place as the premier steel-production plant on the West Coast and Pacific Rim.

It's signed by Lane Peterson.

Johnny's jaw drops as he reads it. Despite the exile, he has gotten cozy and comfortable in the wire mill—also knowing that Velia will be there with him from time to time. However, the wire mill's closing won't affect him as much as some of the other employees. He has seniority among the other millwrights and will be allowed to return to the main plant. But for Velia, it's a different matter. She is pink-slipped right away. It's a tearful Velia that greets Johnny one day as he places his tools, papers, and coffee paraphernalia in a box to take to the main millwright shanty located in the middle of the facility.

"I'm out of here, Johnny," Velia sobs.

"I feared that . . . damn, baby, I'm sorry," Johnny says, turning around to hold Velia. "You can't get any other job in the plant?"

"I was trained in the wire-rope section," Velia explains. "There's no equivalent job in the main plant. Besides, others have much more seniority than I do. I'm fucked, that's all."

A deep disappointment descends on Johnny, which he tries to contain as much as he can. He has gotten used to being with Velia, to those sweet moments below the surface of the wire mill, together in the dark corridors of the tunnel system. Their lovemaking has become frequent and glorious. Days will go by and they won't see each other. But during breaks or days off, they'll find each other in their customary trysting sections of the tunnels. Now all this has been completely ripped to shreds.

Johnny, however, is more in a dilemma than in a funk.

With Velia gone, he has to make a decision—to continue their affair outside the mill or to stop it right there. This weighs on him as Velia tries to reach him at the plant for a few days. Johnny isn't sure he wants to take it beyond the mill. He loves Aracely. He knows what he's doing is wrong; in his guilt-ridden way, he has become more affectionate and helpful to Aracely. But with Velia no longer an employee, he feels the strong urge to cut all ties with her. He likes being with Velia—she brings great comfort and release during the time he most needs it. But regardless of the countless ways he looks at it, Johnny doesn't love her.

He calls Velia early one evening to talk.

"Johnny, I'm so glad you called—I wondered what happened to you," Velia responds, pleased to hear his voice.

"I'm sorry, babe, I had a lot to do since I returned to the main plant. Listen, I think we should talk. How about if we meet at the Norm's Restaurant in Huntington Park? I'll buy."

"Sure, Johnny, I think that would be nice," Velia says although she senses something's wrong. "I can be there in an hour."

When Velia drives into the parking lot at Norm's, she can see Johnny's lone figure through the window. He looks uneasy, nervous—sad. Velia's eyes begin to burn. She pulls in and turns off the engine. She sits there for a moment, wondering whether she should just take off and leave. But a crazy glint of hope that perhaps she is imagining things enters her mind. Perhaps Johnny's in a bad way because of all that's happened at the plant. It may have nothing to do with her. It's the hope of the desperate.

Velia enters the restaurant and promptly sits next to Johnny. She notices right away how uncomfortable he looks. A shine off that glint has been removed.

"Hey, babe, I mean, Velia . . . good to see you," Johnny responds, moving slightly closer to the window. Velia doesn't smile; she stands up and places herself directly across from Johnny. She knows now why he has called.

Johnny's stammering is probably the worst part. It's that point in a closing relationship when a woman grasps more of a man's nature, especially his flaws. Johnny, who seems to have good words when he needs them, is being failed by words.

"Stop it, Johnny, you don't have to say any more," Velia interrupts him. "I know what's up. I'm no longer in the plant. I'm no longer of interest to you. I know I shouldn't have expected anything different. You've got Aracely. But just so you know, I really, really liked you."

At that point, tears form in Velia's eyes. Johnny looks away, toward the parking lot, to a spot far up an alley. Velia continues, trying hard not to unleash the emotions that clamber up her throat.

"Love is blind—that's what they say," Velia manages to say. "So I went blind for a while. No regrets. That's life. You want to end it now. Fine. I can accept that. I just can't stand being here with you right now. I've got nothing to apologize for, but I really feel sorry. I understand if I never hear from you again. I just want to say, it was great, Johnny. . . ."

Velia again tries to contain herself. Johnny looks down at his hands.

"What we had was great, for the time we had it. I thank you for that," Velia adds. "But now I don't have anything else to say to you. You apparently don't have anything to say to me. So I'm leaving. I hope you remember me fondly. That's the way I want to think of you. I'd better go before this turns into something else."

Velia moves out of the booth seat and momentarily stops in front of Johnny, still sitting. He looks up at her, expressionless, a slight quiver on his lips. Perhaps she expects something, some acknowledgment, maybe even a retraction. But hope has died by then. She turns around and walks out the front door.

Johnny sits there, picks a cigarette from his pocket—something he has not done in a long time—and lights it. He has brought this on, and he knows it. Now he'll have to figure out how he's going to deal with Aracely, who as far as he knows has no idea about Velia. But Johnny does, and it's eating at him about how it's going to affect his family, even with Velia gone.

Just then, the thought of Velia gone strikes him in a way he has tried desperately to avoid; Johnny gulps some air as a sense of shame rushes over him and his heart seems to shatter into a thousand tiny pieces.

8

STEEL'S VENDETTA

Turk stops to wipe his brow as he greases couplings and bearings on stainless-steel rollers, many of them gouged from thousands of hours pushing red-hot ingots back and forth on the 32-inch mill. He eyes a couple of men removing the monstrous forge several yards ahead of him. Their effortless collaboration intrigues him. He loves working in the mill; he loves the way the millwrights take apart machines and put them back together, or how the mill hands work in unison as scrap iron, mineral, and ore are melted, poured, and then shaped from malleable ingots into hard steel beams, slabs, or rods.

The two millwrights take different positions as an overhead crane maneuvers a massive ratchet wrench onto a nut as large as a man's waist. One of the millwrights moves his right hand as if it's a quacking duck, indicating the speed the wrench should be lowered, a rhythm the overhead-crane operator sticks to as the powerful wrench gun begins to cover the nut. The other millwright with gloved hands moves the ratchet head so that it fits exactly where it needs to go. With careful handling, the wrench falls right into place.

With a quick motion of the hand, the first millwright has the operator stop the crane's movement. The other millwright climbs higher on the forge, braces himself, then presses the handle of the ratchet wrench that screams with pounds of pressure from an air hose—such hoses are located throughout the plant—as it works to loosen the mammoth nut on the huge bolt that holds the forge down over several sets of rollers.

It takes a few tries, but finally the nut begins to spiral from out of the bolt; the nut is so heavy, a wire rope and chain are needed to lift it up and take it down onto the mill floor.

Turk doesn't even mind the greasing and oiling. His mentor and partner most of the time is Carla, the Salvadoran cutie pie—at least in Turk's opinion—who already has a couple of years' seniority in the oil gang. Her goal is to move up to become a millwright's apprentice, something Turk also covets.

He has heard about Carla's sexual proclivities—steelworkers can be as gossipy as country hens. Carla and Angie had tried to keep their romance under wraps, but things get around in the mill, as if carried by the piping that swirls in and around all the buildings. The mill has eyes. It has ears. It whispers. Secrets aren't secrets for very long.

Angie is already on the 10-inch-mill repair unit as an apprentice. She has become the first woman at Nazareth's Los Angeles plant to work as a millwright's helper. It takes her a long time, but she persists, becoming agile with tools and complicated repairs. It is also quite a feat considering how many obstacles the company and many of the millwrights have placed in front of women entering these positions. The fact that she's a Chicana qualifies this as a double triumph.

Johnny and Ray—the two millwrights working on the forge— move expertly about their tasks. They don't say much. They just know what to do, about who will do what and when. Turk doesn't care that they are Mexicans—after ten years, they are now the top mechanics in the plant; Turk admires them for *that*.

Turk has also heard that Johnny's a rabble-rouser. However, his skills and demeanor earn him respect, despite the fact most of the mill workers don't care much for his revolutionary politics. Turk wants to know more about these guys. These are real steelworkers with style and personalities. They live real lives and care about real issues. His father and uncles are somewhat radical, not Communists but strong union activists. They stand up for the workingman against the corporations and their plant bosses; he sees a link between them and Johnny.

In his Southside Chicago stomping grounds, where Yugoslav, Czech, Polish, and Hungarian immigrants have pushed their way into the giant steel facilities of the Midwest—alongside their Mexican, black, Puerto Rican, and other white brethren—Turk has learned to admire people who have strong, even if unpopular, principles and ideas, and are willing to stand up for them.

Nothing wrong with that, Turk figures, especially if they're into decent ideas like integrity and justice. He has also known too many cowards and shifters—those who change positions depending on whom they're talking to. That really pisses him off; Turk's upbringing won't abide by such nonsense. You have to know what you are about and you have to know how to defend your beliefs. Those who win, in Turk's experience, are those who have more passion about what they stand for *and* who are willing to do more than anyone else to get things done.

No chumps or clowns in that scenario.

When Johnny and Turk finally meet, it's during another drive to win back the union, only this time the issue of the plant's possible closing pulls the vast majority of the mill's employees into the fray.

Johnny decides to go all out behind this new attempt at union power. His dad, Procopio, is on the verge of retirement. His brothers are still in the mill but are no longer the activists they used to be. With rumors of the plant's closing over their heads, he enlists a new slate of union officers to protect as much as they can of the workers' pensions, benefits, and job prospects. They know that in the hands of the old guard, the workers will be left with nothing.

Johnny also realizes that many of the old mill veterans, including the racists in the local union, are being forced into retirement; he concentrates much of his efforts on the younger workers—women, blacks, and Mexicans, especially those breaking into the skilled trades.

"What's up, youngbloods?" Johnny says one day to a group of oiler-greasers in the lunchroom of the main millwright shanty.

"Not much, Johnny, just *refinando*," Carla states while sitting in front of a plate of microwaved enchiladas.

"It's always good to see you, Carla," Johnny says, then turns to the rest of the group. "Listen—all of you—you know we're running a slate for the upcoming union elections. We need your support. The company won't say whether they're closing the plant or not. We need people in the union that can protect what we have—our retirement plans, our benefits, and a way to get training into new jobs if they do close us down. Right now, those *tapados* in the union hall could care less. Most of them are retiring this year. We need fresh leadership. New blood. I'd like to count on your support."

"Sure, Johnny, whatever you say," a young black man answers.

Johnny passes out the flyers with the names of the slate and the positions they are running for. This time Johnny's on top as candidate for local president. Tony Adams, old Robert Thigpen's cousin and Johnny's ally from his first union elections battle, has joined in as vice president. The other guys are some venerable employees from the furnaces, the 32-inch mill, and the 10-inch-mill. And there are a few women as "committeemen," including Angie.

It's a strong slate, a group of workers of different races who can get things done. Who aren't scared of the company or their current union hacks. And they have the support of most employees regardless of race, nationality, or political persuasion.

Turk walks up to Johnny as the veteran millwright begins to leave the lunchroom.

"Hey, Johnny, you don't know me, but I got some experience in union elections," he says.

"No kidding, youngblood? Where at?"

"In Chicago. My dad and uncles are the Corovics of Local 12."

"I heard of them. They're part of the leading opposition group in the international union gatherings. Good, we can sure use the help."

"I can help in plastering posters, getting flyers out, and pulling in the guys to vote . . . whatever you need."

"Great—what's your name?"

"Well, everybody calls me Turk. That's what I've gone by since I was a kid."

"Welcome to our team, Turk," Johnny says, extending his hand. Turk takes it and smiles. He likes being part of these kinds of battles. In Chicago, they happen all the time.

Right after that, Turk hits the ground running. He shows up at the group's gathering spot at a local Veterans of Foreign Wars hall. Late at night, he'll get half a dozen other young bucks and, using milk and sponges, hang posters on telephone poles, fences, and siding. He makes sure flyers show up all over the plant. He talks to as many men as he can. He has a brash and confident style. He also knows how to talk to everyone—blacks, Mexicans, poor whites, racist whites, the women. He makes more than a few laugh and he defends the slate with an intoxicating fervor.

Turk is the kind of support Johnny sorely needs.

Six-year-old Azucena sits in front of the TV set watching afternoon cartoons. Joaquin walks in the front door after playing outside with some friends. He picks up a doll in his path and throws it at Azucena.

"Hey, stop that!" she yells. "I'm telling Mom."

"Go ahead," Joaquin answers, a scrappy boy of eight. "I told you not to leave your sissy dolls all over the place, Chena."

He has called his sister Chena ever since he was a small boy when he couldn't quite pronounce "Azucena." The name took and their parents also use it.

"*Oigan escuincles, no quiero pleitos,*" Aracely yells from the kitchen.

Joaquin and Azucena aren't much into speaking Spanish except when their *lito* and *lita* talk to them. But they also know that when their mother, Aracely, speaks Spanish around the house, she means business.

Just then Johnny emerges from the bedroom. He is back to working rotating shifts since the wire mill closed. He has the evening off until the graveyard starts around midnight.

"What's cooking tonight, *jaina*?" Johnny inquires.

"*Jaina?* You haven't called me that since we were dating. What's up with that, *ese?*" Aracely asks.

"You're my *jaina*, my main squeeze, *que no?*"

"I better be."

"Or you'll what?"

"You'll see—just do me wrong, *ese.*"

At that, Johnny changes the topic.

"Listen, I can't make the CLOC meeting tonight. After dinner we're having a strategy meeting at the VFW. Say *que hubo* to the comrades for me," Johnny says.

By now, Aracely has become head of a growing group of Communists in the surrounding South Central and Southeast Los Angeles communities. The work now is more into study and revolutionary education as well as ongoing propaganda instead of activity. Since Harley's death, CLOC's leading members realize the danger they are in if their members become the "activists" in the struggles for the workers' immediate demands. Instead, they recruit experienced leaders with credibility and give them a highly developed political orientation so that their work does not become dead-end reforms or action for action's sake. It requires more time to have an impact this way, but the idea is that changes would be substantial and long-lasting.

The crazies in groups like Nazareth's KKK have forced CLOC to use stealth and to spread themselves out so that they aren't isolated and picked off.

After dinner, Johnny gathers a notebook and pen and puts them near the door. He strolls up to Aracely, who's already scraping food off the dishes, and kisses her neck. He helps her with the dishes, something he has been doing for years. When they finish, Johnny moves to the dinner table and kisses Azucena on her forehead—she's his *consentida*—and taps on Joaquin's head; the boy only grunts. Johnny grabs his notebook and pen, and leaves.

As Johnny drives off he thinks about his family. Things have always been good with Aracely, but after his affair with Velia, he became filled with shame. So many times he had wanted to confess to Aracely about his indiscretions, but Aracely's good humor and good heart always stopped him in his tracks. This is now something that will have to go to the grave with him, he figures. He doesn't want to hurt Aracely, which the truth will certainly do. What he has done is vow never to step out of the marriage again. By marrying Aracely, he had committed his life to a monogamous relationship. He had committed to being there for his wife and children. But he has violated this trust and now he will have to fight like hell to stay on with his original purpose. And he thanks God that he's learned this before it destroyed the best thing he has in his life. Still, the shame often claws through his insides when he sees how fortunate he is to have such a beautiful and smart companion, to have such great kids.

This doesn't mean he never thinks about Velia. A few times, he'll be working in the mill and almost see her to the side of him. He'll turn that way and find nobody there. Sometimes, he'll take in that scent of hers, but he'll look around and realize this is impossible with the mill's usually skanky odors. Velia comes to him in dreams, in recollections during lulls in the day, or with the tuning of the radio to a particular song.

Velia is a real person, somebody who had given much to him without asking for much in return. Yes, he loves Aracely and will never let that love go—but those moments with Velia will forever be stamped in his soul.

Johnny approaches the VFW hall and sees a large number of men and women—including Carla and Angie—waiting for his arrival. They are brown, black, and white. Johnny feels they are going to win this time. There is more unity among the mill workers, among the Mexicans and blacks, for example, and with many whites as well. The plant closing will affect them all. They are all literally in the same boat. Whatever divisions the company has fostered, everyone now understands that in the end, their fates are tied.

Johnny gets out of the car to scattered applause. He feels self-conscious and embarrassed. His brothers Bune and Rafas are already inside with some of the other strategists and slate members. Junior, however, has stopped being involved with Johnny and the union drive. Over the years, he has developed a serious alcohol problem. He has been let go from the mill on the recommendation of the mill's alcoholic reduction program. Junior now mostly wanders the streets and hangs out at liquor stores in the old neighborhood; sometimes he'll be in the drunk tank of the Firestone sheriff's station or in the county hospital. Most everyone feels he isn't going to last long.

Procopio stays out of the battle this time. Not that he doesn't care. He has decided to take early retirement this year. He supports his son, however, and makes sure the old soldiers who still work in the mill are behind Johnny. He pretty much goes home and watches TV with Eladia or takes care of the grandchildren when needed. He knows that Johnny's going to come out on top this time. He tells him so and gives Johnny his blessing. Johnny, in turn, feels he's finally going to get a measure of justice for Severo and his father's own efforts to create a responsive and egalitarian local union.

But there are still a few obstacles in their path.

Dent and the KKK remain a danger. Threats have escalated during the past few weeks. Posters and flyers put up by Turk and his crew are being painted over or torn down. The old guard has decided to set up a new slate of union officers that consists of whites—younger members of the KKK group among them—but also, surprisingly, one Mexican: Pepe "Mosca" Herrera from the electric furnaces. They finally get a stooge to front for them. But Mosca has little or no support, even from his fellow furnace operators.

In addition, the mill workers aren't standing on the sidelines for this one. A group of Mexican, blacks, and whites walk into Wild Woolly's one night and push a few of the old racist crowd from their stools and tables. They order drinks and dare the bartenders not to serve them. Things may have gotten out of hand, but when some of the old group tries to confront these boys, they face some mean hombres and back down. Pretty soon, Wild Woolly's has all kinds of people coming in on a regular basis.

The integration of Wild Woolly's will precipitate an ugly response, Johnny surmises. He waits to see what will happen. Meanwhile, he pushes forward to become union president and to get rid of the small-minded from local union politics once and for all. He's far from alone in this—as evidenced by the enthusiasm on the parking lot of the VFW hall. That day Johnny walks into the meeting with the men and women who will help make history; Tony Adams is the first to extend his hand.

The mill may close, but the unity they forge in that struggle will last beyond the mill's chain-linked fences and corrugated metal walls. It will resonate in communities throughout Los Angeles and beyond. As far as Johnny is concerned, it's time that a new class of workers—employed and unemployed; undocumented and documented; black, white, and brown—emerge to flex their power. Labor has always been the foundation of society—they've also been the least represented in society's decision-making institutions. For Johnny, it's time this changed.

The 32-inch mill quakes with the rolling of long metal beams on the stainless-steel rollers that push them back and forth into the newly re-furbished forge. All the mill hands and laborers on the catwalks or near the forge have earplugs to protect their hearing; the visors on the hard hats help block flying debris or slag chips from entering their eyes.

The day is nice and sunny. Production demands have picked up for the last few days, giving some workers hope that Nazareth Steel has weathered the worst of an industrial crisis that has rendered once-thriving mill towns into boarded-up rust-belt communities.

A slew of new orders has come in from overseas as well as from do-mestic sources. The soaking pits hold a record number of ingots ready for the forge. As the ingots get pounded into various shapes at the 32, they are then pushed into the 22-inch-mill hotbed that tools them fur-ther into variously shaped rods, some of which end up in the 10-inch mill, where the rods are thinned even more through different-size dies, including one that makes rebar for the construction trades.

Earl Denton walks out of the 32-inch millwright shanty near all the noise and heat. He has a pipe wrench in his hand. He swaggers toward a worn-out coupling on the other side of all the chaos to repair some broken seals. His retirement is coming up in a matter of days. He looks forward to that last day. After almost forty years in the mill, he has put in his time. Now he can finally unwind, relax and enjoy some beers and long quietude, something he could only imagine until then.

Dent has given his all to the mill, taking his beliefs and attitudes to the limit. Nobody can mess with him. He sees the new organizing efforts among the Mexicans, blacks, and their white allies as something that has to pass. He doesn't care as much anymore. Let them run the union and run it into the ground, he thinks. They are fools; they may as well make complete fools of themselves. Running a local union is no party. Besides, in Dent's mind, the mill belongs to him.

In actuality, the mill recognizes no such connections—it knows no chivalry, graciousness, or loyalty. It's a cold lover that will fail to recognize you the day after a sweat-filled night. It's a great mother who often denies her babes suckling, an earth monster who can devour you as soon as birth you. It eventually turns everything it encounters into dust. In the end, it produces steel bars, plates, and beams, not dreams.

Dent places the pipe wrench on the end of a coupling beneath a section of the 32-inch skids not being used. Two oiler-greasers, one of them Turk, are nearby snapping grease-gun hoses onto grease buttons; a number of laborers shovel slag chips and grease piles into large containers next to them.

Suddenly Denton pushes himself out from where he's working, gasping and grabbing his chest, guttural moans emanating from a bluish mouth. He gasps for air, falls to his knees, and clutches at his arm. He tries to hold on to a shaft in front of him, but his fingers, stubby from years of being banged on with ball-peen hammers, only smear the grease.

Turk hears the commotion and looks over to see what's going on. He sees Denton try to get up, then collapse. The laborers also notice the man fall and they stop their shoveling. Turk and the others rush over to Denton, who squirms on the ground, an incoherent sound rising from his throat. Turk steps toward Denton to try and ease him through the heart attack while yelling out to anyone, "Somebody, get help—quick!"

But nobody does anything. Turk stops his movement and looks around. "Come on, man, somebody's dying here."

Nobody stirs. Turk turns toward Denton and a handful of laborers move in front of him. Each stares down at Turk and shakes his head. Turk knows what this means: Leave the KKK man alone. Let his death rattle be the music the mill gives back for treachery, for hate, for pain.

As Denton gasps for the last time, the mill he has lived for, that has carried his hopes and ideals along with its pipes and shafts, the mill that has destroyed lives so he could keep his privileges, belches back his stench. It throws up the years of lies and finger-pointing and threats—and the countless times he has turned his back on other hands who tried to reach out to him.

Turk feels he has to do something.

"He's dying," he screams. "We got to help him!"

But all Turk receives in return are icy gazes from beneath stained hard hats, the twitching of muscles of brown and black skin rippling below drenched shirts—the look of no.

"It ends here," remarks one of the mill hands from the small crowd that has gathered. Turk turns around and realizes he's outnumbered.

Flames thrust out of opened tuyeres on the furnaces. Overhead cranes haul tons of equipment, ladles of molten steel or scrap metal from one end of a building to the other. Gears rip and rattle as supple steel bars thunder down rolls of conveyors in all the rolling mills. Slag chips fly everywhere.

Denton lies stretched out, spread-eagled on his back, a look of agony on his face. It's how he sees his last light. After several long minutes, the row of laborers standing around the body slowly disperses. Someone finally calls the foreman on the 32-inch mill. Turk stands alone as everyone goes back to their stations; tears roll down his dirt-encrusted face.

Elsewhere there is no sorrow. The years of midnight abductions by hooded men, of questionable "accidents" that had removed limb and life, of losing work with the eyes of a hungry child piercing through the skin—that pain died on the floor of the 32-inch mill that day. This is the mill's payback, steel's vendetta, the justice that churns when all else fails.

The day the local union elections are held, swarms of mill hands, laborers, and craft workers gather outside the union hall. They are awaiting the final count. An international union representative is on hand to certify the results. Inside, the members of the slate from the old guard stand around uneasily as Johnny, Tony, and his brothers hang around nearby, grinning and slapping each other on the back. Aracely is also in the room as well as Johnny's father, Procopio.

The first ballot boxes have been counted and the numbers are overwhelmingly in Johnny's favor. But Johnny doesn't want to break out with joy until the last box has been tallied, retallied, and certified. Still, he can taste the sweetness of victory on his lips.

It's not long after dusk when the international union rep steps outside and announces the winners to the swelling crowd—Johnny Salcido and the whole progressive slate he's on have won by a large margin. Howls and hollers fly out of the crowd. Johnny walks out, greeted by thunderous applause, whistles, and more yells. At the same time, the old guard, including Mosca, and their younger slate team slink out the back door.

Johnny is then joined by his wife and election partners. He tries to say something, but the clapping and voices don't stop for several minutes. Finally, the noise subsides and he gets his chance.

"We made it, brothers and sisters, and I thank you," Johnny says, a wide smile across his face, his voice hoarse from so much talking the weeks before, bags under his eyes from lack of sleep. "It was a hell of a battle—in fact, this was many years in the making. My father was around in the 1960s when the last progressive slate held power. We've already tried this since then, as many of you know, but didn't make it. Still, in the end, we didn't give up. I know we're gaining these union positions in precarious times. We don't know how long we'll have our jobs. But I promise you, we'll fight like hell for the jobs you got, and if the mill does close, we'll work on a program that will train you and keep you viable in steel or any related industry. We have a lot of work to do and we're honored to do it. I do want to say . . . I owe everything to my father, Procopio, who came out of his dungeon called home to join us tonight. To my brothers Bune and Rafas—*gracias, carnales*, you've been with me all the way. To my wonderful wife, Aracely, and my children, who stood by me through those awfully time-consuming strategy sessions. To Tony and all the other men and women on the slate, you've proven your mettle and I know you'll help me get a lot of work done. And to all of you for voting your interests tonight and not walking away thinking your vote didn't matter. But I particularly want to dedicate this election to two very special people—to my older brother Severo, who was killed in the mill in 1963; he wanted so much to be one of you. I feel tonight that he is. And to Harley Cantrell . . ."

As Harley's name is mentioned, the crowd falls silent; several men take off their hats. Johnny looks at them and feels a wave of emotion sweep over him, but he holds back any tears. Johnny hadn't realized how much Harley had meant to these men and women, how much he had impacted their lives. Harley was a stone revolutionary, sometimes the butt of jokes in the mill, but he stood by them through thick and thin. His goals were always linked to the betterment of the mill workers and their future. He didn't just live for them—he died for them.

"Harley was a true brother, a true union man," Johnny continues. "You may not have agreed with everything he stood for, but you knew he would give you the shirt off his back if you needed it. I wouldn't be standing here if it weren't for Harley. So, brother Harley, my friend and comrade, I dedicate myself to finishing what you started at Nazareth Steel. I evoke your spirit in the interests of gaining true dignity and voice for every steelworker in this plant. This election, this victory, belongs to you . . ."

Johnny stops then; he puts his head down as the emotions crash through whatever internal barriers he has put up to stop them. Aracely gently places her arm around Johnny's shoulder and weeps.

The crowd erupts into deafening cheers and applause.

Two years have passed since Johnny, Tony Adams, and the other officers of the progressive slate had won the elections at the United Steelworkers of America, Local 1750. Once they took office, things changed radically. The union hall became open for business—meetings, discussions, grievance hearings, committees, and get-togethers. Many mill workers participated in the various structures established precisely to draw out their active involvement.

As local president, Johnny has his own office, which he keeps fairly sparse: a table, a couple of chairs, a file cabinet, and a typewriter desk. On the walls, he tacks up posters with sayings like JOBS AND EQUALITY, IN UNITY THERE IS STRENGTH, and a photo of Cesar Chavez and Dolores Huerta from the United Farm Workers union. He has the UFW's black-and-red eagle flag with those of Mexico and the United States on the wall behind his desk.

A nicely framed photo of Aracely, Joaquin, and Azucena graces his desktop; a photo of Harley and Johnny, smiling at a CLOC picnic event, and an old one of Severo stand nearby.

One day, Johnny's dialing a number on the phone when he spots a familiar face in the doorway, although much older and worn. It's Al Simmons.

"Holy smoke, man, how you been, old friend?" Johnny asks, putting the phone down.

Al walks in slowly, thinner than he ever was. "I'm diabetic—got it real bad, but I just had to come by and say hey," he says with some effort. "I want to congratulate you for taking over this joint. And . . . I want to apologize."

"Stop right there, Al," Johnny says, getting up to shake Al's hand. "No apologies, please. We were young; we made a lot of mistakes, especially me. I'm just glad to know you're still around and that you came by. I hope you stay well, brother. As for me, I'll do my best to represent everyone at the mill."

"I know you will, Johnny," Al says. "I trust you, man. You were always a good brother. I can't stay long—got a doctor's appointment. Just wanted to bring in a ghost from the past to haunt you for a little bit. Remember, whatever happens, stay cool."

With that, Al takes his time walking out the office and the local hall.

Johnny, although glad to see Al, feels bad. Al isn't long for this world, he realizes. Despite their past conflicts, Johnny has learned a lot from him. In a few weeks, Johnny gets the news: Al succumbs to kidney failure. The local union gathers a small fund to help the family with funeral and other expenses. It's the least he can do for a fighter, a black man, a real man.

Meanwhile, the company has its hands full during those two years. Grievances are filed against all kinds of unilateral and unreasonable work requests, discrimination allegations, docked pay, arbitrary days off, forced overtime, and such. Emmett Taylor—foreman on the oil crew—is cited for discrimination by Carla and others, who are then able to move into the repair crews soon after Johnny takes office. Mr. Taylor has to walk carefully after that, not having his cronies in the union to protect him.

The union also takes Lane Peterson to court for violating California's Clean Air Act. Peterson and the company are found guilty and liable. The plant is fined tens of thousands of dollars, and periodic inspections are instituted to keep the bag house in full operation. Peterson eventually resigns, replaced by a mealymouth headquarters guy named Daryl Sherman. Sherman pretty much doesn't know how to circumvent the local union the way Peterson had done.

Peterson, however, is not entirely out of the picture. After Dent's death, someone calls the Los Angeles County Sheriff's Office about Dent's possible participation in Harley Cantrell's murder. That person never reveals who he is or how he knows what he knows. Up to that point, Harley's killing had never been solved. Police go into Dent's sordid apartment in an all-white section of Downey. They find connections between Peterson and Dent, including the solicitation of a hit man, whose name Peterson had provided. Evidence includes notes, audiotapes, guns, and drawn plans on where and how the murder would take place—Dent took sick pleasure in archiving these incriminating items, possibly also to keep Peterson at bay in case he had any notions of betraying Dent.

Peterson is arrested, and after a lengthy trial, a judge and jury convict him and an area hit man for Harley's death based on the secret tapings and notes that Dent had kept; Peterson is sent up to San Quentin for twenty years to life as an accomplice to murder.

The local union sends strong-willed delegates to the USWA International gatherings to fight for jobs, benefits, better pay, and a voice in the international union organization. Local 1750 gains a reputation as a leader among the various union locals facing similar closings and job losses.

But in two years, it's over. With all the rumors, threats, and more rumors, Nazareth Steel Corporation finally declares the closing of its steel-production facility in Los Angeles.

No preparation could truly prepare for the impact of such a decision.

In fact, the company had been slowly removing thousands of workers from the plant over the years—from its peak of twelve thousand during World War II to the last few years when only two thousand labored there.

Soon after the closing announcement, everyone is pink-slipped except for skeleton crews on all the craft units and cleanup teams of laborers that spend another year tearing down the machines, furnace, forges, shears, hotbeds, dies, cranes, scrap yard, and hearths.

It doesn't seem possible, but the expansive, relentless steel city of Nazareth will soon be nothing but dirt and a few leftover fences, structures, and machines. Yet Local 1750 continues functioning for a time after the official closing date of the mill.

Johnny, Tony, and the others create a community center out of the hall, one of the most innovative of its kind. The closing has devastated thousands of families, particularly the Mexican families in the Maywood–Huntington Park–Florence areas. The local union establishes a food bank, one of the largest in the country, feeding some six thousand to ten thousand families a week, including those from other nearby industries that also closed down.

People line up early every Wednesday, mostly women, some with small children, embarrassed at times since these are proud people who'll starve before they'll accept any handouts, but here they are—broken, uncertain, yammering in Spanish, and also a few of the men, the hardened steel men, who have no families or who have families that left them, standing there as well, quietly ashamed but nonetheless gathered, to receive food, to share some gossip, to reconnect, to see if reports of work may come their way.

Around that time, the big plants in tires, steel, auto, meatpacking, weapons production, and aerospace also begin shutting down or are drastically reduced in size throughout the county. Los Angeles, the country's second-largest industrial center—after Chicago—becomes mostly home to small garment sweatshops, bucket shops, fabrication shops, and warehouses. The harbor, the largest on the Pacific Rim and second only to New York Harbor in the United States, loses its mighty canneries and much of its shipyards and container business.

All in all, basic steel loses 350,000 jobs in the 1980s, a large chunk of the more than eight million industrial jobs that disappear nationally in that decade.

Under Johnny's leadership, the local sets up counseling and alcoholics' recovery groups—area health agencies claim a 25 percent rise in alcoholism and at least ten suicides the first year of the plant's demise.

Johnny's aware of the devastation to those who depended on the mill, on those "for life" jobs. These are people who have been used to being secure, to buying homes and getting cars. Sure, they may have accumulated massive debts, and were more likely to drink too much and abuse too much, but they have never been as unhinged as they became when the work stopped.

There were a few smart ones. Johnny knows of a mill operator named Nathan Bueno who used the money he made at the mill to buy a number of apartment complexes. When the plant closed, he had income from the rents and even had enough money to invest in other property. He actually became a major player in local development, partly responsible for building shopping malls, parking lots, warehouses, when other business interests came in to replace many of the empty plants.

But Johnny knew few Buenos coming out of the mill.

The majority were like Wilfredo Lopez, a labor-crew guy and close friend to Procopio. He had four wives and seventeen kids to take care of. He liked to drink and gamble. When the plant closed, he had nothing left to show for the thirty years he worked there.

Wilfredo did have a girlfriend—Johnny remembers meeting her at his parents' house when Wilfredo stopped by for a visit. Her name was Ana, and she was around fifty years old, full of life and very close to her man. But after the plant closed, Wilfredo came home from looking for work one day and found Ana dead in their bedroom—she had shot herself in the head. He'd been going to the unemployment office for weeks to find what kind of work they *might* have for an old man with only labor skills to speak of. There just didn't seem to be any jobs or training for a sixty-year-old ex-steelworker.

One of the things the international union negotiated with the steel companies was educational and job retraining programs. This also included arts funding, which Johnny uses to do theater and poetry workshops so that the laid-off men and women of the mill could express themselves with the help of local actors and writers. Soon afterward, a tour of a play made with the poems and prose from the pens of the steelworkers themselves receives national attention.

For a time, Aracely and Johnny remain pillars of the community; even politicians call them, TV and other media interview them, and their names appear in newspapers and magazines.

But like most such recognition, this is short-lived.

In a few months, the United Steelworkers of America eventually shuts down the local union, closes the hall, and sells the building; it's later torn down to build an apartment complex.

Soon after the plant's official closing, millwrights, other craft workers, and laborers who have elected not to retire or get unemployment benefits—and who have company seniority—stay to tear the mill apart. After removing his things from the union offices, Johnny goes to the mill and signs up for one of the dismantling crews. It's for days only, but the work is arduous, painful, sad.

One day, Johnny's standing on an overhead crane that is about to be taken apart. The mill is silent—the electric furnaces are cold; one of the furnaces even has tons of dust-covered scrap metal still in its mouth. No more thunderous roars. No more furnaces being tapped. No more ladles pouring molten steel into ingot molds. No more sulfurous heats that smoked up the whole building so you couldn't see a few inches in front of you.

Johnny looks out beyond the furnace building, where he can see several buildings standing quiet, while others are in their first stages of dismantling.

Johnny adjusts his hat and safety glasses while watching welders below cut through pilings, corrugated steel, and beams. Johnny thinks about the years he gave to the mill—the many more that his brothers and father had used up. How the mill was supposed to save them all— now here he is, helping tear it down.

He'll never see another generation of Salcidos in the mill.

As it is, Johnny can hardly imagine a future—the world has changed so fast. What will people like him do? He gazes over the scene, his heart aching, his mind racing, feeling like there's no more footing, no more bracing, no more handrails as his life begins to career into the nether spaces of unemployment, underemployment, and different kinds of employment. Something hollow opens up inside of him, an emptiness, void of meaning—only Aracely, his children, and the political work in which he has embroiled himself give him reasons to go on. Only the good things.

Finally, after a year, the place is gone; the plant removed, almost miraculously, from the several blocks of land on Slauson Avenue it once occupied.

The bars, the brick hotels with hourly rates, and worn shanties and housing complexes of mill workers on Slauson Avenue are also bull-dozed, replaced by strip malls, gas stations, small shops, and two-level apartment structures.

Johnny and Aracely become quite the average couple after that. The calls and interviews and invites to special luncheons stop coming. Johnny eventually obtains work in refineries and chemical plants as a maintenance mechanic and sporadically in construction as a mill-wright.

After a few years, they buy a two-story house in Sylmar, at the very northern end of L.A. City. Procopio and Eladia move into a small guesthouse in the back. Bune and Rafas find homes on the other side of the mountains in the San Gabriel Valley. Junior, unfortunately, ends up in the streets of South L.A., abandoning his family, still drinking his life away.

One day, police find Junior dead, his liver destroyed, in an alley not far from the home he grew up in.

Still, whatever happens after Nazareth's closing, nothing in their lives or in their children's lives can compare with the years Johnny and Aracely had known when Nazareth was at its peak, when the electric furnaces rumbled day and night and the rolling mills and forges roared in frenzied intonations; when the zinc tanks galvanized pipes and the spinning machines cranked out miles of wire rope; when all shifts rolled into one another, and the men and women in hard hats and dirty work gear strolled the steel yards and furnace and mill floors; when foremen sent out signals with their hands be-cause they couldn't be heard amid the noise; when production goals were posted on huge plywood signs, and safety messages kept remind-ing the mill hands *they* were responsible for losing body parts or their lives; and when the terrible fate and great fortune of being a steel-worker was sloughed off in the bars, card clubs, prostitutes, and racing businesses.

Every bridge, skyscraper, ship, tank, car, and public art sculpture with steel in it has the stories, songs, blood, hopes, tears, human limbs at times, of the generations that labored in those mills. In the end, more than steel had been created: communities, families, pathologies, triumphs, defeats, great loves, great divorces, values, but most of all character—a character steeled in heat that few people or epochs will truly match, ever again.

Part III

AZUCENA'S FINALE

9

DYING AS SWEET AS THE SUN'S BREATH

Órale, *putos*, that's our car," Pancho declares to a group of Spanish-speaking mechanics at a messy auto shop next to a row of taquerías, hair salons, hardware stores, and bars along a stretch of Pacoima that looks more like a main drag in Tijuana, Mexico, the chaos of signs piled on signs, having no apparent order to them.

"I don't care how you got it, it belongs to my friend here and we want it back."

Let me back up a little. I bought a ten-year-old Honda that broke down about a week after I paid for it. After a friend of a friend, Suzi, tells me about some mechanics she knows, she takes the car, promising to get it fixed, and then nothing, we never hear back from her. I had a hard time getting Suzi to tell me where she took the car. We almost go to blows before she finally coughs up the truth. I inform Pancho and he tells me, "Let's go get it."

Just like that.

Oh yeah—I'm Chena. My real name's Azucena Salcido. I'm thirty and not bad looking; in fact, I think I'm fine—with dark skin, perhaps a little too hefty, but in a good way, *ya sabes*. Voluptuous, as they say. My son's name is Jandro, short for Alejandro. He's twelve. We live in the northeast San Fernando Valley—the "Mexican" side of the Valley, where Pacoima happens to be.

Pancho is . . . well, Pancho's Pancho, *mi mero mero*, my "main squeeze," as they say.

We drive up and down Van Nuys Boulevard, looking for the shop. After several turns around the block, I spot the dusty green Honda parked end to end with some other scrappers in a mechanic shop's lot. We get out and push ourselves into the place. Several *paisas* are standing around, drinking beer, with car parts and body frames cluttered around them. I ask about my car, but nobody wants to say anything. A big Mexicano, with a large potbelly, walks into the shop from a tiny office in back and says to us in Spanish that he won't turn the car over— he'll only give it to the person, Suzi we presume, who brought it in. He's supposedly fixed whatever was wrong with it. I brought my registration and license to let him know it's my car. He still won't budge.

"Fuck you—give us the car or I'm going to beat the shit out of you," Pancho finally cuts in. The other *paisas* put down their cans of beer and surround Pancho. I stand next to him, realizing we're about to get our *pompis* kicked.

Pancho's not dumb, but he is on the hot-to-trot side of things. Impulsive, they call it. You push his buttons, and he's gone. Sometimes I use it to my advantage. He can never win an argument with me because I know how to push all the right buttons—and I've got him where I want him. Now he's revved up again, and I have to figure out how to save our butts.

Pancho's not a *caga palo* or anything. He's an artist and really quite sensitive to what's going on around him. He's thin, all elbows and joints, energetic and creative; he even wears a ponytail, although to me this seems old-fashioned. He eventually wants to be in the movies— some kind of Hollywood producer or director or whatever you call those guys. I met him at a local café where I work—taking orders, making coffee, cleaning up the place, and running the register. It's not even decent pay—and I'm daydreaming half the time—but I have my responsibilities and I come through. I have what attribute tests label "leadership qualities." I was born an Aries—with a mouth to back it up.

"Miren, por favor—ahorita regresamos con la persona que entregó este carro; van a ver que verdaderamente es mío," I say to the men in the best Spanish I can muster.

The Mexican with the potbelly and Pancho are eye-boxing, but I see they're not moving toward each other. The other guys also stay put. Good, I think to myself. I continue to talk, a mixture of Spanish and English. "We'll straighten this out," I say. "Just a misunderstanding. No need for problems. *Nada más queremos lo que es mío*, I just want what's mine. We'll come back"—that kind of thing.

We walk backward as we leave the shop. As we enter Pancho's ride, he's still raging.

"Man, I had that motherfucker; why'd you pull that shit about coming back?"

"Hey, tough guy, if you didn't get that we were about to be part of the decor in that place, we were in worse trouble than I thought," I tell him. "I'd rather buy us some time. I'm thinking we can return tonight and steal back the car. It's parked outside with the other cars, right? I have an extra key somewhere. I'm not messing with Suzi or anybody else. Let's just rip it off tonight."

Pancho and I return to the shop later that night. It's one of those things that you get obsessed about. I want my car, no matter what. I ain't going to die for it, but I'm going to find a way to get it. The car, we find, is not parked outside with the others. We walk up to the shop and spot a window near the entrance. We peek inside. Sure enough, there's the car, parked next to some mobile tool chests.

"Damn, those *chuntarros* brought the car in—now what?" Pancho exclaims.

"Okay . . ." I'm thinking here. "You know what—let's just break into this place, get that motherfucker, and drive it out. It's drivable, I assume, since they got it in."

"There's a lot of question marks there, Chena," Pancho says. "Maybe they pushed the car inside. Maybe they got some guys guarding it—they could be in the back office somewhere. Maybe they got guns now. You're taking too many chances, *preciosa*."

I think Pancho likes it when I get outlaw on him. I walk back to Pancho's car and grab a bumper jack from the backseat, lifting it.

"I'm getting my car."

We break the lock on the door—it's an outside Master lock. There's no alarm in the place. We crouch and slowly walk toward the car. It's dark but a streetlamp just outside the shop is giving us some light. I walk around to the car's driver's side and try my other key. The car door opens and I get inside. I whisper to Pancho—more like a loud whisper—to go to the other side. Pancho thinks he can get the garage door open. He's trying to find the chain that lifts the door. We hear some noise from the back room. A couple of shadows appear at the doorway. I start the car up and yell out to Pancho to get in. He looks around, sees someone, and runs to the passenger side. There's no time to get the garage door open. Two of them come at us. I put the car in gear and drive. The wooden garage door splinters to pieces as I bust through. I hear gunshots—the motherfuckers are shooting at us! I keep driving. I find myself yelling for no real reason. As I speed down the street, I realize that Pancho isn't saying anything.

"*Qué pasa*, killer? Cat got your tongue?" I say jokingly.

"I'm shot, baby," he finally throws in, a strain in his voice.

I look at him and see the blood, mixed through the lengths of his long brown hair. *Hijo de su* . . . I'm suddenly scared and going fucking nuts. I drive crazy trying to get to the closest hospital.

"Go to the county hospital in Sylmar," Pancho suggests, a pained expression on his face.

I blink at his words. Sylmar County is where my dad, Johnny, is getting radiation treatments; it's the hospital where people around here without health insurance go. It's toward this hospital that I turn.

Pancho's closing his eyes, and I'm thinking he's dying. *Fuck!* I mouth with my lips in silence. It seems like forever, but I end up in the emergency room and take Pancho through its double doors.

I wait for a while and finally get the word: Pancho's only been grazed in the head—although there was blood everywhere. He's gonna be fine. The police come by, since the hospital has to report any shootings. We make up some bullshit story—that we're driving down Van Nuys Boulevard, minding our own business, when shots are fired and Pancho gets hit. The police already had a report of a car being taken from a mechanic's shop in the area. They ask if we know anything about it. Pancho and I look at each other and shake our heads. The Mexicans aren't going to come forward. They don't tell the police what the car looks like or about us. I figure they don't have their papers and don't want any trouble. In the end, there isn't much to it. The police say they'll contact us in a few days, for us not to leave town—something like that.

Now I have two people to see at the hospital—my dad on one floor and Pancho on another.

My mom, Aracely, gets wind of what's happened and she lays into me when I see her in Pancho's hospital room. I don't lie to my mom; I even tell her how we fool the police. I love her, but when she's mad she really lets me have it.

"What were you thinking, *m'ija*?" she asks. "Why would you do something stupid like that?"

"I know, Ma, it was stupid. I just really need this car. I can't get to work or school without it. The thing is those guys in the shop stole it from *me*. I think they were planning on moving it somewhere else the next day. We had to try to get it that night. I'm sorry about the mess this has caused."

"You could've gotten Pancho killed," she continues. "Next time, he won't be so lucky."

We don't tell Johnny about the shooting. He's not in good shape—he's on the losing end of a battle with cancer. What happened with the car has a lot to do with me being desperate, confused, and just raging. I'm not good at these things. I'm one of those road fiends who curse out other drivers and give them the finger. Not a good thing to do in L.A. I realize I wasn't just hurting myself but Pancho, too, who I care about. The fact that he stuck by me really gets to me. There are times when I question our relationship. Sometimes I don't want to have him around all the time—he's pushy and jealous. But he's also there when I need him. I have to remember that.

The foothills of the San Gabriel Mountains have never looked as green and inviting as they do this morning, just outside the window of our Sylmar home, where my father, a mountain of a man, is asleep.

I stare at the mountains often, mostly smudged in haze from L.A.'s smog. There are times these humps of trees and stone seem to disappear—making it as if everything around us in the San Fernando Valley is flat. It's not. We really have some heavenly landscape here: fantastic textures, contours; the most amazing aromas, of fruits and flowers, and a slew of birdsongs and crows wailing. Perhaps what clouds my vision is the flatness of our lives, our routines, the predictable shapes of our houses and strip malls. Sometimes I feel each of us is a ship in a bottle, enclosed in glass, cut off, confined, but somehow decorative. It's sick.

Sylmar is in a section of the city so distant from downtown L.A. that people here don't even consider themselves part of the city. Here's where my dad will most likely take his last breath. And I think to myself: Does where a man dies mark his life as a whole?

I hope not.

My father Johnny's life is not the barely audible tones of Sylmar's well-kept single-family homes, of ranches turned into smaller housing units or the outlying barrio dwellings with its vendors on messy dirt curbsides selling *elote, frutas, y tesjuino*. It's not about the undocumented day laborers who gather on Foothill and Maclay soliciting work in house repairs, ditch digging, roofing, and carpentry to anyone who needs them—or the wide-hipped women and their children shopping at Sam's Warehouse and the ninety-eight-cent stores.

It's not even about our favorite take-out place—El Pollo Loco.

Chale. My father carries the raunch and *gritos* of South L.A., el barrio Florencia to be exact, of the tire plants, rolling mills, bucket shops, and foundries that once cut a sizable swath down the Alameda Street corridor from north of downtown to the harbor.

Johnny knew the last days of smoke and dust these plants and mills poured across those graveled streets; he was around when the big plants closed shop in the 1980s—places like American Bridge, the American and National Can companies, Alcoa Aluminum, National Lead, GM and Ford auto plants, Goodyear, Bridgestone, and Firestone tire companies, and the major meatpacking houses. Most of all, he knew Nazareth Steel, where he worked for many years, including the time when my older brother, Joaquin, and I were born.

He may have left those streets and factories some time ago, but that will always be what his life is about—long after he's gone.

Although he doesn't look it, Johnny Salcido is only fifty-four years old. The way I see it, he shouldn't be dying. He's too young. But he's worked in those highly toxic places—as a millwright, maintenance mechanic, and pipe fitter. Who knows what chemicals *y otras cagadas* have scarred his lungs. He smoked, too, as did most of his generation.

I'm convinced the most damaging junk inside my father's system came from the "Big Mill." The Nazareth Steel Corporation was a rambling multiacre facility that once took up several blocks in the town of Maywood. At one time it had thousands of employees. Its electric furnaces rumbled day and night with rows of forged red ingots that were so hot, they forced you to run when you passed in front of the plant—even from across the avenue—or your skin would burn.

That's what I remember about Nazareth.

When I was seven years old, my dad took Joaquin and me to the chain-link fence that separated us from the big open corrugated tin building where the furnaces were. He showed us a massive ladle being tipped over by an overhead crane, spilling its red-orange lavalike contents onto what Dad called "ingot cars."

This is what hell must be like, I remember thinking to myself.

"That's melted steel being poured into those rail cars, *m'ijos*," my dad declared. "We've been in this mill since your grandfather. You'll work here and perhaps your children will, too. It's a mean, hot, dangerous place. But this is what feeds you."

I learned a lot about steel from my dad. How laborers swept and shoveled some really awful materials; how melters and furnace operators rushed about the furnace floor; how mill hands manipulated the forges and rolling mills; how equipment operators, warehouse workers, and skilled craft workers, including bricklayers, electricians, and mechanics, kept everything running.

But it wasn't entirely true what Johnny said. I never ended up working there. Neither did Joaquin—although it was supposed to be our lot in life. We were both expected to be steelworkers—like my dad, like my four uncles, like my grandfather. Although I was born a girl, by the time I grew up, women were being hired into the labor and craft crews. Dad said many of the old mill men hated this, but I think this was "right on," as my mom always said.

Still, there've been a lot of changes since the time my dad brought Joaquin and me to peer into that universe of smokestacks, blaring whistles, rumbling cranes, explosive furnaces on the other side of a metal fence.

The biggest change is that the mill doesn't exist anymore. It's completely gone. If you went back to the same place where we stood with my dad, you'd hardly know a steel mill once flourished there. Rows of pastel-colored warehouses with semis line most of the old streets—and a shopping mall takes up the west end where the old wire mill used to be.

When that mill died, it's like a good part of us died as well.

That's why I've always felt like I'm floating in the world. Even now, as a single mom, stuck in Sylmar, working various jobs, taking classes at Mission College, I'm trying to find my place somewhere. I have one foot on one side of the border, another foot on the other side, and both feet in no borders. We're also at the bottom of the social heap—something I'm working hard to change for Jandro and me. Like all true Chicanas with our borderless souls and endless migrations, I've had to anchor myself in indigenous traditions, healing, and art.

Anyway, my dad's going fast. My mother stays near him as much as she can—now she's asleep in a sofa chair in the living room, gray hairs sticking out of the *chongo*, bun, on the back of her head and along the sides of her face. She's got crow's-feet around her eyes and wrinkles around her mouth. She's still beautiful, at fifty-two, still the mother I only wish I could be.

There's a lot I don't know about Mom and Dad. They're physically strong, bighearted, filled with a deep love. Their generation of Chicanos was so active, both at home and in our communities. They were different from the folks I grew up with. What I do know is they were the center of our lives, the center of the world around us. Everybody knew Johnny and Aracely Salcido. They had socials on weekends. They went to union meetings, community meetings, church meetings, radical political meetings—always a "meeten," as my dad used to say.

My grandfather Procopio—we call him Lito—pretty much stays to himself, especially since my grandmother Eladia, otherwise known as Lita, died almost five years ago of an aneurysm—an enlarged artery in the brain. The one good thing is she died quickly.

Lito doesn't say much, but you can see what the thirty-five years of working at Nazareth Steel did to him. His face is permanently red-brown; smoke and oil seem to be caked into his creases. He's eighty—still kicking. We often wonder how. But he's still hanging on like a single cobweb from the ceiling of an ancient attic.

His son, my dad, Johnny, however, just hovers between life and death—a little closer to death than we'd all like. Lito mostly sits on the front porch of our home waiting for word of Johnny's condition. He lost another son in the mill, my *tío* Severo. Somewhere, family stories say, he had a daughter, whose name I now have, who died when she was two years old. His other sons—former steelworkers—are doing okay. All except for Junior. He became an alcoholic and eventually wasn't any good to anyone; he died, having abused his system far too much.

But his greatest loss is Lita, his companion of more than fifty years.

Now my grandfather watches the world rush past him, fast cars, fast TV, fast kids, *una bola de nietos*, as he lingers, waiting for God to reach out and finally take him.

I know for Lito that would be the sweetest breath of the sun.

"You have to understand, Johnny's done so much for me. He was a real dad . . . caring, hardworking, always there," I tell Pancho after he nags as to why I spend more time with my father than I do with him.

"He won't be around long, Pancho," I continue, looking at my fingernails, which could use some heavy-duty manicuring. "Give me time with my dad, all right? When your dad goes, you'll go through the same thing . . . okay, okay, forget about your rotten *hijo de puta* dad," I add, momentarily hating myself for comparing my dad to his. "My dad's not that way. If you care about me you'll give me this space. We'll see each other soon enough. Jandro is already asking about you. We'll have our good times again. *No te preocupes, mi chulo. Te espero, como siempre.* Don't worry, cutie, I'll always be here for you. Thanks."

With this I hang up the phone.

The last few endearments are to get him off my back. He likes it when I talk in Spanish-tongued love tones. Pancho's a good man. Not the love of my life but the man in my life, for the moment anyway. He gets possessive—like he needs my *pinche* attention all the time. But he's good to me and my son, Jandro. That boy's a handful, so my hat's off to any man who can get Jandro to sit down and listen the way Pancho seems to get him to do.

As for me, well, I was born to talk. *Una hocicona*—bigmouth, if you will. Aracely used to complain about how when I was a kid I talked so much I wouldn't let anyone else get a word in. For a while, I was taken care of by a Mexican lady down the street from our Florencia apartment; this woman had to sit me down in another room with a small TV so I wouldn't bother the smaller kids with all my chatter.

I think her name was Lorinda—a nice person, with a deep brown skin tone, print dresses, and salsa breath. She was the barrio version of day care—some *vieja* from the old country who knew a thing or two about kids and everybody in the neighborhood used her to watch theirs; she could be psychotic, for all anybody knew. Lorinda sure was a big help for all the working families in our barrio, though. Every kid on the block at one point or another passed through her doors. We all did time.

I was an average student in elementary school. I got by using my "gift of gab." Some teachers liked this enough to help me out; others wanted to shut me up so bad they put me in permanent "time-out." But this only got me talking more.

Aracely used to work on the assembly lines until just before my brother Joaquin and I were born; she quit everything to be at home—until she got busy with politics and meetings and things. My mother used Lorinda as though she had a full-time job, but it was really because she was so active in our community.

Johnny brought the money in—only, as I understand it, in the beginning he spent most of it before it ever got to the house. In those early days of the mill, if you listen to Aracely tell it, Johnny liked to gamble, to drink, to hustle pool games, and perhaps a lot of other things he shouldn't have been doing. But the *cuento* is that Johnny got over all that when he became a rebel in the union, helping the guys in the plant. He made a change when he began to think of other people. He even stopped drinking, if you can believe that.

Right now, as my dad prepares to leave us, my own prospects seem hazy. When we were kids, no one cared about anything other than working at home, raising kids, or working on one of the assembly lines. Although I was a discipline problem as a child, I was smart, always have been. But I also looked for something with teeth in it, for life to be more like a vacuum cleaner, something that would suck me up into all kinds of adventures, plans, risks. The reality of my prospects, then, seemed downright deadening to me—I did not look forward to a life filled with such limited choices.

What keeps me smiling is music. To sing—now that's my passion. That's what I want to do all the time. As a kid, I used to drive Johnny and Aracely crazy with my singing acts. But they tolerated it, supported it even. They spent hours laughing, watching me enact an En Vogue song or Ana Gabriel—I could do English or Spanish. I still sit in on bands here and there. I practice my singing at home whenever I can. Now I'm into Mary J. Blige and Beyoncé. But I remember the songs of the eighties I grew up on: Anita Baker, Whitney Houston, or Sade. I try to throw in some of these dusties along with the newer hits. If the place lets me, I also let out a *grito* and belt out a *ranchera* or two.

Joaquin, my brother, who's two years older than me, is another story. Right now he's at Corcoran prison. He drifted through life until he found an anchor in being a criminal. It's easy to do in Florencia. For a lot of young men—and don't get me wrong, many women as well—this was the only life with bite they could find. The problem is they often had to risk jail time, drug use, sexual diseases, and even death just to obtain some deep connection in this world.

Joaquin kind of followed in my dad's footsteps. According to fam-

ily legend, Johnny was a hell-raiser as a teenager. He had been part of
Florencia Trece; this made us a two-generation barrio gang family.
Johnny also went to juvenile hall and eventually a YA prison.

It was the steel mill and—at least as Aracely tells it—his life with
my mom and us children that saved Johnny from going off the deep
end. He let go all that craziness to jump into another kind of craziness—*la vida loca* to *la vida soca* (*soca* being a "put-down," a "wasted
time," a "bad trip"), working in the steel mill. He knew it, too, which is
why after all he'd done and seen in the mill, he had nothing but thanks
for being there.

The mill became his world, his purpose, his place in the universe.
The mill nurtured him like it was a massive womb, and protected him,
too, like he was a baby refusing to come out.

I've kind of shimmied from job to job, relationship to relationship,
not finding anything solid. A lot of things keep me going, but whenever I get a chance to sing at the clubs in Hollywood or the college
bars, I take it. It brings me the greatest joy in a life where weary smiles
are as good as it gets.

"Hey, Chena, whatever happened to the car?" Pancho asks while leaning back against the sofa, the TV in front of him blaring.

"It ran a couple of days and then petered out," I tell him. "I had to
abandon it—the car was going to be more trouble than it was worth."

"Man, you could have sold that damn thing for parts. That's what
those Mexicans wanted. That's why they didn't want to give it to us."

"Listen, just forget about that car. It's gone. *Punto y zas.*"

"You mean I got a dent on my head for a car we don't even have
anymore?"

"Yeah, something like that . . . listen, don't complain. You're lucky
to be alive. If I were you, I'd count my blessings."

I can tell from Pancho's face that he thinks I have a point.

I've had to really assess what I'm doing and where I'm going since
Pancho almost got shot in the head. I realize my stubbornness and ego
had gotten us into this trouble. It grates on me that those *paisas* took

my car the way they did. But it would have served a more useful purpose in their hands than after what happened to it after we drove it out of that garage.

Pancho is recovering well. No bullet or bullet fragments penetrated his brain. We worried about the police for a while, but they eventually stopped hounding us. I end up taking Pancho home from the hospital to my upstairs room in my parents' house.

I feel I owe Pancho something, maybe even a little love.

"Chena, how's your father?" my mother asks from the sofa chair she's been sleeping in. Although she's now awake, there's not much stirring—her eyes are still shut, and there's only a flutter of eyelids and a few words.

"*Está durmiendo*—he's been sleeping this whole time," I answer.

"*Déjalo*, let him be, he's suffered enough. God knows he needs to sleep a long time until he can finally get some real peace."

Lately, Dad's been having a hard time moving around. We're all resigned to his death—not that it wouldn't hurt us to see him go. But the tumors have turned him into a mutant; a creature unfamiliar to us; bloated, twisted, yet inside we know it's him. I hate to see him this way. I'd rather he peacefully passed on than to see those tumors continuing to sprout on his neck, back, arms, and everywhere else.

My mother loves him, but she's also sensible about things, always has been. My dad and mom balanced each other; they were like two sturdy trees with intertwined branches and roots. My dad was funny, angry, active, romantic; my mom just stood *recta*, straight and strong, next to him, dependable but not like those other Mexican women who serve their husbands and kids like slaves. My mom was nobody's slave. In fact, to me my parents are remarkable; they were the most progressive and visionary people I ever knew. I've always felt lucky to have them as parents.

That's why I'm thinking about them so much. Because they've seen things, done things, lived things that I know future generations will never see or live again. I feel like I'm the last of their kind, the last to understand their reality, their struggle, for the generations into the future who will look at this age of industry and its impact as quaint, interesting, and, perhaps, even incomprehensible.

Yet somebody has to remember. Especially for those people who are no longer tied to that complex industrial world. Of course, you still have rulers of industry who believe they can dictate our lives, although their lifeblood—the blood profits off the sweat of people like Lito and my father—will no longer feed them, vampirelike, in their continuous quest for immortality. Like my dad, they're bloated with tumors. Unlike my dad, their tumors are on their souls.

As I watch Johnny resting, bald head with spotty hair from all of the radiation he's been undergoing, I realize how valuable his life has been. I *have* to remember. Otherwise he'd die in vain—otherwise he'd be just another forgotten peon or nameless worker. My thoughts run with words that I heard my parents use. I knew the concept of the *proletariat* before I ever knew a decent nursery rhyme.

And I think of my poor Pancho, with grazed head and bruised ego.

He reminds me that I also have to remember what I've been through. It may not be pretty, but that's how I may find something worthwhile in all this.

Where to start? Ah, I know—it's best to start with love.

10

LIKE LOVE

Sometimes you place your heart in a box, wrap it up with a perfumed hand in silk ribbons with glitter on the edges, then hold it delicately on your lap. I've seen girls like this— waiting for this box to be gingerly opened by an attractively quiet man who would know how to unfurl the ribbons, ever so gently, lift up the top, and linger on the glowing object inside with loving awe.

I almost puke at the thought of it.

Love to me is a drunkard hanging on to a lamppost in the early-morning dark. It is chaos and hangovers, sweat and sweet pain, yelling and slammed down phone receivers. That's all I know about love. That *telenovela*, woe-is-me, *arráncame el corazón* crap doesn't work for me.

It's odd since my parents are loving and kind to each other. They're not mean or abusive. I didn't get my ideas about love from them. Aracely respects Johnny. And Johnny never even yells at Aracely. The fact is they never really yell at Joaquin or me either. They are stern, sure, letting us know where things stand. It's always clear what they expect of our behavior. It never occurs to me to cross them.

I had no problem coming home and doing whatever homework I had to do and then going to my room and playing with my dolls or games I made up from painted cardboard boxes and other stuff I saved from the trash. I didn't really play with ready-made toys and dollhouses. I liked getting things from the backyard or the kitchen and creating my own toys and play houses. Aracely encouraged me. Johnny patted me on the head. It was great being with them. I felt safe, except for the times

Joaquin picked on me, which he did all the time. But I learned to stand up to my brother. I cried a lot when I was smaller, but Aracely or Johnny wouldn't really do anything. They'd tell Joaquin to stop, but as soon as they turned around, he'd be at it again. So in time, I would stomp around and yell and he would roll his eyes and leave, calling me names on the way out. I'm sure he wished I was a younger brother.

Overall, though, I was happy at home. I was happy with myself. Like I say, I did well in school. Teachers liked me because I would give the right answers all the time. I loved the attention. There was nothing better than raising my hand and reciting the right answer. I didn't even care how the other students felt; I mean, the ones who didn't have the answers. They probably hated my guts. But that was okay with me. I wanted the teacher's approval. I wanted to be recognized. I wanted to be the one that knew everything.

All this changed when I turned twelve. Something happens to a girl when her body changes and you feel like a monster, like an alien has taken over, like your heart and mind belong somewhere else. I grew big in all areas. I wasn't fat, but big; I grew breasts like you wouldn't believe. My hips and thighs widened. There were curves on me everywhere. Other girls still had their stick-figure bodies, their little-girl bodies that much later flared up with breasts and pubic hair. I, on the other hand, became King Kong. Thick hair blossomed down there. My periods came on hard and strong. I smelled like menstrual blood for days. Boys could smell it because they'd say "P.U." to me when I first started to bleed. I didn't know much about what to do at first. Boys, what the hell did they know anyway? Boys are boys far longer than girls are girls. If other girls were barely developing when I started to sprout, boys were in the Jurassic age.

So when I first showed up to seventh grade, I was the monster kid, a hybrid woman/girl. My mother worried about me. Dad never said anything, but sometimes I'd hear them whispering about me in the kitchen. Aracely showed me what to do about my periods. She'd have my grandmother heat up some *estafiate* tea, a Mexican herb good for just about anything. She'd put hot towels on my stomach for the cramps. And then she'd put this diaperlike thing on me to catch the blood.

Seventh grade was a living hell. The boys my age laughed at my breasts, at my butt, at my womanhood. The other girls were mostly jealous—walking away from me, staring me up and down, a couple of times picking fights. I got stares from the male teachers that made me feel uncomfortable. I'd see them looking between my legs when I sat down on my chair during class. They'd get close to me when they walked over to see how I was doing with my work. I even spied them staring at my behind as I walked past. I felt grossed out. Men smell different when they are turned on. It's disgusting to me; well, at least it was then. Women teachers were also affected, but in a different way. They stopped calling on me—I guess to prevent me from getting any more attention than what I was already getting. They hardly spoke to me. I got the sense they shook their heads in disapproval behind my back.

I was what they called "big-boned." Lots of strong woman muscle—shapely and hard. I also got horny as hell. This happened during and after my periods when the cramping began to fade. I seemed to swell down there. I sat in class and squeezed my thighs, trying to rub them in my seat so that it pushed up against my privates. I'd get these urges to rub it often. At home, it was easy. I'd rub myself in the bathroom, before my bath, or at night, with the blankets over me and my hands between my legs. It felt so good to come. I felt like I was falling out of my skin when it happened.

Sometimes, I rubbed myself in school, when I didn't think anyone was watching. I did this mostly in the girls' restroom. I didn't want anyone around so I could make all the noises I wanted. But this was hard—some girls at that age practically lived in bathrooms. It was a big chance on my part, but I never got caught. I wasn't stupid about it. It just felt good to rub myself whenever I could.

By that time, Joaquin started hanging out with older guys and getting into trouble. His partners were Florencia Trece guys, with plenty of muscles and mustaches. They had short hair or no hair at all—we called them *pelones*—and wore oversize khaki pants with Pendleton shirts and beanie caps. On their arms and chests were homemade tattoos, with gang names and images of Mexican sombreros, *cholas*, crosses, ribbons, hearts, and *cholo*-style calligraphy. I was drawn to them, for some reason. They seemed like men to me, not like the seventh graders I went to school with.

Joaquin was *trucha*—he knew what these guys were about, so when they came around the house, he noticed how they noticed me. He'd mad-dog them with looks that could kill. "Don't fuck around with my *carnala*," he'd say, and his homies would make faces as if to say, *Not me.* But they were sly *perros*, let me tell you.

That's when I met Trigger. He was a solid *vato loco*, one of the main callers in the barrio. He was sixteen and didn't say much. When Joaquin brought him around, he looked serious in a thick Pendleton flannel shirt, always cleaned and pressed, with baggy gray Dickies cut off below the knees and long white knee-high socks beneath them. This might have looked funny to some people, but to me it was real sharp. Trigger had a spiderweb tattoo below his left eye and F13 on his neck. He was in and out of *campo*—the county youth probation camps—or in juvie.

I'm not sure why I was attracted to these roughnecks and knuckleheads. But I was. They seemed in control. Able to do anything. Unafraid and exciting. I wanted some of this in my life. And the fact that I attracted them made them attractive to me. Sometimes at night I'd rub myself and think of Trigger or some of his homies kissing on me, on top of me. When I was done, I'd yell out extra loud and have to put the end of my pillow into my mouth to keep quiet.

Eventually, it wasn't a fantasy. I often walked home from school, which was hard at first since I got so many stares and whistles, especially from the *paisas*, the Mexicanos, freshly wet from over the Rio Grande. There were run-down motellike apartments on Florence Avenue that I had to pass by every day. Nothing but newly arrived men lived in them. They worked in local construction and factory jobs. By the afternoon, many of them were hanging out, already drinking beer, with their shirts off, wearing Mexican vaquero hats, a type of cowboy hat. They always yelled and whistled at me. They used nasty words and gestures and I just yelled back at them to stop, which they seemed to like. Once I shook my ass as I passed by, mostly to say, *You see this, but you can't have it.* This really got them going. After that, they kept ask-

ing me to do it over and over. The men in the barrio seemed to sniff
out girls like me. You could see the desire in their every step, in their
eyes, their smiles.

One day I turned the corner and bumped into Trigger, standing
there with a stick in his hand, poking it at the ground for no particular
reason.

"Hey, Chena, what's up?" he said, looking at my breasts. I didn't
mind.

"*Qué hubo*, Trigger, nothing much," I responded, a smile on my
face that I wished I didn't have. I just couldn't help it—I already had
thoughts of him putting his mouth all over my body. "Going home.
What's going on with you, *ese*?"

I learned that talk from Joaquin. I wasn't really into the *chola* thing.
The *cholas* I knew were like guys—walking tough, dressed like *vatos* but
with a lot of makeup and teased-up hair like you wouldn't believe. I
called them *payasas*—clowns, what my mother called them, but they
seemed to know that. I actually knew one homegirl named Payasa. I
didn't think much of them, but that didn't mean I wouldn't use the
lingo to get close to their men.

Trigger walked up to me and placed his hand around my waist. He
talked real slow and low, sexy even. We talked for a long time, about
nothing in particular. Nothing deep or important. But it just seemed
like the more we talked, the hornier I got. I wanted to stay there talking to him forever. I eventually left, Trigger eyeing me the entire time.

A couple of days later, I came through Florence again and saw
Trigger standing in the same spot, minus the stick. He was wearing a
black-and-white football jersey with 13 in big numbers, front and
back, and *Florencia* in Old English letters across the back. He had on
long Dickie pants and tattoos on his arms. He was a walking drive-by
shooting target. Any of Florencia's enemies could have cruised by and
made shredded cheese out of him. But he didn't seem to care. That day
we talked, but this time he moved his hand down to my butt. I pulled
his hand up, but he moved it back down. I smiled and asked him what
he thought he was doing.

"I think I'm going to kiss you," he said, and then bent down—I was smaller—and kissed me. We kept at it for a long time. I couldn't stop myself from moaning.

In my third meeting with Trigger, I went with him to an abandoned old house behind a boarded-up storefront. He had cleaned up a room there and placed a clean mattress—at least it looked clean—in the middle of the floor with a bottle of Tokay wine next to it. We talked and shared some of the wine. He gently laid me down on the mattress. Before you knew it, he had taken off my blouse and pulled down my pants. He was all over me. I was drunk, not with the wine but the sweat of his face, his lips, his touch, his moans, his words. He loved to talk dirty. And I wanted to hear it. I was so into this. He moved so he could put his thing inside me, but I stopped him. I told him to touch me, lick me, do anything but that. He was disappointed, but he got into it. I also licked him and played with his thing. I was twelve years old. Joaquin never found out about us. If he did, I think he would have killed Trigger.

Unfortunately, things didn't go well for us. Trigger got busted after shooting two *vatos* from 38th Street, one of whom died. He ended up in state prison, tried as an adult, and I never saw him again.

But I recalled those tender moments with Trigger for a long, long time. I started seeing a few other dudes that my brother knew, but he found out and forbid anybody from coming around. I guess he saw how stacked I was and got worried.

School became a waste of time for me. I didn't study. I didn't care. Sometimes I wouldn't even show up. I hated it when the school officials called my parents and worried them. Aracely and Johnny had serious talks with me. I felt bad because I really respected them, but I just couldn't fit in at school anymore. Those schools were nothing but "factories" for factory workers. You didn't learn more than you needed to get a job and work with your hands. Most kids dropped out before they got to high school; most of them ended up working in those factories since they didn't need schooling for that. Others got into drugs and jail and the street life. I knew I couldn't drop out—my parents would have gone nuts. But there was more than one way to drop out of school, believe me.

I was around fifteen when I met my next great love. Once I had a taste of what guys like Trigger could do, I wanted more of it. I hung around older guys and some men. They were nasty but also more experienced.

I even got me a *paisa* once, one of the good-looking ones from the motels on Florence Avenue. He was younger than the other men but a lot older than me, like eighteen or nineteen. I tried to communicate with him in my street Spanish. He said I talked all *mochada*—cut up— like I'd forget certain words in my sentences. But he liked it and even encouraged me to keep talking that way. The thing he really liked was feeling me up and seeing my body. I was fourteen then—all boobs and booty. By then, I had learned how to use my body, not like that awkward twelve-year-old who didn't even know how to walk. Now I knew how to move my hips, to lift my breasts with my posture, and to look straight into a guy's eyes as though he was the only one in the world. That was the trick: eye contact.

If you looked straight at a guy, with a slight smile on your face, he'd fall apart. It also helped that I had a pretty face. I got the best of Aracely and Johnny. My mom's always been beautiful, and Johnny had been the most handsome steelworker in the mill. Face is everything since I truly believe that's the first thing guys go for. Sure tits and ass is what they want—and this may get most of their attention—but if you don't have a sweet and pretty face, they'll always think twice about it. If the face is nice—and you also have the rest of the package—you have power. I know now this is false, this power, this game. It took me a long time to figure this out, but at fourteen and fifteen it gave me an edge.

By the time I'm fifteen, some girls began to catch up with me. Many of these girls have led troubled lives. Rape, abuse—I know because they've told me. They used their bodies like weapons. There was a lot of competition for the few guys worth going for.

Another factor is that guys don't last too long in this barrio. They get shot. They OD on *carga* or go nuts with *la pipa*. They are *torcido*— busted and put away for a long time. Most girls weren't easy like me. So that left a few of us to make all the moves, and we often stepped on each other's toes. I had my competitors: La Marlene, Yasmin, and Iselda, and some of the *cholas*, too—La Green Eyes, Moni, and Triste.

They were all *firme*, real fine.

Anyway, at fifteen I met Ricardo. He wasn't a gangster. He was a quiet, handsome young dude from El Salvador. Salvadorans started moving into the neighborhood when I was in grade school, refugees of a civil war that began in 1980. Most of them were like the *paisas*—kind of out of it. A few of them became stoners, with AC/DC T-shirts and *wango* dirty Levi's pants. But then they started to get picked on and beaten up by Chicanos. Some of these Salvadorans got into trouble and ended up in juvie. Before you knew it, they came out looking all *cholo*. The Florencia guys started jumping them into the *clica*. Some of these Salvadorans claimed to be killers because of the war. They tried to prove how hard they were to the Chicanos. In the end, Chicanos taught them how to be hard-core, putting in work and getting all tatted and shit.

Ricardo stayed out of all that. He played soccer and ran track. He would have been a jock, but we didn't really have that in our school. He just liked sports. I used to see him after school with a few friends. The *cholos* and *cholas* were on their own corners. Ricardo and his friends were on another. They were fairly good students and *futbolistas*, mostly Mexican and Salvadoran.

I started to leave notes for Ricardo. I wrote and told him that I liked him and wanted to talk to him. I was bold. If I wanted something, I'd go and get it. Something about the Salvadorans intrigued me. They were different, that's all. I mean, not really, because they ended up being like us Chicanos in the end, but just the fact that they were from somewhere other than Mexico. I wanted some of that. Something different.

Ricardo was extremely shy. We started to talk after school and on the way home. One time when I was walking with Ricardo, a carload of my brother's friends drove up and honked their horn. They asked me to get in; they'd take me home. I could tell that Ricardo was scared. He didn't say anything, but you could see it in his face. This really got to me. Normally I didn't like guys who reacted like that, but I felt something for Ricardo. I told the *vatos* I'm fine. But they kept insisting, as if they owned me. That's when I got mad. "No, already, I'm walking home, okay?" This didn't sit well with those guys, but they took off anyway.

It was hard to get Ricardo to open up. It turned out he was shy for a reason. When he was young, he witnessed his father's murder, cut up by the machetes of uniformed soldiers in the small village where his family lived. His mother ended up taking the kids—he had five brothers and sisters—and sneaking everyone over three borders to end up in Los Angeles. He said he had shut down. He felt safer if he didn't say much and put all his energies into soccer and the other sports he liked. He rarely talked about what he witnessed as a kid. He told me, though, in a few words.

I really got to like that one. I mean, to be honest, we didn't do anything sexual. We kissed. We held hands. Once I even took Ricardo to a picnic that Aracely and Johnny had organized with other community people. It was the first time my parents ever met any boy I had anything to do with. I mean, everything I'd done up until then I had to sneak around to do. I was good at home. I never talked back to my parents. But sometimes I'd come home late, and they'd believe what I told them, even though it wasn't true most of the time. I'd tell them I had practice with cheerleading (something I wouldn't do for all the weed in Mexico), or that I had to stay at the library to finish some schoolwork, or that I went to visit some girlfriends. That kind of thing. They believed me for years because they thought I'd never lie to them, poor things.

Still, I felt safe to have Ricardo meet my parents. Joaquin wasn't too keen on him. He'd give him dirty looks and silently challenge him. Ricardo shied away most of the time. At the picnic, though, Joaquin started to talk to him normallike. I figured that my brother was trying to jump him into the 'hood. When I caught Joaquin by himself getting some *carne asada* from the grill, I told him in no uncertain terms: "Don't fuck with Ricardo, stupid—I don't want him with your friends." But Joaquin never listened to me.

Sometimes I want to blame him for what ended up happening. But I know it really wasn't Joaquin's fault. It was one of those fluke things. Joaquin invited Ricardo to come to a nearby house where the F13 guys were throwing a party. I didn't want him to go, but Ricardo thought it was a good idea for him to be there. I didn't think he wanted to cross Joaquin. So Ricardo went. I stayed up watching TV, then went to bed. I didn't think much of anything until my mother, with tears in her eyes, woke me up in the middle of the night.

She told me Ricardo was killed at a party. Later on I learned that a carload of *vatos* from 38th Street had pulled up, their headlights off. Somebody yelled out their barrio name and then several rounds from an AK-47 tore into the porch. Everyone hit the ground. Others pulled out Glocks and Uzis and started firing back. Joaquin ran to a window with his own handgun and blasted off a few. When the car sped off and the smoke cleared, five people were shot. Only one died. It was Ricardo. The innocent one, the quiet one, the one who didn't want anything to do with gangs. He'd seen a lot already. He understood war—what he witnessed and fled from in El Salvador. But this, he'd told me often, this kind of warfare with its drive-bys and people dying for street names, he never understood.

I cried so much for Ricardo. I really loved him. At the funeral I couldn't stand his mother's *gritos* and the many people from his country who came to weep and see him off. It was tragic to me—mostly because I felt responsible. I brought Ricardo into my world and therefore to the edges of the street world that eventually claimed him. It was hard for me to want to love anyone anymore. That's the way I felt at the time anyway.

Unfortunately, he was only the first of my boyfriends to get killed.

Most times I feel like my parents didn't deserve the kids they got stuck with. They tried hard to make a good home for us. But they have always been needed by their fellow revolutionaries; there have always been so many demands on them. Before Sylmar, we lived in extremely poor areas, surrounded by massive mills, factories, and assembly lines. There was so much injustice, with police abuse, bad schools, lousy housing, and lack of decent services, that people *had* to get involved. But sometimes that meant their children fell through the cracks. Joaquin and I were two of them. Joaquin got pushed further and further into the barrio life. I started drinking, at first, then drugs, then more drinking.

I learned to live a double life. Good parents have to go through this. I'm sure it would have been worse if our parents were terrible, if they didn't care or didn't expect more from us. But even with such great people like Aracely and Johnny, my brother and I dropped into the abyss.

After Ricardo's death, I hung out with some of the people from the funeral. They were F13 dudes and some Salvadorans. We drank a lot—40s, cheap wine, jugs of vodka and juice. We smoked a lot of *mota*. It was a way to forget, to let the world drain from under you. Joaquin knew about this. I didn't think he liked it, but he didn't really stop me after Ricardo was killed. I think he also felt guilty. He knew I was angry at him for a long time. Man, I regret that, my blaming him. Joaquin and I used to fight a lot when we were kids, but I really love my brother. I looked up to him. And, in his own way, he tried to take care of me. We were both trying hard to hide behind masks at home so that our parents wouldn't worry; but in the streets we were wild children.

I really made Joaquin suffer for what happened to Ricardo.

There was an abandoned hotel along Florence Avenue that some teenagers stayed at. It was in Huntington Park, the other side of the Alameda tracks from Florencia. So many Mexican and Central Americans moved out there, although in the fifties and sixties it was mostly white. By the 1980s, the main drag, Pacific Boulevard, had around a million people shopping there every weekend; it looked like Mexico City or San Salvador. F13 guys hung out on several corners. They had enemies everywhere: 18th Street guys, 38th Street guys, you name it.

The hotel was boarded up, but we broke through the back and lit the place up with graffiti and shot holes through the walls. We left bottles of beer and wine everywhere. Some brought in crack pipes and syringe needles. I stuck to drinking and weed mostly. I still wasn't one of these *locas*, although they were all around.

The other girls here with these guys were game for anything—they fucked and sucked and got messed up on pills, dust, and rocks. The guys were mostly strong and good-looking, but they'd get fucked up with us and lose it. Sometimes they'd fight with each other over some *jaina*—a girl. Many times they fought over me.

Man, I felt guilty hurting my parents, though. I was still in school in those days. My dad had already left the steel mill—he left in 1982, when I was around eight. So during my teen years he went from job to job—there were so many layoffs then because more plants were closing. He had skills, so he was kind of a gypsy. He had tools in the back of an old truck. He'd solicit work. He'd get jobs in a few big plants, but he had already been labeled a troublemaker from his union-organizing days at Nazareth Steel. Once he worked in a chemical refinery, but they fired him before the six-month probation period ended so the union couldn't help him. They set him up by accusing him of abandoning his post inside a boiler while a welder was working inside. You weren't supposed to leave anyone alone in those places, ever. They would take turns welding, and when one wasn't doing it, the other was keeping watch. But it was all a lie. Johnny had asked permission to go to the restroom. But when the foreman questioned the welder as to why he was alone, he claimed that Johnny left without saying anything.

The truth was that my dad was helping undocumented workers who had been hired to do elaborate mechanical work and weren't being properly compensated. The company got wind of this and set him up to be fired.

My father had problems like these ever since the steel mill went down. He had gotten a reputation, and some managers, especially in big plants, didn't want anything to do with him.

There were times we couldn't pay rent or buy food. Sometimes the gas and light bills didn't get paid, and we had to use candles and take baths in cold water. Aracely tried working again, in an assembly line, after Joaquin got sent up and I was out on the street. I got lost in the shuffle. All this work and community activities made it harder for them to keep track of me, although they tried. My mom would run around to various neighbors' homes looking for me. I'd show up and she'd sit me down to talk, worried. I tried to come home sober, which took me a few days. I just didn't want my parents to see me drunk. But they knew I was doing something—I felt they sensed my pain.

It was around that time—I was sixteen—that Johnny and Aracely proposed we leave Florencia. We were going to take my Lito and Lita with us—they were old and pretty much by themselves. My uncles Rafas and Bune had already moved out to the San Gabriel Valley; Junior, on the other hand, stayed in the old neighborhood.

I didn't want to leave. It was the first time I actually challenged my parents. They were extremely disappointed in me. But I was losing it, let me tell you. I stood up and yelled at them. They were so good despite this, so patient yet firm. *I'm still their daughter. I'm still underage and therefore under their control. Wherever they went I had to go.* That kind of thing.

I was prepared to run away. I could hide out with the F13 dudes, I figured. For example, in the abandoned hotel or somebody's *chamba*. I made my plans, but like most of my plans, as stupid as this one was, it wasn't meant to be.

One night, I walked into the abandoned hotel. By then, strangers were hanging out there. I didn't know most of those kids. They were all lost teenagers, using drugs, having sex, tattooing themselves, fighting. Not just at that hotel either. They were in the streets, in the alleys and parks. They were abandoned not only by parents but by an economy, by a culture, by a convergence of circumstances where adults walked away from the youth, adults who didn't want to rock any boats, who themselves had fled war and hunger, forcing their young to carry the weight of creation and discovery, a weight they couldn't possibly carry alone. They sacrificed these children to the gods of conformity.

The whole thing got too sad for me. I wanted to get out of there. I felt suffocated in those graffiti-covered rooms and busted-up hallways. I didn't want to go with my parents, but my other options were starting to feel worse to me. Either we were enslaved by old ideas, morals, and responsibilities forced on us in our homes, at school, in the workplace, to homogenize and "normalize" us—or we moved toward the junk: the drugs, the sex, the uprooted and unconnected "just go for it" mentality that most of us thought was hip and revolutionary. For me, it wasn't freedom anymore.

The problem was I didn't leave soon enough.

One night, I stayed around at the hotel, drinking like I usually did.

I found an empty mattress to lie down on. There was a guy to talk to. I didn't know who he was, but he seemed friendly. Not good-looking, but talkative. I don't know when I actually blacked out. He may have put something in my drink. I was out cold. It was during this time that several guys took off my clothes and raped me. A few of the *jainas* showed up at the hotel the next day and found my naked, dirty, and bleeding body curled up in the corner of the room. I had been punched in the face. Somebody wanted to hurt me. I had a black eye and a fat lip with scrapes on my face and neck, bruises everywhere.

I never did find out who did that to me. I knew it wasn't F13 dudes. One of the *jainas* claimed some 18th Street guys had come in and fucked me up. I didn't know for sure—I doubt it was them, too. I was unconscious during all of it. I was taken to a hospital, a county facility since my parents didn't have any health benefits like they did when Johnny worked at Nazareth Steel. My parents used to brag how Joaquin and I were born healthy because of that health plan. In the county hospital, they fed me through an IV, took tests, and tried to help me recover. I had to file a police report for rape, but it was just a waste of time. Whoever did it got away, free as fucking birds.

We moved to Sylmar after that—way on the other side of the world as far as I was concerned. Its big claim to fame is that one of the county's juvenile halls is located there (it also has one of the world's greatest classic car collections at the Nethercutt Museums). The community is much calmer than South L.A., where Florence is located and where our family began life. But Sylmar's still a working-class neighborhood with a growing number of Mexicans and Central Americans. It has its share of gang and drug problems. It just happens to be quieter. I had gotten used to the yelling in the streets, the glass breaking, and the gunfire in South L.A.

Sylmar was so quiet when we moved there; I had a hard time getting any sleep for the first few weeks.

A short time after we moved to Sylmar, Junior died. He was my uncle, a few years older than my father. Junior really got into drinking way before the Nazareth Steel Plant closed. But it got worse after that. Like I say, when the mill shut down, I was old enough to be aware of the impact its closing had on our family.

Junior had a wife with three kids, all born after Joaquin and me. Junior's wife was African-American. MerriLee was her name. She was tall, pretty, with coffee-and-cream-colored skin. She kind of looked Mexican, but her family came from Louisiana. She always said she had French and Spanish mixed in with the African. She talked black, although it was more Southern than, say, South Central. I believe she really loved Junior. But Junior deteriorated after the plant went down. Many businesses vanished with the mill, but the bars continued to thrive. In fact, there were more liquor stores and bars, it seemed, after the plant was gone than before.

With so much unemployment in the area, people had to deal with their economic, social, and domestic problems one way or another. They could organize and fight back, which some people did, like Johnny and Aracely. Others took to drowning out the pain.

Once, I asked Aracely why Junior drank so much after I had spotted him teetering near the entrance of a liquor store on Florence Avenue. He was in wretched shape, unshaven, in extra-long dirty clothes, red-faced. He looked like one of those drunken Indians you see on TV.

"It's the way the system kills off those who it can no longer accommodate," my mother said.

"Say that again?" I asked.

"I'll try to explain this to you," she said, sitting in front of me at the kitchen table, getting all serious, the way she does whenever she gets political. "There are cheap bottles of wine like Muscatel, Night Train, and T-Bird. These have higher alcohol content than other bottles of wine. They cost a lot less than regular wine—for years, they went for less than a dollar, although now they're just under two. These cheap bottles are often made by the same companies that make expensive liquor. They're created to make alcoholics out of people."

"You mean it's done on purpose?"

"Yeah, that's why in Florence and Watts and places like that you have liquor stores on every block. We can't get any decent grocery stores, but we can sure get some booze," she explained. "In other words, some liquor companies purposely make sure there are enough cheap bottles in the poorest neighborhoods to keep many of the men—and lots of women—from doing anything but drink their life away."

Junior was one of those men.

In time, Junior abandoned MerriLee and the kids. He couldn't hold a job. He pretty much hung out by the railroad tracks or derelict hotels, with the homeless and hoboes, the winos and *tecatos*.

The sad thing was that Lito had to let Junior go. Junior would come around when we still lived in Florencia. He'd be drunk, asking for money so he could get more booze. Johnny tried to help, to talk to him, get him food. But one day Junior went to Lito's house and they had a terrible fight. Johnny and I were visiting, so I saw what happened. Junior picked up a lamp and threw it against a wall. Lita got a broom, bless her heart, and tried to hit Junior with it. Lito got into his face, yelling and daring Junior to strike him. Johnny tried to calm things down.

I had never seen Lito or Lita act this way before. But to see their son just lose it like that was too much for them. Lito declared Junior was no longer his son. He didn't want anything to do with him until he stopped drinking. Johnny, Bune, and Rafas had already stopped drinking—although at one time they were all going that way. But Junior never did stop.

MerriLee was really hurting because of this. She dropped off the kids so Lito and Lita could take care of them. We heard that MerriLee started selling herself around Western Avenue. We heard she was on crack. That she ended up in Hollywood and downtown. I saw her once when she came to the house to get money. She was frazzled and almost incoherent. In time, Lito and Lita took care of those kids until Rafas's family decided to take them in. The kids turned out okay, although you never know how all this will affect them later. But MerriLee—she didn't make it. Years later, a friend of hers found her dead, a drug overdose, in the bathtub of a sleazy Hollywood dive.

And Junior, poor Junior, fell out before all of this.

There's another side to this story: Junior once tried to have sex with me. I was fourteen years old. I never told my parents, like the many other things I didn't tell them. I was alone in the house. Junior came in like he always does—all my uncles could walk into anyone's house, no big deal. I had the TV on and was in the kitchen making a sandwich. I had on denim cutoff shorts and a halter top. The way my body was then, it was really too much for anybody to bear. But I was home by myself. I wasn't wearing this for anybody but me, for comfort. Junior didn't take it that way. He waltzed into the kitchen and kept staring at me.

I looked over at Junior. At first I didn't think anything of it. But I could smell the alcohol on his breath from the other side of the room. Then I started to feel that something wasn't right.

"What can I do for you, *tío*?" I asked. "You want a sandwich?"

"No, no sandwich," he said, but nothing else.

"Well, Mom and Dad ain't here. You want to write them a note?" I was trying to get him to leave in a good way.

"They're not here, huh," he said, as if thinking out loud.

I turned around and saw Junior come closer. His eyes were bloodshot and his mouth was watering. He took out his thing from in front of his pants, withered and dark, and waved it at me.

"Come on, baby, lick this back to life," he muttered.

I never heard my uncle talk this way. He wasn't himself. He wasn't even aware of the terrible thing he was asking. I threw the sandwich at him—I didn't know what else to do. He then rushed me, put his arms around me, and pulled down my halter top. My *chi-chis* fell out, round with those large dark nipples of mine. I covered up but Junior tried to pull my arms out. I looked down and saw his thing flopping around, so I kneed him—real hard. He moaned like a mangy dog and fell to the ground. I picked up a chair and then hit him over the head with it; Junior sank farther onto the floor. He was a big man, strong even when drunk. But after the wood pieces broke around him, he looked like shit. He tried to get up. I put my halter top back on and ran to the hallway closet where Johnny kept a shotgun.

I pointed the shotgun toward Junior and told him to leave. I knew there were no shells in the gun, but I figured Junior would get the message.

"*Tío*—I don't want to ever see you again. Get out of this house—now."

My uncle looked at me, tired, sad, angry, and confused all at once. I felt sorry for him but also fucking pissed off.

"Get out!" I yelled. "And don't ever come back here!"

Junior backed off into the living room, gave me one more puzzled look, then put his thing back into his pants and walked off.

It was a long time before I saw Junior again. When I knew he was around at Lita's or at the house, I'd go someplace else. Again, I never told anyone this story. Nothing really happened as far as my uncle getting to me. But it was devastating, nonetheless—my trust in men really fell apart then. My family is family. My uncles had always been kind and decent with me. I remember Junior when I was small, and he wasn't married. He'd take Joaquin and me to the show from time to time. He wasn't drinking that much—or at least only as much as everyone else. He never tried anything like that before. Never. But after that incident I just stopped seeing him as my uncle. Later, when I got raped and then into the drugs and the drinking and the rotten men, I thought of Junior, but in a bad way. I wanted to shoot him. I wanted to cut his heart out. It didn't stop me from doing what I was doing. But I hated that I couldn't trust my uncle anymore. Although my other uncles, Rafas and Bune, have always been good to me, thinking of what Junior did to me caused me to shut myself down around all of them.

Only a few years after he tried to mess with me, a couple of police officers driving through an alley just off Florence Avenue found Junior splayed out on dirt and overgrown weeds, among strewn garbage, next to graffiti-scrawled cinder-block walls.

Everybody felt bad—I didn't know how to feel. I still harbored something mean and ugly: I secretly hoped this had happened to him because of what he did to me.

11

THE FLOATING WORLD

o, no, *m'ija*, don't come out with more of your craziness,"
my mother yelled from the kitchen when I stepped out of
my bedroom not long after we moved to Sylmar.

"What are you talking about—this is nothing crazy, it's
the fashion, it's cool, it's everywhere," I responded, my lame excuse for
the way I dressed: all in black, with black eye makeup, black lace
gloves, and my brown, straight hair dyed black. It was indicative of the
next phase of my adolescence, short as it was, as what some people
called a "goth girl."

For some reason, I got this notion I needed to be something completely different in the San Fernando Valley. The houses are more
spread apart. Few people walk the streets. People are more TV- and
mall-oriented. So why not make a change? I sure needed it.

I first saw this style after we moved in and three strangely dressed
kids walked by—two boys and a girl. It was a hot day, but the boys had
on long torn black coats; the girl wore a black skirt, black blouse, had
unevenly cut black hair, over pale skin—as though she stayed inside
her room for months before finally coming out.

I came across this again when Aracely and I drove twenty minutes
one day to the Northridge Mall. The so-called goth kids were few in
number—most of the teens there were sunny California types, with
skimpy halter tops, long, many-times-brushed hair, and below-the-
knees Hawaiian-style shorts. The goths were mostly white, morbid-
faced, with dark makeup on both girls and guys. The darkness

appealed to me—darkness in the light, sunny, and patently phony suburban world we were in.

I found some black duds in a shop that catered to goths and punks in the mall. I figured this must be okay, considering they had a store for this stuff. I didn't tell Aracely what I bought, although earlier she had given me money for clothes.

But when we got home, and after I took an hour to get ready, I walked out my bedroom and Aracely just about flipped.

Johnny walked in just as Aracely started fiddling with my hair and calling me a tramp.

"Whoa, there, horsey," my dad said, trying to be funny. He got into this cowboy thing after we decided to move out here. Sylmar used to have many horse ranches, before developers came in and turned most of the large spreads into housing lots. Somehow, the neighborhood history worked its way into my dad's vocabulary.

"Just look at your daughter," Aracely said, shaking her head. "I'm not going to have this—this is not healthy."

"Well, babe, hold up now," Johnny responded while looking at me with a strained expression. "I don't see anything really bad about this—I mean the kids who dye their hair, get piercings, and dress in black are not the worst kids out there."

"What are you talking about?" demanded Aracely, now turning her attention from me to my dad.

"Where did we just come from? From the barrio, *qué no?*—now, those are some troubled kids. Look at Joaquin. Look at where we grew up. Look at what happened to Chena over there. I'm for letting her express herself. I don't want to judge her by how she looks—I'm sure she knows we expect her to do well in school, act respectfully, and do her chores. But for now, let her find her way around."

"No way," Aracely insisted, but then she looked over to me and says, "Go to your bedroom for a while—me and your father have to talk."

"Oh, man, why does everything have to be so much drama," I said as I went back into my room, closed the door, sat on the bed, and put my Walkman on, the Cure blaring into my ears. I had even picked up a few CDs—including Echo and the Bunnymen, Thrill Kill Kult, and the Ramones—at the mall record store.

I could hear my parents talking in the living room—they were adamant, but they didn't yell or lose it. I couldn't actually hear what they were saying—but their angry tones came through clearly.

After a long while, there was knocking on my door.

"Yeah, I'm still here," I answered, tired and expecting the worst.

My dad walked in. Aracely had gone back into the kitchen. He came over and sat down next to me.

"How you doing, *muñeca*?" he said (he always calls me *muñeca*, which means "doll").

"What did you two decide?" I asked, resigned to being squeezed out of my new identity.

"Well, your mother and I had a long talk," my dad began. "You can wear this stuff, if you want. Again, what we expect at home is for you to be respectful, do your work, do well in school, and not hang in the street. We don't want a repeat of what happened to you in the old neighborhood. Your mom only wants to protect you—she's worried, and you know with your brother still running the streets, it's not easy for the both of us. But you are our precious girl and we don't want you to feel like you're not appreciated. Just, for your mom's sake, keep it down a little. Don't go way out with this stuff, okay, *muñeca*?"

I had to agree; it was actually a nice gesture on their part—by rights, they shouldn't have let me do anything odd after the mess I'd put them through.

I ended up at Sylmar High School, a mostly overcrowded Chicano school—I mean like 99.9 percent—with bungalows and narrow halls. I stood out like a freak—but there were a few kids like me, and we began to gravitate to one another.

The school allowed me to catch up on my school credits so I could graduate on time, despite the fact I had missed a lot of school in South L.A. But I was smart—and when I wanted to, I could do the work. Wanting to—that was the problem, but by that time, I really made a point of trying.

I was rather quiet and alone at that school. I was seventeen, although I still looked older. I hid my body with my long black dresses and blouses. Kids still stared at me, and I still felt self-conscious. But looking like I might be a witch's disciple might have kept more kids away from me.

After a while, my new scene got old. I didn't like being with those goth students anymore. They were way too cynical and confused for me. I let my hair come out natural and started wearing some color. After a while, they didn't want anything to do with me.

One day a group of girls began talking to me while I sat alone eating lunch. Not goths—they were Mexican girls not far removed from the old country: Xochitl, Melinda, and Rosalia. The Three Stooges, I ended up calling them. One was fine; one was slightly on the heavy side; and the other was skinny and too much dork from my point of view. But they were cool when together. They had recently acquired a good command of English and we got along—I spoke my Spanish and they tried out their English and we communicated *de aquellas*.

In time, I told the girls my story. They were enthralled, awakened perhaps, since they seemed like good Catholic girls who had never done much of anything. They asked questions about the men I'd been with—I could tell they didn't have these experiences yet. I thought they might get weird with me and never come back, but every day they came by my sullen spot on a bench and listened. I kind of relished this.

"With men, I gave too much—and got little in return," I said.

"That's why you should have held off sex until you got married," Rosalia, the dork, remarked with confidence.

I looked at her with a slight smirk of disdain—but I didn't really think less of Rosalia; she just didn't know any better.

I told them about the rape. But as I went through the incident, I realized that even this didn't swear me off men. It should have. My parents suffered a lot in the aftermath. But somehow, I still got the notion that I'd find me another fool somewhere.

One night, the girls and I decided to check out a teen *pachanga*—a barrio dance—in San Fernando, the one independent city here, surrounded by L.A. communities like Pacoima, Sylmar, Sun Valley, and Mission Hills.

At the dance, I stood alone with Xochitl, Melinda, and Rosalia. Unfortunately, we mostly stayed away from the others. There was a *montón* of hardened *cholos* and *cholas*. I wasn't worried about them, but my friends were. I wasn't trying to be in a gang or to be a *chola*, but I got attracted to their style, their intensity, their danger.

"Let's get out of here," Melinda suggested.

"No, *quédense*—we'll find somebody to party with soon, just wait a bit," I managed.

"I'm not sure I want to dance with these *vatos*," added Xochitl, who was the prettiest of us four. "They look like *chunts* to me."

"I think I'll call my dad to pick us up," Rosalia offered.

I didn't want to go, but I wasn't sure I could convince the girls to stay. Just then this well-dressed Chicano in fly beige coat and pants walked up to me. He was dark brown with a chiseled *cara de indio* and hair cut to his scalp. He looked sharp. He asked me to dance and I looked at the girls, gave them a wink, and said *"simón"* without looking away from them. Melinda sighed in disgust.

The dude told me his name was Raton Moreno. We talked some more, and I got a pretty good idea of who he was. His real name was Gabriel. He was a *cholillo* from Pacas, one of the oldest barrios in the northeast San Fernando Valley. A gang war between the San Fer barrio and Pacas had been going on for several generations. I didn't realize this until we ended up in Sylmar. There were other gangs in this part of the valley: Blythe Street, Varrio Van Nuys, Astoria Gardens, and more.

Not so different from South Los Angeles, it turned out.

Raton and I danced through about ten songs. He was an okay dancer—he did the same move over and over again, but it was a good one. I was all over the place. I loved to dance, to shake everything to the beats, heating up my skin and watching others admire my efforts.

After a while I glanced over at the girls and saw that two of them were also on the dance floor; Rosalia, the homely one of the bunch, stood alone, but I felt she'd find someone soon. Sure enough a small, nerdy-looking dude came up and asked her to dance. A little while later, we were all up, *moviendo la cadera*.

When the slow dance came, the DJ picked one of my favorites—"Always and Forever" by Heat Wave.

Raton grabbed me with a combination of confidence and tenderness; I could tell he liked pressing close to my chest—I felt his thing get big under his pants. That happened a lot with dudes whenever I slow-danced with them. I didn't mind, only it had been several months since I had been with a man—ever since the rape. Instead of making me recoil, I realized how much I missed it. We danced very close and slow; I felt his warm wet cheek next to mine. I could see the throbbing of his vein along his neck, which also sported a barrio tattoo. Our sweat became one. The smell of his manhood, mixed with cheap cologne, was soothing and sensuous to me. I placed my hand on his head and moved my hand over his bald pate. He didn't mind. He got closer to my neck and his breathing freshened up the humidity in the stifling room.

After the dance I just held on to him. He liked that, smiling large. He had a great smile. Kind of strange for a *cholo*, but that was okay with me. When the *pachanga* was over he asked for my phone number. I told him it was best if I called him (I didn't want my parents to worry about some *vato* calling). He gave me a number and said I should only call during the day and on the weekends. I could only imagine what he was doing the rest of the time.

Afterward, in the parking lot, there was a huge brawl. I saw Raton jumping up and throwing some mean blows. Someone pulled out a gun and police arrived. It was time to go. I saw Raton leave with several other *vatos*. I knew he was trouble. But for some reason, even after Florencia, I fell deep into trouble once more.

Speaking of Florencia, my brother, Joaquin, didn't come to live with us in Sylmar. This caused Johnny and Aracely a lot of grief. But he absolutely refused to leave the barrio. The fact he was nineteen years old didn't help. He was a legally independent adult. He found homies to live with and he stayed in the old neighborhood. I kind of missed him.

This made it hard for me to get around since Joaquin used to let me drive his *ranflita*. But I was determined to contact Raton again. The girls tried to talk me out of seeing him—they knew being with Raton was a mistake. Bless their souls. But I was a hardheaded *hija de mil brujas*—I wasn't going to listen to them.

One day, Raton took me to his barrio, to hang with some of the Pacas dudes in a worn-out section of neighborhood off of Van Nuys Boulevard. On the corner was the famous Bobo's food stand that had hamburgers *and* tacos, where we'd go to late at night.

With enemies everywhere, the dudes from Pacas constantly watched one another's backs. Their biggest enemy was the local LAPD—they were like the Big Gang around here (this also happened to be the same police division that later beat up Rodney King).

If Joaquin had moved out with us, he'd kick my ass for being around these fools.

Since Johnny and Aracely were "keeping an eye on me," I could only get out of the house by pretending to hang with Xochitl, Melinda, or Rosalia—whom they liked—although I always ended up with Raton.

Then it happened, even though part of me dreaded it: Raton made a move to get into my pants. Again, I wanted it—it had been so long. But I wasn't sure how it'd work out. I told him one day while we sat alone in his car—vigilant against enemy intrusions—that he had to go slow. I told him I might have to stop him at some point. I didn't really know what I was saying, but I felt it wouldn't be an easy time.

To Raton's credit, he was a lot nicer than I thought he'd be. I truly believed he liked me, for what that was worth in a barrio relationship. He was questioning me so I could feel comfortable—"Is this okay? . . . How about that?" The more we talked the better everything became. The first time we actually made love, in that burned-out heap of his, it wasn't so bad. I found it hard to come, that's true, but I felt cared for—held and alive. Being in a man's arms, living in his eyes and in his laugh, did this to me more than anything else. It was a kind of addiction. I started too young with men and now found that during my loneliest and trying times, only male fingers and the hot smell of male breath could satiate my hungers.

Then the rages began.

I can hardly explain them. After we made love, for example, and we were together in the quiet, something inside me began to explode. Sometimes it'd happen as we talked. I wanted to break his face. Break the windows. No particular issues sparked my moods. If he mentioned any other woman, even if it was his sister, I'd go off about other women. If he mentioned his homies, I'd go off that he loved his homies more than me. I called him *puto* and *joto*—terrible things to say to a *vato loco* from the 'hood.

Raton had his own rage issues, but I think I took it over the top. Mostly he tried to calm me down—to hold me, to talk to me. Sometimes he just walked away, which drove me to greater heights of fury. I'm telling you, I became possessed, out of control, a drama queen supreme.

I think a lot of this came from stress. The stress of hiding this relationship from my parents, whom I honestly didn't want to hurt despite my impulses; the stress of trying to finish high school, which I promised myself I would do no matter what; the stress of remembering— the rape, my brother's gang life, hurting my parents, and so many other things that invaded my head and caused me to explode in screams.

That's when Raton began giving me weed, pills, and then blasts from his crack pipe. I guess he tried to medicate me or something, to make me feel better. But it only made things worse—especially that pipe. I called it "my glass dick." I took puffs of it, burning my throat and causing me to cough some shitty-ass *flema*. But soon I wanted it all the time.

It was the beginning of the end for me.

I didn't think Raton was trying to fuck with me. I honestly believed he was trying to help. But that's all he knew. He sold rocks on the streets. He helped make the crack and crystal meth in somebody's garage. He sold it and he used it. The rages, on the other hand, didn't subside with all the drugs; they just took uglier turns.

Sometimes, Raton could see I needed it too much, and he kept the pipe away from me. Big mistake. I'd be pissed off for days. Finally, after I couldn't take it anymore, he shared a pipe smoke with me. *Pinche puto*, I thought. Then we'd make love and it all seemed glorious and otherworldly. I got stuck on him. I was addicted to him because I was addicted to the crack we shared. The only real thing we shared together.

Coming down on the crack after such an intense high, however, really hit me hard. I got depressed, disoriented, suicidal even. I needed more crack to get going again.

My parents tried to rein me in. But they also had their own troubles with my brother, Joaquin. Some of these more pressing matters pulled them away from dealing with my shit.

At times, Raton would lose it and knock me on my ass. I always felt I deserved it somehow, which everyone says you shouldn't do. Not to say I should have gotten hit—no woman should—but I kind of got him going. I threw things and yelled my lungs out. He'd finally had it with me and punched the side of my head. Man, he could hit. I flew back against the wall with a loud thump and slid down to the ground. I struggled to get up, cursing that Raton hit like a girl, like a *joto*, and that I was going to stand up, that's how lightweight he was in knocking me down. Only now I had a monstrous welt on my temple, a black eye, and a wobble.

I wouldn't go home for days after that. I wore shades all the time, even on cloudy days. My parents asked me about them, but I wouldn't say a word. I found out if I didn't say anything or if I changed the subject—to other issues we had between us—they'd stop asking me about the shades.

I thought I had this all figured out. A system, my system. What an arrogant fool I was.

I tried to leave Raton, thinking it'd be for the best. But with the pipe and then later crystal meth, I always came back. We were yin and yang, push and pull, fuck you and *please fuck me*. We were no good for each other, but we couldn't stop being with each other.

One day, in one of my worst rages, I went off: breaking the windows in his car with a tire iron, yelling in the middle of the street, the neighbors hiding behind their curtains and slightly opened doors. Raton came hard out of his house and I swung at him, but he pulled back in time. He jumped on me and pushed me to the ground. I yelled and kicked, but he wouldn't let me go. The drugs made me feel like I could do anything, beat up on anybody. Only Raton could actually stop me. Later that night, we smoked some crack and made love.

School became a disaster. I still tried to go because I had this thing that I had to finish. But, honestly, I just stopped going. Xochitl, Melinda, and Rosalia pretty much went about their business—they didn't want to bother with me after Raton and I first hooked up.

The thing that stopped this madness was my getting pregnant. I didn't want to be pregnant at first. I didn't expect it. I didn't think about it. The fact that I didn't use condoms or any safe-sex measures only proved how stupid I was. AIDS hit the big time back then. I trusted Raton that he didn't have HIV. Thankfully, he didn't. Yet my getting pregnant was a whole 'nother matter.

Something happened to me when I found out I was pregnant. I went to the free clinic in San Fernando. I'd been feeling extra tired before then, getting sick and gaining weight. They did the test and later told me the result. I was nine weeks pregnant when I got the news. I hated to say this, since I don't recommend anybody doing this, but that baby was what stopped my drug use and helped me from going over the edge.

I know women on crack and other shit who've had tons of kids—that doesn't stop them from using drugs or living the street life (I'm thinking about MerriLee, Junior's wife). But not me. With my pregnancy, I woke up from the inside. This was something I treasured, that I wanted; something I could say is mine and would take care of. It's the most precious of all things precious. Perhaps this is where good parents like Johnny and Aracely come in, even if we give them hell for trying. Some of their love of life, of nature and children superseded my own destructive and selfish behavior. Maybe it's from our culture, how most Mexicans love their babies (unless they become sick in the head, like many I know, and abuse the shit out of them). I wanted this baby. I wanted it to be healthy. I wanted to be healthy so that I could help the baby be healthy.

Raton took the news of my pregnancy in stride. I find out later he already had two other kids from two other women. I became a whole new person after I'm aware of the baby forming in my womb. I asked

Raton to be there for me, but to let me have this baby my way. To not push the pipe or the meth or any of that shit on me. I wanted my baby so bad. I never thought I could want anything as much as I did my baby.

Raton backed off around that time. He stopped calling. He stopped his loving ways. Fortunately, this meant he stopped slapping me around. For me, it wasn't about Raton. It just wasn't. I didn't care if he came by or not; I didn't care if he wanted to be a daddy or not. I felt it would be fine just me and the baby. That might have been dumb, but having to deal with any guy felt like a burden, especially guys like Raton. My focus was on my child. If Raton wanted to help—to change diapers, to clean the house, to make sure I was comfortable and well fed—sure, why not? I had no problem with that. But if the guy wanted attention, to be held, to have sex or just to talk, fuck that! I only had time to be a mother. Maybe that's the selfish part—who knows?

I was seven months pregnant when Raton got shot. He was still in the street, slanging and dealing, probably making it with other *jainas*, doing what a *vato* from the barrio would do. I was home, out of school by then, getting help from my mother and father. The shooting happened late one night. He had burned some dudes over packages of crystal meth—that's what I heard anyway. They came to his house and ambushed him as he walked out the door. It wasn't like a gang war. It was a drug deal he fucked up. They confronted him where he made all his *movidas*. In the end, they pumped five bullets into his brain.

I heard his family planned a big funeral. I didn't go. I didn't want to deal with his homies or his exes. I didn't want to hear his mother crying and all the screaming that happens in funerals. It wasn't that I didn't care. I did. I liked Raton to a point. But in the end, we weren't about each other. It was about the *pipa*. The one good thing he did was give me my son. That was all I cared about. To me this was our fate. That was why we came together, why I suffered the beatings and drug use—so that this one little guy, this special, incredible human being, would be born. This child wouldn't be this child if I had a baby from any other man. It had to be Raton, as fucked up as he was, although it didn't mean I owed him a tear at his funeral.

I finally told Aracely about Raton and what we went through. I had to. I wanted my mother involved in my pregnancy. Of course Johnny and Aracely got pissed to high heaven after I told them. They wanted to wring my neck. But they also have so much love for me. And I love them. We argued, we cried, but in the end we came together as family and did what we needed to do to bring this child into a better world.

I did promise to go to a recovery program while attending birth classes—Aracely was big on the birth classes. I wasn't convinced the recovery group would be of any help, but that was the one thing I agreed to do so Johnny and Aracely could work with me. Fine, I went to a recovery meeting at a local barrio evangelical church—the Victory Way—in Pacoima. It was recommended to me by Melinda, who had begun to get all Jesus on me. I thought it was worth a try. Like I say, I didn't have many friends—and Xochitl, Melinda, and Rosalia were as close to me as anyone has ever been. In time, we drifted apart. The girls found their great loves and married and had their own kids. We'd stay in touch for a bit, but since I pretty much left them during my *fracaso* with Raton, we lost much of our closeness. Melinda's last act as a friend was to get me in this Christian recovery group.

I attended meetings once a week. Aracely didn't like me going there. She wanted me involved in her Communist group. I've known about them since I was a baby. She had a core group of people who hung together through the years and the various battles around Los Angeles—the 1992 riots, the bilingual education struggles around Proposition 187, the earthquake, the Ramparts police scandal, and all that. Aracely thought their revolutionary outlook would be good for me. I actually picked up a lot from them as a child, forced to go with Aracely to meetings. My mother thought I was just playing or watching TV while she held court with her comrades. But I listened. It helped organize my thinking, sometimes my decisions, especially when I needed to get away from some bad thoughts and bad decisions.

But to be an active Communist—*chale*, I wasn't into that. I respected them, but they were also too old school for me. The world was changing. More and more young people like me weren't anchored or set in our ways. The culture was pushing so much junk at us—either conform and fall into line, or distance ourselves from adults, from teachers and mentors, and live for today, to have all the fun you could while it was still possible, and only with one another. I went the latter way. And I paid the price. I didn't want to do this anymore, but I also questioned how the heck stodgy old Communists who organized during a different time, when industry was happening and they were the *vanguard* of the working class, could possibly influence and lead this new generation—Generation X, the "slacker" generation, generation "whatever."

Don't get me wrong. I didn't disagree with the revolutionaries and their core ideas. I just felt they were too stuck in another period to really impact the "floating" world the rest of us were all standing on.

And just to be clear, I'm not saying that young people today are less intelligent or less interested. They're aware of what's going on. I know I am. And they definitely care—I know I do. But there are many ways to get pulled off track, to forget, to lose perspective. That's true for anyone. If Communists are going to be any good for this generation, they have to be relevant, invigorating, and flexible. I'm for it if they can do that.

So I don't have any problems with Aracely and her Communist friends—I just want to know how to weave myself in without losing my own patterns, particularities, and passions.

Alejandrito came into this world full of vigor, with a pair of great lungs, seemingly angry—which made me think that at least he had a fighting chance in the world. My mother was by my side the whole time. Johnny showed up after the birth. He hugged me, and when he let go, I saw a tear in his eye. A nurse brought the baby and Aracely started with her baby talk, "*noni, loni, caboni*"—whatever that means. Johnny had the baby wrap his small hand around his pinkie finger. The boy was small—he was premature—but he was going to be fine. Making Johnny and Aracely grandparents became a source of pride for me—I finally felt like I had accomplished some good. They really seemed to enjoy this. Aracely, who was tired from my birthing, turned out to be the best birthing coach ever. She knew this stuff so well.

The other people who showed up to visit were from my Christian recovery group. It was a mixed group of Mexicans, blacks, and a couple of whites. Many of them were heroin and crack addicts, ex-*pintos* or alcoholics. With Jesus in their hearts, they were now drunk with the Lord. They came with their Bibles and prayers, laying their hands on my head and on my son's. Pastor Roy Velez came, too. He was an old gangster who brought in "lost souls" on a daily basis.

As you can guess, I became "born again" not long before Alejandro's birth. I had gone to several meetings, where we talked about our lives, read the Bible, and prayed. One night during Sunday service, I walked up to the pulpit and stage area of the small storefront church on Van Nuys Boulevard. I wobbled to the front, holding on to chairs, my womb like two days ahead of me. I followed another group of ex-druggies, bikers, and Chicano gang members. A really sorry bunch. But I liked that this church catered to them. Nobody was turned away. A few hands helped me up a couple of stairs as I got close to where Pastor Roy was putting his hands on people. I got up there with my arms out and palms opened in front of me. I closed my eyes and Pastor Roy said a few words of praise, some things in tongues. When he placed his hand on my neck, I felt the power, the electricity, the Lord's grace enter my body. He was blessing me and my baby, I just knew it, and my tears began to flow.

"Praise Jesus," I said, as if it wasn't my voice. It just came out, and as I did, others echoed my words back to me.

When I told Aracely this, she wasn't happy. Johnny, as patient as he tried to be, kind of smiled and said he hoped I was happy. But I knew that Aracely, although she'd never told me this, was kind of an atheist. I remember how she often railed against churches and religions that enslaved the mind, and how they blinded people and kept them stupid. I believed her for years. Until I joined the church group. I then saw how much I had missed. There was spiritual power there, and I had been removed from it so long. I now believed that's why I started all the drinking and drugging. But Aracely thought my need to be drunk or drugged was also behind my need to be a "Jesus freak"—her term for my newfound spirituality.

"Mom, you shouldn't say those things without knowing what you're talking about," I responded, in my usually contrary style, while we were driving to the store one day and having another one of our heated discussions.

"I know what I'm talking about—you think I don't know how these religions work?" she said. "I grew up Catholic. I did all the sacraments—baptism, first Communion, confirmation, and all that. I just got dirty-minded priests and mean nuns and a lot of rules without any sense of why or what for. I saw the hypocrisy, the lies, the way us poor people were supposed to swallow a lot of indignities and injustices—and not complain. Meanwhile, the rich and powerful had everything. It's a trap, a prison for the poor. At least I finally freed my mind."

"This is different, Mom," I tried to argue. "This is not a big church or religion. It's a small church with ties all over the country and the world. They follow the Bible, not the pope. They make Jesus come alive. He's not a statue on a cross to be kneeled down to. He's in our hearts. That's a big difference."

"Yeah, and then we'll see what this does—I've been around born-again Christians before," Aracely insisted. "They're the most conservative and the most willing to accept the capitalist system. They are rabid anti-Communists—even more so than Catholics. At least some Jesuits are among the poor in Latin America, trying to throw off the oppressors. Let's see how they twist your mind around to think like a Republican."

I didn't quite get that. Nobody was trying to make a Republican out of me in the prayer meetings. But this kind of exchange between Aracely and me was far from over.

12

HEALING

Jandro was a yeller. He could scream the paint off walls. The screaming got on my nerves, but after I held him and placed my nipples near his mouth, which he opened wide, he began to calm down. I fed him the old-fashioned way (I may as well use these clunkers). I was now staying in the upstairs bedroom with the baby—there was more room for the both of us. My mom and dad moved downstairs. Aracely helped me with Jandro anytime I needed her, although she and I were icy toward each other.

"Jesus loves you," I greeted her after coming down the stairs with a much calmer Jandro in my arms.

"He should, considering how much patience I need to deal with you," she remarked.

"No matter—Jesus will take care of it. Whatever problems, He'll handle it—He can handle anything."

"Get off your high horse and check reality every once in a while, will you?" she said while nonchalantly pulling Jandro from my arms and starting in with her baby talk: *"noni, loni, caboni."*

Despite his screams when he was hungry, Jandro was a sweet and happy child. I'm aware, however, that I could have harmed him for the rest of his life if I had continued using and continued hanging around Raton. I'm not saying that Raton *should've* been killed—that's not right. But the best thing I did was get out of that situation.

I continued with my prayer meetings. I didn't have any desire to take drugs or even drink, oddly enough, but I did have to hang around my newfound friends at the Victory Way. Pastor Roy said the temptations will always be there, so I had to surround myself with a strong support network. Besides, only Jesus can drive the temptations away, he explained, the way He turned away from the Devil, who tempted Him for forty days in the desert.

The prayer group was made up mostly of Mexicans from Pacoima. Pacoima is mostly Mexican, with a smattering of Central Americans, but there has always been an important, even if dwindling, black community there, mostly in and around the San Fernando Gardens Housing Projects.

I hung out at the church three times a week, not including Sunday services.

One evening, I heard Johnny and Aracely talking about me—they didn't always know when I stood at the top of the stairs, picking up on what they were saying.

"She scares me with that Jesus talk," Aracely told Johnny.

"Well, look at it this way—she's off drugs, she's healthy, she's a good mom. Sure, I don't go for that Jesus stuff myself, but she's doing a hell of a lot better than before. Be thankful for that," Johnny reasoned.

"I am, believe me, I am," Aracely continued. "But she doesn't need Jesus to be healthy, off drugs, and a good mother. She'd be fine if she wasn't pushing that stuff on us and everybody else she meets."

As I listened to them talk, I realized my mother is partly right. I was talking Jesus to everybody now. It was just my way—my talking way. Whatever I'm into, I *really* get into. Soon I was trying to convert friends, family, even strangers.

I did make the mistake one day of trying to get Lito into Jesus. He and Lita lived in a small guesthouse behind the larger front house. They were happy there—Lita tended her small garden, and Lito walked every morning, read the newspaper, and watched his Spanish-language *telenovelas*.

Finding him rocking on the front porch of our house—something he loves to do—I sat next to him and said, "Lito, do you know that

Jesus died for your sins. And that if you accept Jesus Christ as your personal savior, He'll grant you eternal salvation."

Lito looked at me like I was a creature from another planet.

"*Azucenita—házme un favor*, do me a favor: Keep those *pinche babosadas* to yourself, okay?"

My grandmother just listened to me and smiled. My grandparents were raised Catholics—although they didn't go to church. Lita had an altar in her house with a large framed portrait of La Virgen de Guadalupe surrounded by various saints and candles—the Indian way. She probably thought I had lost my marbles, too, but at least she was willing to humor me. Lito never did.

A couple of years passed before DeAngelo entered my life. I was still into the church, and one day, a new guy showed up to our recovery group. He struck me as handsome and self-assured. He had battled into drugs and alcohol before he began his road to recovery. Older than me—by ten years—he was African-American, which for me was no problem, but for others, especially my brother, Joaquin, could prove intolerable. Of course Aracely and Johnny didn't care about this kind of thing. They'd be leery of any man, of course, but not because of his race.

His full name was DeAngelo Stone. He seemed wise and experienced. I could see right away how he could be a big help with my recovery and my trying to make myself a better person. At the time, he had a twelve-year-old daughter, Keisha. They both lived in a modest home in Pacoima near Humphrey Park. His daughter's mother was a white woman he met in the music industry, where he was a composer, musician, and producer.

DeAngelo was the first man I dated outside my *raza*.

I sought love and tenderness in DeAngelo and I sought it in Keisha.

DeAngelo and I began to see each other. He started by asking me to dinner. He took me to a fancy Brazilian restaurant along Pasadena's Old Town section of Colorado Boulevard, which we could get to in twenty minutes on the 118 and 210 freeways without traffic. The Old Town area was packed with people, waiting for valet service, lining up for restaurants, clubs, bookstores, movie houses, and cafés that adorned its streets. It's real chic, real yuppie, and sometimes real weird, too.

But DeAngelo was right at home. He was a tall man, well built, with nice threads. He loved good food and good conversation. We didn't drink, but other than that, we enjoyed each other's company quite well.

At one moment while eating, we began to talk about our interests.

"What do you like to do besides take care of your son?" DeAngelo asked.

"Oh . . ." I tried to say in between mouthfuls of spicy fish and black beans. "Believe it or not, I like to sing. I really do. I have lots of great albums and tapes. I play them and sing along whenever I get a break. I don't even like watching TV. But put me next to my sound system, with my collection of soul and jazz CDs, and man, I'm like in another world."

I didn't mention that I also owned heavy metal, punk, and alternative rock CDs from my goth days. I didn't want DeAngelo to know that part of my life.

"That's funny, Keisha is into the same thing," DeAngelo said. "She wants to be 'famous,' she tells me. She thinks she'll be like Whitney or Janet. She's got the looks and the voice; she just has to grow up some more."

"It's good you support her," I said. "I'm not saying my parents oppose my singing or anything. But they are into different things. They don't exactly encourage me. I do this mostly on my own. I even have a few songs memorized."

"Man, I'd sure like to hear you sing."

"Here?"

"Yeah, not too loud, just enough to see what you got."

I thought about this while staring at DeAngelo. I could see he was truly interested. He had large expressive eyes and a well-formed face that didn't hide his emotions well. He was the kind of guy whose face matched exactly whatever he was feeling. I put down my fork, wiped my mouth with my napkin, picked up a glass of water, and drank. Then I began a slow and fairly quiet version of the Sade song "Cherish the Kiss."

When I finished, DeAngelo was silent, his eyes wide open.

"Well," I finally said. "What do you think?"

"Honestly, and I'm not lying to you, but you really can sing," DeAngelo responded. "Usually when people say they sing at home or in the shower, it's time to duck out. But you have potential, my dear. You can use some voice lessons, mind you. That's where the skills are taught. But you have the raw talent, the seed that needs nurturing. I'm truly impressed."

"Why, thank you," I said. "I try really hard to sing well, but I also know I don't know what I'm doing. I need feedback from somebody like you."

"Listen, I didn't tell you this because we barely got together," DeAngelo said. "You know I have ties to the music industry. I've also told Pastor Roy I'd help him get a praise singing group at the church. And, if you're interested, I'd like to help you and perhaps record your singing. We can start with the songs you memorized and then maybe some new ones, including a few songs I've written."

"You write songs? Man, you're a man of a thousand talents," I responded. "I'd like for you to help me out if you can."

About a week later, I was in a studio owned by DeAngelo's cousin, Matthew Stone, who also worked for a major label. I was nervous. Luckily DeAngelo brought Keisha along—we encouraged each other. They put me in a room with a drum set and foam-padded walls; several microphones stood around me. I had a sheet of paper with lyrics on them. They were DeAngelo's words, a song he recently composed.

"You're just going to sing a few lines," DeAngelo said through a microphone in the mixing room. "We're back here checking levels. I'll tell you when to start."

After a short while, DeAngelo gave me a one-two-three signal through the glass then pointed his index finger toward me. It was my cue. I cleared my throat and sang the words to the song over a track of music they piped into my headset. Matthew sat in front of the mixing board, adjusting dials while I sang.

After a while DeAngelo asked me to step into the mixing room.

"You can sing, girl," DeAngelo said as soon as I walked in, his enthusiasm written on his face. "I like the way your voice interprets my lyrics. It has a soulful, raspy sultriness to it. You sure you ain't a sister?"

I laughed, turned to Keisha, and winked at her. She gave me a smile and two thumbs-up. I had been practicing so long by myself; I had no idea whether I was any good or not.

We recorded a few cuts that DeAngelo said he will hold on to until he could figure out how we could get the songs into development. He also suggested I sing in a few clubs around L.A.

"I don't know about that," I said, although the prospect was exciting to me. "Do you think I've got the presence to perform?"

"You got what it takes, girl," DeAngelo assured me. "What you don't have we'll teach you. The kind of music we're talking is slow and jazzy. We can help you with phrasing, style, and delivery."

This possibility was so far out of my imaginative reach—I didn't even know if I really wanted to do it or not. I never dreamed I'd be in this position. I knew I wanted to sing—but to sing at clubs, to record, to probably get an album out—that was something else entirely.

Jandro was still a toddler. I had to think about babysitting and practice time during the day. I felt bad about this. Jandro and I were inseparable until then—especially since I didn't work. We loved each other's company. He was becoming a playful child with long dark hair—it looked like a girl's—and honey-brown skin with smooth round features. He was a pleasure to hang with. But now I had to think of turning him over to a babysitter when Aracely couldn't watch him. Keisha helped a lot when I needed her to watch the boy. But leaving him was still a hard thing to do.

But to sing—sweet Jesus!—to bare my soul in melody, to make poetry with lyrics and voice, to tell my story with all its fuss and froth, with all its pain and poignancy, while honoring the greatest singers in the world by interpreting their work with my own experience—now, that was healing.

The nightclub's main room was small, intimate, and noisy. Smoke curled up from various tables. Conversation was in a loud drone—a woman laughed and glasses tinkled with ice. When the lights dimmed, people's faces appeared less clear, at times less real.

I was set to perform in minutes. This was my first public singing event. The place was called Blue Dog's in North Hollywood. DeAngelo had arranged the gig after we worked for weeks on my voice, trying to get me to have a better command of a few key songs. The way DeAngelo put it: I had to own these songs.

The band was made up of studio guys that Matthew knew—real musical geniuses. These guys could play anything. Three African-Americans, one Chicano, and a Korean. There was guitar, bass, sax, keyboards, and drums with other percussion instruments, including congas.

Aracely and Johnny sat at a table near the front of the stage—I wanted them to be part of my first break. When I told them I had recorded songs with DeAngelo, they lit up—they were so proud, I could tell. It seemed that the church and the people I met there were good for me, after all. While Aracely still challenged my thinking on Jesus, she was more accepting of the way I had changed my life.

I made sure Jandro was in good hands—Lito and Lita were more than willing to help. Jandro was normally a handful, but with my *abuelitos*—that's why we call them Lito and Lita, short for *abuelito* and *abuelita*—he never crossed any lines.

So there I was, sweating the big one, waiting to be called to the mike. I learned some unusually fresh songs—some of my old favorites—from artists like Ronnie Laws, Patrice Rushen, the Jones Girls, and Flora Purim, an eclectic list that DeAngelo was willing to help me with. I also knew some Mexican standards like "Los Laureles" and "Amor Eterno," but this was mostly an English-speaking crowd. I didn't mind. Whenever I did get in front of *mi gente*, I belted out a few of our beloved tearjerkers.

I tried to keep my mind off the fact that I was standing in a bar. Although my urge to drink or take drugs was curtailed by the prayer group and people like DeAngelo. But every once in a while I'd get that feeling, like an itch I needed to scratch but couldn't, to hold a glass in my hand and let the sting of a gin-and-juice or Tequila Sunrise slowly grease my throat.

I fought it—what I wanted more than anything at the moment was to sing.

With bottled water in hand, I strolled from the backstage area into the small performance space. I had on a long black-and-white dress that accentuated my still-curvy body, although I had gained a few pounds after Jandro's birth. My hair was short and wavy, after I'd spent most of the day with curlers affixed to my head. The lights shone bright onto my face. I could barely make out the people in the audience, although I could tell it was a decent crowd. I even managed to contact my old high school friends—Xochitl, Melinda, and Rosalia; only Xochitl said she might make it, but I couldn't see if she had or not.

"Hello, everybody," I said in a breathy voice, once I made it to the mike; the audience, in turn, became strangely quiet. "Thank you for coming to my singing debut. I have some friends and family here—I truly appreciate your support. Right now I'm kind of nervous . . . but anyway, my name's Azucena Salcido. The band behind me is called Walks of Life. I hope you like what we have to offer."

I then kicked off my first song, a mostly obscure but sweet composition by Stevie Wonder that I always loved: "Golden Lady." My parents used to say it was one of "their" songs—they had many—when they first hooked up. I sang it with as much emotion as I could muster. I heard it a lot growing up—my dad still had those ancient vinyl LPs that he tried to keep in good shape, although over time many of them were scratched and some not even playable. When CDs came out, he replenished many of his favorites and I learned to sing a few cuts from these mostly 1970s soul, as well as Chicano rock acts—like Santana, Malo, Azteca, El Chicano, and Tierra—that Aracely and Johnny always loved to play.

Accordingly, my next number that night was "Sabor a Mi," a Mexican standard that El Chicano brought back to the barrio those many years ago. Some people still call it "the Chicano National Anthem."

I sang a few more songs and the response was incredible—"Love Will Follow" by Kenny Loggins, "I Try" by Angela Bofill, "You Are My Starship" by Norman Connors, and "Give It All Your Heart" by Herbie Hancock. The band played smooth and just right—I tried to interpret each song as if it were mine. Because many of the songs were not very well known, it was as if they were originals. I didn't want to play popular songs—anybody could do that. I wanted to perform songs that weren't always appreciated, that were often ignored. It was just something I could identify with.

After the first set, we got a stirring round of applause. I felt so alive and necessary, almost as if I were born for this. I thanked everybody and walked backstage.

Aracely and Johnny came back to the dressing room to congratulate me. I felt so much love for them. I had given them hell for years, but they never gave up on me. They smiled and laughed—they seemed truly happy with me, their wayward daughter.

Xochitl also wandered in. I was surprised to see her. She had gotten so fat. I mean big, big, not just plump, as they say. But her pretty face still shone brightly. I stood up to greet her as well as her husband, an equally big Mexicano who seemed out of place in this situation and not very interested in its happenings. They said they had to leave right away, and were gone before we could talk about anything important.

After the second set, DeAngelo and I left Blue Dog's for his apartment. By then we had become lovers. I say that because he was a romantic gentleman. Even though he had once abused cocaine and the highest-priced booze back when he was deep into the music business, he still maintained his sleek demeanor and good taste far into his well-earned sobriety. That night, however, he was damn eager to get me out of my clothes. I was tired, I mean really pooped. But I figured I owed him what he wanted. I didn't mind, but I also have this thing: My mood determines what I want to do. I'm in the mood for love most of the time, thank God, but if I'm not, I become as limp as a wet towel. That night, our lovemaking seemed mediocre, just so-so.

The next morning we had our first major argument.

"You did great last night," remarked DeAngelo, talking directly to the omelet he made himself for breakfast. I wasn't that hungry, so I sat in front of him, a cup of coffee and a glass of orange juice near my hand.

"You mean *you* did great, D." I called him D. "Thanks for everything you've done. I never thought I would ever have a chance to do what I did last night. But it felt so natural, like I had been doing it for years. I never realized how comfortable I'd feel being up there in front of all those people."

"Yeah, the Blue Dog owners were also pleased. I'll be talking to them about having us do this on a regular basis. It'd be good to do a regular gig for a while. Afterward we can jam in other venues around town. You have a unique style and you have some strong material. We should be on our way."

I turned to DeAngelo with a tentative gaze. He liked to manage things, which was fine, but sometimes that meant telling me what to do. I felt as if he saw me as someone he could mold, an idea I didn't care for.

"Chena." D paused to consider his words. "Last night when we went to bed, you were different. Like you weren't really there. Is anything wrong?"

"Just tired, that's all."

"Tired? You seemed like you weren't into it at all. That's not like you. Everything cool?"

"It wasn't about the relationship," I said. "I was just tired. I sang two sets and had to entertain my family and friends. You were at a table hanging out. This was my first gig and I had pumped myself up so high that when it was over I crashed too fast."

"I mean, we're going to go far, you and me, but I don't want to feel like I'm not really what you want," he threw in.

"What are you talking about? I told you I was tired. End of story. Don't make this into something else."

"It *is* about something else." He raised his voice. "I'm not just here to get you gigs and record your stuff. If you wanted to have someone do that, you should get somebody else. I happen to be your man. I don't want to be just for show, you know."

My anger began to rise. I could feel it from the pit of my stomach. I tried to remain calm, but just hearing him say this brought to the surface tons of issues. I tried to back them off as much as I could.

"Listen, nobody here is using you," I said. "I'm not just doing this because you have these great connections. Remember, you offered me this; I didn't go to you. In fact, I wasn't sure I even wanted to do this. This was all your idea. So don't make it sound as if I'm pushing any of this on you. Don't do nothing for me if you don't want to."

"Hey, I'm doing this because I care. I believe in your gifts and beauty. What I'm saying is I don't want to be neglected. Last night was the worst sex we've ever had. It was your singing debut—it should have been our best. And don't tell me you were tired. I was tired, too. But I could still manage some passion. You, on the other hand, were practically asleep."

"Man, if I'm tired, I'm tired. I told you that last night. But you insisted. I told you wait until today. Everything would have been okay today. I just wasn't in the mood last night."

"You weren't in the mood? You have to be in the mood to make love?"

"Yeah, doesn't everybody?"

"Man, if I love you I don't need a mood. I just love you. I'm there."

"Who's talking about love? We're dating. We're seeing each other. I like you, but love—that's something else."

"You don't love me? Oh." He paused. "You using me, maybe? Maybe after, you'll get rid of me. Is that your plan?"

"What in the world are you talking about?" I said, exasperated. "I don't have any plans. I like you; I'm willing to see how far we go with this relationship. But I'm not going to bullshit you and talk about love when I'm not there yet, when we're not there yet."

DeAngelo stood up. I'm not sure why, perhaps my past, my issues maybe, but I thought he was going to hit me.

"Sit down," I said sharply. "What, you gonna hit me?"

"Now you've got it all fucked up. I'm just walking into the living room. I'm not going to touch you."

"I've been fucked up before—I'm not afraid. You try it and I'll come back and kick your ass. I've been in a few fights, D."

"Fights? Are you crazy? We're just arguing here. Who's talking about fights?"

"Don't call me crazy, fucker," I stammered.

Now I was getting tight with rage. I didn't know why; I should have just let this go. But somehow our simple disagreement escalated into a full-blown "fuck you" session. At least on my part.

"I'm not your 'fucker,' my dear. I could hardly get a nut off last night. I'm far from that."

"Don't start throwing that shit at me again. Can't you respect my space?"

"Maybe you better have a two-sided sign around your neck that says, 'Come Get Some,' and 'Don't Bother.' "

"Fuck you!" I yelled, and then threw my glass of orange juice on him. We both stood there, shocked. A bird chirped outside the kitchen window.

"What's everybody yelling about?" D's daughter, Keisha, asked as she walked into the kitchen in her pajamas, rubbing the sleep from her eyes.

DeAngelo looked at her, wiped his face with a napkin, and walked her back to her bedroom. He helped her get dressed and then they left.

"You know how to lock up when you're ready to leave," is the last thing DeAngelo said before walking out the door.

I was so livid I didn't know what to do. I got into the shower, hoping the water would cool me down. I didn't know why I got so mad. Maybe because I don't like to be smothered, to be told what to do, to be challenged. I know that's my problem, but you'd think DeAngelo would know not to go there. I mean, why do that? But he didn't know when to stop. I would have stopped challenging him if he just backed off about my being tired the night before.

I didn't hear from DeAngelo until later that afternoon. I told him

I'd be at my parents' house if he wanted to reach me. I wondered, however, if this meant he wouldn't help me with my singing or getting any more club gigs. I almost didn't care anymore. He tried to apologize, but I hold my grudges long and tight.

Two days later, I tried to call DeAngelo, only to hear his answering machine. I didn't leave a message. I felt terrible that things had gotten so bad. I feared I wouldn't be able to relate to Keisha anymore. I also sensed that I blew my chance at ever singing in public again.

I spent most of the next few weeks with Jandro. That's how I get out of most funks. Jandro brings me immeasurable joy. DeAngelo and I talked a few times. But the fight created a massive gulf between us. He was just more into the relationship than I was.

One morning, we met for coffee in Old Town Pasadena, where he liked to hang out. I made a suggestion to him.

"D, listen, maybe we should let go of the singing thing until we get to a point where our relationship is stronger—or let's just forget the relationship for now and concentrate on the singing. One or the other—right now it's too stressful to try and do both."

"How 'bout we just forget about both," DeAngelo retorted.

"Oh, that's how it is now—it's all or nothing. Okay, D, I was willing to step halfway into this relationship, but you want it that way. Then fine. Don't help me with the singing. And let's drop this relationship thing. That's what you want? I'm not standing in the way."

"That's not what I want. I want us to have a mutually beneficial and loving partnership while also working on your singing," DeAngelo intoned, using a phrase he'd learned from our recovery group. "You say we can't do both, okay then, let's not do either."

"What sense does that make?" I countered. "We can still work on our songs and gigs. That's got its own life. And maybe, later, we can come back together again."

"That sounds so practical, so correct," stated DeAngelo. "I'm not about that. Love ain't got no practical steps. It happens or it doesn't. You, on the other hand, can turn it on and off like a faucet. Well, I can't. I want more out of my women—you seem quite comfortable taking what you can't give."

"Don't tell me what I'm comfortable with. You don't have any idea about what I can or can't do. I'm only saying there's a way through this and you're saying you're not having any of it. That's your decision. But don't put it on me as if I didn't try to salvage what we had. I gave you my idea of how we can make something of this. You don't want to listen, okay, don't waste my time."

We didn't talk for the rest of the morning.

It was clear to me then that D and I were finished as a couple. I tried to put up a strong front, like it was no sweat off my back, but I did so only to protect myself. Later that night I cried, I mean a lot. I felt alone and unfulfilled. I cried for D and Keisha, I cried for Raton and Ricardo and Trigger and people I cared about in middle and elementary school but who didn't care about me. I cried because I felt like I was born to be alone, unloved, to raise Jandro by myself. A loving relationship like what Aracely and Johnny have, which is my ideal, didn't seem to be in the cards for me. And I felt sad, broken-down tired, so much like dying.

Days after D and I broke up, I was in the kitchen with Aracely. While I washed dishes she prepared ingredients for her hot and tasty one-of-a-kind salsa. I had already told her that DeAngelo and I had broken up.

"I wish I could still sing," I said. "But DeAngelo only wanted to help me if I loved him. I can't just make that happen. I was just falling in love; we still needed more time and intimacy. He just couldn't wait."

"I understand, *m'ija*, men are usually the impatient ones," my mother said. "But the other thing is maybe you shouldn't worry about the singing for now. Get a job. Or go to school and find yourself a career. You need to have something solid to fall back on, for you and Jandro's sake."

"Singing *is* solid," I responded. "It's a career. It's also something I'd rather do. I can work in many jobs. But nothing is as good to me as my singing. I know if I stay with it long enough, I'll make enough money to survive."

"Sure, *m'ija*, but it's unrealistic right now," Aracely explained. "What have you gotten for the recording and singing you've done so far? If you work and maybe go to school, you'll have your bills paid and some left over for clothes and things—for Jandro's schooling even. I think you should let the singing go for a while."

"Mom, I can't believe you're saying this." I turned around, irritated. "You know how much I love to sing. Now is the time to do something about it—I may never get this chance again. I want to really do this. Maybe I don't make it. Maybe I don't get enough pay for doing this. But I'll never know unless I try."

"I'm just saying, I know how hard things can be. You have to be realistic, too. Neither your father nor I did what we *wanted*. That was never an issue for us. We did what we had to do."

"That's the problem—too many people in this world doing what others want them to do," I responded. "There's no life in them. No passions. They're just taking up space, living in bodies without souls. Most of them become naysayers. The gatekeepers. They don't want to see anyone else find their happiness. To fulfill their dreams. I may be wrong, but I've had a taste of what singing can be; I've heard that applause. I'll never be the same. This is what I have to do, Mom."

Aracely stood there, an irritated look on her face.

My mother and father lived that hard factory life—you had to do practical, reasonable things in their world. Dreams were frivolous and pointless in their world. It was better to destroy them than to have the world crush them for you. That was what schools did, the priests and nuns, the neighbors. I heard this my whole life, and it had gotten me nowhere.

I couldn't really blame my mom and dad. I knew they were shaped by the circumstances of their environment. I just felt I had to try something else. I knew I looked more lost than focused, more confused than clear—a result of my own environment, one that's chaotic, uncertain, shifting by the minute. This was the only reality I knew.

I wanted to make something happen before I got stale, before I got as tired and dreamless as everyone else seemed to be.

Things fell apart for me after D and I finally broke up. It wasn't so much about him. I could live without his companionship. It was just that my hopes of singing onstage and recording were tied to DeAngelo—and when that ship sank so did those hopes.

As much as I wanted to get back to singing, I needed help from people like D who knew the industry, the venues, and how to promote. I wanted to sing but I didn't know how to get the gigs, to do demos and talk to industry people. That wasn't what I was interested in. Singing, that's all I cared about—but it wasn't going to happen.

Unfortunately, I also stopped going to the recovery group and the church. I found it hard to sit through meetings with DeAngelo sitting right there. I felt like letting this go for a while. Pastor Roy called me, so did some of my friends in the group. They'd come to the house. I told my mom not to answer the door, and she was more than happy to comply. She never liked my turning to Jesus in the first place. I now saw the hollowness of loving Jesus more than valuing myself. In the church I looked away from me—that's what this church thing does. Jesus is both resurrection and the life. What about me? Where's my resurrection, my life? They taught me to look up, away from the world, but I wanted to find a way to walk in this world, with balance, strength, confidence, and love. I didn't want to keep isolating myself because I was scared of everything I touched.

I stopped going to church altogether.

Because Aracely was adamant about me working, I tried to get jobs. I'd go from crap job to crap job. Once I sold tacos at a local food stand where the owner one night tried to corner me in the kitchen when no one was around. He fired me when I didn't give in. I did some office work but was promptly let go due to jealousy on the part of the other women who worked there—apparently, I was getting too much attention from the men.

I also waited tables and worked the cash register at a clothing store. The money was okay, not great, of course, but enough to help me catch up on a few bills and make sure Jandro had clothes and school materials. Nothing fancy, let me tell you.

It wasn't long before I ended up back in those clubs, just me in some corner booth, looking at up-and-coming singers, wishing it were me, while ordering gin-and-tonics, one right after the other. I went back to drinking. It was my solace for a while. I turned my back on everything I learned about recovery and Jesus. I knew this was a mistake, but I was just too pissed off and depressed to do otherwise.

I went to the clubs on weekends, after I made sure Jandro was okay and asleep, and Aracely or Lito and Lita were around to watch him. I then started going during the week. The jobs stank. My life stank. I just wanted to hide in my beer-and-bourbon washes.

That was when I started hanging out with bad men again. Men I met in the bars. I wasn't even sure they were cute or had any redeeming social value. If I drank enough, though, whoever happened to be talking to me when I got plastered was who I'd be with. I call it "crossing over," that point while drinking when you lose consciousness but you keep talking, walking, and acting like your mind is still there, present, alive, even though it's not.

I'd go to their homes, have sex, at least I think I had sex, and end up getting dumped back at my house in the morning. I still had to get ready to work at the restaurant, food stand, or store—depending on the job I had that week—so I was dead tired and good for nothing most of the time.

Sometimes, I'd wake up thinking I was in my bed. But I'd look over and spot a strange man lying next to me. I'd try to focus my eyes and wouldn't recognize any of the furniture, the walls, the floor or ceiling. I'd get scared. I wanted to cry but I didn't want to wake the guy up, whoever he was. I felt like shit. What happened to me? I was getting big around my thighs, my stomach and arms. I began to lose the smoothness in my face, the sparkle in my eye, the jump in my step. My panties would be on the floor. My panties! My most private things, on some fool's grimy floor. I thought about how gross I had become, how I couldn't stop. I thought about how many countless pairs of panties I'd left on nameless floors around the city.

This lasted for years. I refer to them as my lost years.

Poor Jandro suffered during those years. I seemed to have missed most of Jandro's childhood. I yelled at him a lot, many times for no reason. I want to cry when I think about it. He didn't deserve any of this. He was always a good boy, a sweet and caring kid. But I began to turn him into something mean and distant. He'd go to his room and listen to CDs, watch TV, or play video games whenever he came home from school—most times not talking to me at all.

I didn't know what to say to him anymore, either. When he wandered into the kitchen or the living room, and I happened to be there, I'd say mean things. I didn't even know why. I'd question how he was doing—about his schoolwork, if he took out the trash or cleaned his room. We had nothing else to talk about. I knew this aggravated him. He'd argue with me. In turn, I got *brava* with him, into his face, looking him up and down, as if I were going to hit him. It was hard for Jandro to stand up to me, but he was doing it more and more. Slowly, but ever so surely, I was losing my son.

One day, I got a phone call. It was the police.

"We have your son, Alejandro Moreno, at the station," the female officer stated. "We'd like you to come by and take him home."

"What happened?" I asked.

"We found stolen items in his possession after we stopped him and a couple of other kids at the park," she said matter-of-factly. "We know this is his first time. But we could get him adjudicated and sent to juvenile hall. I'd just like to talk to you to see if this is the best way to go."

I drove to the police station, upset as hell, and picked him up. I let him know I was pissed, but he just looked away, tired, not even afraid. I grounded him for a month. He didn't seem affected. I tried to stay home during that month, but I still found my moments to sneak away and get plastered.

Not long after that incident, I came home early in the morning, around 4 A.M., and I walked up the stairs to the second-floor bedroom. To my surprise Jandro was still up, standing at the head of the stairs. He had a glass of milk in his hand. He seemed bigger, taller, looking too much like Raton, if you ask me. I felt bad seeing him there. I walked up the stairs as he stood there and hugged him. I was drunk but hadn't blacked out yet. I can still remember Jandro recoiling from me, grasping that glass of milk with trembling hands as I tried to hold him, weeping into his hair. I was sure he was disgusted with me. But he didn't say anything. He didn't have to. It was the way he shut down. The way he hid from me. Even with us together, he knew how to put his mind into another place, off into a distant land, far away from this house, this reality—from me.

I didn't want to see him this way anymore. I had to stop. Jandro wouldn't reach out to me. It was on me. I had no one to blame for this. If Jandro went off into the world, joined a gang like his father, and drank like I did, who would be responsible? Even if I wasn't ready, I had to be the stable and mature person here. I had to wake up from this illusion—it didn't mean sacrificing my dreams, it meant going toward them, making them happen, by healing myself, and becoming what I knew I was supposed to be so that Jandro could look at me with eyes I had not seen in many years—eyes filled with respect and love.

It was time for me to sober up. To live up to what I wanted my own son to do. To stop living two fractured and irreconcilable lives. It's funny how we, as parents, are supposed to save our kids when they need it. But most times, they end up saving us.

I decided to quit drinking on my own. I didn't want to go back to the church. It was years since I was last there—I really felt like a failure. Yet I wanted to control this thing. The recovery groups were good for strength, for guidance, for support when you needed it. But I'd turned them into a crutch, into my religion—into my everything. It was good I wasn't drinking. When I was active at the church, life was healthier and I was calmer. But I was mainly going to meetings three times a week and even on weekends just because I was afraid to be alone.

This was when I went to Johnny. I had rarely talked to my father the past few years. I mean a good heartfelt daughter-and-dad talk. We interacted briefly from time to time, but he was into his work and pretty much left most of the talking to my mom. I had heard from her how he had stopped drinking those many years ago. How he did it mostly by himself, since he didn't trust the rehabilitation program at the Nazareth Steel Mill—or treatment programs outside the mill, which were nonexistent or limited to those who could pay.

One day on a hot summer's afternoon, I saw Johnny sitting on the front porch, drinking some of Lita's *té de limón*. That's a tea made from lemongrass, good for many ailments, but also just to enjoy. On a hot day it's better than a soft drink.

"Hey, Pop. How're you doing?" I asked, standing next to his rocking chair.

"I'm good, *m'ija*, just relaxing on my day off. How about you? I rarely see you anymore."

"I've been working, been partying too much, too, but I'm trying to stop that." I looked at him, wanting desperately to tell him everything, to confess, hoping that if I did, my life, Jandro's life, could somehow finally make sense to me. "Dad, I need to talk to you."

"Chena, of course, anytime. I'm always here for you, you know that. You're always on my mind and in my heart. What can I do for you, *muñeca?*"

"Well, this is hard to talk about but let me try," I said, pulling up a wooden chair next to the rocker and leaning close to my father. "I'm having problems with Jandro. I mean, he's a good boy and all, but we're not close. We don't talk. He stays aloof from me, in his room, sometimes with his skater friends. I'm trying now to invite him to places—to the park, the museum, to a movie. But he's not interested. I know it's my fault. I work all the time, but then afterward I go to clubs and drink and—well, you know how it is. I wasn't there for him. I want to change this. I'm trying to stop drinking. I know this will help a lot. But I need your advice, you know, to be more in control. Sometimes I just get these notions I need to lose myself, to forget about the important things. I know it's selfish. I want to stop being selfish. I want to be there for Jandro and even for myself. I'm desperate, Dad, otherwise I wouldn't talk to you like this. I didn't want you to know some of these things, but I need a major change in my life. I need it right now."

Johnny looked at me with those lived-in, watery eyes and his hard-

ened face, softened by a wry smile and a well-worn finger scratching
the stubble on his cheek.

"Well, *m'ija*, I've learned a few things in this world, having been a
mechanic all my life and a Communist for almost as long. Sometimes
they follow the same principles. When something breaks down you
stop and have to check out where the problem is. If you can't see it
right away, you take things apart until you find it. Every problem has a
source. You have to trust that's true. You also have to trust that any
problem has a solution right next to it. Sometimes we don't see it because we're looking the other way. It seems to me you've figured out
the problem—and, from what I can tell, the solution as well. The only
real issue is what to do next. Good mechanics know how all machines
generally work, so they can tackle any machine, even if they've never
laid eyes on a particular machine. This problem you have, many of us
have had. It's not just you. And many of us have gone through it
enough to find ways out."

Johnny then raised his callused hand and spread out his fingers.

"Let me tell you about five things, five lifelines, five points to
remember to keep your life on track. It's helped me when I've felt disoriented, after falling down and learning again and again how to
get myself up. Now listen: There's a reason we have five fingers. Five
senses. There are always five things to everything you want to know. In
your situation, *m'ija*, the first thing is to find your art. There's painting,
dance, music, poetry. Even teaching, carpentry, and mechanics are
arts—they shouldn't just be a job. I remember your singing. You were
truly in your element there. I don't think you should give it up—"

"But mom says—" I tried to interrupt.

"I know what your mother says," Johnny continued, over my
words. "She's not wrong. Just listen to what I'm saying right now. . . .
Next find your spiritual path. Some people become Christians—like
you did. It's better, in my opinion, if they really follow what Christ says
rather than what some church, preacher, or institution says He said.
But there are many other paths as well. They're all different, they're all
beautiful, and they're all valid. The point is all of them lead to the same
center, the same 'God,' if you will. This center is too big to fit into any

box or category. The Creator doesn't care how you paint Him, imagine Him, or believe in Him. Or even that you think it's a 'Him.' Beliefs are man-made issues. There are, however, principles of life, of balance and coherency, that most spiritual paths contain, which lead to the same light. I know you think I'm an atheist, but even atheists can be spiritual, if you want to know the truth, whether they know it or not. The point is I'm not religious. I'm not against it for others, but not for me. But I still think you have to develop a healthy and vibrant spiritual life."

"Man, Dad, that's great to hear from you. What else?" I asked, really interested since it echoed much of what I had learned in recovery groups, only without the moralist rhetoric.

"Next—and mind you, these don't have to go in any order—find your cause. This is something beyond yourself. I found mine in the struggle for justice and equity. I call it communism—others may not agree, but this is what I'm about. I'm not about the Soviet Union or China or even Cuba. Those countries are doing their own thing and some are doing better than others, but they also have big problems. Still the road to communism is real regardless of what some so-called Communists have said or done. We say in CLOC that we reserve the right to support states or parties conditionally while supporting revolutions unconditionally. Just because most people think communism is no good doesn't bother me—our aims are similar to any decent, caring, and intelligent revolutionary: to remove the power of private property to exploit, enslave, and manipulate the world for the gain of a few, and to create a world where everyone cooperates for the benefit of everyone else. Your cause for now may be to become a better mother. That's a great cause. I also have that as a father. Find a cause or causes, but apply your art, your dreams, to bettering the world—your family and community included.

"The fourth finger represents finding help. This is important. Nobody can truly live full and complete lives all by themselves. Sure this culture pushes the 'rugged individualist.' The self-made man. But that's mostly BS. They're more like the 'ragged individualist.' Of course, having individual interests, initiative, and discipline is important for any of us—just remember you are part of the human family. Others have been where you're going. Find a mentor, a teacher—get help. The fact you asked me for advice is a big start, *m'ija*."

"Next"—here Johnny held up his thumb—"whatever happens, you have to own your life. That's something your brother, Joaquin, didn't understand. I was just like him as a kid. He turned his life over to the barrio. He didn't have anything left for himself, for his mother, for you or me—for his own kids. When the gang goes down, he goes down. Now he's in the perfect place for those who give up their core being—in prison. He thinks he's his own man, but we all know he's trapped like a spider in the web. He's not a fly in the web—he's the spider, making it harder for him to unravel since he's also put himself into this trap. In your case, you've turned yourself over to the drugs, the alcohol, and, if you don't mind me saying, to men. You gave too much of yourself up for some of those men. You tend to let go of the good guys and get stuck with the rotten guys. Lots of girls do that—turn everything over to some *pendejo*. So when a guy abuses them, ignores them, or leaves, they don't have anything left for themselves. Make your mistakes, *m'ija*, own up to them, and make your successes—revel in them, 'cause they're all yours."

When Johnny finished, I stayed quiet. Speechless actually. In a few minutes my dad changed my life. I was twenty-eight years old. Maybe he couldn't tell me any of this until I asked, until I had reached the end of my rope, until I had matured enough to even care. That's the mechanic's way, I suppose. They don't tell you outright how to do things. But when you need to know, they're there. They know.

"Pop, I don't know what to say, but thank you," I finally responded as Johnny went to drink more of his *té de limón*. "I'm not going to take all this in right away; I feel like I have a way to go. But I'm going to be a better mother. That'll be my cause for now. I'm going to show Jandro that even though I've made mistakes, big ones, some of which I'll never be able to make up, I can also change. I can also become the mother he deserves and I know he wants." I started to cry. "I love you, Dad. I love Mom, too. I know she was right. I see that now. She was trying to get me to think of some immediate things and not use my singing as an excuse to get away from my responsibilities. I now have to find a way to do both—not sacrifice my child for my dreams and not sacrifice my dreams for my child. But something has to come first. Right now Jandro has to be my focus and purpose. I feel great just saying this. Thank you, thank you, thank you."

I got up to embrace my father, who placed his strong hand around my shoulder, closed his eyes, and smiled. I hadn't felt this close to him since I was a little girl. Somehow, I forgot to turn to him during my teens and twenties when I should have. I wondered how that happened. I thought about Jandro and realized it will be the same for my son unless I build those bridges now. What my dad said was fantastic. The hard part was putting it into practice.

Just like putting a broken machine back together again.

13

HEAT

"Go back to where you came from!"

The words cut through me like a knife. It was not long after my talk with Johnny. I needed to find a way out of my lethargy, the stagnation that could pull me into the booze, sex, and the neglect of my son again, unless I made some kind of move. Any move.

My dad told me, "To make a change, all you need is two steps—the first step, then the next step."

I understood—just do something. I began looking for a job, a direction, a miracle maybe, walking down Glenoaks Boulevard in Sylmar, one of the main streets here. I was in my thoughts, thinking about Jandro, about my parents, about working, and maybe taking community college classes at night. Sylmar has a great low-fee working-class school called Mission College. I felt good, that I might actually stay sober, remembering my dad's advice, and looking forward to new things, new openings, new risks.

Then this guy said it again from the back of a pickup truck: "Go back to where you came from!"

I wanted to yell back: *I am where I came from*, cabrón! *This is my land. It was my land before Columbus made a wrong turn, before the Pilgrims sailed in on the* Mayflower, *and before European immigrants landed at Ellis Island.*

But I didn't get a chance to say this. I was just able to flip him the bird before the pickup truck flew past me.

I'm aware that this beautiful, sunny, golden state, California, has always been a place of conflict, but it had become particularly divided in the past twenty years, let me tell you.

I was seething over what that nameless guy in the truck yelled at me. But I kept walking, only now I was practically stomping my feet. I crossed through a strip mall that sported a small grocery store, a hair salon, a ninety-eight-cent store, a manicurist, and a pizza joint. At the end of the mall was a funky little bookstore and café. It had a painted sign that said LO NUESTRO, which means "Ours."

I walked up and looked at a wall plastered with flyers about local readings, musical events, talks, art receptions, and workshops. A display of Chicano books graced its window. I went inside—the place was rustic, kind of *rasquache*, and painted in warm earth tones. There was explosive art on the walls and Mexican-style gifts and Chicano *movimiento* T-shirts. On one wall were shelves with books, in Spanish and English, on Chicano literature, indigenous culture, history, politics, and colorful bilingual children's books. A pretty young teenager was at the counter, taking orders for espresso coffee, including cappuccinos with Oaxacan and Guatemalan coffee beans. The voice of the Mexican singer Lila Downs emanated from the speakers. I'd never seen a place like this.

Go back to where I came from!—yeah, sure, just look at this place. I felt here was where I belonged. Here was proof this *is* home.

A good-looking older woman in her fifties, with long braided hair and a colorful *huipili*—an indigenous Mexican blouse—emerged from the small kitchen. She said something in another language, which I assumed was Aztec or Mayan, and then greeted me in English and Spanish with a smile.

"*Gualli tonalli . . . Good day . . . Bienvenidos*," she burst out.

"Wow, this is something else—when did you open this up?" I asked.

"We've been open a few months. My name is Xitlalli—what's yours?"

"I'm Azucena," I said.

I told her about the guy in the pickup truck. Xitlalli motioned for me to sit down while I was still talking. She had one of the counter girls make me any kind of coffee I wanted. I asked for a mocha. Xitlalli listened to my story, and then explained why Lo Nuestro was created.

"We are under attack—by racists, as well as others, even some racist so-called Hispanics," she said. "We need to have a place where we can sit down, talk, share ideas, and maybe learn about our history, languages, and indigenous teachings."

"Okay," I said. "I'm interested." It was the door I was looking to walk through.

I eventually got a job working at Lo Nuestro. It doesn't pay much, but I felt like I was in the right spot. Although I was older than most of the Chicanos and Chicanas who hung out here, I paid attention to the heated discussions at the tables about indigenous consciousness and community events.

This was where I met Pancho Reyes. One day, he walked into the café while I was in front of the espresso machine making a latte. He had a large black portfolio under an arm—an artist trying to get the gallery here to show his work. He appeared closer to my age than the other people sitting around. Pancho looked around, then spotted me in a black apron with the words *Lo Nuestro*, written in colorful lettering.

"Excuse me, miss, who can I talk to about showing my art?" he asked.

I turned around and got a good eyeful of him. He seemed kind of weird at first—with long hair, pierced lower lip, Aztec sun calendar tattooed on his arm. But that was who walked into Lo Nuestro—the creative, way-out youth activists that I hadn't seen anywhere else. They stood out, but they were also smart and terribly engaging.

"You can talk to me," I said to Pancho.

Pancho smiled while placing the portfolio on the counter. He opened it to show several photos of paintings—they were alive with bright colors and images of animals, shapes, faces, as well Aztec and Mayan motifs. His art had a kind of urban-graffiti style to it. I really didn't know much about art, but I was beginning to get a feel for it.

"You're good," I responded, flirting.

"I live in the neighborhood—just around the corner," he said.

"Ummm," I replied.

"Well, I'd like to show my work at the café. I've only had a couple of exhibits, but I've been painting for years, mostly doing this on my own. I walked by one day and checked this place out. It seems perfect for what I do."

"Okay, but the owners aren't here just now," I said. "But I like what I see. Can you leave the portfolio and a way to contact you? I'm sure we can work something out."

Pancho hesitated—like he didn't want to let go of his portfolio. Maybe he saw how truly moved I was by his work.

"Fine," he said. "I'm sure I'm leaving these in good hands."

After our initial encounter, Pancho came into the café almost every day. Soon he was asking me to see a play or a movie. It was dating but it felt friendlier and natural—I began to like his company. He was into books, music, art, movies—the kind of things I had mostly neglected, but now felt compelled to reach out for.

He also got along with Xitlalli. In a couple of months, his art pieces ended up gracing Lo Nuestro's peeling walls.

One day, Xitlalli invited Pancho and me to a purification sweat-lodge ceremony. I had no idea what this was, but according to Xitlalli, she only invited people she felt were ready to learn and participate.

The lodge was built by Xitlalli's companion, Omar Cuevas, and other Chicano/indigenous activists in the northeast Valley. It was situated behind Omar's mother's house in the Pacoima barrio.

To get to the lodge, you walked through a rusted black wrought-iron fence onto a long driveway—up to then the place looked like any stuccoed-over barrio home with three different apartmentlike rooms, housing various families. But then you entered the backyard, where piles of wood and lava rocks surrounded by tree-trunk benches sat, all near a metal-covered fire pit. The frame of the lodge, in willows, was on the other side of the fire pit, its entryway facing east. A garden of cornstalks, *nopales*, and medicinal herbal plants were against a cinder-block wall. Next to the wall, a *huehuetl*, or Mexika (Aztec) vertical drum, was being made by placing hot coals in the middle of a tree trunk, letting them burn all the way through, hollowing out the trunk. A wooden shed held blankets and tarps that were used to cover the lodge for our ceremonies. Beautifully painted and stained homegrown water gourds hung from the sides of the homes.

When I first met Omar, he sat Pancho and me around a fire he had going in the backyard. He told us that the sweat lodge is the oldest continuous community ritual in the Americas—the sweats go back tens of thousands of years. Other cultures had them, but the native peoples on this continent perfected the spiritual and cleansing aspects that are vital to the ceremony. These lodges have different names depending on the tribal groups. The Lakota call it an *inipi* (most people in the United States do Lakota-style sweats). The Mexika—the so-called Aztecs as well as most Central Mexican cultures—call their sweat lodges *temescalli*. California Indians, Navajos, and others have their own styles. The differences include how they are built—some with earth or willows or stone—but their essence is the same.

Omar pointed out that in the indigenous Chicano circles we incorporated the *inipi* and *temescalli* styles. The *inipi* is generally made with river willows that are carefully formed into a round lodge. Prayer ties, in red cloth bundles, are hung from the top of the lodge to carry our prayers to spirit. Blankets and tarps are used to cover the lodge just before a ceremony. Several lava rocks—these are the best to retain heat and not crack like other rocks—are heated in an intense fire for at least two hours before the ceremony. An earthen altar is placed in front of the lodge opening, or door, usually facing east in the Mexika style or west in the Lakota style.

I learned that urban sweat lodges had become common by the early 2000s—although there are people who say the lodges should always be set up in nature, in the mountains or in an open clearing. But with many Chicanos getting into the sweats, it makes sense to have sweat lodges in the 'hood. The only major issue is that sometimes you get people from the neighborhood who don't respect its sacredness. Neighbors peered over the fences and even laughed at us as we lined up to enter the lodge. These same neighbors threw weekend parties with *norteños* and *cumbias* blasting from a boom box and *carne asada* on the barbecue grill with lots of beer, laughter, yelling, and a *pleito* or two.

We learned to push these sights and sounds away, to concentrate on our prayers, our chants, our songs. After a while we didn't even notice we weren't surrounded by nature—although we brought nature into our world with the rocks, the feathers, the fire, the smoke, and sitting on Tonantzin, our Mother Earth. It goes to show that the sacred can happen anywhere, any time that you bring the right intentions, the right teachings, and a good heart into whatever you do.

That blistering summer we had a number of sweats. It was tough, considering how intense the lodge can get with the water poured over the red-hot lava rocks. But it taught us a thing or two about endurance. It was helpful for my recovery—Omar is also a recovering addict and ex-*pinto*. I ended up going to sweats once a week or more. Whenever someone needed healing, we'd pull together whoever was available and get them into the sweat. You have to make time for ceremonies; you can't plan anything around them. Sweats don't run like mass on Sundays. They are indigenous rituals and therefore run on ritual time. You think you're in the sweat for an hour or so only to find out that when you emerge from the "womb," two or three hours have gone by.

And the sweats are helpful for anyone in AA or NA—we worked with many recovering addicts and alcoholics. While we gathered in a circle with our friends and family, we also called on our ancestors and all the elements, the Great Spirit and all its manifestations to gather among us. There are a variety of energies to draw from.

For the most part, the men did their sweats separately from the women, but every once in a while we'd come together in community sweats. We also had talking circles with an eagle feather so we could interact, express, and share.

A legitimate pipe carrier—such as Omar—will sometimes facilitate the lodge proceedings, but most are run by local teachers and elders. Fire keepers and cedar men—they bring in the cedar as medicine—help out as well. The fire keeper maintains the fire and brings in the red-hot stones to the middle of the lodge, where a hole has been excavated.

The stones are people, too: They're called grandfathers and grandmothers—our ancestors. All the elements of nature are used in the lodge: Water is poured over the fiery rocks, causing the steam; earth, our mother, is beneath us; the rocks hold our memories and stories; air is alive through the tobacco smoke and the steam; nature, also known as change, is represented by the sage, cedar, tobacco, and *copál*, the sweet-smelling resin from trees in Mexico and Central America; and fire, which heats up the rocks and provides the steam that heats up our bodies and heals spirits. There are four rounds in which the "door" is opened to let out the steam. We're supposed to stay for the whole four rounds; each round has a different healing purpose. But sometimes, especially for first-timers, people leave before the four rounds are finished. They can't take the intensity.

The point of a sweat lodge, I learned, is spiritual cleansing. Purification and balance. The intensity is as great as using drugs and alcohol, but with none of the negative effects. We drink herbal teas, including the Navajo lightning tea, which really packs a wallop. Some people throw up after drinking it. All of this is good—it's the toxicity in our bodies that is being removed. The sweat from our bodies helps to carry out this toxicity, this negativity. You can't go into the lodge if you use drugs or have been drinking. Because of the lodge's use in recovery, we know people relapse, but they have to wait at least forty-eight hours to several days from their last drink, or even longer for drug use, before they can come in.

Because there's a community and a facilitator, it's always monitored. The grandparents, the stones, talk to you when the water is poured. Sometimes you see things in the red-hot stones—faces, devils, angels, your kids, your fears, whatever you need to see. You pray in the lodge. You chant and sing in the lodge—there are many beautiful

Lakota songs and Navajo peyote songs. Some people know songs and chants in Nahuatl, the language of the Mexika people. Female and male energies are brought to bear. Nature and spirit. You feel like an ancient Indian. You feel like your ancestors must have felt thousands of years before, going through what they were going through. Mostly you feel like you're back in the womb, in the embrace of our mother, the earth, since the idea is to be reborn again when you emerge at the end of four rounds.

Not everything in the sweat is serious, though. I mean, you're supposed to go into the lodge with solemn intent and awareness. You're supposed to not curse or joke around. But sometimes we share a laugh or two. Like when we're in the sweat earnestly praying, and someone lets out a loud fart. That's nature. You can't help it. But it's still funny.

One time a young guy entered a particularly crowded lodge of at least thirty people. He was eighteen or nineteen years old and had never been to a sweat ceremony before. When you have that many participants, everyone has to be packed tight with two or three rows of people. Often legs would cramp if the people weren't used to sitting in the same position for a long time. Anyway, this guy was scared and talked a lot and generally annoyed everyone. We were patient, explaining things to him, getting him to calm down. I think he thought he was going to die. He complained about the heat. He complained that he couldn't breathe. He complained that everyone's prayers were sucking the air out of the place. Then he really lost it—in the middle of somebody's fervent expressions, he yelled out, "I can't feel my leg! Something's wrong, man, I can't feel my leg!"

Omar asked him to relax and take his time in explaining what was happening.

"I went to rub my right leg and I couldn't feel nothing, man!" he shouted, his voice in a panic.

Then someone next to him responded in a rather nonchalant way, "You were rubbing *my* leg, dude."

We laughed for the longest time after that.

One of the funniest things to witness is when Omar brings these real hard-core gangbangers—they've seen it all, done it all, right? They're heavily tattooed and scary looking. But as soon as they get into the sweat, inevitably one or two of them fall apart. Not all of them—most of them can take a lot of heat. But you get that one guy who thinks he's all "gangsta lean," but as soon as the water is poured over the rocks, he's ready to get out, although he's only been in a couple of minutes. I've had middle-school-age girls enter the sweat and go through all four rounds without any complaints. But a couple of these so-called killers begin fainting or running out of the lodge as soon as they feel the first beads of sweat on their skin.

In the sweat you really get to find out what people are made of. You can't BS in there. You can't play games—the sweat will get you in the end. A couple of people try to come into the lodge loaded on drugs or booze—they don't last long. The sweat knows and makes it extremely uncomfortable. As Omar says, the facilitator can only do so much— the rest is in the energies, the male and female energies, which are evoked and then adjust themselves to what the sweat participants actually need.

"I just don't want to, Mom," Jandro yelled out from his chair in front of the TV.

Jandro is now eleven, a killer age for any kid in any city.

"Listen, son, I think you'll like what I'm doing," I said, walking toward him. "I know I haven't always been there for you, but you know I'm making some big changes here. Most of this has to do with the sweat lodge—I'd like for you to check it out."

"Mom, I'm tired. I have tons of homework."

I started to get mad—*yeah, he doesn't seem to have "homework" when he's invited to the mall or to hang with his friends.* But I stopped myself. I knew in my heart it would be wrong if I did that.

"I only want you to share this experience with me—it's really something. . . . I can't do it justice by just talking about it."

"Is this like the Christian thing?" added Jandro, sarcasm in his voice.

I realized he was judging me from my past behaviors. I knew it was going to take a while before he could truly trust what I said and did.

"It's all right, son, I'll be leaving then for about three hours. Lito and Lita are in the back if you need anything, okay?"

Jandro didn't say a word.

My authority as a mother was being questioned most of the time. But it was Pancho who helped me realize how important a decent and strong man was for a boy like Jandro. Mothers can do a lot—and when the men aren't around, we do just fine, thank you. But you also know there's something missing, something vital that can't be substituted. There has to be a way for a boy to see a man, a noble and caring man, to know what that's like to emulate. It wasn't easy since Jandro and I continued to have a hard time communicating, although I had made major leaps in this regard. I could still be a guiding force for my son as a woman—single mothers have done this since time immemorial. But nothing beats having an emotionally open and wise man in a boy's life.

That's why I was glad Pancho was around—it turned out to be the best thing for Jandro just then.

When Pancho visited, right away he acknowledged Jandro and talked to him—about school, video games, the music he liked, and skateboarding—my son's favorite pastime. Jandro wasn't forthcoming at first, replying mostly with burps of *yup* and *nope* to his questions. But Pancho didn't get fazed. He kept talking with Jandro until finally the boy started taking his guard down.

Now don't get me wrong: Johnny and Lito are good men to have around. Jandro picked up mechanical and yard skills from his grandfather and great-grandfather. Maybe that's what helps keep Jandro from really losing it. I've brought so many unhealthy and immature men into his life that he has to have a corrective to go by—and my dad and Lito have done a good job.

But there is also a need to have a man outside the family, someone who can bring other kinds of knowledge and skills essential for the boy's path toward manhood—a mentor.

After that exchange with my son, I asked Pancho to help get Jandro to a sweat.

"I know what you mean," Pancho said. "Kids nowadays don't have any grounding, any sense of meaning or lasting values. There are so many other distractions, but almost all of them are superficial. Let me talk to Omar and see what he thinks we can do."

The strategy they came up with was for Pancho to take Jandro to meetings of men and boys Omar had set up called "warrior circles"— they taught about living in one's word . . . about dignity, respect, and indigenous concepts of manhood (not the macho nonsense most men got in our society).

"You don't think I know you—let me tell you what I know," Omar said during a heated talk Omar, Xitlalli, and I had one crisp night.

"There is a deep dark core inside you, a destructive part that keeps sabotaging your life. This core is dense and it's powerful. But mostly it's negative—we all have this. We have it in different ways. You may never get rid of it. But for sure, you'll have to learn how to carry it—to balance it, to not let it dominate your life."

I was listening, but I was also angry. I didn't like to be told I was wrong. Yet with Omar and Xitlalli, I couldn't avoid this discussion. They are my elders, my mentors and friends.

Omar, originally from Michoacan, Mexico, is of Purépecha indigenous descent. He is a graying, long-haired fifty-five-year-old former addict who rediscovered his indigenous roots in prison and learned enough to teach the rest of us. He is now a Sundancer in the Lakota tradition—a role he has lived for fourteen years—and also participates in a Danza Azteca group.

Xitlalli—a Nahuatl name meaning "star"—is about two years younger than Omar but looks like she may be ten years younger; her family is from Jalisco, linked to the Huichol people. She's beautiful, with long black hair, a strong brown Indian face, and usually wears *huipillis*, with many beads and bracelets on her neck and wrists. She's strong in a quiet sort of way, but also knowledgeable and patient— somebody I can go to when I need to talk.

"This core Omar is talking about . . ." Xitlalli explained that night while burning more sage in the middle of a clay pot so that it would help the healing needed for our talk. "It's that part of you that wants to hide, to not take risks, to be safe and comfortable in mediocrity and anonymity. There's another part of you that wants to live, to break out, to tackle the world and all its wonders. You have to let this become the most dominant and active part of who you are, *mujer*. We know many women who don't do this—male-dominant society has withered their dreams and their strength. Some of them become the *chismosas*, the scared ones at home, living their lives through talk shows and soap operas, and other people's fantasies. They're spectators of a world that goes on without them. Don't be like this—you have to be the center of your life."

"Okay, okay, I get it, but I can't do this if you're fighting me," I responded. "I feel like I'm under attack here."

"You think we're fighting *you*," Omar patiently answered. "We're not fighting you. We're fighting this core, this ball, this corpse of a bitter life—whatever you want to call it. I call mine a beast. It's vicious. It lashes out. It hurts people. It's impulsive and mean. It's that part of me that wants to shoot up heroin, drink all night long—that wants to walk in front of a moving vehicle and get hit. I won't necessarily put a gun to my head, but I'm like one of those walking suicides. You know what I'm talking about: those people who walk around in the world dead inside, their spirits crushed, unable to see the beauty and hope around them. All they see is the negativity, the misery, the worst of people and things. I have to get up every morning and pray that this beast doesn't come out today. I pray every day, sometimes in tears. Yeah, I even cry about this. I'm ecstatic that it's dormant. But anything can get it going. I have to be conscious of this every day and every minute of the day."

"What do you call your core, your shadow, that dark side of you?" Xitlalli asked me. I had to think about this for a while.

"I don't know . . . I see it more like a black hole," I told her.

"That's good. That's a good metaphor," Omar interjected. "That's a good image to help you understand what you're dealing with. It's a black hole that sucks all the life out of you. It ruins your relationships, where you don't connect deeply with anyone. You wonder why you don't have any close friends. Why you're not close to your own family. That's because you give so little to anyone. You're not generous. You're like the tip of the iceberg—we want more of you. But you're selfish that way. You only give us a glimpse of who you are. You've said you don't trust life. Yes, I know life has been rough for you. But it's also been good. You have people who love you. You have a son who loves you so much but is frustrated that you don't give him the best that you have. You need to learn how to trust people and life. I've known people like you, who've felt nothing but abuse, humiliation, degradation— terrible mishaps have occurred their whole lives, but they still manage to care, to give of themselves. Others are generous to you, but you only respond this way briefly, in few and far-between moments. We're asking for more—give us more of who you really are."

"I never saw it that way," I conceded.

"Listen, Chena," Xitlalli added. "As Omar says, we're not fighting you. We're fighting this black hole. But, honestly, it's not really our fight. It's yours. I feel like you're a boxer in the ring, but sometimes you're just sitting on the stool while the black hole's knocking you around. We're like your trainers. We're talking to you from the out-side because we know it's not our fight. We have our own fighting to do. But you won't stand up and take this thing head-on. So we get frus-trated. We end up entering the ring and fighting this thing for you. This isn't right. But that's what's happened. You have to do the fight-ing. We'll encourage you. We'll support you. We'll be there for you. But this is your life. It's your fight, not ours."

They were really letting me have it. But it was all good. It was what I needed to hear—sometimes I can dish it out, but I can't always take it, even from those who only want what's good for me.

It's great that a number of Chicano/indigenous recovery circles have been created since my father's time. These circles are organized around the premise that our culture and values are incompatible with the driving values and needs of the capitalist, dog-eat-dog, immediate-gratification reality we are surrounded by in this country. The kind of linear and psychological model of most recovery groups is geared to mostly white people. Sure, many blacks and Mexicans are in them, but many more aren't. People have begun to create their own healing and recovery circles that include the principles from indigenous traditions. They emphasize natural healing, powerful herbs, teas, and ceremonies like the sweat lodge.

I had done many things to find my way in this world—most of them wrong. But until I met Xitlalli and Omar, I had never tried to reach back to my own roots in Mexico and in this country, too. Omar told me before the borders came, we were all in one land. The Mexican migration patterns to the U.S. have been going on for tens of thousands of years—way before the Spanish came; way before *la migra*. Lito and Lita have Yaqui and Mayo roots from the state of Sonora, where they're from. Raton was part Chicano and Hopi. These ways are real to me. I'm not playing "Indian," as I've heard some people say about Chicanos—although we look more Indian and have more native blood than most card-carrying Native Americans in this country.

It's strange, then, to think all this knowledge can penetrate my thick head—I'm the one who stole back my car and almost sacrificed Pancho, even after having had many sweat ceremonies under my belt.

I'm the one who hated schools and rules and ingested all kinds of dangerous drugs. I'm the one who rages and doesn't always think straight. I'm broken. I'm wounded. I know, I know, but that's who all these ideas and thoughts are made for—for the lost, the confused, the pissed off.

For people like me.

The intensity of the sweat lodge reminds me of the heat of the steel mill, from the descriptions my father has given me all these years. The difference between a steelworker and us sweat-lodge participants, however, is that we are the drive and the momentum; we are the doing and the undoing; we are the subject and the object. The sweats and other rituals are *our* way of sustaining our courage, of developing our character, and of achieving coherency without the outside industrial world encroaching in a contrived, exploitive, and intolerant manner.

This heat is ours, of nature and the spirit world. Some of us have remade ourselves through this tempering. At my age, I've wasted so much time, so many relationships, to finally find true beauty and innate wisdom. I'm still young enough to do something with it. I'm still capable of positively changing the world around me.

I also eventually realize I don't have to abandon Jesus Christ to participate in these ceremonies and learn these teachings—there's an indigenous Jesus in the Bible, Who walked among the poorest and the hurt; Who challenged the hierarchies of the Temple as well as of society; Who healed in the way healers have done through time—with words, touch, ideas, stories, and love. I see Jesus as the earth, expansive, inclusive, wise, welcoming, and brown, not the idealized, whitewashed Jesus that some people use to excuse their own intolerant and constricted natures.

Jandro finally saw how I had changed.

"Mom, are you feeling okay?" he asked one day after school.

"Yeah, sure—why?"

"You didn't lose it when I came home late the other day. Or even when I didn't finish my homework yesterday. Or when I stayed up in my room later than I was supposed to. You just said what was wrong and offered to help me. So I'm worried—are you really okay or are you hiding something?"

"What a cynic," I said, with a smile. "I'm not hiding anything. What you see is what you get."

"Wow, that's great, Mom," Jandro said as he walked away from the kitchen to the outside door. "I'll be back soon. I won't try to worry you either."

Jandro is a great kid. We've had our run-ins, a lost and destructive single mom and her son. Now, when Jandro is in trouble, we take him into a sweat. He didn't want go in at first. It's hard, and I even thought he was too young. Omar told Jandro he'd be fine. Jandro now comes regularly. He's learned how to set up the fire for the rocks and to put the heated stones into the lodge. He still does weird things from time to time, but it's just natural kid things. Mostly he minds what I tell him. He doesn't hang with bad people. And he studies hard.

When Jandro reached twelve, Omar suggested a rite of passage and naming ceremony that included a sweat with his family and "uncles" and "aunts" (adults outside the immediate family willing to guide him along his life's journey). For the first time, Aracely and Johnny came into the sweat—they were hesitant at first. My parents are community activists, revolutionaries and leaders, devoted to social reality and practical political outcomes. A good part of their lives they've taken issue with "mysticism" and religious precepts. That's okay. I told them to just open up their hearts and let spirit go where it goes. In the end, they didn't seem to find the ceremonies or the words counter to what they're about—they came through like champs.

For this ceremony, we also brought in Pancho. We ended up in the sweat for five hours. Jandro suffered, but he hung in there through the four rounds. I was so proud of him. All the men and women said beautiful prayers and spoke wise words. They recited heartfelt songs and chants.

Later on, Omar and Xitlalli presented Jandro with his Nahuatl name, Ocelotl, which means "the jaguar." This is a very powerful symbol. Jandro actually smiled when he was told of his new name. This must be cool after all (and not just another one of his mother's crazy notions). Almost everyone in the circle eventually gets a Mexika name. The names are determined by one's birthday, year of birth, and, if possible, time of birth. This information is recalibrated to the Mexika calendar, known as the Tonalmachiotl, which is considered one of the most accurate calendars in the world, and is a round, carved stone that was found in the ruins of Tenochtitlán in the 1970s.

Its origins go back thousands of years, linked to the Mayan and other Mesoamerican calendar systems. The calendar actually consists of two separate time references that line up at various times of the year. The stone itself is huge, weighing several tons. Small clay replicas can be found hanging in people's homes or as images on posters or *manteles*. I know *vatos* who've had the whole Tonalmachiotl—we're talking something intricate here—tattooed on their backs or abdomens. Believe it or not, the calendar still works. Someone can get their new name based on how the month and day of their Gregorian-calendar birth date aligns with the more accurate and complex Mexika calendar.

There are other ways to obtain your name—on your personality, your *tonalli* or destiny (which is also based on the *calendario*), or the animal or object representing your qualities as a person.

The same day that Jandro was renamed, I also received a new name. It's Mayahuel, which is the "goddess" energy of the maguey plant, provider of a precious drink from the carved-out heart of the cactus plant, also known as Aguamiel—"honey water." She is the deity for the day of Tochtli. By the way, we don't "worship" these entities—we recognize the energies they represent, energies present in all life, and use them to balance and guide us.

Everyone—including adults, teens, and children—given a new name is encircled by the rest of us. Omar and Xitlalli light *copál* and then blow a decorated conch shell before pronouncing each new name and the meaning behind the name.

Pancho's Mexika name is Omecoatl or "two serpent," which is derived by drawing on his parents' and grandparents' birth dates as well. This is another way it's done if such information is available. Although some Mexika groups insist that you replace your European names (the Spanish ones) with the Mexika ones, Omar doesn't force any of us to do that. We can if we want to; regardless, it's a name we use in ceremony, in prayer, and in the circle—using our Mexika names outside the ceremonies is solely up to us.

I like my name Azucena. Always have. But increasingly, I've been moving toward using Mayahuel. Who knows, someday that may be the only name I use. But not yet.

One day, I came across my grandfather rocking away on the front porch. I walked up to him while he sat with his eyes closed.

"Hey, Lito, you want to know my new name?" I blurted out.

He opened one eye and stared at me.

"I'm Mayahuel now," I said. "It's Mexika for 'lady of the maguey plant.' You think you can pronounce it?"

"You're Azucena," he countered. "Don't ever forget that. That's a special name. A name from God. Azucena—that's your name. You don't have any other name."

I had forgotten how important the name Azucena is for Lito. It was the name he had given his only daughter before she died. Although I was kind of eager to use my new name, I decided not to use Mayahuel at home after that: Lito will be too hurt if I change what to him is most hallowed.

My impulsiveness was still a part of me—probably always would be. I was glad I had people like Lito around to let me know what was what. I had a lot to learn, I knew, but I was happy I was making progress. Relieved, actually.

14

DEATHLESS

Johnny lies in a drug-induced sleep in his bed—morphine drops putting him into a death dream before his actual body gets there. The roads of his life line his face. He doesn't look like Johnny anymore. I recall his once sharply defined, handsome features—the way he was when I was growing up, in photos, and when I think of him and the mill.

If he was about anything, it was about sacrifice. Omar says the words *sacred* and *sacrifice* are linked. And I get it now. Johnny gave his life to the mill. And somehow, in a strange way, it became a sacred act. He did it for his father and mother. He did it for himself and for us. He wouldn't have had it any other way. Yet here he is, a dying testament to the power of industry to enter our bones, our cells, our life genes, and nuclearize them, alter them, to tear up our basic compositional structure and send it careening into the other world.

Johnny's been bedridden for a week—all treatments have become pointless and only his death can repair what's diseased him. A nurse has come to administer the morphine drip—there's nothing else left to do.

Now we're closing in on another long night, weighty with colliding emotions, after weeks of anticipation, of prayers and songs, of stories and memories, of wanting my father to go, of not wanting him to go.

Aracely is here by his bedside. Tonight, so are Jandro and Pancho, who stand up, walk around, watch TV, or sit in chairs scattered around Dad's small bedroom. Also coming in and out are Rafas and Bune with their wives and children. At times, we converge around the kitchen table, exhausted but still small-talking or eating from perpetually heated pots of beans and rice that my mom and I keep filled, next to handmade tortillas wrapped in towels.

Lito wanders in, humorless, tired and silent; he grabs a tortilla, makes himself a taco, and then sits down. He won't enter Johnny's room.

Night is the worst time for my father—he once told me how he dreaded working the mill's night shift; he said he felt as if he were treading in and out between life and death. I also read how some cultures consider night a period of great mystery, a time of ghosts, when the other world overlaps with the living world.

My father must have known he'd die at night.

Before tonight, Johnny had been confused and difficult to understand. The drugs kept him from expressing anything meaningful, of being fully conscious and engaged in his death. With morphine, he can't acknowledge the ancestral world he's moving toward—or the material world he's leaving. All this has been taken from him. That's what this culture does—it deadens our lives and then deadens our impending birth into another life. We don't want any pain. No struggle. I think that maybe we need to get my dad off the drugs, but Aracely makes the strongest case to ease him into the inevitable. The pain is unbearable, she argues. "No more suffering," she mutters, "no more suffering." So I relent. We all do.

Still, I witness a moment of surprising coherency when no one is around. I'm standing next to Johnny, holding his callused but diseased hand, bruised from needle punctures, when he unexpectedly moves his lips. The word isn't audible, but I know what he's attempting to say: *Aracely*.

"Hey, Mom—somebody—come here!" I yell out.

Aracely rushes in, a sea of concern on her face; Jandro, Rafas, and Bune follow close behind. Pancho is knocked out on the living-room sofa. My father has now fallen into his last and deepest slumber.

"He tried to speak," I say, now whispering, although this doesn't make sense since nothing is going to rouse Johnny now. "He said your name, Ma. He said, 'Aracely.' "

Aracely's eyes water. She walks up to me and places her hand on the small of my back. We stand together around Johnny's bed, waiting as night draws itself over us.

Just before Johnny worsened, I had made plans to visit my brother Joaquin at Corcoran prison. By now he has been in and out of prison and juvenile facilities for some ten years. This last time, they give him a "three strikes" life sentence for robbery. According to California law, he's not going anywhere.

We scarcely visit him anymore. In the beginning, we'd come often—Johnny, Aracely, and I. He'd been in a few places already: the notorious Twin Towers County Jail (high-powered unit), Wayside, Chino, Mule Creek, and finally at Corcoran. The last time I saw him, he was placed in general population, where we could spend hours with him in a large visiting area. There we hugged and talked and had a good time. But the last couple of years, Joaquin has been locked down in the SHU (Secured Housing Unit), the segregated section at Corcoran for the "worst of the worst" prison offenders.

Joaquin has been called a "shot caller" for the main Chicano prison gang. He supposedly led a riot that involved several stabbings. The prison tries to isolate these guys by putting them in tiny individual cells for twenty-three hours of the day—they only get an hour to exercise and maybe shower. They eat in their cells and are watched every minute of the day.

Most of the guys in the SHU are Chicanos, alleged prison gang leaders. Many of them are into Mexika indigenous consciousness, even learning Nahuatl and the Mexika and Mayan cosmologies. But to the California penal system, just studying these things, sporting Aztec or Mayan tattoos, or even speaking Nahuatl, is tantamount to being in a prison gang. So it's outlawed.

I know some of these prisoners who claim to be Mexikas are not really serious about this; many continue their criminal activities. But I also know there are those who are really into it—reading books, doing prayers, following the Sun Stone, practicing the Nahuatl language. But they're treated as if they are devil worshipers.

Some *vatos* become born-again Christians, which has helped many addicts and bangers, and this is acceptable in the prison. But to study and follow your indigenous ways is not. What a world.

The previous summer, when I got deep into my heritage and its teachings, I sent Joaquin papers and books on indigenous practices that Xitlalli and Omar gave me. In his letters back to me, Joaquin showed interest. For years, he had already drawn elaborate black-and-white ink works of Aztec and Mayan figures and symbols. It turns out Joaquin has been working Chicano-style art for years. His drawings include prison scenes, barrio scenes, *cholos* and *cholas*, and masterly de-tailed images and vibrant lettering. Although in the SHU, they're not allowed paints or brushes, the Chicano inmates scrape colors off mag-azines and playing cards; they get wet toilet paper and shape it into a drawing utensil so it can be used when it dries. With their elaborate and amazing drawings and paintings, they find a way to be human.

I encouraged my brother with my gifts. But beyond that, he didn't seem to show any interest in anything else until I started sending him the Mexika books. Then he wrote asking for more materials and even to send books to other prisoners. I couldn't send all that he wanted, but I sent him as much as I could. The prison administration soon stopped these materials from getting to him.

Unfortunately, since he entered the SHU, we've failed to visit. A visit to my brother was long overdue.

The trip to Corcoran from Los Angeles is a boring three-hour drive. The prison is located in a dusty rural community deep in the heart of the state, off Highway 99 near Tulare. It looks like any other prison—guard towers, concertina wire, and flat block buildings. The place is actually two facilities housing some twelve thousand prisoners, including the world's largest addiction treatment center (Blocks F and G). You have to get your identification checked at the parking gate, then again after you enter the prison. You're searched and then monitored as you walk through doors, which automatically lock behind you.

Corcoran State Prison has gained a measure of notoriety over the years. Eight guards were once indicted for allegedly setting up prison-yard fights pitting warring gangs against each other for entertainment—one 1994 incident led to a riot that forced guards to shoot and kill a prisoner, the seventh prisoner to be killed that way in five years (those guards were later acquitted). There have also been investigations into staff misconduct, medical neglect (an extraordinary number of prisoners have died of AIDS and other ailments in their medical facility), physical and verbal abuse of prisoners, and health and safety violations. At Corcoran, many prisoners, like in all prisons, have also been stabbed and killed by fellow inmates.

I don't like that Joaquin is incarcerated there, but also that he's locked down in the SHU. This special unit is so sensory-deprived it's known to drive prisoners crazy, and Joaquin is already touchy as it is.

While a family can meet with a prisoner for several hours in the main visiting area of the prison, the SHU's visiting time is limited to an hour (which is why many people don't visit more often—to drive six hours, back and forth, for only an hour makes for a lot of wear and tear). Visitors here are set apart from the prisoners by thick glass. We sit in a cubicle in front of the prisoner and talk into phones, all the time the prisoner's shackled by his legs and arms.

The last time I visited, I sat in the booth waiting for Joaquin to show up. Finally, the guards brought him in. He looked even harder than when I'd last seen him. His head was shaved bald. His dark skin sported new tattoos on his neck and arms. A faint F13 is tattooed above his left brow, one of his older markings. Three dots in a pyramid shape are tatted below his right eye. This is the universal symbol of *la vida loca*. On his thick neck is a scene of barrio life with low-rider cars, guns, prison walls, *cholas*, and the words Chicano gangsters made famous (from an original song by Sunny and the Sunliners, a Chicano band from Texas): SMILE NOW, CRY LATER.

Joaquin is still handsome—his face is well defined and his body muscular. He's thirty-two years old already—a grown man who's been shot and stabbed. Who has committed robberies and drive-bys. Who is now considered one of the most dangerous prisoners in the California correctional system.

"*Qué húbol carnala?*" Joaquin greeted me in that *pinto* graveled drawl we have been hearing from him for years. On his hands were other tattoos including his gang moniker: SLEEPER.

"Hey, bro, I wanted to say hello and to let you know how much we love you and miss you," I said into the phone. "Mom says hi. So does Jandro, who wanted to come but I told him maybe next time. He needs to have an hour with you while I'm not around—you understand."

"*Simón*, no problem. I'd like to talk to him. He must be huge by now."

"No lie, he's enormous—already taller than me and he's only twelve."

"What're you feeding that kid?"

"Must be them tacos and burritos . . . He's doing well, though, in school and around the house. I wrote you about the naming ceremony and how much he got out of it. He's come to more sweats. He wasn't into it at first, and I didn't want to force him or anything. This is the kind of thing that has to come from him. But he knows it's there when he needs it."

"A real Mexika warrior, *qué no*?"

"Yeah, he's on the right track. How about you? How're you doing in this place?"

"Ain't no big thing. They try to break us in here, but the Chicanos are hanging in tough. The more they take away from us, the more we can take it. Some guys crumble under the pressure—you know, the *tintos* and *gabas*. But we just laugh at the guards and their fucking system. They ain't men. You get them in this situation and they wouldn't last a minute."

"Yeah, but it must be hard. You don't get any human contact, right?"

"Nah, just fucking bulls to deal with. They throw everything at us—electronic cells, all manner of weapons, elaborate ways to keep us from coming together. Goes to show how scared they are. But we find ways to communicate. The more they split us up the more we figure out how to go around them. But, yeah—it's not right. Nobody should be treated like this. But we're united. Our spirits are strong." Joaquin looks me straight in the eye as he says this. He stares into me, his eyes allowing very little of the world to interfere with his gaze. "I'm really glad you sent me those books and articles. You know a lot of them books got confiscated—we can't have any books with Aztec or indigenous writings in them. But the articles are cool. And the *National Geographic* magazines—man, they're the best."

I thought about how smart Joaquin is—he loves to read, write, and draw. I know he's got his bad side, but you can't take away his intelligence. He knows more shit than some professors I've known.

As we talked a guard brings in another prisoner and marches him to the farthest cubicle from Joaquin. This *vato* had his prison number tattooed in large numbers around the front of this neck—a lifer. His arms were full of intricate tattoos, so much so that he appeared to have blue skin over his natural brown skin. It looked like his girlfriend or wife had come to visit with him. She looked pretty beaten up herself. I ignored them when I saw that Joaquin did.

"So, Chena, how's Dad—I know he can't be doing well," he said.

"He's not going to make it, *carnal*," I responded, with emotion in my voice. "The cancer is all over his body. He may only have a few days to live, if that. He's now in bed all the time. They tried all kinds of treatments, but it didn't make a difference. Now we wait. . . ."

Joaquin didn't say anything. He didn't show any emotion—being in prison forces him to push his feelings down so deep that I'm sure there are times he doesn't know where to find them. He leaned back in his chair, his eyes still locked onto me. I know he loves Johnny. I know he's never had a gripe against Mom or Dad. But I'm also aware how much he's hurt them.

Joaquin moved forward toward the glass that separated us, and asked, "There's nothing left to do—nothing to save him?"

"No, Joaquin, we've looked into it. Even natural healing. We've even consulted with *curanderas*, like my friend Xitlalli I wrote you about. You should see what's happening to him. He's bloated inside and out."

"Give my love to Dad," Joaquin responded. "Also tell Mom how much I love her. I really miss them. I can't go back to the past and make anything right. That's not going to happen. This is my life now. But I think of them all the time. I'll pray for him and the family."

Joaquin had started to do Mexika ceremonies in his cell. He commemorates special days like the Mexika New Year in March, the solstice and equinox days, the Day of the Dead in November, and other Mexika ritual dates with prayers and fasting. He says he gets in trouble for this, but he's determined to do it no matter what.

"I have nothing but respect for Pops," Joaquin continued. "I remember how strong and patient he always was. Remember when we were kids and he'd come home from work? How we'd look out the window waiting for his car to pull up and then jump up and down until he opened the door? He had his hard hat and safety glasses, dirty clothes in a bag, and steel-toed boots. He loved to pick us up over his shoulders—remember?"

Joaquin paused, then turned his thoughts to another subject.

"I know I was a pain in the ass—especially to you, sis," he said. "I apologize for that—I don't think I've ever apologized to you before."

"You don't have to."

"I don't—but I want to. Believe it or not, I've grown up in here. I got nothing but time. So I do a lot of thinking. I wasn't such a good brother. I'm really sorry. I've always loved you."

"I've always known."

"*Tlazohkamati*," he said, the Nahuatl word for "thank you." "The thing is I've never really apologized to Mom or Dad neither. I was a lousy son. I think they know I appreciated them, but I never really told them. My problems had nothing to do with them. Despite everything they tried, I always felt lost. Nothing had meaning until I got jumped into the barrio. Then, for once, I felt accepted in a way that brought me something to die for, which meant something to live for as well. I was a soldier with a soldier's heart. I learned to fight and not give up the fight no matter what. I wanted nothing more than to die in a blaze of glory. I didn't die like that, of course, but it wasn't for lack of trying. Remember how I used to do drive-bys and then stand on the street corners, throwing hand signs and yelling out the barrio's name? You better believe I was ready to die. I never hid from anyone. We all got shot, almost all my homies, but I survived and most of them didn't. I always felt bad about that. I wanted to be the one they cried for in the cemetery, the one they gave the gun salutes to. I remember going to the funerals and you once asked me if this didn't make me think twice about being in the *clika*."

"*Simón*, and that you wanted a funeral just like all your homies got—with everyone crying, the girls and mothers and other homies," I interjected. "You wanted a funeral just like that, with all that love."

"We were at war. We'd kill our enemies. They'd kill us. There was nothing to be scared about. Also the *pinta*—what deterrence was that about? We all knew we'd end up in the joint. It was a rite of passage. Prison was built for us. We weren't scared. And the *drogas*—the heroin, PCP, crack, and meth—that was also part of this life. If someone OD'd, we didn't question what we were doing or think of getting out. Maybe a few did, but most of us were thinking, 'That must be some good shit. I want some of that.' "

"It's another way of seeing the world," I said. "I've been through this with drugs and booze, too. Most people can't understand this, so they fear it. They want to destroy the *cholos* and the graffiti and our barrio culture. Or to put it away behind prison walls—they don't understand how much they contributed to creating this life. It's their world; you just figured out a way to dwell in it on your terms."

"I don't know about all that," Joaquin broke in. "But I know we aren't going to put down roots, to have families, to get jobs like Pops did and make a living. That ain't in the cards for us. We are all *caga palos*, misfits, outcasts—the ten percent who won't go by the rules. Who'll hire us? We won't take shit from bosses, police, or schools. We can't get any skills or become regular guys. For many of us, there is no time for love, for marriage, for normal relationships. We've turned ourselves over to *la vida loca*. And that's the only God we'll follow out of here."

"I understand, but I want to know . . . didn't you worry about how Johnny and Aracely suffered for you—that they put so much behind you and you stepped all over them?" I asked, for the first time since Joaquin's been in trouble.

"Sure, but if you get jumped into the *clika*, you've made a decision to do whatever your barrio expects of you. I love you all, but I can't stop what I'm doing. As they say, 'Can't stop, won't stop.' No family, job, school, or *jaina* can change that."

With his hands still in handcuffs, he lowered the top of his blue prison shirt revealing elegant, swirling lettering across his clavicle that read: PERDÓNAME MADRE POR MI VIDA LOCA—"Forgive me, Mother, for my crazy life."

"Sure, we love our mothers, our dads," Joaquin explained. "We love our girlfriends, but the barrio becomes everything. Nothing else matters. Sure, some of us have good parents. But in the streets it's 'kill or be killed.' You can't be weak. Early on, I had to make a decision—be a predator or be someone's prey. Everybody is fighting for the little bit that's there. So I made my choices, now I have to live with them regardless of the consequences."

"That's why you guys are hard to break," I said. "You accept whatever they give you because you expect this is what you deserve for what you do. Most people don't live that way. They still have expectations outside the reality. But you guys have reconciled your actions—no matter how atrocious—with their outcomes."

"I mean, we don't try to get caught when we do our crimes and shit," he added. "But when we do get *torcido*, we don't cry about it. Hey, they busted us. That's what they're supposed to do. I'm supposed to do whatever I can *not* to get busted. If they get me, they get me."

"So let me ask you, *carnal*—what's your future?" I asked.

"Future? Look at this place. This is it. I'm not getting out of here," Joaquin exclaimed. "With my third strike, they gave me twenty-five-to-life. There are people fighting it, and if they win, fine. This is a lousy deal for anybody. But I'm not crying about it. I can take whatever they want to give me. Once the system started me on this track, I've never looked back. If I have to die in prison, so be it. I'm living a strong

Mexika warrior way now—I'm not into that gangbanging shit anymore, no matter what the prison thinks. I do my prayers. I follow my *tonalli* in the Sun Stone. I read and write and do my art. They're trying to take all this away, but like I say, they ain't going to take my spirit."

"How did we get to this point, Joaquin, us Chicanos?" I asked. "We take everyone on. We don't get along with nobody. Yet we don't have any way to go but down. I'm with your Mexika ways, but I'm going to make something beautiful and grand out of all this. We're going to raise families that won't have kids make the choices you felt you had to make just to find some respect in this world. We don't need any more Chicanos in prisons—we don't need any more addicts or kids dead before they're eighteen."

"I'm with you," he agreed. "Like I say, I made my choices. But if you haven't noticed, more *morrillos* are coming in here every day. There are baby lifers in the *pinta*—*vatos* like eighteen and twenty years old. They want to make a name for themselves. They're not listening to nobody. Someday they'll understand all of this, but for now they're just wrecking."

"Well, that's what I want to change," I responded. "To help them find their roots, their destinies, so they don't go full-fledged into this purposeless intensity, like lambs to the slaughter."

"You're right—you got some smarts in that big head of yours." He laughed.

"Shut up."

"I just like the way you think—your letters, Chena, I'm telling you, they've been like food for my soul."

"I've learned a lot from Xitlalli and Omar," I explained. "It ain't just me. They even help me understand the link between the mill's closing and the growth of violence and drug wars over the past twenty or thirty years. When that big industry died, the gangs got bigger and deadlier. So did the drug trade. That's when L.A. street organizations like the Crips and Bloods, Maravilla and Sur 13, 18th Street and Mara Salvatrucha, and hundreds more really took off."

"Yeah, most people forget that with all the jobs gone, most drug sales and robberies are to pay rent and feed families," Joaquin threw in.

"Prisons are now the fastest-growing industry. I read in a magazine that California had fifteen thousand prisoners in the 1970s. Today there are more than a hundred and sixty thousand. Close to a hundred thousand of these are Chicanos."

"Hey, you got some brains, too."

"I read a lot."

"But it's true what you're saying, *carnal*," I said. "Look at how schools went from looking like factories to prisons with no windows, gated entrances, and police and community patrols. A lot of these schools don't even bother with books, sports, music, or arts. You know where those students are gonna end up."

"Well, keep teaching those youngsters, Chena," Joaquin said. "If the Mexika consciousness can get to them before they get here, so much the better. I wish I had this knowledge when I was a kid. I was lost, but now there are so many. I'm talking thousands. It's not just Chicanos. You have Central Americans, blacks, Cambodians, Armenians, even whites. Poor people. That's all what's in here. We may hate each other but, damn, we all have to look at the same empty walls with the same futureless eyes."

"I want to help change that," I stated. "I see now that's what Johnny and Aracely were all about—in their own way, they were giving our *gente* something to fight for, to get strong for, and to help them connect with the poor and despised everywhere. You just made me see that—I think you just recruited me into your army, *ese*."

"As long as it's the army of the mind, with ideas, poetry, and art—the army of Ometeotl," Joaquin commented. "The army that's in here, well, we'll do anything for a little slice of respect; we don't have the time or the mind for anything else. But if you can, reach the youngsters before they get their brains and hearts closed off in places like this."

Joaquin and I had the best talk of our lives that day. I feel bad he's never going to grace our household, to actually hold us and spend holidays and birthdays with us. But despite all the rotten things he's done and seen, he still has a dignified soul. Sure, society—this punishment-obsessed and narrow-minded world we're in—will never fathom this, will never grasp Joaquin's true depth. But I do.

Finally, it was time to leave. Joaquin gave me a slight smile—and a little of what he used to look like as a boy. He still has it in him, I thought, he's not all dead inside yet. The guards pulled him up and out of the cubicle. I placed the phone down and told my brother with the movement of my lips, "I love you."

Joaquin winked, then turned around toward the exit, moving slightly back and forth as he walked due to the shackles on his legs. A tattoo of the Mexika symbol for movement—OLLIN—adorned the back of his head.

Days after seeing Joaquin, Aracely and I are moving some of Johnny's things—boxes of papers, his tools, his political booklets and personal artifacts—to the garage. We had piled them into the living room to clear up the bedroom for Johnny. At one point, one of the boxes falls from my grasp. Among the papers on the floor, I notice a letter. It's written in Johnny's hand. I pick it up and read it. Right away, I can tell it's a love letter.

Oddly, it's addressed *Dear V.*

This isn't right. At first I think it's a letter to an old girlfriend before Dad hooked up with Mom. But there's a date—November 8, 1979. They were already deep into their marriage then. Perhaps it's a letter he wrote but never got to send. I don't know what to do. I want to show this to Aracely, but I'm not sure if I should. I start obsessing about it. I realize then that I don't know everything about Johnny; I suppose he's had his vices. God knows I have mine. I probably should let it go. But still—to think my father may have been romantically involved with another woman when he was married to my mother? I don't know, but I have to find out. I have to get the nerve to ask Aracely.

"Mom, I have something to show you," I later pronounce at the kitchen table—and already regretting my decision to raise this. "I'm not sure how to do this, but I better just let you see it. I found it in one of Dad's boxes."

I hand the letter to Aracely.

She doesn't say anything. She opens the carefully folded letter and reads. She closes the letter and then looks at me.

"I'm sorry you found this," Aracely says. "I would prefer this part of your father's life was long buried and forgotten. But I'm going to be honest with you. I knew about this affair. . . ."

Aracely stops, her eyes staring off into space.

I say nothing, waiting for her to begin again.

"Listen, I was very much in love with your dad and devoted to him, but I wasn't stupid," Aracely explains. "I never let on that I knew. There's something that a woman's heart can see, even when her eyes can't. He was different, distant, although he was so attentive. I knew something was wrong. Whatever was going on, though, it wasn't happening after work. He always came home and always made himself available. So I figured he was having an affair with someone on the job. I knew a lot of women were coming into the plant. Sometimes your father would talk to me about these women. He felt they were getting the wrong end of the stick, and he was trying to help a couple of them. The whole thing really felt strange to me after he was sent to the wire mill. Not at first, but after a while he became quite content being there. It wasn't like him. At first he saw the wire-mill assignment as punishment. He was isolated. He couldn't get any help for repairs. He was bored a lot. But then he started to act like everything was fine. He even seemed to like being there, alone, working by himself, not a care in the world. One day when I left you and Joaquin with your grandparents, I took a bus to the wire mill. You can't just go in there—there's a security guard that keeps away nonemployees. But I watched to see who would come and go. Then I saw her—it had to be her. A pretty, long-haired Chicana. She was trying to look so fine in her work clothes. That's when it hit me. I could read her like a book. I later found out her name was Velia. Again, it's not anything I could prove. It was something I knew deep inside. Call it intuition, or something even stronger than that—but I just knew."

"What did you do, Ma?"

"I didn't know what to do. I was tempted to just let Johnny have it. To let him know what I knew and see how he wiggled out of it. But I didn't want to do that. I figured he'd deny it. He could just call me a paranoid idiot—what did I have to show him?"

"That letter," I suggest.

"I didn't know about this letter. This is the first time I've seen it."

"I'm sorry, Mom, but if it were me, I would have thrown the whole thing into his face."

"Well, *m'ija*, as you know by now, I'm not you," Aracely emphasizes. "What I did was talk to my old friend Nilda—this was just after her husband, Harley was killed, you remember that case?"

"Sure do."

"Nilda was getting ready to leave L.A. So I had to talk to her right away. She said if it was worth destroying my marriage, go ahead and let him have it. If he was a terrible guy, he probably deserved losing me. But she said if not, I had to weigh my long-range love for him with the immediate pain of my suspicious. It probably was a fling. But since she had just lost the man she loved, she didn't want me to do anything to take Johnny for granted. She suggested I talk to Johnny, to get him to come clean and to work on making things better. Or to ignore it and see if it blows over. Again, I wasn't sure what to do, so I decided not to do anything. I bided my time."

"So what happened?"

"Well, it was a few months later, but then the wire mill closed . . . yeah, I think that's when," Aracely says, struggling to recall the actual time frames. "The closing took up most of the conversations your father and I had for a while. But then I began to feel something else. Johnny became more involved with us. I don't mean to distract me. I mean for real. Then the realization hit me: He was no longer with this woman. Again, I didn't know for sure. But my heart knew. I had to make a decision—to pursue the matter, although by then the affair was over, or to let it go. I can tell you now, I cried about this for many nights. I was in a terrible bind. Yet I saw how you and your brother were so in love with your father. I saw how much love Johnny had for the both of you. I didn't want to destroy that. He may have been the stupid one, but I had to be the smart one. I also knew he loved me. That's something I always understood. It was a difficult thing, but I decided to never mention this to Johnny. Maybe I was wrong, but I had to live with that. I also promised myself that if he did it again, if I ever got that feeling that he was sharing his love with another woman, I wouldn't let it slide. I'd leave him. Who really knows if he did or not, but in my gut I know he never did. That's the end of that. I never thought about it again. I'm sorry you found this letter, but the best thing right now is to forget this ever happened. You understand, *m'ija?*"

Before I can say anything there's a long silence, which I know has to irritate my mother—but she doesn't show it.

"Mom, I don't know if I do," I finally respond. "I'm still confused and hurt by all this. But I also trust you. I trust that you somehow did the right thing. I guess I wouldn't have done what you did, but then I've made a lot of mistakes in my handling of men. So I don't know. Who am I to judge? In principle I think you were wronged and you needed to do something. Yet I also know, as hard as it may be, you would do what was right for all of us."

"I'm not sure this is something I would recommend to anyone else," she adds. "I don't think women should just stand around and take nonsense like this. But it was a decision that at the time I felt I had to make. I was at war with myself. But now, especially that your father's almost gone, I'm convinced it was the right thing. Somehow I believe Johnny knew he did wrong. Johnny knew he was on the verge of destroying his family and all that was dear to him. And somehow, he found a way to change that. That's what matters in the end—that he never again made that mistake."

I don't know what to say. I smile and hold my mother's hand.

"Mom—I know I don't always say this—but I'm honored to be your daughter . . . thanks for being open with me."

"Good . . . then I can do this," Aracely says while walking over to the stove and turning on a burner. She places the folded-up letter over the flames and it catches instantly. She grasps the edge of the burning letter and takes it to the kitchen sink. She throws it in and, after a few seconds, turns on the faucet and watches the ashes disappear into the drain.

Lo Nuestro Café becomes popular after more than a year of business. More people get wind of its existence, even though it's kind of hidden away. College and university students hang out here—particularly Chicano activists. But we get people from all over L.A. and even as far away as San Francisco and Chicago. On Friday nights, we decide to create an open mike, where members of the community can recite poetry, tell stories, play instruments, or sing.

We get all ages—one young poet who likes to read is only eight years old. Even the lady who makes tamales in the neighborhood comes in and belts out a few *rancheras*.

One Friday night, Pancho is sitting at a back table enjoying the words and songs of the patrons with a cup of our steaming-hot Mexican chocolate in his hand. I'm behind the counter, listening to a teenage girl recite some angst-ridden poetry, reminding me of the silly verses I used to write when I was in high school—only hers are pretty good.

Pancho stands up and walks over to me; he puts his face next to my ear and whispers, "Why don't you sing?"

I make a face, then turn around to face him. "Are you crazy? I haven't sung in years. I probably sound like a croaking frog by now."

"No, I'm not crazy," Pancho insists. "I never saw you perform before, but I've heard you sing when we go to the clubs or when there's a song on the radio you like. I know you got it in you. And I know how much this means to you. Please, do it for me. Or better yet, do it for yourself."

"I don't know, Pancho," I say, half pondering the possibility. "What if I make a fool of myself? I work here. I'll never hear the end of it."

"Come on, hard-ass—you know you won't make a fool of yourself. You may feel rusty but you can do this. You're as good as anyone in here."

"Let me think about it," I say. "Now go sit down before I 'accidentally' spill a hot pot of coffee on you."

Pancho laughs and walks back to his seat.

There are times Jandro comes into the place to hang out—there are now a couple of computers for Internet access, and he likes to play video games on the Web. Even Aracely comes in once in a while to get some warm *cafecito*. But this night they're not around. I'm thinking this is probably the best time to try out my voice. If I suck, at least they won't have to bear it.

During the break, I slowly walk over to the open-mike list. I see a string of names, most of which have been crossed out after they've done their thing. I hurriedly put my name at the bottom and scramble back to the counter. The rest of the break I'm making coffee until the open mike starts up for the second round. I feel like a kid again.

The emcee is a young Chicano rapper named Xol-Dos. He does his rhymes in hip-hop style—in Spanish, English, and some Nahuatl. He then announces the next person on the list.

After a while, he looks at the list, his brow scrunched up. "I'm not sure what this says, but it looks like Mayahuel—will Mayahuel please come up?"

I walk around from the counter and approach the microphone stand on the small stage in front of the café. Xol-Dos looks at me, does a double take, then feels compelled to make a big deal out of this.

"Well, what do you know, it's one of our own. This is Mayahuel, also known as Azucena Salcido. Please, everybody, give a round of applause for Mayahuel."

I feel like tripping him as he walks off. But I decide to go through with this. I step to the microphone and see a respectable crowd looking at me. Pancho is in the back with a huge grin on his face. I'm thinking I'd like to find Xol-Dos and Pancho walking down the street someday so I can run them over.

"Thank you all for your support," I start, mustering up as much courage as I can. "I haven't done this for a long time, but I'd like to sing a song for you. I have a whole mess of songs I've sung over the years, but today I feel like singing one of my favorites, 'Constant Craving' by k.d. lang. There are no instruments, so please bear with me while I find the right key."

I take a few seconds trying to hum the melody with my head away from the microphone. I then clear my throat, drink some water, close my eyes, and begin the first lines in a plaintive voice, pulling up all the longing, hurt, and trouble that this song reflects.

When I'm finished, a roar of applause and cheers fills up the room. Pancho is standing up and whistling—my handsome fool.

I look at everyone and I feel real good. I make that connection always there when I perform—that undeniable force of a voice that swirls through the intricacies of anyone's life, even strangers, and finds home.

Rain begins to fall. My parents once told me I was born in the rain. As my dad lies still, we pull up chairs and gather around. I stay up, listening to the rain's melody on the roof and gutters. I can't sleep anyway. Jandro curls up and then snoozes in one of the chairs. A tall twelve-year-old, he looks like a small child just then. I reach over and gently muss his hair. Pancho strolls in and out of the room, half asleep, unsure of what to say or do. It's probably better that he doesn't say anything. Regardless, I'm glad he's here. My uncles stick around for a while, talking among themselves and to Lito, who's in the kitchen, mostly just listening to everything around him.

Johnny's breathing has been shallow all night. Sometimes it's hard to tell if he's breathing at all. After a while, the rain stops. In moments, I hear a single bird chirp. Then the sun bursts through the clouds. Just as the dawn breaks, Johnny breathes in deeply. Aracely reaches out to me with one hand while she places her other hand on Johnny's chest. In that inhalation, my father takes in the room, the smells, our presence, our sorrow, and our love. I'm hoping it carries him wherever he's going. Then he lets out a long, drawn-out breath.

Emotions begin to rise within me, uneasily at first, then in torrents. Aracely cries softly—I envision Johnny and her in each other's arms long ago, back when they were young, full of fire and verve. I glance over at Jandro—I don't want to wake him; I'll tell him later about his grandfather's last breath. Pancho walks in; he appears sad but is now fully awake. He walks up behind me and gently places both hands on my shoulders.

In a watery moment, time wanes, it reflects, sitting in the room with us, and just stares. In that pocket of held breath, I think about death with more concentration than I've ever done so before—despite all the death I've known in my life. People die, but then they don't die. They leave ideas, impressions, remembrances, art, words, and this is how they live forever. My father used to think the steel mill would never die—he couldn't imagine that steel was an exhaustible commodity, or that the march of technology and market conditions could destroy his precious mill once and for all.

Johnny may have had his battles in the mill—he may have disagreed with how things were done, how people managed the plant or the way they broke workers down, misusing them, dividing them, scaring them, and then lying to them. But he learned to love the work; he learned to love the machines and the way steel's properties were melted, poured, shaped, and hardened. Perhaps he saw a similarity to human beings there. Johnny grew up, he matured in the mill. He found his heart and his life there. Yes, Nazareth had to die, but the deathless push-pull of humanity and nature, of mind and matter, of fiery creativity against finite reality, would continue to clash, curl, connect, and grow. This would always be there. In the end, I think this is what Johnny loved.

Soon enough, time reels itself in, becoming real time, where again you notice life, where you again hear the talking and the crying. Lito walks in just then, his face drawn, his steps halting. He stops next to us and looks down at his son. I see tears flow down his wrinkled face, coming on, not like in a storm, but as if they are the rain after a drought in a dry desert, a place of withered plants, intense heat, waterless horizons, where even tears drift like dust. I imagine a land and time far away from here and yet somehow tied to all of this, to what all of us have come to witness and carry, and never, ever forget.

ACKNOWLEDGMENTS

Thanks to my agent, Susan Bergholz, for believing in my voice and vision; to René Alegria and everyone at Rayo Books/HarperCollins—*un millón de gracias*. To my fellow steelworkers at the former Bethlehem Steel Plant of Maywood, California, many of whom are no longer with us, as well as steelworkers everywhere who know the fury of furnace and forge—in particular my friends Tony Prince, Lee Ballinger, Frank Curtis, George Cole, and Rueben Martinez. Special thanks to Francisco Chavez, a Yaqui who grew up in East L.A., for research information on the Yaqui Indians of Mexico and Arizona, Susan Franklin Tanner of the Theater Workers Project, Dave Marsh of *Rock & Rap Confidential*, and Bruce Springsteen. To the Sweat Lodge Circle in the barrio of Pacoima, in particular Luis Ruan—*tlazohkamati*. And to the artists, musicians, writers, dancers, actors, filmmakers, healers, staff, supporters, and partners of Tia Chucha's Café & Centro Cultural—the bookstore, café, art gallery, performance venue, cybercafe, and workshop space we created in the Northeast San Fernando Valley section of Los Angeles: Your spirit and commitment keep me emboldened to tell the stories of our fathers, our mothers, grandparents, *tíos* and *tías*, stories rich and invigorating, necessary and sad, painful and triumphant.

And to my family, always my family, for the love, patience, and generous time they've allotted me to write this novel—*no hay palabras, pero también palabras son todo lo que hay*.

bonus PAGES

LUIS J. RODRIGUEZ is the author of the memoir *Always Running: La Vida Loca, Gang Days in L.A.*, which won a Carl Sandburg Literary Award and a *Chicago Sun-Times* Book Award and was chosen as a *New York Times* Notable Book for 1993. His books *Poems Across the Pavement* and *The Concrete River* have won the Poetry Center Book Award from San Francisco State University and the PEN West/Josephine Miles Award for Literary Excellence, respectively.

Rodriguez is a recipient of a Lila Wallace–*Reader's Digest* Writers' Award, a Lannan Literary Fellowship, a Hispanic Heritage Award in Literature, a Dorothea Lang/Paul Taylor Prize from the Center for Documentary Studies at Duke University (with Donna DeCesare), and a National Association for Poetry Therapy Public Service Award and fellowships from the Illinois Arts Council.

QUESTIONS FOR DISCUSSION

1. *Music of the Mill* is structured in three parts: Procopio's story, Johnny's story, and Azucena's story. Why has the author structured it this way? How does the structure help tell the story?

2. The first two parts ("Procopio's Prelude" and "The Nazareth Suite") are written in the third person while the last part, "Azucena's Finale," is written in the first person. Why? How would the novel feel different if all three parts had been written in the third person, or the first person?

3. All three generations of the Salcido family have drug and alcohol problems. How do they deal with their substance abuse issues differently? How do their struggles with addiction reflect society's evolving attitudes toward addiction?

4. Rodriguez has created characters that are anything but stereotypical. They are multidimensional and very real. Discuss some of the characters and their good qualities as well as their flaws. What about the minor characters? Are they also fully realized, complex people?

5. The Salcido family members go through many changes at the mill, in American society, and in their relationships with each other. In what ways do their struggles get easier, from Procopio and Eladia's to Johnny and Aracely's to Azucena's time? In what ways are their struggles harder? In what ways are they unchanging?

6. The mill is a powerful presence in the Salcido family history. Discuss the ways in which the mill was a force for good in their lives. In what ways would their lives be different if Procopio had never secured a job at the mill?

7. On page 271, a group of teens in a pickup truck yell at Azucena, "Go back to where you came from!" How does she respond? As a reader, how does this bigoted incident bring you into the realities of modern America? How does it figure into Azucena's struggle to figure out who she is and where she wants her life to go?

8. While her brother Joaquin is in prison, Azucena is working to stay sober and pursue singing as well as being a mother. What is Rodriguez saying about the role of art in communities and cultures?

9. There is a history of American writers exploring the changes in urban environments as industry "created" and "destroyed" cities as Luis J. Rodriguez does in *Music of the Mill*. How did writers like Nelson Algren, John Dos Passos, James T. Farrell, Sinclair Lewis, Ayn Rand, John Steinbeck, or Richard Wright deal with these issues? How are they different or similar to the approach Rodriguez takes?

10. Many industries were automated, downsized, or shipped overseas during the 1980s; cities like Detroit, Chicago, Pittsburgh, Cleveland—the so-called Rust Belt—were hit particularly hard. We learn in *Music of the Mill* that other cities, namely Los Angeles, were also negatively impacted by the dramatic shift from a mechanized industrial economy to a high-tech electronics economy. Did this affect your community on a short-term or long-term basis? How so?

11. How does the very real and devastating deindustrialization of the country in the 1980s affect the Salcido family in the novel? How do you think it has changed the way people in this country now work, live, and think? What does the novel indicate may be our future as globalization and technology become the next stage of economic development around the world? How do you think these developments will shape your life in the years to come?

AN INTERVIEW WITH LUIS J. RODRIGUEZ

How many years did you work at the Bethlehem Steel Plant in California? Where does your experience fall within the spectrum of what we see in Music of the Mill?

I worked at the Bethlehem Steel Plant from 1974 until 1978—four years. I was also one of the few people of color at the time entering the mostly white skilled-craft jobs. Like Johnny Salcido, I served as an oiler-greaser and millwright apprentice. I knew the mill inside and out—oiling and greasing its massive and complex machinery, and repairing many of them, particularly on the electric-furnace floor. Much of what I remember and experienced was reimagined in the novel. Many of the characters were fashioned after the real, often amazing, characters whom I worked with. The beauty of fiction is that these characters take on a life of their own, shaping the world around them, forcing me to let them go from trying to fit them into preconceived notions about who they are. They begin to speak in their own voices, telling their own story. This is where the imagination becomes as real a force as reality.

The conversation between Joaquin and Azucena at the end of the book is very powerful. Both are young, intelligent Chicanos trying to navigate through American society and figure out what their lives are about. Was it intentional that the young man is incarcerated while the female is out in society? What are you saying with this final image?

They are both imprisoned—one literally. When a society centered on an "incarcerated" mentality is created, whole families end up serving time. Joaquin, while a criminally inclined gang member, is very aware and conscious of the world around him. He's no dummy. But his physical incarceration has also forced his mind to lose much of its imagination for anything outside his prison reality. Azucena still dreams of a life away from drugs and other "incarcerated" holds on her life. She wants to help others embrace their own dreams, break their own chains, and remake their own world. When the mills, auto plants, textile factories, and other industries died in the 1970s and 1980s, people like Joaquin and Azucena faced fewer options that would help shape them into full and complete human beings. In this scene, we see how Joaquin, full of spirit despite the bars that confine him, and Azucena, filled with spirit, pulling away from her own psychological prison, are both aspects of the future we all face. Consciousness, awareness, and a fullness of spirit and creativity are the keys to open any prison door (including jail and other forms of imprisonment, like substance abuse).

The comparisons to John Steinbeck are natural since this book revolves around people trying to make a living in very difficult conditions, and it takes place in California. Have you thought of Steinbeck as an influence? Can you discuss some of the writers whom you admire?

I've always loved writers like John Steinbeck, Theodore Dreiser, and James T. Farrell. They wrote epic novels of real American working-class life. They created amazing characters with many flaws, but who, challenged by a cruel and heartless world, were often able to find their own hearts and capacities to hope, to grow, to thrive. These are important stories and we connect with them because they represent issues we all have in our lives—can we live meaningfully and with purpose in a world that in many ways drains much of the spirit and meaning from all life? How can we go out into the world, lose ourselves, get back up, and then help make the world a better place? The hero's journey in any myth, story, or novel is a guide to our own hero's path. These are great books, wonderful literature, but also filled with teachings from the imaginations of great writers that show us that we, too, can be worthy of our gifts, our challenges, our dreams.

Music of the Mill *is very poetic and has a rhythm that feels like spoken word. How does writing poetry affect your prose writing? Do you think the book has a musicality to it?*

I started out as a poet and journalist at the same time some twenty-five years ago. Two contradictory writing streams—but in my case I think this helped. In the novel I was able to bring out the music that language inherently has, and which thoughtful poets work with. But I also try to view things with a journalistic eye: to describe in vivid detail, as well as to juxtapose one truth with another to create a powerful third truth, allowing for the story to ebb and flow into a kind of orchestral connection between character, plot, setting, language, and delivery. The more literary—in a vital sense—a book is, the more it can hook a reader, including those who normally don't read. It's the balance between the poetry/musicality of words and the concrete details of things and people, threaded by story.

The difficulties young men face trying to stay alive on Pacoima's Van Nuys Boulevard feels very much like the plight of the mill workers trying to make it through the night in the often dangerous, often deadly bowels of the mill. How do you compare the struggles of today's young men with those of the men who had to face unsafe factory or mill jobs every day?

In the factories and mills, everything was placed on the line— one's dignity as well as one's life. The mill exacted a certain loyalty, cosmology, and relationship that also required great sacrifices, including the caring and communal traditions that Procopio and Eladia understood from their native Mexico. Families were given options to be materially better off, but they were also mutated—fathers' schedules were not based on the needs of their children or their wives, but on the needs of the mill to produce profits. Mothers were pushed away from their own capacities to meet their callings, forced to work in lesser jobs or to maintain the households while their men worked hours upon hours—including sixteen-hour days. In the poor barrios of L.A., like Pacoima, the streets demand its own sacrifices and loyalty for whatever excitement, escape, and survival can be wrought from the little at their disposal. Alcohol and drugs become the main way the spiritless cycles can be dealt with—of course, forcing more sacrifices and even greater upheavals. Many of the youth of mill families ended up in the gangs and drug worlds that filled the vacuum created when the big mills and factories closed, particularly during the 1980s.

The book is an "easy" read in that it is so enjoyable and provocative. The journey of the Salcido family and the world of the Nazareth Steel mill are compelling and vividly described. The book seems a natural for the big screen. Is there a movie in the works?

Any good book can translate into a good film if the dynamics of both are understood and addressed. The dynamics of a novel, with language and plotting as its principal palette, can be realized on the screen only when the dynamics of film, the visual and sound aspects (dialogue, action, image), are properly taken into account. It is not a one-to-one relationship. But there are threads that tie both genres together—the most important being: telling a great story. A novel does this primarily with words; a film with what you see and hear. I would love to see a film made out of *Music of the Mill*—but only if the qualitative differences of the genres are adequately understood and a fantastic script is properly executed. The rest I leave to the artistry of the filmmakers and actors.

Azucena's son Jandro is about twelve at the end of the book. He is just about to go through puberty and become a man. The next generation of Salcidos. His future is unknown. Is he a symbol that represents the future of the Chicano people? Were you tempted to write his story, or did you want to leave it a mystery?

All good stories leave some mystery. The future is mystery to us all. We can read the patterns of people's lives and determine where we think they're going. But imagination changes the equation. Jandro is further removed from the steel mill than his mother, Azucena. He does not carry the burden of trying to meet others' expectations. At the same time, he can be more lost, unless, as Azucena finally tries to do, he's guided into what his own particular destiny is crying out for him to do. When Azucena finds her way, rebalances her life, and places her parents' and grandparents' realities in proper perspective to her own, she can be the powerful and connected mother that Jandro has been missing for most of his young life. He's young enough to know and feel the difference. Jandro, as a fourth-generation Chicano, must now forge a new path, not by denying his past, his family, or his indigenous roots—but from this deep and rooted ground, to reach levels of accomplishment they couldn't even have imagined (without sacrificing his ancestors or his destiny in trying). In indigenous thinking, the ancestors are the guides to destiny. In the Nahuatl language, it's called *tonalli*—the path the sun has chosen for him. In a community of conscious indigenous people, this also means he will break new ground. He must enter what is called the "pathless path, the gateless gate," where he will occupy a space only he was meant to occupy. Jandro is being asked to embrace the imaginative possibilities that the steel mill or the streets could never, ever, do.